the *Bennet Women*

the Bennet Women

EDEN APPIAH-KUBI

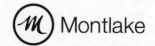

Text copyright ©2021 by Salima Appiah-Duffell
All rights reserved.

Published by Montlake, Seattle

www.apub.com

Amazon, the Amazon logo, and Montlake are trademarks of Amazon.com, Inc., or its affiliates.

ISBN-13: 9781542029179
ISBN-10: 1542029171

Cover design by Faceout Studio, Lindy Martin

Cover illustration by Jordan Moss

Printed in the United States of America

For Momma, who gave me everything,
including a deep love of books,
and my John, who kept me believing in this one.

THE FALL FORMAL

EJ

"What fresh hell is this?" EJ exclaimed, entering the common room through wisps of white-gray smoke. It was a little early in the morning to be referencing Dorothy Parker, but she couldn't help herself: the couch was (ever so slightly) on fire. She ran out of the room and quickly returned with the fire extinguisher, unloading at the flames until they were smothered by the foam. EJ took a moment to be grateful the fire alarm hadn't gone off before she located the source of the mini-blaze: a flat iron resting on the threadbare arm of the sofa. It was set to high, and still plugged in. Shaking her head, EJ turned it off and set it on the floor.

Bennet Women are better than this, she thought, shaking her head.

The term *Bennet Women* was not simply the collective noun residents of the dorm used to describe themselves, but an ideal and an identity. There were several contributing factors.

The first and most significant factor was Bennet House itself. It had been a gift from Dorothea Bennet, the school's first female math professor. She'd offered her palatial family home as the school's first female residence when Longbourn finally went coed. The former mansion was the most beautiful building on Longbourn's quaint, but otherwise unremarkable, campus. The house was a long walk from the rest of the school, save for the Physics and Mathematics Buildings. This remoteness helped give the house its own subculture, especially in the winter, when people did all they could to avoid being outside.

Another factor that went into shaping a Bennet Woman were the many house rules. There were the official sexist ones set down by the school's trustees that were somehow never changed (more on those later). On top of those there were many unofficial rules, customs really, that might have annoyed your average college student: residents received a copy of *The Second Sex* with their keys and were prohibited from referring to themselves as "girls." (Each such infraction cost the guilty party a quarter.) And then there were the house commandments, something between an honor code and a set of guidelines most Bennet Women held sacred. They were reviewed annually by the house's resident advisors and presented at the first house meeting.

EJ had inherited a beautifully calligraphic poster of her first commandments from a graduating RA. It now lived on the wall that faced her love seat:

THOU ART A BENNET WOMAN, FULLY GROWN AND RESPONSIBLE:
ACT THINE AGE, NOT THINE SHOE SIZE

THOU SHALT KNOW THINE WORTH AND ACT ACCORDINGLY

THOU SHALT LOVE THINE BENNET SISTER AND
SUPPORT HER IN HER ENDEAVORS

THOU SHALT TAKE NO MESS

The last three commandments had survived from its very first iteration. Across the decades they were deemed the most important:

THOU SHALT TRY, EVEN WHEN AFRAID OF FAILURE

THOU SHALT ASK FOR HELP; THERE IS NO SHAME IN THIS

THOU SHALT PARTICIPATE IN AND EMBRACE THE ADVENTURE THAT IS LONGBOURN COLLEGE

The type of woman who was attracted to the house for its architecture despite the drawbacks tended to be a little more romantic, a little more feminist, and a little nerdier than the usual woman who would ordinarily be drawn to a single-sex dorm. (Nerdier because of the proximity to the Math and Science Building—not to say that STEM automatically equals nerdy, but . . . STEM ≅ nerdy.) This mix of personalities turned Bennet House into something between a sorority and a benevolent cult. For EJ it was simply home. As one of about a dozen female engineering majors, EJ spent most of her time surrounded by young men. When not in class, she desperately needed a break from men and their nonsense. Bennet House was a refuge. It provided an oasis of positive femininity.

With a final look at the foam-covered couch, EJ left another voice mail for janitorial services. Then she sighed and hurried back down the hall. For a moment, she wondered why she'd signed up to be an RA. Then she remembered that (1) she got paid in room and board at her small, but criminally expensive, liberal arts school, and (2) since tuition went up every year and her aid package stayed the same, she probably couldn't afford Longbourn without the RA gig. Still, even if it was worth it, there were times when it didn't *feel* worth it—like this morning, when she'd had to defuse three different crisis situations before 10:00 a.m.

Let me get back to my room before anything else happens.

EJ's day had started with an SOS call to janitorial services, too. One of her residents had attempted to make herself a redhead in the floor's shared tub—it now resembled a bloody crime scene. Later, her breakfast of yogurt and Netflix was interrupted twice: first by a screaming argument over an eyeshadow palette, then by an actual fistfight over a missing pair of heels. And then there was the fire. EJ returned to the sanctuary of her single and closed the door with an authoritative thud. Getting ready for the annual Fall Formal had always thrown the inhabitants of Bennet House into a tizzy.

But this year her dormmates had lost their damn minds.

She fished her smartphone out of her bra and texted this sentiment to her best friend, Jamie.

> I'm a feminist and all, but women be crazy.

She took a moment to lean against her door and sigh in weary relief; then she walked to her window and peered out. Ordinarily, on sunny Saturdays like this, EJ would throw on her hoodie and go for a long walk in the nearby woods. The west side of the campus was at the edge of a wooded nature preserve, home to a remarkable owl, or something small and endangered. From her window, EJ could spot the lightly worn path where the bed of fallen pine needles would have made her steps almost silent. Unfortunately, the cell phone coverage was spotty in the preserve, and due to the dance, she was on call through the weekend. EJ dreaded these big party weekends because of the sexist rules mentioned earlier.

Because the trustees back in the day found women drinking "unseemly," Bennet was—and remained—a dry dorm. The same fight against "unseemliness" meant that men could not be anywhere in the dorm but the main common room after 10:00 p.m. EJ didn't love busting girls for hiding marshmallow vodka in their shower caddies or emailing her floor after spotting empty bottles of Goldschläger in the hall trash cans. But the absolute worst was being forced into her residents' personal lives. She'd likely have to drive out any leftover boyfriends / male hookups tomorrow morning. That wasn't fun for anyone. Yesterday, she'd sent a house email asking her hetero residents to "just crash at his place" and hoped for the best.

Shaking her head at the thought, EJ opened the window and took a deep breath of fresh air. Then she stood and looked around the room. Her eyes landed on her giant whiteboard, where she'd drawn the timeline for her senior capstone project. While most of her fellow engineering students were just submitting their project proposals this semester, EJ had set an ambitious (or "nuts," according to her advisor) goal of getting her project finished and defended by Winter Break. That meant the responsible thing to do now was get back to designing her models.

But just because she was working didn't mean EJ couldn't get into a party spirit. She crossed the small room to her record player, which was balanced on two milk crates decorated with a scarf from Barcelona. Going into grand plié, she thumbed through her small album collection until she lifted her Harry Belafonte best-of album with a victorious cry. Lovingly, she withdrew the album from its cover, blew away any suggestion of dust, and dropped the needle. Her room was filled with the bouncy opening guitar notes from "Jump in the Line." EJ eagerly kicked off her flip-flops and samba-ed to her bed. She grabbed a bath towel, stretched it taut, and danced it around the room.

Midway through the song, EJ gave up the towel and the pretense of steps, letting her body do what it wanted, as long as she moved. This took her back across the room from her closet to the "inspiration station" at her desk. As the song ended, she winked at the Rosie the Riveter poster above her desk and gave finger guns to her signed and framed pictures of Dolly Parton, LeVar Burton, and Misty Copeland. Thus energized, EJ fired up her laptop, only to hear a soft knock on her door.

That had better not be a noise complaint, she thought.

"Eej? Help?" pleaded a small voice from the hallway.

"Coming." She closed her laptop. It looked like working on her project was not in the cards, for now.

"What's up, buttercup?" she asked, opening the door. Quickly she bit down on her lower lip to stifle her laugh.

It was Dayspring Kaylin Shumway, better known as Dia, a petite, chipper freshman with—in EJ's opinion—an endearing but excessive enthusiasm for new experiences. This morning it had apparently led her into a losing battle with false eyelashes. One strip seemed to have sealed her right eye shut; the other was glued halfway up her left eyelid, creating a jaunty mustache effect.

"Oh dear." EJ forced a sympathetic tone. "You'd better come in."

"I only wanted some vintage glamour." Dia pouted as she stepped inside.

"Don't we all?" EJ replied reassuringly. "That"—she gestured to the sequined dress carefully draped over a chair—"is the closest I think I'll ever come to looking like Dorothy Dandridge or, more accurately, Jessica Rabbit."

"I don't know who either of those women is," Dia said, sitting down on EJ's cozy hand-me-down love seat.

"Of course you don't—it's the freshman's job to make the senior feel ancient." EJ chuckled, then sang, "You're my pearl, my twenty-first-century girl."

Dia looked up at her, perplexed. Her wonky lashes made her look like she was raising three eyebrows. "Sorry, what?"

She couldn't be mad at Dia. It was unreasonable to expect people their age to know T. Rex—or any glam rock besides David Bowie, really. Also, since her pop culture knowledge was, in the words of her best friend, Jamie, "abysmal," she had no right to complain.

"I'll send you a link later." With that, EJ walked the short distance to her narrow dresser and grabbed a sizable Caboodle off the top. Dia filled the gap in conversation as EJ rummaged for makeup remover and cotton balls.

"That dress will look so, so great against your dark skin!" the freshman offered brightly.

EJ stiffened. Between her time at an elite ballet academy and her three years at Longbourn, she'd seen/heard/experienced that many well-intentioned white folks could and did say cringe-inducing stuff to their nonwhite friends. She braced herself as the younger woman continued.

"Anything metallic makes me look like an ice cube, but you're like . . . Lupita! You can wear anything."

Oh bless. That could have been worse.

"I also get Issa Rae. We're both tall and have warm undertones."

It was nice to live in a time when there was more than one dark-skinned female celebrity EJ could say she resembled. She pulled over her wheeled desk chair and gestured for Dia to take a seat. "I like to think I have her hustle, too."

Though EJ couldn't tell a Kardashian from a Cardassian, she'd grown up in an *Ebony/Essence/Jet* household and could identify who most black celebrities were—if not always why they were famous.

"Who?" Dia chirped.

"She has her own show on HBO and—oh, and she did *The Misadventures of Awkward Black Girl.* It was a web series. It made me feel very seen."

Dia giggled. "Well, she sounds great, but if it had sex or swears, I wasn't allowed to watch it growing up. That cuts out a lot."

"That sounds rough," EJ said and bent to examine the younger woman's face. It was strikingly expressive with large, wide-spaced eyes, an anime mouth (very small when closed but somehow gigantic when open), and a slim, crooked nose—all under a mop of curly blonde hair. Dia wasn't traditionally pretty, but her look was distinct. This face would serve her well as an actress.

After tilting Dia's face left, then right, then left again, EJ made her diagnosis. "Doing ballroom team, I've seen some false-eyelash application go really, really awry. This isn't that terrible, hon. I can get you fixed up in no time."

Dia brightened. "Oh, thank goodness!" she exclaimed. "I was afraid I'd miss the dance, which would be the ultimate disaster. I mean, it's the social event of the season!"

"So they say." EJ gave a wry smile. This year's dance had a Victorian theme promoted with the tagline Dia had just quoted. EJ was sure that somewhere the English major who'd thought it up was quite pleased with herself.

"I wouldn't have thought a few posters could be so persuasive. I mean, sure, it's a bigger deal than Homecoming, but your hallmates are acting like they've never been to a school dance before." She clicked her tongue. "The floor's been wildin' out today."

Dia blinked questioningly. "C'mon, you know this isn't any Fall Formal, it's Lee Gregory's Fall Formal. The posters say it's 'A Lee Gregory Joint.' That's why everyone's excited."

Now it was EJ's turn to tilt questioningly. "Lee who?"

"Are you kidding? He's like *über*-Longbourn famous. He's the president of the Gordon Campbell Society, and he's got three solos in the BournTones. Plus, his parents are ultrafamous Hollywood people. Their divorce got its own profile in *Vanity Fair*," Dia exclaimed.

"That's sad," EJ said. She doused two cotton balls in makeup remover and handed them to Dia. "Close your eyes, hold these on your eyelids, and hum your favorite song."

As Dia obeyed, EJ whipped out her phone to text her best friend.

> Who dafuq is Lee Gregory

Jamie texted back a shrug emoji.

> I'm actually having my own teensy crisis

> Can you come over?

> As soon as Dia stops humming

> Umm, what?

> Nm, I'll be over soon.

Jamie

Once she confirmed that EJ was coming, Jamie turned to her mirror and went back to brushing her hair. She had copper waves that she'd grown to almost her waist through a considerable amount of time and effort. This included brushing her hair one hundred times daily, which she'd been doing when Ma said she'd sent her a dress for the Fall Formal via her cousin—an act of surprise kindness that took about five minutes to send Jamie into a blind panic.

Thankfully, Dia didn't take too long with her humming—whatever that meant. EJ was knocking at her door before Jamie had plugged her phone back into its charger.

"Hey girl, hey," Jamie said, answering her knock.

"Hey girl, hey," EJ responded, coming into the room. It was how they said hello, only to each other, at twenty-five cents a pop. Jamie forgot how it had started, but it was a necessary step in the move from friendship to best friendship. Jamie was pulled into a strong hug, and she felt herself relax; it was what she needed most. After a moment EJ squeezed her hands and sat on the bed.

"J? What is it?" EJ asked with a touch of concern.

Jamie sat next to her and said in a low tone, "Ma bought me a dress for the Fall Formal."

EJ frowned, looking as confused as Jamie felt. "When, today?"

"Essentially." She nodded sadly. "My cousin Davey brought it by, unwelcome as bad news," Jamie confirmed.

"But aren't you wearing the jumpsuit?"

"Yes!" Jamie burst out. She'd known EJ would get to the heart of the issue. "I spent literally two months on Rent the Runway trying to get the jumpsuit. I have shoes for the jumpsuit. I planned my hair for the jumpsuit. I even got a gel manicure in matte Orchid Petal for the jumpsuit—you know how picky I am about my nails!" She huffed a sigh. "But my mom wants me to wear that!" Jamie pointed an accusatory finger at the garment bag.

EJ craned her neck to see her closet door and glanced back at Jamie. "Can I take a look?" she asked.

Grudgingly, Jamie unzipped the garment bag to reveal the floor-length column dress with an apron neckline. To her dismay, EJ's eyes widened.

"What a pretty green! Is it silk?" EJ was a sucker for nice fabric. When they went thrifting, she shopped by feel, running her hand along racks until something made her say "Ooh!"

Jamie nodded, disappointed that EJ might like the dress. She watched her friend's face intently and released a breath as she frowned, first thoughtfully, then critically.

"It's not your style—at all—though," EJ added. "This looks like it's for an Irish debutante."

"Thank you!" Jamie interjected.

EJ gave a quirk of her lips. "I would've expected something . . . paisley, to be honest. Your mom is still a bit of a hippie."

"Oh, she knows better than that." Jamie took a step back and EJ followed. They gazed at the dress like a painting in a gallery.

EJ bit her lip thoughtfully. "So the problem is that you don't want to wear the dress?" she asked, going to sit on the bed. Jamie settled next to her and rested her head on her friend's shoulder. They sat like this until Jamie spoke again.

"It sounds so simple when you say it like that, but . . . Okay, remember the summer after I came out to you and Ma?"

EJ winced and nodded but didn't say any more. They both knew the memories still hurt.

Jamie had been through it with her mom after coming out as trans. Her liberal, feminist, NPR-loving mother had spent a month convinced that Jamie was just "confused." Then another month being weirdly silent. This was as surprising as it was disappointing. Ma had been a super PFLAG parent in high school and even threw Jamie a *RuPaul's Drag Race*–themed birthday at fifteen. But when she wanted to transition, it was like her mother's reservoirs of support were all used up from back when she came out as gay.

Jamie sighed heavily, and EJ slid an arm around her waist. Silent encouragement. "Anyway, that summer I had the tutor/nanny gig with the family near Harvard Square. Sometimes walking to the T, I would pass the mothers and daughters with their shopping bags, and I would get so sad." Jamie swallowed.

"All I wanted was to get to the point where she could see me as her daughter. That we could, like, do something as simple as going shopping. At the time it seemed like too much to hope for."

EJ shifted and wrapped both arms around Jamie. It was still hard to talk about that time. Jamie and her mother had been very close since she was born and became nearly inseparable after her dad left when she was ten. Transition was hard, but what made it nearly unbearable was doing it without her mother's full-throated support. Thankfully they were beyond that now.

"Flash forward to this August," Jamie began again. "The weekend before I come back to campus, I get my wish. We go to the Cambridgeside Macy's for winter coats. They're having this nuts sale. Ma has her coupons, and it's great. It's her and me laughing and shopping like I've always wanted. I don't think I can explain what it's like to crave something so ordinary. It was so nice."

She sighed deeply but continued at EJ's encouraging squeeze. "We get our coats and are heading out when we pass the J.Crew. Ma sees this gown on a mannequin and gasps. 'Jamie, that would be perfect for you! Don't you have that formal dance in October?' I say yes, but I already have something in mind. Then I take out my phone and show her the jumpsuit on Rent the Runway. And she's like, 'Oh. Isn't that a little casual?'" She affected her mother's artificially bright tone.

EJ choked out a laugh and looked up at Jamie. "Your momma, who doesn't own shoes that aren't Crocs or Tevas, said the jumpsuit was too casual?"

Jamie nodded, annoyed. "Ma insists I try on the green gown. I'm not going to ruin our good day, so I do. It looks good, but thank God it's a little too expensive because I don't want the dress.

"Since then it's been 'Isn't that outfit a little too low cut?' 'Will you be able to dance?' 'What if one of your boobs falls out?'—every time I call home." Jamie paused to roll her eyes. "I had no idea why she didn't drop it, until now. Ma seems to have bided her time, gotten some coupons, and hey, presto." She gestured weakly to the dress. "Now the green gown is here. I don't know how she can afford it. Coupons or no, she had to have been saving up.

"And part of me is like: Why not wear it? It's a nice dress." Jamie leaned back against her wall. "It's just . . ." She knew EJ wouldn't judge, but this was still hard to say. "I was envisioning tonight as sort of my debut." She rested against EJ again. "I mean, I only started coming out to people—besides you, Ma, and my roommate—spring of sophomore year. Then I left for junior year abroad.

"I can't say what it was: maybe having ID that matched the real me or just getting to be young in Paris, but that year was the freest I've ever felt. It was like I stopped trying to convince people of what I already knew and started figuring out *my* femininity and *my* style—when I wasn't camped out in the library or attending seminars on Molière. Point is, I know that beautiful silk dress is not me. The woman who I am, who I've been waiting to be on this campus for so long, she wears an ivory jumpsuit with a high ponytail."

The declaration took all Jamie's strength, and she drooped. "But I don't know how I can reject the gesture. That shopping trip was the first time I felt like her daughter." She put her head in her hands despondently.

EJ patted her friend's knee. After a thoughtful silence, she spoke. "First of all, I don't think you're overreacting. Clothes are all about expression, and like you said, you spent a lot of time figuring out what you want to communicate. You get to wear what you want."

She squeezed Jamie's hand and sat up. "Now, I've got regular news, bad news, and good news. The regular news is that this sounds like a classic mother-daughter dispute over clothes. The bad news is your mother is a ninja at maternal manipulation. The very good news: there's an easy solution to this problem."

Jamie tilted her head. "Why would she care what I wear? Ma's never expressed an opinion on anyone's style in her life—especially mine. Plus, she's all about women's agency."

EJ responded with a maddening smirk. "*Au contraire, ma soeur.* Your mother still has a distinct sense of propriety—and a tinge of puritanism that runs through a lot of second-wave feminism. She doesn't like the idea of women dressing sexily because she thinks it's for the male gaze. That's why you're getting all the neckline comments."

Jamie skeptically arched an eyebrow. *Uh-uh. Ma is no prude.* Back when all the high schools had to go abstinence only, Ma had convinced their rabbi to offer a sex-ed course through the temple. She thankfully had stopped teaching when Jamie came of age, but the class was there. Ma had fought the high school's PTA on banning *The Color Purple*. Jamie read it for ninth grade English, lesbian sex and all. Ma was sex-positive before it was a thing. Usually Jamie trusted EJ's judgment, but this seemed pretty far off base.

EJ chuckled at her friend's expression. Then she did some ballet/contortionist shit and ended up facing Jamie from the back of the bed. "Do you remember the first time she came up for Parents' Weekend? It was late September and a solid sixty degrees. I wore a sweater and those formal shorts you convinced me to buy with sheer black tights. We walked to Cousin Nicky's for brunch, and your mom asked if I was cold seven times over two hours."

Oh shit. Jamie's eyes popped open at the memory. "Oh my God. I'm like retroactively mortified."

EJ shrugged. "It's easier to pick up when you're raised with it. Back when people were shaming you for being too femme, most cis girls were being lectured on how to be modest—or at least not look slutty."

Another thing to figure out, Jamie thought, stifling a sigh. It was hard enough just getting people to accept her as a woman.

"This is . . . exhausting." She groaned, rubbing her eyes.

"What?" EJ asked.

"Misogyny!" Jamie said, waving her arms. "There's just . . . so many flavors."

"Internal, external, cool ranch," EJ offered sardonically. "Some days being a woman is choosing the cherry for your shit sundae."

Jamie laughed, in the grand feminine tradition of laughing to keep from crying. "Well, today I choose the jumpsuit. I just have to tell Ma before I post my pics tomorrow."

"Don't worry, J," her friend began. "I've been working around my mother's interference for the better part of a decade." She unfolded her legs, sat up, and put on her best TV announcer voice. "And for only three payments of nineteen ninety-five, I'm willing to share my patented system of wearing what you want—most of the time."

Jamie tossed her head back and laughed. EJ waggled her eyebrows, and she laughed some more. It didn't matter if EJ's advice was bad—she'd gotten Jamie out of her anxious mood. The big green dress wasn't a burden; it was a surmountable problem.

"Okay, friend. Please enlighten me with your hard-won wisdom."

EJ held up three fingers. "Step one: say thank you. What your mom wants most is to feel like you appreciate what she got you—are you writing this down?"

Jamie snorted. "Don't worry, it's all going up here." She tapped her temple and winked.

Her friend continued. "Step two: provide a plausible excuse for not wearing said thing. Your green gown is easy. The formal is in a tent on the quad; that dress is silk. If you wear it tonight, you'll only get to wear it once because it rained this week—"

"And water will ruin it!" Jamie interjected. "That's brilliant."

"I know." EJ smiled. "Now we come to step three: take the L another day. Think of some point in the future when you could wear the dress and promise to bring it back out then."

Jamie thought for a moment. "With my scene presentation for drama and my thesis for French next spring, I think I'll be too stressed out to shop for Senior Gala next May, so—"

"The system works, especially for double majors," EJ confirmed. "Now go call your mom and thank her. Then we can get lunch."

Jamie smiled, her good feeling mostly restored. This wasn't going to be the last time she and Ma fought over her clothes, and developing that mother-daughter relationship was going to be tough. Still, for tonight, this was enough: she was going to be attending the Fall Formal as the truest version of herself Longbourn had ever seen.

"Thanks, Eej," Jamie said as they rose. "Oh! And about that Lee kid, you should ask T. She knows everything that happens on this campus."

"T" was Tessa Ocampo, Bennet House's Renaissance woman. The junior was an astrophysics major, a nature photographer, and the biggest gossip on campus. If anyone knew why their floor was going crazy, it would be her.

EJ slapped her forehead. "Of course! I'll ask about it when I see her later. She's going to do something cool with my Senegalese twists." She patted her messy bun of extensions.

Just then EJ's phone buzzed. She glanced at it and rolled her eyes. "Duty calls. Someone may or may not be having an allergic reaction to a face mask. You okay, love?"

Jamie nodded. "I'm good. I'm gonna call Ma."

The friends blew kisses to each other and waved, their standard goodbye. Then Jamie reached for her phone.

EJ

It was a truth *not* universally acknowledged that a black girl at a mostly white college, in an even whiter college town, must befriend someone who can do her hair. EJ's someone was her very close friend Tessa. You wouldn't expect it, because Tessa (1) was Asian American (Filipina, specifically), and (2) had had the same bob since freshman year. She said that she got good at styling black hair when she got a younger black stepsister in elementary school. After YouTube taught her how to do cornrows, she kept learning so her baby sis's style wouldn't get stale. Tessa said by the time she graduated from high school, she could install box braids, do flat twist updos, and even do finger waves—she'd pulled them off when her sister played Josephine Baker in a school play.

EJ was very grateful for her friend's talents and, in exchange for a styling session, would let Tessa tell her, in great detail, about the latest bullshit her boyfriend had pulled without screaming "Just fucking dump him!" She considered it a fair trade.

That was why EJ was sitting on a fluffy orange rug in Tessa's single, biting her tongue as she heard another story of Colin's ridiculous lack of consideration. She looked around her friend's room and marveled at her ability to stick with a theme: there were butterfly-patterned curtains, a butterfly bedspread, and a photo of Tessa and her stepsister, Zenobia, in a butterfly-shaped picture frame. Even the aforementioned rug was butterfly shaped—Tessa didn't do anything halfway.

Eventually, they moved from the subject of Tessa's crappy boyfriend to war stories from the morning. Tessa's floor had been going nuts, too.

"I just don't understand why, T! No offense, since I know you're part of the Gordon Campbell Society, but this dance happens *every year*. I've never seen it cause fights. And before you say *Lee Gregory*, let me say that the name means nothing to me, so I'm going to need a thorough explanation."

Tessa took a hairpin out of her mouth and looked down at EJ. "Well I know why you, in particular, don't know him, but you're not gonna like it—he's a cappella famous. He's the reason the BournTones won their first IVC Northeast Championship—"

EJ waved her hands in surrender. "You know I can't deal with this school's a cappella obsession. It's so weird!"

Tessa chuckled. "Okay, okay, anyway, while he's famous on campus, his family's famous in the real world. His name isn't just Lee Gregory; it's Lee Gregory *Engel*. His dad is Anders Engel, the music producer." Tessa paused while EJ figured out the rest.

"Wait, wait, wait!" EJ straightened with interest. "So is his mom Diana Gregory?"

"Ding! Ding! Ding!" Tessa confirmed gleefully.

"Oh. My. God!" EJ twisted around, bouncing with happiness. "His mom is *the* Diana Gregory—as in the director of *Lima* and *South Bronx Symphony*." EJ let her head be guided to the right as Tessa continued pinning.

Tessa laughed. "Frankly, I'm shocked that you know who she is. You're the same person who thought *The Office* was an actual documentary."

"Only until my junior year of high school, and I had never watched it. I merely heard about it." EJ sniffed. "From age two until twelve, my life was dance, piano, Girl Scouts, and church. After that, it was pretty much ballet, ballet, and more ballet until my junior year. Then robotics team, show choir, spring musical, and piano again, until graduation.

And a job. You'll forgive me if I didn't have time for reruns of a Bush-era sitcom."

How had she been going to school with Diana Gregory's son and not noticed? EJ shook her head in amazement. "I didn't know someone with those kinds of connections went here."

Tessa paused. "Lee tries to keep a pretty low profile. I've known him since my freshman year, and he's never named his parents or discussed their work. Also, he's mixed race, but like Halsey or Vin Diesel. Most people can't tell he's half-black, let alone see his mom's face with his freckles and the hazel eyes. I think that's why he started growing out his hair into an afro. When it's super short, he could be anything from swarthy Italian to South Asian."

Tessa put another pin in EJ's hair. "Now, for the reason everyone has been losing it: Lee promised to bring a 'special celebrity guest' tonight, someone who is good friends with his mom. Since word got around about that, speculation has been building—especially since a hot guy was spotted parking a new red Tesla near campus on Friday. I think people are trying to look their very best, just in case."

EJ's shoulders slumped. "So this is all about trying to hook up with some rich and/or famous friend of Lee's? I'm so disappointed. Bennet Women are better than that."

EJ was one of the house's strongest boosters. She maintained its traditions and upheld its commandments—especially the one about supporting her Bennet Sisters. She was also extremely biased in favor of her fellow Bennet Women.

Tessa tapped the updo she was creating so that EJ looked up. "I love that you believe that." She chuckled. "But ninety percent of your fellow Bennet Women would not say no to a rich husband if he came along. You gotta pay your student loans any way you can."

EJ opened her mouth to object, but Tessa continued. "You're just hopelessly blind to the ways people show off here. Remember when I had to explain Burberry scarves?"

That made her groan internally. EJ knew she was solidly middle class, and she liked to think she was pretty sophisticated: she played piano, spoke French, and even embroidered a little—like accomplished ladies in old novels. But every so often someone or something at Longbourn would make her feel like the poor country cousin.

"All those people started wearing the same ugly plaid scarves that one weekend," EJ huffed. "I thought they were a gift with purchase from American Eagle or something."

Doing elite ballet had shown her how wide the gap between the middle class and the upper-middle class could be, but Longbourn revealed the yawning chasm between someone like her and the very rich. Her deficiency in the language of luxury goods was a particularly sore spot. She knew the designers who got name-dropped in rap lyrics or referenced on *Project Runway*, but that didn't count for much. There seemed to be a whole other code of luxury (mostly hideous prints and boring jewelry) that existed to maintain a fence between those who were raised with money and those who found their way to it by other means.

Tessa barked with laughter, her arms shaking as she pinned the last bit of EJ's hair into place.

"Anyway, I think it's a credit to my own character, and to Longbourn, that I haven't had too many run-ins with showy, rich assholes," EJ added. "It also helps that I don't have a WASP-y finance major for a boyfriend."

Tessa stuck out her tongue. "And for that, I'll offer no more information, and your hair may be crooked."

EJ didn't even pretend to take the threat seriously. Tessa took too much pride in her updos to make her worry. In any case, she didn't have long to wait.

"Hop up!" Tessa commanded, giving her masterpiece one last pat. "Tell me if you like it!"

EJ got up and looked at herself in the mirror on the back of the door. "I love it! I look like Audrey Hepburn in *Breakfast at Tiffany's*. It's perfect." She whirled her head around. "And it doesn't move! You're a wonder." She turned back to Tessa and gave her a big hug. "Well, rich randos or not, we're going to have so much fun tonight."

Tessa squeezed her back. "I think this might be the most memorable Fall Formal Longbourn has ever had."

EJ at the Dance

She knew it was a little silly, but EJ couldn't get ready for a big campus party without thinking of her parents. As the frequently retold story went, they met at a house party during Howard's homecoming in the early '80s. Momma was sitting on the couch wearing espadrilles, a floral sundress, and giant round glasses. She was a music major and hadn't been to many parties where there was no band. She didn't really know what to do with herself at these things if she wasn't playing piano. Her friends left her to go do the Electric Slide and had been gone for some time. She was deciding whether to stay or go when this guy in a vest offered her a drink. Daddy had seen Momma from across the room, looking like she was trying to camouflage herself in the near-matching couch. He handed her the drink and said, "A pretty lady like you can't fade into the background."

At this point Momma always interrupted. "I thought he was corny—but he also was fine, so I let him sit down." Then they'd kiss, Maya would groan, and EJ would find it sweet or sweet but embarrassing depending on her age/mood. From that initial meeting came dating, then marriage, then her sister, Maya, and finally EJ. The story never lost its magic for her. Maybe that was why she always put a little extra effort into getting ready for campus parties. A little part of her was always hoping that someone would see her from across the room.

Tonight was no exception, and in EJ's opinion, she and Jamie looked really fucking good. She'd found one of those stick-on bras actually in her size and decided this year she'd try her first backless dress, C-cup be damned! The sequined gown also had a scandalously high slit that wasn't visible until she walked. EJ topped off her look with a white faux-fur stole cape for vintage '30s glamour. She worried that the fur made the whole thing a little too much, but Jamie approved.

"You are rose-gold sex in that dress, mama," she said before bending to reapply her lip gloss in the rearview mirror. "Seriously, seriously, absolutely no joke—what is wrong with Longbourn boys? You should be fending them off with a stick. I look at you, I see how cute you are every day, how hot you look when you turn it out, and then I remember that you're single. So are the guys here blind or what?"

"It's not my market," EJ said with a shrug. She knew she was pretty, funny, and a catch. She also knew the prevalent ideal of feminine beauty at Longbourn was white or light skinned, no more than five feet two, and slender—preferably with long hair. EJ was the opposite of pretty much all those things: tall with dark-brown skin, an hourglass figure, and hair that was either in braids or an afro.

During her freshman and sophomore years, she'd caused herself a lot of pain by trying to overcome her obstacles with sheer force of personality. Unfortunately, when she flirted brazenly, she got a blushing rejection that embarrassed them both. When she was subtle, guys just thought she was friendly. At Longbourn she was romantically invisible. It was a phenomenon most black women in white spaces had experienced—dark-skinned women especially. She had to live with it the way she had to dodge the occasional stranger trying to touch her hair.

Eventually she decided that looking for love at school wasn't worth the effort. When she was quiet and rational, EJ knew the magic her parents found just wasn't on this campus for her. She wasn't one to sob into her soup, though. EJ still dressed like someone a guy might notice from across a dance floor. And if that didn't happen, this was still her last Fall Formal. All she wanted from tonight was to look stunning and have the best time with Jamie and Tessa. She just had to end this conversation in a way that didn't completely kill the vibe. "I'm a Joan Holloway in a world where all the guys seem to want Megan Draper."

Jamie faux gasped. "Wow, you made a pop culture reference. It's even from this century!"

EJ rolled her eyes. "At least I got a chance to make up for lost time in Scotland. They were buying what I was selling." Not only did EJ have some enjoyable hookups during her time abroad, but she'd had something close to a boyfriend for a month. They broke up right before exams after ruling out a long-distance relationship.

"And Paris. And on a ferry to Mykonos, if I recall correctly." Jamie snickered.

"Hey! I was heartbroken and emotionally recovering," EJ protested.

"And missing getting it *regulah*," Jamie added in a cartoonish Boston accent.

EJ gave a slight tilt of her head. "That too."

Jamie returned her lip gloss to her clutch. Then she straightened and posed for her friend's approval.

"Goddess," EJ exclaimed. Jamie looked powerful and also feminine and sophisticated. Every detail was perfect. "You look like you could walk out of a *Vogue* cover."

"Thanks, I feel like a cross between Lindsey Wixson and Lana Del Rey." She did a brief runway walk up and down their parking space.

EJ blinked and tried to recall either name. "I got nothing. Would you like to know who got the best cinematography Oscar last year? Because I can tell you who it was and who got robbed."

Jamie blinked at her and then leaned in, whispering, "You know, doll, you can tell me if you were homeschooled in a cave or reanimated in a lab two weeks ago after being frozen since 1972. I won't judge, I promise."

EJ rolled her eyes again in response, mostly because she had no comeback.

"Not knowing Lana is unforgivable," Jamie continued. She seemed to love educating her friend. "But Lindsey is a bit of a deep cut. You'd know her face. She was a supermodel from when the term meant something—before Kendall Jenner and the Hadids took over."

EJ still had no idea what her friend was talking about. "You look beyond hot. Ready?"

They followed the sound of music to the main quad. The dance's organizers had thoughtfully and literally rolled out the red carpet on the moonlit grass. At the mouth of the party tent, someone checked them in, and another person got them to pose for a photo. Amber light spilled enticingly from the entrance.

Inside, the space had been impressively decorated in a reasonable approximation of Victorian style (for a school fundraising dance). At one end, there was a long banquet table groaning under donated snacks from local restaurants. At the other, an empty dance floor and DJ booth. Artfully strung Christmas lights gave the impression that an elegant swarm of fireflies was attending the party.

Before she could put down her beaded clutch, EJ felt her arm being lifted into a spin. It was her ballroom partner, Franz. (That was just how he said hello.)

They were joined by Vanessa, his girlfriend and EJ's old lab partner. She gave EJ a hearty wolf whistle. "Damn, girl. I feel like a detective should be describing you in voice-over." She gestured to EJ's slinky sequin dress. "We've been in half the same classes for all this time. How did I not know you had all that going on?"

"Because in engineering classes I dress like Ernest Hemingway," EJ said, laughing. In the department, she was known for her wardrobe of clever hoodies and giant sweaters. "I had Samuelson freshman year, and he doesn't think you can do math and have boobs at the same time. God bless the minimizer!" The women laughed in commiseration.

"Seriously, though, he needs to get fired," Vanessa said darkly. "Wanna check out the food?" The three of them wandered over to the dessert bar and chatted about their capstone projects until the mirror ball started to spin and the opening notes of "Canned Heat" began to play.

"Fun throwback," EJ chirped, pitching her voice above the music. The song always made her think of the movie *Center Stage* and doing fouetté turns in a red tutu.

Franz held out his hand and nodded in the direction of the mirror ball. "Let's go put on a show." EJ smiled. With a wave to Vanessa, they hurried onto the dance floor.

She was giddy as she let Franz spin her around in the fast, whirling steps of the hustle. A few more ballroom friends joined them, and other students formed a small circle to watch them show off.

Before long the song changed, and EJ spotted Jamie across the room. As if on cue, Jamie mimed casting a fishing line in her direction. In response, EJ pretended to be caught and "swam" over to where Jamie was dancing with some of her fellow French majors. Wordlessly the pair got in sync swaying and shimmying to a dancehall-EDM hybrid that neither could identify.

About an hour in, they'd just finished scream singing Beyoncé's "Run the World (Girls)" when Tessa materialized beside them, looking gorgeous in a fringe dress. She'd volunteered to be the handler for the special guest, after Colin launched his one-man boycott. Now it appeared to be showtime. Tessa said something into her walkie-talkie and looked over at them.

"You are gonna flip," she squealed, vibrating with excitement.

EJ didn't have a chance to react before the DJ's voice filled the tent. "Longbourn University, make some noise!" The crowd clapped and cheered obligingly.

Now let's see who all the fuss is about, EJ thought.

"Please welcome . . . star of stage and screen . . . Za . . . ra . . . Her . . . nan . . . dez!"

EJ staggered and clutched Jamie's arm. *"What?"*

Jamie looked back at her with wide eyes. She looked to Tessa, who gave a Cheshire cat smile, somehow smug and pleased at the same time.

"I told you," she laughed.

Standing before them was Angelica from *Hamilton at the Hollywood Bowl*. "The Girl" from the very first production of *Everybody Taps*. Mia from *La La Land—on Broadway*. Dr. Bev from freaking *Dr. Bev*!

"Is this happening?" Jamie cried.

EJ couldn't respond. She was in a full Beatlemania-style freak-out. Luckily for her, everyone around them was screaming, too.

Once the cheers died down, Zara launched into a rousing appeal that flattered the students while reminding them of their immense privilege. As she spoke, Tessa fired up an iPad with a credit card reader and held it above her head. Jamie looked around and saw other Gordon Campbell members with giant plastic buckets. It was smart—they were ready to take additional donations in any form. She returned her attention to the stage. Zara, again *wow*, seemed to be wrapping up. The star went to the side of the stage and dragged a tall, furiously blushing guy into the spotlight.

Jamie leaned over and shouted into EJ's ear. "Who's the cutie?"

EJ, now calmly fanning herself with her hand, chuckled. "He's Lee Gregory. Tessa has all the details."

"I have to embarrass this kid right here," the celebrity continued, "who I've known since I was his babysitter—which is how his mom discovered me, but that's another story. Anyway, Lee, your Gordon Campbell Society president, has the best heart I know. He cares so much about this school and about making your volunteering projects valuable and meaningful."

There was another surge of applause.

"When Lee called me and told me about the goal of doubling the number of alternative Spring Break projects this year, he was only asking for advice. Lee wanted to know how I pull in the big funds for my charity." Zara looped her arm around the tawny young man's waist. His unruly brown hair was like a lion's mane. "What did I say you needed, sweetness?" She tilted her mic toward him.

After a fit of nervous giggling, he replied, "You said something about a celebrity endorsement." Zara bowed to a mix of laughter and applause. "And an incentive."

Zara kissed him on the cheek and spoke into the mic again. "Since we know one is taken care of, here is your incentive, Longbourn. If you guys give a minimum one thousand dollars in this room, I will add ten thousand dollars to whatever is raised here, tonight."

Lee gasped in happy surprise and hugged Zara as the rest of the service group's leadership cheered especially loudly. Now Tessa was the one screaming and jumping up and down.

Lee took the mic, still looking amazed. "Zara, thank you!" He turned to the gathered students. "I had no idea she was going to do that!" He caught his breath. "You heard the lady. Get giving, Longbourn— and let's dance!" The lights went down, and the music started again. EJ fished out her emergency twenty-dollar bill. Looking around she saw many other students reaching for their wallets. Zara Hernandez was a smart woman.

Not long after all this excitement, the DJ put on something slow and romantic. Everyone *not* in a couple drifted away from the dance floor. Tessa had already dashed off, probably to celebrate with Gordon Campbell leadership. Most people grabbed snacks from the back tables and went out to the quad. The formal needed a sort of intermission after Zara's appearance.

Jamie at the Dance

After getting some fresh air and fixing their makeup, Jamie and EJ went looking for Tessa. They spotted her under a lamppost on the other side of the party tent. (T was wearing a rainbow fringe dress that was *ev-ery-thing* and so was pretty easy to spot.) EJ pulled off her heels and rushed over to give Tessa several hugs in rapid succession. Jamie followed at a more measured pace. She squeezed Tessa's hand and congratulated her on the evening's success.

"Everyone I saw was emptying their pockets," Jamie said. "Seriously so, so impressed."

Tessa beamed and did a small victory dance. "Thanks! It was so exciting. I had the craziest afternoon."

She was beginning to tell them about her day with freaking Zara Hernandez when Jamie spotted someone approaching their trio. It was that cutie-pie Lee.

God, he's so attractive he's almost sparkly.

Tessa brought him into the circle. "EJ, Jamie, this is Lee."

He greeted EJ warmly; then he turned to Jamie, stuttering slightly before saying, "Hi."

If you asked Jamie what she felt in that moment, she wouldn't have been able to describe it. It was the chill of anticipation on a hot summer night before a fireworks display, or the bright spark of exhilaration that rushes up your spine when the house lights dim in a theater, or the moment on a roller coaster when you put your hands in the air and get ready to scream. That feeling of magical possibility had somehow been turned into a human—and he'd just said "Hi."

After a moment of smiling, Jamie realized she hadn't said anything yet. This pause was too long—why couldn't she speak? EJ must have sensed her panic. She gave Jamie an imperceptible nudge.

"Hi, Lee," Jamie almost sighed in response. He was tall with long limbs and warm hazel eyes, wearing a stylish all-black tuxedo that someone had obviously picked out for him because he didn't seem to remember where the pockets were. Jamie found this adorable. She also loved how the lamplight on his afro gave him a sort of halo. His smile was slightly crooked—and he had freckles! Lee seemed like the romantic hero of a YA novel come to life—perfectly imperfect.

She heard a giggle behind her and caught EJ exchanging glances with Tessa.

"Well, I've been working this party for two and a half hours," Tessa began. "I'm gonna go dance. EJ, coming?" she asked pointedly.

EJ was too nosy. "In a minute," she said sweetly.

"Okay, I'm requesting 'the Wobble' for Zara, so I know I will see you soon." With that, Tessa disappeared into the tent.

Jamie laughed internally. EJ could no more resist a line dance than Tessa could a spin-off of *The Bachelor*. They all knew each other too well.

Tessa went inside, and EJ made small talk with Lee. It took a moment for Jamie to realize her friend was giving her time. Eventually, when Jamie could remember how to be clever and charming, she joined the conversation.

"So you're a psych major? How long after you declared did you start diagnosing your roommate?"

Lee laughed, and Jamie felt a hundred feet tall. "Almost immediately, but I had my reasons. He was collecting PEEPS."

Jamie frowned. "Like to eat?"

He shook his head. "No, like, pathologically. He only bought the chicks—hundreds of them. He would arrange them on every surface he had in the room. After he started making them little wigs out of Starbursts, I decided I was getting my own apartment."

They all laughed. This was good; EJ was talking less, Jamie was talking more, and they kept laughing. Then, of course, someone had to come from the shadows and rain on their parade.

"Yo, Lee! We done here or what?"

Jamie and EJ turned to face the human record scratch. Lee blushed and seemed to force a laugh.

"Hold your horses, Will." He stepped to the side to allow the newcomer in.

First thing, Jamie was sure Will had money. He was very expensively dressed and distressingly handsome. *That man has never bought his own groceries in his life,* she thought. He seemed to be about their age and looked kind of like an Asian Christian Bale: slim and well muscled with a face that could slide easily from cruel to kind. At the moment, he seemed set on "sardonic."

The new arrival rocked a blue suit of intimidating style (Tom Ford, maybe?) and designer sunglasses, even though it was after ten. He paused a moment like he was waiting to be photographed before he spoke again.

"Zara and her people are ready to go," Will said blandly, folding his arms.

"Actually, she just asked someone to request a song for her," EJ observed archly. "So you sound mighty misinformed. Perhaps you should go check your intel."

Shit. Jamie heard the challenge in EJ's voice. This guy was exactly the kind of person her bestie could not abide. And EJ had no poker face. She bit her tongue so much in class and labs that she had zero fucks left to give with rude strangers. Jamie needed to tread lightly here and get EJ away before Lee's friend did something offensive. Fortunately, a distraction presented herself.

"Hey, Eej"—Jamie directed her friend's attention to the far wall of the tent—"isn't that Tinkerbelle? I think she's looking for you." God bless that little Mormon pixie; she'd turned up at the exact right time.

"Our song is next!" the petite blonde cried.

EJ blinked in surprise. "I can't believe she got the DJ to play 'Sister Kate.'" She nodded to Lee and his friend. "Excuse me, gentlemen, I promised that young lady a Charleston, and a Bennet Woman always keeps her word."

As she departed, shimmering all the way, Jamie and Lee chatted for a bit. "We're both seniors, right?" Jamie began. "I'm amazed we haven't met yet. Longbourn's only a couple thousand kids."

"I know, right?" Lee linked his hands behind his back and rocked on his heels. "You might have heard me, though. I had a show for Longbourn's radio station until a cappella and *The Bugle* took over my life last year." Lee paused and shifted to his radio voice, which was a twenty-two-year-old's passable impression of Barry White. "Hey, funky cats and disco kittens, it's time for another Wednesday night dance party—"

Jamie gasped. "Oh my God, you're the Funkmeister?"

Lee gave his best courtly bow, in response. Out of the corner of her eye, Jamie could see Will smirk sarcastically, but she decided to ignore him. "I loved your show! I tweeted requests every week from @ DiscoJew, and yes, I've had that handle since high school."

"That's awesome." He laughed.

He thinks I'm funny, Jamie said to herself. The thought warmed her.

"Teenage you and teenage me would have been friends," Lee said with a shy smile.

Jamie flicked her ponytail back. "Only if you were also into reading *Steven Universe* fan fiction." *Oh God, that was too much. Abort! Abort!*

Just then the music went up several decibels. Though Jamie couldn't hear Lee's response, she knew it was something very sweet from the way Will rolled his eyes. Unfortunately, between the loud music and Will's sourness, conversation became too difficult. She made her excuses and prepared to leave. "Hate to keep you from your evening plans, so—" She began walking away, sparing a glance at the still-fuming Will.

"Wait!" Lee called after her. "What are you doing afterward?" The dance ended at eleven, which was when most Longbourn students started their nights out.

"We're heading over to Cousin Nicky's. It's kind of a tradition," Jamie responded. "You're more than welcome to join us." Well, Lee was more than welcome. Zara (!) would be amazing. This Will character, Jamie could take or leave.

EJ at the Dance, Later

The dance had just ended, and people were pouring out of the tent. EJ grabbed her wrap and went to the bathroom to repair her hair before the after-party. She could feel Tessa's elaborate creation starting to list to one side. It took a little time, but she successfully stabilized her hair with the addition of a skinny headband and a well-placed pen. "Structurally sound," EJ said approvingly to her reflection.

On the way back to her car, she heard Lee's voice. He seemed to be heading toward the tent. She hung back, not wanting to disturb the conversation.

"Come on, Will, would it kill you to hang out?" Lee pleaded. "You're going to be here for a year."

The other man audibly huffed. "I can see why you want to go: the girl in the white outfit is the kind of angularly pretty you like. I can see why Zara wants to go: she loves playing Evita. But why should I go?"

"What about Jamie's friend?" Lee offered. "EJ, I think. She's pretty cute."

She suddenly felt even more warmly disposed toward her new acquaintance.

"The rando in the rose-gold sequins, with the fake fur?" Will asked acidly. "She's . . . fine, great if you like lady pimps."

EJ's jaw dropped. She could see Will's shadow shrug insouciantly.

"She's definitely not interesting enough to drag me someplace called Cousin Nicky's. I can smell the grease from here."

Before EJ could respond, she heard an aggrieved squeak followed by someone trying to stomp in the grass.

"Hey, jerk! If anyone's a rando, it's you!" Dia stepped into the light and glared as ferociously as her short stature would allow. "I don't know who you are, but you insulted one of my favorite people and my favorite diner! Both are way more popular around here than you'll ever be, mister, so shut up or go home."

Will coughed uncomfortably at her while Lee offered an apology for his visiting friend.

"Whatever," said Dia with an admirable finality.

Even in the middle of this horrible situation, EJ had to smile. *Though she be but little, she is fierce,* she thought, silently applauding her resident.

Her smile faded quickly, though. She felt exposed. She was suddenly aware of how she must look to the rich kids at Longbourn. It was a truth that she really didn't need to know. Her walk across the campus slowed to a trudge, though she tried to put on a brave face at the car, where Jamie and Tessa were waiting.

"To Nicky's!" EJ cried with false brightness.

Her friends' faces creased with worry from across the roof of her car. "What happened?" Jamie asked.

She sighed and signaled for them to get in. "I'll tell you later."

As the trio entered Nicky's, EJ was infused with warmth. First, her old manager greeted her with a big hug and asked her if she wanted her job back—an old tradition. Then Tessa wasted no time firing up the jukebox, and Jamie secured their favorite booth at the back. More friends came. Tipsy milkshakes were made.

Later, when most attendees were either dancing (EJ, Vanessa, ballroom friends), talking intensely about abstract things (Jamie, French major friends), or leaving for the night (Tessa, after a tense phone call with Colin), the door gave a particularly portentous jingle. Then Zara (!) entered, greeted by applause and shouts of surprise. She was followed by Lee, whose eyes were searching the crowd, and a gloomy-looking Will. EJ smiled as she saw Lee spot Jamie and, seeing her receptive smile, race over to her booth. Then she felt a tap on her shoulder.

"Oh my God, that dress!"

EJ turned. To her amazement it was Zara. She'd come right over to the impromptu dance floor in time to catch the vamp from "Try a Little Tenderness."

"Thank you!" EJ cried over the surging horns.

"All I did was speak the truth, hottie. Wanna take a selfie?" Zara whipped out her phone.

"Yes!" EJ moved into frame as the star took several pics. The best one was the last—an accidental candid of the two of them laughing. Naturally, most of the room wanted to dance with Zara, so the booths—and everyone else—rushed to the front. (Everyone but Lee's friend, of course, who seemed a little dejected as he sat down in the last unclaimed booth.)

After someone killed the dance floor with an obscure folk selection, EJ followed Zara to her seat. They were infused with the best effects of alcohol and the camaraderie that can only be formed by extroverts on a dance floor. They were making amicable small talk when a groan came from across the table. Will emerged grumpily.

"Oh!" EJ exclaimed. "I thought you were a coat." She congratulated herself on not screaming and running away. He grunted in reply.

"Will, this is EJ," Zara said. "She's really fun. EJ, this is Will. He's usually fun but has had a rough few months. We're old work friends."

"We've met, in a way," EJ responded.

"My condolences—you met him in the middle of his audition for 'world's biggest asshole.' He's really going for it," the actress added with a slight glare across the table.

Shrugging at EJ, he addressed Zara. "I bought you a caramel coffee milkshake. I hope it makes your ass fat." Zara, for her part, flipped him off and took a long sip of the milkshake . . . before setting it at the far end of the table.

Zara pointed at the milkshake. "This is what I mean by *asshole*. Homeboy knows that I start filming a spandex movie next month and that I'm force-feeding myself enough kale to turn green. What does he do? Orders me my diet kryptonite because he's in a bad mood. This is the problem with befriending spoiled little rich boys. They only know how to fight dirty."

Will responded with his own middle finger and snuggled into the corner of the booth.

Zara turned sharply away from him and faced EJ. "Let's you and I talk," Zara said. "Where were we?"

EJ had already decided that Will didn't matter, so she happily took up the conversation. "You were about to share some juicy theater stories, I hope. Please excuse this bit of fangirling, but I have to tell you, I thought *Cosplay: The Musical* was brilliant! I was one of the lucky few who caught it off-Broadway because my mother is awesome. I also saw you in *The Taming of the Shrew*, at the Shakespeare in DC—I'm from Maryland—and you were incredible! I'd always hated that play, but you were so compelling as Katherina, even her surrender felt like strength."

"Thank you. Truly." Zara seemed pleasantly surprised. "I consider the theater my home, so that means a lot." As they talked, Will grabbed Zara's milkshake, splashed a bit of something from his flask into it, and sipped until he slumped, thoroughly passed out, milkshake in hand. Unfortunately, he hadn't emptied the glass. Slowly, the sticky concoction seeped out onto his jacket and then his shirt.

"Should we . . ." EJ wasn't quite sure what to suggest, but she felt obliged to ask.

"He's fine," Zara said abruptly. "He can afford whatever will happen to that tux."

"He must have been real annoying tonight," EJ observed.

Zara watched the dripping milkshake, and EJ watched her. "He's been a pain in the ass for two restaurants and a bar. Actively getting wasted, then cutting everyone with that patrician passive-aggressiveness. He's more like his dad than he thinks."

The words spilled out before EJ could contain them: "Why is he here when he so obviously doesn't want to be?"

Zara sighed and reached for Will's abandoned flask before squeezing her hand into a fist and returning it to her lap.

"He says he's 'rebranding,'" Zara responded. "'Creating a new, intellectual persona.'" EJ had never seen such sarcastic air quotes. "I keep trying to tell him he can't win the breakup. But he never listens to me."

EJ shrugged and adjusted the strap of her dress "Fuck him then, you're great."

Zara responded with a snort of laughter. "I am great, thank you." She sat up and squeezed EJ's hand. "And thanks for not asking about Carrie. Most people would."

That's 'cause I have no idea who Carrie is, EJ thought. Context clues gave her enough, though. It was clear that Will was some kind of celebrity, who dated a more famous celebrity. The other thing that EJ understood clearly was that Zara was somewhere between tipsy and drunk.

"Do you want coffee?" EJ offered. "It's surprisingly good here, even at God-knows a.m."

"Yes, thank you." She leaned back against the leatherette seat of the booth. "Despite all appearances, I'm having a blast."

"I'm glad to hear it," EJ replied.

When the coffee came, they clinked mugs.

"To new friends." Zara smiled.

"And Shakespeare! And the theater!" EJ added.

As they drank their coffee, across the booth a dozing Will shifted. There was an audible crunch, which he didn't seem to notice.

"What was that?" EJ asked.

Zara peered over Will's side of the booth and giggled. "He sat on his sunglasses. Oh no, those were vintage. He loves those . . ." The actress started to shake with laughter. "He's going to be so pissed tomorrow."

EJ tried and failed to suppress a laugh. "Oh! That is unfortunate."

THE MORNING AFTER THE FALL FORMAL

(And a Little after That)

Jamie

It was Sunday, and Sunday meant waffles. Jamie and EJ had established this early in their freshman year.

"We eat. We bitch. We let it go," Jamie had said. "Waffles and whipped cream are cheaper than therapy but equally necessary." Since then she, EJ, and now Tessa kicked off every week by eating carbs and venting about whatever flavor of bullshit (racist/sexist/transphobic, etc.) they'd dealt with over the past seven days. Occasionally they celebrated their victories, too.

Walking to their usual table, Jamie felt split two ways. She was so excited about Lee, but she wanted to ask EJ what had upset her at the end of the dance.

"Give me good news!" Tessa demanded. "Who's got it? Who's got something to report from last night?"

"Jamie does," EJ prompted.

Okay, that meant she still wasn't over whatever happened. Jamie soldiered on. She knew EJ would be excited for her no matter what.

"Lee might have given me a little kiss last night, outside of Nicky's," she began. "And he sent me a text this morning asking when we could see each other again."

EJ beamed from across the table. "Oh, J, I'm so happy for you!" she exclaimed. "I'm not even going to ask you to rate the kiss. If it was bad, he seems teachable."

Tessa clasped her hands excitedly and bounced. "Hooray, Jamie!" She cried, "You're so great, and he's really so great—this is so great!" She gave Jamie a congratulatory squeeze of her hand.

Jamie didn't expect to feel relieved, but she was. Being trans, sometimes you found the limits of a friend's support only when it ran out. With both of her friends excited with her and happy for her, she decided to gush. "I'm not exaggerating when I say he is the sweetest guy that I've ever met—gay or straight. He's also smart and idealistic, in a useful way."

She was about to take a big bite of waffle when she exclaimed again. "Oh! I didn't tell you the best part: no disclosure! Lee found my IG—"

"@BookishTransAriel," EJ piped up with a giggle.

Jamie laughed and nodded. "Yup, with my, like, seven pride flags. Anyway, he DMed me when they were heading to Nicky's. Basically, he made it clear that he understood everything and was very in."

"That's the best!" Tessa said happily.

EJ's eyes danced with excitement. "Oh my God!" She took Jamie's hands. "I don't want to overreact, but I'm so excited for you! I have such a good feeling!"

Jamie sighed. She could hardly believe it herself. "I don't want to say anything more than that yet—but I have a good feeling, too! Hooray for possibilities!" Her face felt like it could crack in half, she was smiling so hard. Sure, it was right at the beginning, but it felt so good. Jamie looked to Tessa, then to EJ, and decided to get up right then, before she started babbling about Lee's dimples.

"Okay, loves, I'm going to refresh my coffee," Jamie said before dashing back to the cafeteria. She returned moments later with her coffee and a soup bowl filled with dessert.

"Cannoli!" she exclaimed, lifting the bowl. "They just put these out." She set the dish on the table.

"Perfect! Every waffle needs a cannoli chaser," Tessa agreed.

EJ nodded and went for another mug of coffee, as well. There was a period of dedicated chewing until she returned. Once EJ was back in her seat, Tessa straightened up and seemed to remember something.

"Eej," she began gently. "What happened last night, before you got back to the car? You were so happy and then so down."

Jamie was grateful Tessa asked, even as she watched her bestie's face fall.

EJ leaned back in her chair and groaned. "It's so stupid. I can't believe I let some random dude get to me like that."

"Don't downplay it, Eej." Jamie reached out and squeezed her hand. "Just tell us what happened."

EJ sighed and then repeated what she'd overheard. Tessa gasped, and her eyes got as round as saucers. "I'm so sorry," she breathed.

Jamie swallowed hard. "Who the hell does that guy think he is?" She slammed down her mug. "Where do you want him buried?"

EJ waved her off. "Don't go to war for me, J. For one, Dia already told him off—it was amazing. And Zara Hernandez herself said my dress was fly and took a selfie with me." EJ couldn't help smiling as she scrolled through her photos, then handed Jamie her phone. "Take a look."

On-screen, there were Zara and EJ laughing together, looking like the best of glamorous friends.

Yes! Jamie silently cheered. This was the perfect antidote to whatever that Will guy had to say. She handed the phone to Tessa, who nodded in appreciation.

EJ leaned back in her seat again, but this time she looked as content as a cat in the sun.

"My night got better, and his got worse," she chuckled. "I'm not usually one to revel in this kind of schadenfreude, but when I last saw Lee's arrogant friend, he was passed out drunk, covered in leftover milkshake, and sitting on his designer sunglasses. Seeing him like that, I was much less concerned with his good opinion."

Jamie was mostly, but not completely, satisfied. "I still say a hearty 'Fuck him.' I don't know who this Will guy is, but he must be both blind and stupid."

"This was Lee's other friend, right?" Tessa asked. "Zara mentioned that he was hard to deal with right now. I'm sorry you guys had run-ins with him."

"You didn't?" Jamie asked, pushing her tray away.

Tessa shook her head. "Didn't even see the guy. He wasn't with Zara at the Airbnb, and I left the diner right before Lee and his friends turned up—which I will *never* forgive Colin for."

Jamie sighed. "Unfortunately, we're stuck with him for the year. Lee says that Will's here to finish up his undergrad degree. He's going to be at Longbourn until the spring." He'd also said that Will was going through it right now because he'd lost his job, or his pilot didn't work out. Whatever. All Jamie heard was a good guy covering for his bad friend. It was a relief to know that Lee had flaws.

"I overheard that, too," EJ groaned. "Lucky us." She rubbed her neck the way she always did when something stressed her out. "Wait, why didn't he just finish up remotely?" she asked.

The women paused thoughtfully. Tessa drummed on her chin with her fingers. "Eej, did Lee's friend say what he did? Can you describe him?"

EJ thought for a minute. "He was Franz's height, so medium tall. Asian American, black hair. Attractive but in a mean, bro-y way—kind of like a hot stockbroker. Or the young villain in a Korean soap opera."

"Anything else?" Tessa whipped out her phone and was searching the internet for EJ's clues. Jamie just looked on in confusion.

EJ finished her cannoli and went on. "Probably rich. Probably the most arrogant person I've ever met. Oh! Zara mentioned he had some huge public breakup. She had the impression that I already knew about it, so I guess he's famous and his ex is megafamous? Kyrie? Kylie? No . . . Carrie!"

Tessa choked on her coffee "I think you were insulted by Will Pak." She showed her friends the picture on his IMDb page.

EJ tilted her head and blinked. "That's definitely him—and I know none of these shows."

Jamie scanned the screen. "Same."

Tessa groaned. "Oh, come on, guys. The Wolf Pack Trilogy made half a billion worldwide. *Forensic Team: Hawaii* is one of the top ten shows on TV."

Jamie and EJ looked at each other and shrugged.

"Doesn't make me feel better," EJ said.

"Nor does it provide an excuse," Jamie added.

"I know, but . . . you snobs!" Tessa cried. This broke the tension. "You have to at least know *Band Camp*. It was a musical. You love musicals, for some reason."

EJ took a sip of her water and gave a half shrug. "We didn't have cable before cutting cords was popular. My parents thought it was a waste of money when you had PBS or DVDs from Netflix. To their credit, everyone in my family plays piano and one other instrument. If that makes me a snob, oh well. *Je ne regrette rien.*" She gave a defiant shake of her shoulders.

Jamie chuckled. *When I have kids, I'm going to make sure they get enough pop culture to hold a lengthy nostalgic conversation with their peers.* "All right, EJ, we know; you spent your childhood under a rock for only the best of reasons. Now can we please focus?"

Jamie folded her hands and looked at Tessa in amazement. "How did you guess it was Will from the useless clues EJ was giving?"

Her bestie squawked in protest, but Jamie just laughed. "Honey, there's a reason no one wants you on their team for Taboo."

Tessa snickered before she spoke again. "I'm never one to shy away from praise, but the one useful clue she gave was kind of obvious. The only famous Carrie that had a big breakup recently is Carrie Dean, duh."

Jamie suddenly had a vision of a blonde woman with blue lipstick sobbing on the beach with headlines like: Carrie Is Blue Crushed or An Ocean of Tears. That story had been everywhere, just a month ago.

"Even I know who Carrie Dean is!" EJ exclaimed. "Dia's talked my ear off about her new album. She won't stop playing it."

Tessa, who'd been scrolling nonstop since Carrie's name came up, gasped and pointed at her screen. "According to the *Hollywood Rag*, the second verse in her new song 'Dumb Blonde' is probably about Will; it calls him a boring snob she met on the job. Oof, I'd hide, too. Carrie fans are intense. Like a white-lady Beyhive."

Jamie winced. "I don't think anyone deserves the attack of a stan army, but I'm going to save my pity for someone else." She was still irritated with Will on EJ's behalf. "Carrie Dean didn't force him to act like an ass last night."

"This is so disappointing," Tessa said. "There are only so many Asian faces on TV. He has a responsibility not to suck." She paused to eat a miniature chocolate chip. "Then again, he didn't say anything about Carrie Dean doing that problematic geisha photo spread—and it was after they broke up! I guess he doesn't care *that* much about representation."

EJ started stacking her plates on her tray. "The only thing I need to know is that Will Pak has bigger problems than me and I've got bigger problems than him. I consider this done. Will's easy enough to avoid. And please don't hold grudges against this man for me, especially you, Jamie. You've got a relationship to grow." EJ smiled warmly at her and Tessa, then squeezed Jamie's shoulder.

And just like that, Jamie's anger at Will melted away. She had her friends, and maybe, possibly, she might have a boyfriend soon. Because God had a sense of humor, as soon as this thought passed through her mind, Jamie's phone chimed with a text.

> Hey, gorgeous, want to hit up the farmer's market later?

> Show me how a real New Englander does fall.

Jamie couldn't help her grin. She looked up from the screen to the knowing faces of her friends. EJ squealed. Tessa waggled her eyebrows. "I know who that's from," she said in a singsong tone.

Jamie giggled and texted Lee a flirty yes. Then she put her phone facedown.

"Enough about Lee, enough about Will," Jamie began. "We need to know why you ran off during the best part of the after-party. What's going on with Colin, T?"

Tessa dropped her head back and groaned. "Where do I even begin?"

EJ

It was a gorgeous fall day. The maples that lined the quad shimmered in deep reds and oranges. The gingko trees by the Administration Building were bedecked in buttery yellows and more strident goldenrods. Even the neatly trimmed bushes by the library had joined the spectacle in shades of plum. Since the weather was bound to be abysmal for the next four to eight months, days like this were to be savored. EJ had been forced to spend the morning inside: first doing some work on her capstone, which was progressing smoothly, then fulfilling her duties as a senior on the ballroom team teaching the newbies rumba and swing.

Done with everything she *had* to do, EJ hurried back to Bennet House to do something she *wanted* to: take a long walk in the nearby woods. It was sunny and warm, which kept her going even though the ground was still soft—and a little slippery in places—from several recent days of rain. She'd been walking for a good twenty minutes when her phone buzzed with a text from Jamie.

> At the hospital. Can you come

She gasped and, fingers flying, texted Jamie. Even though they were in a really liberal college town in pretty progressive Western Mass, EJ always had a little extra tinge of worry for Jamie when her friend was off campus. It took one hateful lunatic, and there were a lot of them around, these days.

Sure thing, J. What happened?

Lacrosse ball + my head=possible concussion

Might have blacked out for a second

EJ almost collapsed with relief. She responded quickly.

OMG! On my way.

I'll be ready to hold your hand.

Thx you know how much I 💜 hospitals

Lee is here, tho

Yay Lee. What a sweetie!

I just don't want to go into my whole thing/
phobia/whatevs

So I'm pretending to be bored, not terrified

Insisted on calling Malfoy, btw

He gave us a ride over

& he's still here

Boo Malfoy

I'll be good—see you soon.

When EJ got to the emergency room, she found Jamie looking on as Lee made a fuss in the waiting area.

"It's outrageous!" Lee fumed.

"It's routine, Lee," Jamie reassured him. Will said nothing to help, either, instead tapping idly at his phone.

"What's up?" EJ asked, putting her things down next to Jamie.

"We're looking at a three-hour wait," Jamie replied, resigned but not surprised.

"How is that even possible?" Lee exclaimed. "There are only like twelve people here."

EJ rubbed the back of her neck. His mood was not helping Jamie, who was successfully hiding her anxiety from anyone who didn't know her well.

"Lee," EJ began with quiet firmness, "it's a small public hospital on a Sunday afternoon. Not a high-danger time. Twelve patients are a lot. We"—she gestured to those in the waiting room—"are a tour bus pulling into a McDonald's at two a.m. They are slammed, but they are doing their best. May I suggest you accept things you cannot change? Take a lap around the floor if you need to?"

She sat next to Jamie and drew her friend close. She just needed to keep Jamie calm. Lee gave her an embarrassed smile. "My yelling isn't helping your head, is it?" He looked around. "I think I saw a soda machine when we came. Let me see if they have any Diet Dr Pepper."

"You remembered!" Jamie said happily.

"You did just mention craving one during our walk," he replied. "I don't think I get brownie points for that."

EJ smiled at the obvious warmth between them. "Hey, now," she interjected. "I was a Girl Scout until middle school, and I say the brownie points are yours."

"Can I get you anything, Eej?"

EJ thought it was cute that he already used her nickname. "I'll have the same, thanks," she said.

"No problem," Lee said before jogging down the hallway.

"Thanks, Lee," the young women sang after him.

"How are we doing, J?" EJ asked, gently moving Jamie's hair out of her face.

"Hanging in there." Jamie rested her head on her friend's shoulder and sighed. "I know it's an unlikely, unlucky mistake, but you remember Aunt Pauline. She's never been the same." EJ shook her head. She remembered thinking those stories about doctors leaving their keys in people were kinda funny. It never occurred to her that sometimes the patient almost died for no reason. That was exactly what had happened to Jamie's aunt—who, even though she got a nice settlement from the hospital, still had stomach trouble from her medical accident. Jamie said she hadn't looked at a hospital the same way since.

EJ gave her friend a squeeze. "I came as soon as I could."

"Clearly," Jamie said, looking pointedly at her friend's clothes.

EJ looked down too, shaking her head. "I didn't think I hit that many mud puddles." She stood and stretched. Then she unzipped her Longbourn hoodie, revealing a clingy yellow T-shirt, leggings that were similarly stained with grass, then dirt, and then mud. Her sneakers were more mud than shoe.

"You are phenomenally dirty," Will said bluntly.

"Excuse me!" EJ flinched, startled by his presence. She'd been so focused on getting to Jamie that she hadn't noticed that she was standing in front of Will. Why was he even talking to her? Her head whipped around, a frown etched into her brow. Something in her expression caused him to backpedal.

"But it works," he added hastily. "You look earthy and refreshed— like a wood sprite."

EJ looked to Jamie. "Well, damn. That must be the charm that made him the toast of the Teen Choice Awards." She tossed her hoodie down on her duffel and retook her seat.

Will looked around, alarmed. "Lower your voice, please."

EJ couldn't help her snort of laughter. She opened her mouth to say something cutting but noticed Jamie's discomfort and changed her mind.

Will continued speaking to her for some reason. "So you're familiar with my work."

EJ shrugged. "Not really, no. But my friend recognized you by description. She said you did some teen werewolf something. I wouldn't know; I don't watch much television."

"It was a movie," Will corrected. "Three, actually."

"How nice for you." EJ coated her words in honey, switching tactics. She wanted to adopt the particular brand of southern passive-aggressiveness her mom had perfected during her Tennessee upbringing. EJ had seen it deployed with everyone from annoying family members to useless store managers to great effect. There was a long silence, and then Will finally returned to his phone.

She turned back to Jamie and mouthed, "I'm being good." Then she explained her appearance. "I was walking through the nature preserve when I got your text. The shortcut back to campus was still muddy from all that rain last week. What can I say? I'm messy but I'm here."

"And I'm grateful," Jamie replied softly.

"I even brought distractions." EJ grabbed her duffel and began fishing out her offerings, one by one. "I've got *Rent* on Broadway on my laptop. I've got a bunch of theater-nerd podcasts queued up on my phone. And I found that issue of *i-D* you lost in my car." EJ fished each item out of her duffel bag as she named it.

"The thing about *Rent* is that the whole show falls apart once you realize all their art is bad," Will offered without looking up from his phone.

EJ forced a laugh. "Hey, look: a man with an opinion no one asked for. Haven't seen one of—"

Before she could say more, Jamie pulled EJ down into the seat next to hers. She took the magazine, eagerly.

"You are the best," Jamie said with a small smile.

"Yes." Will had decided to chime in again, for some reason. He tapped at his phone and spoke distractedly. "It's clear that you're a good friend, dropping everything to rush over here."

"Thank you," EJ replied with a new quizzical frown. She braced herself for a barbed insult and was confused when it didn't come.

Lee had just returned to the group, a soda can in each hand. "I could say the same thing about you, Will." He distributed the drinks and then settled on the other side of Jamie. "Thanks for the ride. Will's always been there when I need him, ever since we were kids."

EJ gave a short smile to Lee but then shot a skeptical look to Jamie. It was nice of him to try and remind them that Will had good qualities— even when they weren't anywhere to be seen. Will didn't seem to notice Lee's efforts on his behalf.

"No big deal," Will said, gaze still fixed on his phone. "I live in town, and I wasn't busy. Besides, your friendship is its own reward." He offered this sentiment in the same bored monotone one generally reserved for a bank's automated phone system. Even Lee didn't seem quite sure if Will was being sarcastic. He, Jamie, and EJ exchanged looks.

No matter how confusing Will was being, EJ needed to change. "Lee, are you good to hang out with Jamie for a bit?" she asked.

"Wild horses couldn't drag me away." He took Jamie's hand and gave it a warm squeeze.

Look at this mensch! EJ beamed at him. "Great! Since my dear friend and your dear friend have pointed out exactly how gross I am, I'm going to change. I have my ballroom practice clothes in here." She patted the duffel.

As she stood to look for the women's restroom, Will piped up, again. He looked up from his phone with interest. "Ballroom?" he echoed. "I love the Viennese Waltz. Do you do that?"

EJ rubbed her neck. She was too internally perplexed to answer with anything but honesty. "It's my second-weakest dance, but yeah. I have a respectable V. waltz." *What is with this guy?* she wondered. *Boorish and insulting one moment, quiet and awkward the next.*

Will nodded to himself. "Good to know," he said before returning to his phone.

She blinked at Will, then turned and looked questioningly at Lee. He shrugged.

"Okaaay." She squeezed her eyes shut and tried to shake off the whole exchange. "Like I said, going to change." EJ turned toward the hospital lobby and walked rapidly away, all the while thinking, *Will Pak is a fucking weirdo.*

Will

A week or so after he gave Lee and his love interest a ride to the hospital, Will invited his friend over for Scrabble and pizza. Lee shot back a text that said:

Yes, we need to talk.

Will groaned and sighed. Lee was going to try and pry the truth about Carrie out of him. He'd been hiding behind Carrie's brutal NDA to avoid discussing the subject. The truth was the whole thing was still too painful to talk about.

That evening, after he'd *trounced* Lee but before the food arrived, Will noticed his friend looking distinctly uncomfortable.

"Okay, do you want to talk about Carrie?" he asked Lee, who was sprawled on the adjacent leather love seat. The younger man visibly tensed but shook his head. Lee was hideously conflict averse due to living through his parents' divorce—and the many years before it, when they should have stopped being married. It took Lee several false starts before he got out his first sentence. Will knew he must seem in bad shape since Lee was treating him like a Fabergé egg.

"It's just—you're my best friend. You're lonely, Will, and you're sad, so I have trouble saying no to coming over anytime. I'd be lying, though," Lee continued with difficulty, "if I said I didn't feel torn between you and my school life."

He glanced from the coffee table to Will, then back to the coffee table. "I need you to start making friends who aren't me."

Will nodded, silently absorbing the fact that despite his best efforts, he'd become a burden to Lee.

"And you need to stop actively pissing people off," Lee continued.

Will sat up straight. "Who have I pissed off? I haven't been here that long."

Lee replied with a list. "Well, I'd be shocked if the staff of Cousin Nicky's isn't spitting in your coffee."

"They are pretty icy," Will said, considering. "I just thought that was 'northern hospitality,' so to speak."

Lee hadn't stopped talking. ". . . and yes, he was totally making fun of your name-dropping. Plus, Jamie's friend EJ clearly isn't your biggest fan—"

"Miss Rose Gold? What about her? She wasn't too friendly at the dance, or the hospital."

Lee gave his friend a long look. "Do you not remember the dance, or the after-party? You were in rare form that night. You managed to annoy Zara more in one night than her fiancé has in three years."

Will winced. So that was why Zara hadn't returned any of his texts. He'd have to send some flowers tomorrow. "I don't remember much," he admitted, "but I can definitely recall my hangover."

He knew Lee's sighs. This one contained a long lecture that his friend wasn't prepared to give. "Anyway, I know it's early, but I think I like Jamie a lot, and I like EJ, too, as a person. You're going to have to get used to hanging out with them or get some new friends—or both."

There was a tense silence. Will could tell Lee was not going to back down. When he created a "boundary," he stuck with it. Lee took a sip of his Pellegrino and slipped the dagger in. "I actually think you'd like EJ if you got to know her."

"You've been hanging out with her?" Will couldn't rationally explain this feeling of betrayal and tried to push it down.

Lee nodded, oblivious to Will's turmoil. "Yeah, a couple lunches with Jamie, but we get along. She got really into the Premier League on her year abroad, so we talk soccer. She supports the Gunners but shares my hatred of Chelsea, as any good person should."

Will frowned. Why had Lee taken her side—on everything? Had he truly been *that* terrible since his arrival or . . . were he and Lee just growing apart?

As if he'd read his mind, Lee looked him in the eyes and spoke seriously. "You're still my brother, Will. You're still the most important person in the world to me besides my mom. It's just that—I thought that the arrogance, the jerk behavior, that was all because of Carrie. It's so disappointing that you brought it here."

Will was glad to be sitting down. *Okay, this is bad,* he thought. *Lee thinks I'm an arrogant jerk—and he said so.* In the entire history of their friendship, Lee had never called him on his shit so directly.

Will sighed. "Have I really changed that much?"

Lee looked at him, scrubbed his hand over his face, and sighed. "It was like you joined a cult." He sat up. "Like, before Carrie, you took on acting projects for your own reasons: the character was interesting, or you liked the shooting location—that kind of thing. You were in Hollywood but not of it. It helped keep you interesting and wonderfully normal. With Carrie, you started buying into all the bullshit. You got a public Insta and talked about building followers like you used to talk about books. You showed up to parties for the paparazzi." Lee looked at Will directly. "You were talking about moving to LA, dude! You hate LA! You barely tolerate California."

Will was forced to laugh. "But really, it's a stupid, vulgar city. All the charm of Las Vegas without the sense of humor."

"I refuse to be derailed into defending my hometown when you were looking at buying a house there." Lee sighed and squeezed his temples. "Seriously, though, what happened? What did she do to you?"

Will sighed and melted into the sofa. He'd never fallen so fast, or had a relationship so thoroughly blow up his life before. He tried to speak but felt the hot prick of tears in his eyes. *She saw me, but then she used me.*

He'd met Carrie at a time when he was starting to get dissatisfied with his career. Despite refusing to play nerds or stereotypes, Will was still being cast as "the token Asian." His characters never got any depth or development. He knew he was one of the hottest guys in the *FT: Hawaii* cast, but he never got a romantic subplot. They wouldn't even consider giving him a solo for the musical episode—and he could sing! That was why it was so gratifying when Carrie noticed him. She was the one who insisted on their on-screen kiss. She was the one who made other people see him. But that was what made it so crushing to find out he was her token Asian boyfriend.

Will sat up and reached for Lee's phone. "I'm just gonna write the whole thing down. Please read it, away from me."

Lee nodded. He was used to Will's rambling emails. They'd met on Martha's Vineyard when Will was twelve and Lee was ten. Of course, neither of them lived there, but they kept their friendship going through emails and actual letters. Will liked those the best.

After rapidly typing on his phone for a few tense minutes, Will stood up. "Read that email draft, then delete it. I don't want to actually send it and violate my NDA."

"And you still can't talk about it?" Lee ventured.

Will shook his head. He felt his cheeks flush. "No, I can't."

The buzzer sounded. "You take a moment, I'll get the pizza," Lee said, leaving Will in the living room. Will didn't know whether to cry or laugh. He still hurt, but getting the whole thing out felt good. Cathartic, even. *This feeling is why people go to confession—or therapy.* Maybe *he* could go to therapy? It would give him someone to talk to besides Lee. And even if he made some new friends, he couldn't really trust anyone who wasn't legally bound to keep his secrets. As Will warmed to the idea of therapy, he also came around to Lee's point about making new friends. Why not try? He said, quoting Voltaire to himself, "If we do not find anything very pleasant, at least we shall find something new."

A GODDAMNED COSMOLOGICAL EVENT

EJ

Just two weeks ago, EJ had thought she had the modeling for her capstone pretty much wrapped up. Then she noticed a small error (she didn't fully integrate the current climate change projections), and as though she had pulled the wrong Jenga block, everything fell apart. She had to shift into full "grind it out" mode, especially since she wanted to get the modeling done before Halloween weekend. There was nothing quite as depressing as working in your dorm room when everyone else was out partying.

To reach her new mental deadline, EJ chucked out any sense of work-life balance. If she left Bennet House, it was only for class or the computer lab. When she was at home, she worked until she fell over, subsisting on protein shakes, frozen peas, and the occasional tangerine to prevent scurvy. (It was like being fifteen again: living in her toe shoes, rehearsing four hours a day and squeezing meals between homework and her studio time.) Finally, at the last possible moment, she had a breakthrough.

It was 6:00 a.m. on the Wednesday before Halloween. Bennet House, on its lonely hill, was hushed and dark—save for the light coming from EJ's desk lamp. Sometime in the small hours she'd awoken with a fully formed idea that proved to be the key to fixing her capstone project. She sat up, grabbed her laptop, and began reworking her bridge model. By sunrise, her model was complete. An hour later, so was the outline to her presentation. EJ ensured that her work was safely in the embrace of her hard drive, then backed up. Once all this was done, she stood up and did an ungainly but ecstatic happy dance. Then, as was her practice when anything good happened, she called home.

"Hi, Ella!" her mom said. At home, EJ was known as Ella to everyone but her father, who called her Lizard. She hadn't adopted EJ as a moniker until college, when she thought something more gender neutral would be helpful for a budding engineer.

"What are you doing up at this reasonable hour?" the older woman asked. Jokes about EJ's love of sleeping in were more tradition than comedy.

"I fixed my bridge!" EJ cried happily.

"Wait, wait, give me the context again, darling. Your mother is not a young woman."

"You're not old, either," she retorted. "Anyway, remember for my capstone, I'm doing a project on methods of improving failing infrastructure? Well, my second case study, the Bassington Bridge, was not coming together, at all—not for my ideal scenario, not for my practical scenario. Then, I don't know what changed, but when I woke up, it was like the solution was right before my eyes; all I had to do was write it down. Which I did!"

"That's tremendous, Ella!" her mother exclaimed. "I knew you could power through."

"Thanks, Momma. I'm so relieved. I thought I'd still be untying this knot in the middle of finals."

"Here's your dad. I'll let you tell him your good news."

After some rustling, she heard her dad's voice. "Hey! How's my Lizard?"

"Hi, Daddy!" she replied cheerily before telling her story a second time.

"That's wonderful, dear, truly," he said after EJ finished. "But what happened to doing your project on restoring the Old Stone Mill? You were so excited when you talked about that this summer."

"I know, Daddy, but I decided to do something a bit broader. Engineering for climate change is going to be a big industry. Historic building conservation is sort of a niche area. Since my capstone presentation is also my project submission for the Black Engineers conference, I want to cast a wide net for employers."

EJ had it all planned out. If the National Society of Black Engineers really liked this project, she could get a chance to present. If she got to do a presentation, even a poster, she would get interviews. If she got interviews, she could have a job lined up before graduation.

"There's a career fair, and many good employers participate the whole weekend," she added. "If I play my cards right, I could leave with a good offer."

EJ heard her father hesitating. "I understand that impulse, but you already compromised once when you switched away from aerospace engineering to civil for better job opportunities. Now you're compromising again, and I don't know why. It's not often that you get to pursue your specific interest or to spread your wings creatively in the working world. You should be grasping that opportunity."

Daddy sighed, and EJ ached at the sound of it. When she was little, EJ always thought she understood her dad best because of their shared scientific aptitude. Maya got his idealism, which seemed to matter more now. EJ remembered how overjoyed her dad was when her older sister announced that she was going for a degree in social work.

"There'll be more opportunities than you think, Daddy. I can always build sets for community theater or join a historic preservation group. Best of both worlds, right?" Her dad made some noncommittal noises. EJ soldiered on. "For now, my goal is to get the best job I can, pay down my loans. Maybe even travel a little, too. I just want to do good work, for a decent amount of money."

She at least had her mom's approval; she was thrilled by her daughter's career pragmatism. She'd often told her children, "I don't care what you do—actress, lion tamer, sea captain—as long as you have a salary and retirement plan by thirty. Broke in your twenties is an adventure. Broke in your thirties is a crisis."

"Anyway," EJ continued breezily, "I was hoping I could do my presentation for you and Momma over Christmas Break. Also, since I'm asking favors: Could you keep your ear out for any babysitting or dog-walking opportunities? I know it's some ways off, but I'll be right at the end of my stipend when I get home for three weeks and . . ."

"Sure thing, Lizard," her dad replied. "In fact, we just had an architect couple move in up the road. They mentioned needing someone to walk their Ms. Fifi then."

EJ relaxed. Even when her dad wasn't the most enthusiastic, he was supportive. "I think Mom mentioned her. She's a giant poodle, right?"

He chortled. "Oh yes. If you ask Kurt and Jerome, she's *the* giant poodle. Ms. Fifi's a pageant dog. Did you ever see that movie *Best in Show?*"

She chuckled. "No, but you can tell me all about her." EJ clutched the phone to her ear and relaxed as her father filled her in on the neighborhood gossip.

Later that day EJ met Tessa for lunch at Cousin Nicky's to celebrate her escape from her academic prison. When she sat down, EJ's stomach let loose an audible growl that made her entire body rumble. She had never been so hungry. She felt like food was just invented yesterday and she was finally getting her chance to try it.

EJ ordered her "special" (buffalo wings and a bowl of cucumbers with Old Bay Seasoning), then added curly fries and a double strawberry malt. Amelia took their orders and said, "See what happens when you don't visit? You get too skinny."

"Sorry, Amelia. I won't stay away so long next time." The older woman left them, and EJ slumped back into the booth. "I'm so relieved. It had only been two weeks, but I was just like, 'This can't be my life anymore.'"

"Welcome back to the land of the living!" Tessa cheered, raising her coffee mug in a toast.

"Thanks," EJ said, clinking mugs. "It's good to be back."

Tessa drummed her fingers on the chipped Formica table. "So that means you're definitely down for tonight?"

EJ gasped. How could Tessa think she'd miss tonight? (Well, to be fair, she'd pretty much bailed on all her other obligations for the past couple of weeks, so it wasn't unreasonable.)

"You bet your buns! This is a goddamned cosmological event—an actual, literal once-in-a-lifetime thing . . . I was always going to be on that roof, no matter what. I just would have brought my laptop with me," EJ added quietly. "What do you say to meeting at the main library at eleven? I'll bring my famous cocoa; you bring your sleeping bag for us to sit on."

Tessa nodded enthusiastically.

EJ picked up the check. "I got this one," she said, sliding out of the booth.

"Thanks, Eej. Oh! Don't forget your umbrella," Tessa advised. "It looks like the rain might kick up again."

EJ nodded, lifting the bubble gum–pink umbrella to reassure them both. Soon, with a friendly wave and a jingle out the door, she was gone.

Will

Damn, that's good coffee, Will thought, draining the last of his mug. He was sitting in the back of Cousin Nicky's diner with his sketchbook, drawing his surroundings. He hadn't had much time for just sitting and drawing until he came to Longbourn, always too busy with filming or TV appearances or his hot superstar girlfriend. So what if he'd lost all that in a matter of weeks? He had time to draw now. And play his piano. Silver linings, right?

All this time also meant Will was out of excuses; he seriously had to work on his physique. His agent had been quite insistent on this point since he left LA. "Look at Bradley Cooper; look at Chris Pratt," Katerina said. "They go from character actors to leading men. All because they got diesel." She said that Will could break out of ensemble TV with a new body. He could even get into movies again. "We'll carve you a new lane," his agent promised. "And we'll do it despite that fickle blonde girl."

That fickle blonde. Katerina wouldn't even say Carrie's name. But he couldn't talk. He hadn't told Lee the full story until a week ago. Instead Will had fled LA, set his social media to private, and started school in middle-of-nowhere Massachusetts. All he wanted to be was a quiet student who kept to himself until graduation. He was growing his hair out; he dropped his contacts for glasses; he even toned down his signature style. That was his biggest sacrifice; he had been on *Vanity Fair's* best-dressed list three years running. Now none of his friends would recognize him. *I'm wearing a hoodie, for Christ's sake.*

Will signaled for a refill. The manager came by and filled his mug without glaring. Progress. It had taken only a formal apology, overpaying for the booth he had ruined, and tipping 200 percent every time he came—but it was worth it. The diner had the best coffee in walking distance from his sublet. He'd walked there this morning.

That was one thing he didn't miss about LA. So much of your life was wasted on the freeway. And you couldn't even draw, not safely anyway. Will put his sketchbook to the side with its half-finished drawing of the tree out the window. Then he pulled at the hem of his beanie and picked up the menu. Hopefully, there was something that his trainer would approve of.

Will was busily calculating the calorie count of the salmon salad when a noisy conversation from a nearby booth broke into his thoughts. Why couldn't these people talk at a normal volume? Will had forgotten his earbuds at home and couldn't tune out the world, as was his practice. He returned to the menu, but it was no use—the rambunctious girls were thoroughly distracting.

Will thought he'd lean out from his booth and give the loud talkers a prolonged scowl. *Maybe they think they're alone. I'll start with an annoyed look,* he decided. It seemed like a sufficient rebuke. He put on his new sunglasses so he wouldn't be recognized and prepared his most unimpressed face.

He moved to the edge of his booth and leaned out; then he internally gasped. *It's that girl from the hospital. EJ, I think.* Will dropped his scowl and sat up.

Should I say hi, though? he thought. *Lee asked me to be nice—but she was weirdly standoffish.* After a few more moments of indecision, Will decided to say nothing and sip his coffee. This quickly turned into eavesdropping. *What are they so excited about?*

He waited until EJ left to inquire further, moving to the booth across from the other girl after the door jingled with the taller girl's departure. He pulled his Longbourn hoodie forward in the hope of passing for an ordinary, if shy, fellow student. "Excuse me, what were you talking about? What 'once in a lifetime' thing is happening tonight?"

Tessa

Tessa was leisurely sipping her coffee refill when a deep voice shook her out of her thoughts.

She jumped. Will Pak had just materialized on the spot, dressed as a TV executive's idea of a college student. It was slightly surreal seeing in person someone you'd watched on television. Her younger sibs were big Wolf Pack fans. Okay, she was a fan, too. *Would it be weird to ask him for his autograph?*

He looked at her expectantly—right! He'd asked her a question. For a moment her loyalty to EJ warred with her inner fangirl. The fangirl won, and she answered enthusiastically.

"The universe has conspired to give us a spectacular light show, a once-in-two-hundred-years meteor shower," she explained. "We're especially lucky because of our time zone and weather: nighttime with no clouds."

"So people are watching from the library?" Will asked.

"People are, but we're going to . . ." She looked around before whispering, "The roof of the Physics Building. It's at a slightly higher elevation than the library, and the crowd will be more hardcore enthusiasts than tipsy amateurs. If you're at all interested, you should come with us. Physics kids won't put you on TMZ."

Will's eyebrows shot up to his hairline, and Tessa struggled not to laugh. *Who does he think he's fooling?*

He removed his sunglasses and set them down with a sigh. "It seems my subterfuge is ineffective." He let down his hood and unzipped the sweatshirt.

Tessa decided to help him out. "Okay, number one: the sunglasses inside—never done unless you're hungover. This is New England in October. There is not that much sun to begin with. Two: there are several cute Asian guys on campus but only three, including you, who are movie-star hot: Tony Keng has a beard and like five visible tattoos, and David Cho has an English accent. The sweatshirt doomed you from the start." Tessa opted not to mention that she'd seen almost everything Will had starred in since he was fifteen. Instead, she added, "And three: you dress like an adult. I mean, I'm pretty sure you iron your jeans."

Will pursed his lips. "I send my clothes to the dry cleaner. Most real New Yorkers have their clothes cleaned."

I guess all those laundromats are just decorative, Tessa thought snarkily. She didn't get a chance to reply, though. Will was talking again.

"The guys here are in for a rude awakening once they leave this campus. Most women develop standards by the age of twenty-four. The wanton slovenliness that's so pervasive here will *not* fly," he said, shaking his head.

She laughed. "I think half the point of going to college is doing stuff that you wouldn't get away with in the real world."

Will didn't seem to be listening; he was staring at his immaculate boat shoes. "What if I wore sneakers? I could have passed for someone's visiting boyfriend, right?" he protested mildly.

"Nah, I'm Filipina, dude. That would've made it through the Asian grapevine in about six seconds. I would have a dossier on you by now."

Will chuckled, and they lingered in that odd conversational place where each had more to say but didn't know where to begin. No longer starstruck, Tessa dove in first.

"Look, you seem concerned with being inundated by unwanted attention, but there have been a lot of rich kids and even a couple of famous ones that have passed through this campus unscathed. Act normal, and people will leave you alone. At most, you may feature in an anecdote or two over Thanksgiving dinner, but no one here wants to make their name on you."

"Like fame in New York," Will inferred. "Some people might care a little; most don't give a shit."

Tessa nodded encouragingly. There was another beat of silence, and Will seemed to be getting up to leave. She spoke again.

"Do you mind if I say one more thing?" Gathering her courage, she slid to the edge of her booth. "So, freshman year: despite being super excited to be here, I was really homesick for the first month, and I didn't really get into campus life. After a while, I realized I had missed this crucial window where you could trip into a big pile of friends with, like, no effort. Well, I kind of gave up. I'd just go to class and then go back to my room to study. The most social thing I did was play video games with my high school friends online, like I never left home." Tessa spoke quickly to her coffee mug, occasionally darting glances at Will to see if he was listening.

"Thankfully, when I finally made an actual friend, she was a great one. At first, she'd just come over to play *Portal* or we'd stargaze from the Bennet House balcony. Then she started inviting me to things, like all the time. She was a sophomore and seemed to know everyone. I'd never say yes, but I'd also never say no. Finally, we were walking together between classes, and she says, 'I'm not going to pressure you into accepting any of my many invitations, but here's the thing about Longbourn: for the magic to happen for you, you have to show up. It's not going to come to your dorm room.'

"I don't know why, but something clicked. I started trying things. I joined clubs. I organized nature photography hikes. I got a flipping boyfriend." She giggled. "Once I started showing up, the Longbourn magic started happening."

"I didn't really come here for the magic," Will replied with a small smile. "Just to wrap up my BA."

Tessa let her face express her disbelief. "Okay, I'll pretend to accept that . . . and forget that there aren't lots of college courses from great universities online—that there are colleges in New York, LA, and Vancouver where actors usually work. I'll even forget that someone with your resources could have banged out your last classes over a con-centrated summer session."

Tessa looked at Will directly. "I'm going to forget all that and say this: you're here. Try showing up."

She shrugged as if to say, "Think about it."

Will nodded as if to say he would. He went back to sketching, and Tessa got ready to go. As she made her way to the door, he called, "Eleven, tonight?"

"Yup, we'll meet up at Cassler Library—it's pretty central—then head to the Physics Building."

Will thanked her. It was noncommittal but sincere. Tessa would take it. Now she had to figure out how to tell EJ about their possible guest for the evening.

EJ

After meeting with her delighted advisor, EJ took a short victory lap in the nature reserve and returned to her room. Now that her capstone fog had lifted, she could see her single with fresh eyes: it was a mess. Protein-bar wrappers were scattered across her desk. Various plastic bottles rolled on the floor, rattling stray cans of soda and seltzer. Her trash overflowed with tangerine peels and takeout containers. Her laundry pile was inexcusable. EJ's standards had more than slipped; they'd taken a nosedive off a cliff.

"The universe is telling me to get my life together," she said to herself. She hung up her jacket, threw on some neon leggings and her gray "Model, Analyze, Repeat" tank, and got to work. First, she carried a couple of loads of laundry down to Bennet House's creepy basement and, after a prolonged argument with the washing machine, started her darks and colors. When she returned to her room, EJ attached her laptop to its external speakers and scanned through her music selection for something energetic but encouraging. She settled on the soundtrack from *The Young Girls of Rochefort*. Cheerful, brassy French jazz was just what she needed.

A swept floor, a clean mirror, and four trips to the creepy basement later, EJ was folding her laundry to SZA's *Ctrl* when Tessa's face appeared on the screen of her silenced phone. She frowned and put the phone on speaker. "You're calling," she began cautiously. "You hate talking on the phone. What's wrong?"

Tessa's reply was too cheerful. "Wrong? Who says anything's wrong? In fact, things could be very right."

It was times like this EJ wished she could raise a single eyebrow. "If you want to convince me of something, you'll do better in person," she responded flatly. "Plus, I finally cleaned, and it's not gross here anymore."

"All right, I'm coming over," Tessa replied. "And I promise it's nothing horrible." Her friend disconnected the call.

That means it must be something only I think is truly horrible, like a cappella.

EJ shook off that thought with a shudder and took a moment to look around her freshly tidied space. She was proud of how she'd decorated her little single. She didn't (and couldn't) point to a page in the Restoration Hardware catalog and have her parents purchase everything, like her freshman roommate had.

But even if she had the money, she liked stuff with more personality. She liked thrift shops and Etsy. She liked old things. She liked that everything in her space had a story: her grandma Elizabeth's quilt on her bed, the trio of her completed embroidery projects on her wall, the record player she got from a garage sale and learned to repair via YouTube. These days EJ needed a very good reason to buy something wholly new. Researching climate change for her capstone made her really want to consume less.

Laundry done and put away, EJ was watching *Tiny Desk Concerts* on her laptop when Tessa knocked on her door. Before EJ could say "Come in," Tessa had entered and started explaining.

"First let me say, I didn't approach him, he approached me. He was hanging out in Cousin Nicky's—he must tip well if your old boss hasn't poisoned him—anyway he was asking about the meteor shower, and you know how I get so excited, explaining things—" She was pacing the length of EJ's bed now.

"And he was clearly super sad. He's lonely. Like, I never bought hot people being sad and lonely, but he definitely is. He just works really hard to hide it. Like, he is arrogant, but the arrogance is definitely a shield, and maybe there's a good guy under there—"

EJ held up a hand. "T, stop explaining. Summarize."

Tessa sighed. "I invited Will Pak to watch the meteor shower with us."

EJ's face fell. "Ew! Boo! Ew and boo!"

"Oh, come on, Eej," Tessa complained. "It's just one night, and there'll be a ton of other people there."

EJ closed her laptop and pursed her lips. "Just tell me one thing: Would you have invited him if you weren't a fan?" Again, she really wanted to raise one eyebrow. Tessa's motivations were probably *mostly* noble, but she sincerely doubted that her friend would be making the case for your average annoying prick of a senior.

The question burst Tessa's balloon. She stopped pacing, and her shoulders slumped.

"Then you're just asking me for a favor. In that case, I can be bribed," EJ said plainly. "It's not a matter of principle, only personal taste. I don't like Will Pak, but I can put up with anyone for the right price."

Tessa's expression wavered between hope and skepticism. She slumped into EJ's desk chair. "What's it going to cost?" she asked impatiently.

EJ sat up and crossed her legs, humming thoughtfully until she landed on an idea.

"Since this is about having to quietly grin and bear something, you must accompany me to the following: one a cappella concert, the fall musical, and Mime's the Word's fall performance. There are Bennet Women in all three shows, and they must be supported." The sharkiness of EJ's smile belied the sweetness of her words.

"Mime? *Mime?* I have to endure the garbage breakfast of musical theater, and you add a silent, boring cherry to that crap sundae?" Tessa cried. "I didn't kill anyone."

Shifting on her bed, EJ looked at her friend without pity. "My dude, you're asking me to play nice with someone I know was actively talking shit about me. Besides, it's not like I'm not going to suffer. I'm putting myself through a whole a cappella concert because Tiffany started a new group that sings sixty percent medieval music and forty percent renaissance music." She frowned at the thought. How was she ever going to stay awake?

"That does sound rough for you," Tessa admitted. "Not as bad as a Longbourn musical, though."

EJ snorted. "The fall musical is always well done. It's the spring musical that gets wacky."

"The problem isn't the fall musical," Tessa growled. "The problem is all musicals!" She huffed.

EJ couldn't control her giggles. "I'm sorry, I don't get how musicals are your cultural bridge too far. You are the person whose senior quote was from *CSI: Miami*. You hold *90 Day Fiancé* watch parties. You have a *Real Housewives* and a *Bachelor* fantasy team."

Tessa huffed and rolled her eyes. "God save me from the tyranny of good taste," she muttered.

"Oh, don't give me your snob talk. You make fun of my lack of pop-culture knowledge. I get to make fun of the stuff you like. Fair is fair."

"Fine," Tessa huffed. "I don't like musicals because there's no reason for the people to be singing! I have never received a satisfying answer to the critical question 'Why are they singing?' Ugh." She drooped at EJ's desk.

EJ looked away from Tessa's forlorn face and addressed her framed, autographed photo of Dolly Parton. "What do you think, Dolly? Should I be merciful? Should I be kind?"

Tessa turned to the photo. "Dolly, please. EJ tells me you're really great, and I've never made fun of her for being a black girl into country music—"

"Hey! I'm fine being a weird black girl—it's like my brand. And also, I'm only into *good* country music: Dolly, Patsy, Reba, the Chicks—"

Tessa interrupted her with a cough and, hands still folded, turned back to the photo. "Anyway, Dolly, if you could get her to take mime off the table, I'll be so grateful, and I won't complain, out loud, about the other stuff she makes me sit through."

EJ smiled at Tessa, genuinely this time. "All right, hon, how about this: you get to swap the mime for an unnamed event in the future. Think carefully, though. That mystery show may involve *slam poetry*."

Tessa swallowed hard and stuck out her hand. "I'll take my chances. So we have a deal?"

"Yes," EJ confirmed as they shook on it. "I will not make Will Pak feel unwelcome. I will share cocoa with him, and I will tolerate him." She couldn't help grumbling the last part.

"Thank you," Tessa cried. "I can't wait to tell my brother! He's a huge *Wolf Pack* fan! He's gonna die! Maybe I can get a picture?"

EJ raised her eyebrows. "Of course, all of this assumes that he'll show up."

Will

It was only after EJ's friend left that Will realized he didn't know her name. Her words stayed with him, though, through his salad and his walk home. Even as he tried to get a little coursework done back at the condo he was renting, Will simply couldn't concentrate. *That was like the intro to a TED Talk,* he thought, revisiting the unsolicited advice. Maybe he should go. The event sounded like a good idea: intellectual but fun—perfect for the image he was creating post-Carrie. He could even snap a few photos for the 'gram. His sister, Lily, had called his campus sunsets "basic" and his bookshelf photos uninspiring.

But he didn't want to go alone, and if he went with . . . that girl, it would definitely involve EJ, which could be uncomfortable. Conflicted, he sent a text to his sister. She was a freshman at the Fashion Institute of Technology and was navigating a similar social minefield with the grace he lacked.

> Hey, Tiger Lily!

> Hey, big bro. What's up?

> Okay . . .

> So . . .

Spit it out!

Got invited to meteor shower watch thing.

2 issues:

Katerina still wants me to lie low.

Also, weird vibe from friend of inviter

She's friends with Lee's new g/f, so can't ignore.

OMG!

JUST BE A PERSON!

You've forgotten how unfamous ppl work

Friends once removed are often awkward

It happens when people aren't in the habit of faking nice.

But!

NO!

Go be awkward

See some stars or whatever

But . . .

Tiger Lily out

Will looked at his phone screen quizzically. "What does she mean?" he complained. "Katerina says I'm remarkably grounded, and so did *Us Weekly*." Reflecting on the fact that he'd just cited his agent and a gossip magazine as his evidence, Will realized his sister might have touched on something.

As evening fell, he found himself pacing the length of his sublet's kitchen. He wanted to call Lee but remembered that he had a cappella rehearsal tonight. As his fingers hovered over the screen, Will realized he had no one to call. He hadn't made any real friends yet. It was harder than he'd thought.

One thing that was certain: he needed to get out of his apartment. The surrounding decor did nothing to lift his malaise. He was renting a condo from a Longbourn anthropology professor currently on sabbatical in Belize. She had a large collection of tribal masks from her trips around the world. They were on literally every wall—even in the bathroom. When he first saw the place, Will thought the masks added a cultured charm. He insisted that Dr. Blakenship leave them up—he might have promised to dust them.

Will shook his head. Now their silent faces peered from every wall. They seemed to judge him. Something needed to change, and soon. In the absence of another idea, he grabbed his coat and made his way to the library.

EJ

That night, EJ sat on a ledge of planters adjacent to the library steps, next to a small bronze statue of Longbourn's mascot, Wally the Walrus. She tugged on the sleeves of her superwarm ballroom hoodie and riffled through her duffel bag, making sure she had all the evening's essentials.

"Binoculars? Check. Water? Check. Massive cocoa thermos? Check. Flask of Baileys? Check. Flashlight . . . flashlight? Where is that thing?" She dug into her duffel bag and started searching in earnest. EJ was so wrapped up in her search that she didn't notice a figure approaching in the dark until he said, "Hello there."

She started and sat up. "Jesus Christ!" she exclaimed. "What are you, part ninja?"

"Oh, sorry. I didn't mean to startle you," Will began, seeming genuinely apologetic.

EJ waved away his words, impatiently. "Don't worry about it. I'm sure you took two years off my life, max."

Will shifted uncomfortably, and EJ released a soft sigh. *Be nice,* she chided herself. *You made a deal.*

She spoke again, injecting some warmth into her tone. "Ready for a goddamned cosmological event?" she asked cheerily.

Will gave a puzzled nod. Then EJ's phone buzzed with a text. "Tessa's running a little late. She'll be here in a few."

"Cool." He patted his jeans. "Thanks for letting me tag along."

EJ gave the ghost of a smile before looking at the night sky. "I think conditions are optimal for gazing tonight: perfect darkness, perfect clarity. We should have quite the show."

"So I've heard." He nodded and shoved his hands deeper into his pockets. "I've never seen a meteor shower before . . . or, now that I've thought about it, really looked at the sky for any sustained period of time. Growing up in Manhattan, you get used to not looking up."

EJ groaned internally, prepared to be lectured on pizza or bagels or dim sum until Tessa finally turned up. "Native New Yorker, then?"

"Born and bred. Though I'm not one that thinks it's the center of the world. I prefer London. It's like New York but with a bit more history and charm."

EJ nodded. She could handle basic small talk, "I'm from the DC area, and I love it there—but I'd move to Edinburgh in a heartbeat." She rhythmically tapped her chest for emphasis. Will didn't have a chance to respond as EJ spotted Tessa over his shoulder.

Before long, they secured a spot on the roof of the Physics Building. They unfurled Tessa's unzipped sleeping bag on the ground to block the cold from the cement. EJ sat down at one end; unzipped her duffel bag; and unpacked her thermos, flask, and binoculars.

"Tessa, cocoa now or later?"

"Ooh, now, please," she replied, rubbing her hands together.

EJ called across to Will: "Tessa and I can share the thermos. You can drink from the cup—I can even spike it a little," she added, waving the flask.

"I'm feeling chilly and a bit adventurous, so yes," Will said.

"So, Will," Tessa began as EJ poured. "Let me ask you a question I bet no one has yet: What's your major?"

He laughed. "Art history." Both ladies raised their eyebrows in surprise. "Really," he insisted.

"Why art history?" EJ asked. She was expecting drama or finance. Then again, she'd met rich girls who studied art history so they could one day "manage their husband's collections." Will seemed like one of those husbands.

He ran his fingers through his hair. Apparently, he'd been growing it out. It was almost to his shoulders now. EJ thought it was a better look than the Patrick Bateman Special Will had been sporting at the Fall Formal.

"I love art; it's that simple," he responded, giving a slight nudge to his glasses. Those were new, too. Between his new hair and his glasses, you could see how someone might mistake Will for a nice, normal guy.

"My mother gave that to me," he continued. "She used to take us to the Met, the Frick, and the Whitney so often that just going to the museums feels like going home."

Tessa nodded. "You're lucky to have so much easy access to that kind of thing. My hometown is an hour from Princeton and a little more than that to the city, so we don't have our own museums. I have been to the Museum of Natural History on a field trip, though. It was great . . . until we got kicked out. Someone from our class tried to light the fire in the cavemen exhibit." She sighed dramatically. Will and EJ laughed.

EJ remembered her own early exposure to art. "Even though I was in the burbs like you, T, we could at least metro down to the Smithsonian museums and the National Mall."

Passing the carefully prepared cup, EJ added: "It also helped that they're free. In the summers we would go almost every week. Each of us got to pick a museum: Maya, my older sister, liked the art museums, especially the modern stuff like at the Hirshhorn or the National Gallery's East Building. I loved Natural History and Air and Space. Mom loves history and modern architecture, so she chose the African

American History Museum almost every time. Dad was the X factor. He was the one who took us to the Anacostia museum, or the National Zoo. Once he even surprised us with a trip to the Great Blacks in Wax Museum, in Baltimore—he thought it required a visit. The rule was, you couldn't complain during someone else's turn or yours would get skipped. Together we got pretty well rounded."

She watched Will sip the cocoa. His eyes widened. "This is fantastic! What's in here?"

EJ smiled to herself. It was a small thing, but she was quite proud of it. "My three favorite brands of hot chocolate mix, plus a pinch of cayenne, and a secret ingredient. The goal is to get a creamy taste, but with just adding water so the cocoa stays hot. I got this down to a science back when I was in Girl Scouts."

"EJ introduced me to her hot chocolate during our first long hike together," Tessa added while adjusting her high-powered camera, "but cruelly she won't give me the recipe."

"Then what would I give you at Christmas?"

"A Christmas card with the recipe?" Tessa suggested.

They laughed; EJ felt herself relaxing. *Maybe this won't be so bad after all.*

Slowly, more science students joined them on the roof. EJ and Tessa waved at their classmates as they passed. At first, Will was embarrassingly uncomfortable, jumping at every camera flash, but once he realized that no one was photographing him, he seemed to calm down. He even took a couple of selfies on his own. EJ and Tessa briefly surrendered the sleeping bag so they could be safely out of frame.

A little after midnight, Tessa got them on the subject of their favorite artists. First, she recalled how a high school project on Ansel Adams had led to her taking up nature photography. Then EJ chimed in, describing her revelatory experience at the Van Gogh Museum in Amsterdam. Will was in the middle of an impassioned argument for the relevance of the English Romantics when voices called to Tessa from across the roof.

"Benny! Sara!" She waved, then turned back to EJ and Will. "I'll be right back. Two shakes, 'kay?" Both watched her go, longingly. It was hard to find something to say without her. They stared off into the distance. After a few moments, Will cleared his throat, then broke the increasingly awkward silence.

"So what's your major, EJ?" he asked.

"Civil Engineering," EJ replied, taking another swig of cocoa. She held the thermos up in offering.

Will shook his head. "I'm still working on my first mug." He took another sip. "So is that like, bridges and tunnels?"

"Yes, among other things: roads, canals, levees." She set the thermos to the side and sat in a butterfly position, pressing the soles of her feet together and sitting up straight. "We basically create the built environment." She rolled her neck slowly: right, then left.

Will continued drinking his cocoa again, thoughtfully. "Civil engineering," he repeated. "That's surprising."

EJ froze. Would he follow up with something racist, sexist, or both? Why did people think that they were complimenting you by saying stuff like "I didn't think women / black people were smart enough to do science, but you're the exception"? It frustrated her to no end. She waited for him to complete his thought, so she knew exactly what she was dealing with. After no words came, she picked the scab.

"Surprising how?" EJ ventured, willing her tone to be neutral.

Will gave a sort of half shrug. "It sounds kind of . . . I don't want to say *boring*, but not creative. And you strike me as creative."

EJ gave Will a long look across the sleeping bag before responding. He was drinking the last of his cocoa and rocked from side to side. He seemed to think this conversation was going well.

"All engineering is creative problem-solving," she began. "Sometimes that problem is 'How do we build that bridge?' Other times that problem is 'Can we make that bridge beautiful?' Just because a career isn't artistic doesn't mean it lacks in creativity."

"I get that," Will said, setting down his mug. "So why engineering?"

"It's simple," she began. "I like it. I'm good at it. And engineers don't starve." This was her "cocktail-party dum-dum" response. The one EJ gave when she was over explaining her field or her place in it. She gave a little laugh as punctuation. Now, hopefully, they could talk about something else, anything else.

"Are you doing anything for Halloween this weekend?" she asked. "Even though we don't have fraternities at Longbourn, things can get pretty crazy. Last year the Matisse House—"

"No frats? That's interesting," he interrupted absently. Will ran a hand through his hair and hummed. "But going back to engineering, I still—you don't seem very passionate about it."

EJ turned toward him, brow creased. "How on earth would you know what I'm passionate about?" she asked crisply.

Will gallingly shifted toward her on the sleeping bag. "It's just . . . you and Zara talked Shakespeare for quite a bit at that diner. You seemed really passionate about theater. I thought you had to be an actor or a playwright. Something like that."

She swallowed hard. She'd been doing her best to forget Will from that night. She considered her options and ruled out loudly telling him off in favor of icy passive aggressiveness.

"Oh? I didn't think you were paying attention. You seemed thoroughly absorbed by your milkshake." There was enough ice in her tone to skate on.

"I'm observant by nature," he said, becoming the living incarnation of dramatic irony. "It comes in handy."

EJ rubbed the back of her neck and adopted a slightly bored tone. "Observation is good, but I hope tonight has shown that asking questions like a normal person is a better—less creepy—way to learn things about people." She smiled at him perfunctorily and turned away. This seemed like a good time to do a little passive-aggressive stretching. In her former life as a wannabe ballerina, nothing had said *go away* like going through your whole stretching routine without making eye contact.

Will uttered a surprised "Creepy?"

"Creepy," EJ insisted. She sat up straight, then leaned into the pike position, reaching forward and grabbing the soles of her feet. After feeling the kinks in her spine release, she sat up again and began her shoulder stretches. "What else would you call sullenly pretending to ignore a conversation two feet away, only to pipe up, weeks later, with random tidbits you picked up like some discount Sherlock Holmes? Weird? Off putting?" She didn't look at Will but could feel him watching her.

"Effective, mostly," he offered jokingly.

EJ faced him again. "Many a stalker is effective, but also creepy. But I'm sure you know that much better than I. Being a famous person and all." She ceased stretching and set the thermos between them.

"Here, have some more cocoa," she quietly ordered. Then EJ pulled out her phone and began checking her email, effectively ending the conversation.

Will

Will sipped his refill slowly, relishing the warmth. He hadn't thought to bring gloves, and his hands were freezing. His leather jacket wasn't the best idea for tonight, but at least it kept the wind out. His scarf was warm, too. Discreetly, he stole a glance at EJ. He didn't understand her. It seemed like they were finally having a conversation about something real, and then she went and called him creepy. Evidently engineering students could be as shallow as everyone else, too. His eyes bounced around the roof, scanning for Tessa. Maybe if she came back, right now, he could turn the night around.

He'd been really enjoying himself up until about ten minutes ago. Tessa and EJ seemed genuinely interested when he was talking about his major. EJ even asked some intelligent questions. Her tastes were a bit pedestrian—Impressionists, Van Gogh, and the like—but at least she understood that art could be fascinating, that it was worth talking about. (Unlike Carrie, who knew only the auction values of the paintings she bought and talked about them like stocks.) The point was, he was having fun. He was getting to be an ordinary student on an extraordinary night. And then things went off the rails.

Still better than being home with the masks, Will thought.

He looked over to EJ again. She'd put down her phone and was now taking a few nips straight from her flask.

Perhaps that will put her in a better mood, he thought. Will glanced at his watch. The meteor shower was half an hour away. He sighed and looked up at the sky. At least it was a pretty night, as promised: white diamonds scattered widely on a black blanket. But there was nothing revelatory about this night sky. It was certainly better than New York and Vancouver but nothing to write home about.

Someone on the roof interrupted his thoughts with a cry: "Did anyone bring red Saran Wrap?"

"Right here!" EJ called. Will watched her dig into her bottomless duffel.

"Wait, who said that?" responded the voice, searching the roof with a flashlight.

"Look left, toward the front." She waved the package over her head. The light shone on EJ's face. "Aughh," she cried, covering her eyes.

"Oops! Sorry." The light went out, and soon a slim South Asian face appeared above them. "Eej, is that you? You're a lifesaver!"

"Yup." EJ smiled. "Here you go, Arun," she said, proffering the roll. "Do you need a garbage bag, too?"

"Let me take it, just in case." As she dug in the bag, her friend noticed Will. "Hey, dude, sorry I didn't see you there. I'm Arun." He gave a small wave.

Surprised, he reciprocated without thinking. "Will. Hi."

"Nice to meet you. Oh hey, I didn't see *The Wolf Diaries* or whatever, but it's always good to have an Asian guy on-screen who's not 'the nerdy friend.' Thanks for that."

Speechless, Will nodded as EJ handed over the black garbage bag. Tessa was right: people noticed him but truly didn't care. Will felt a weight lift in that moment. Though he wasn't anonymous, he wasn't the focus of anyone's attention. That could make a nice change, for a while. EJ and Arun carried on and finished up their conversation without him.

"Thanks, Eej," Arun said, lifting the items. "See you tomorrow?"

"You know it! Every day I'm modelin'."

Arun laughed. "I still have that shirt," he said before making his way back across the roof.

Will thought he might try starting over with EJ. "How'd you know they'd need that?"

She responded readily; all it took was the right subject. "When there was talk about viewing from here, we thought we'd try to block the security lights. White light blows out your pupils so you can't see as much," she explained, pointing toward the artificial light. "They're low enough for a tall person to reach. True Girl Scout, I thought I'd pick up some garbage bags in case people remembered the conversation, but not the items themselves."

"Always be prepared. Right?" Will said with a laugh.

"Be prepared," EJ corrected. "'Always' is the Boy Scout motto."

Will looked back at the lights for a bit before turning to EJ with another question. "I understand the garbage bag. But why the red Saran Wrap?"

"If you wrap your flashlight in red and keep it on low, your pupils stay dilated, and you'll be able to see more of the sky. I mean, we can't have it completely dark up here." She laughed. "Don't want kids falling off the roof just to avoid light pollution."

Will blinked in response. "That's brilliant."

She shrugged. "It is—but it's not my idea. I learned that little life hack from my first stargazing trip." A small smile crept onto her lips.

"What was that like?" Will asked, moving a little closer to her.

EJ gazed up at the sky, dreamily. "I don't think I really saw the stars until I was about twelve," she began, leaning back on her hands. "We had this field trip to the Goddard space center—it's a part of NASA about half an hour from my middle school—anyway, they helped work on the Hubble and had opened this huge exhibit for its twentieth anniversary. For the first time I could really see how amazing and complex stars are." She shivered as a strong breeze swept across the roof.

"Would you like my scarf?" he offered.

EJ smiled at him, genuinely. "No, thank you. I think I've got something in here." She reached into her bag and felt around until she retrieved an old flannel blanket. She snapped it like a sail and then pulled it around her shoulders.

"Anyway," she said, returning to the story. "My little mind is being blown by all this when I spot a panel on the opposite side of the room explaining light pollution. Mind double blown: now I know—supertelescopes aside—why I've never seen what's truly visible from Earth." EJ tugged at her hoodie, then continued.

"This is all I can talk about for like a month. Then one Saturday my dad says, 'There's a new moon tonight, little Lizard. Let's go see some stars!' The whole family piles into the car, and we drive an hour plus to somewhere in Virginia for this park's family stargazing night. There's no light on the path between the parking lot and the gazing park, so we rent flashlights wrapped in red plastic." She closed her eyes with the memory.

"When we got to the clearing . . . I don't think I truly understood wonder as a concept before. I just looked, looked, and looked, trying to memorize the sky. It was literally awesome." She opened her eyes again. Something about EJ sparkled when she spoke like this. Will found it intriguing.

"Honestly, I've never experienced anything like that," he replied. "But the way you describe it sounds amazing."

"Maybe it will happen tonight." She turned away from him to face the sky. Whether it was the Baileys in her flask or the conversation, he and EJ had moved past the earlier weirdness. Perhaps it was just the feeling of experiencing a "goddamned cosmological event" together. Whatever the reason, this was nice.

"Lights out, lie back!" someone ordered. Across the roof screens were darkened, and devices were stowed away. Tessa made her way back to the sleeping bag by the red light of her plastic-wrapped phone. EJ fished a travel pillow from her duffel and lay back. Tessa gestured for Will to do the same.

"This is easier on your neck," Tessa explained.

"And you won't accidentally block anyone else's view," EJ added.

Will did as he was told; everyone around him was already lying on the hard cement roof.

This is how cults are formed, he thought as he lay back. Conversation on the roof dropped to a murmur. EJ and Tessa were silent. Everyone was looking up. Then, one by one, they each started to see the sky, *really* see it. Tessa gasped happily as EJ breathed an awed "Hot damn!"

Will was agog. The night sky wasn't black at all. It was purple, and blue, and crowded—and the stars . . . they were so much more than distant diamonds; they were a glittering snowstorm frozen in midair. Points of light were scattered across every bit of the sky: some pulsed, some winked. It was all so much more than he'd expected.

"This is here, all the time?" Will surprised himself by asking.

"Incredible, right?" EJ confirmed. "This is how people saw the sky hundreds of years ago."

"And this is still with a fair bit of light pollution," Tessa added. "I got a chance to visit Bryce Canyon. It's what's called a Dark Sky Park, no light pollution—like nothing you've ever seen. I'm gonna try and get a job there next summer."

"I'm jealous," EJ replied. "Can't imagine a better summer than one under the stars." She sighed. "If everything goes right, I'll have a new grown-up job and new grown-up life. Which is not at all terrifying."

Will was silent, still taking it all in. He turned to EJ, who was searching the sky with binoculars. Happy and unguarded, she was radiant in the darkness.

EJ

EJ turned and looked at Will briefly, then looked back to the sky. She was thinking about supernovas: how they burned brighter than whole galaxies. How the remnants of long-dead stars hung in the universe like glowing ghosts. She thought of how cultures, long ago, had looked to the stars and seen gods. Mostly she thought of the hugeness, the vastness of it all. It gave a scale to her many plans and decisions. Even if she fucked everything up, the stars would be the stars. In that, she found a peace that generally eluded her.

"Isn't it wonderful," she said quietly, "how little we matter?" Almost simultaneously, the roof gave a collective gasp.

"Showtime," EJ whispered happily, as the first streak of light crossed the sky.

HALLOWEEN AND AFTER

Jamie

I'm on the pooch, Jamie texted Lee drowsily; white wine made her more sleepy than tipsy. She went outside to avoid falling asleep on a stranger's couch. Inside, the party was ending the way a cappella parties always ended: with the arrangers arguing over music like it was life or death.

*porch

"I'm not disrespecting Beyoncé; I just question her importance," insisted one voice.

"She's our generation's Michael Jackson!" That was Lee.

"She can't be! Michael Jackson is still Michael Jackson," the other voice was shouting. "That's what makes him Michael Jackson!"

It was *the* party of Halloween weekend, the BournTones Masquerade—an ostentatious way to say *costumes required*. Most people didn't wear masks. Jamie and Lee had gone as Raggedy Ann and Andy—his idea, of course. He showed up at her single with a rented costume, a yarn wig, and a huge, persuasive smile.

"We both have freckles! This will be great!"

Even though her soul cried out against putting so much gingham on her body, she couldn't say no to her first couple's costume. Well, romantic couple's costume. She and EJ had besties costumes every year. As for EJ, she'd had enough enthusiasm about their costume for everyone involved.

⟋⟍

"A couple's costume?" Jamie had smiled at EJ's gasp. "That's like a pro-posal!" she squealed. EJ was helping Jamie get her hair under the red yarn wig. Even though Jamie had naturally red hair that would have suited the costume, Lee was really fixated on the idea of them wear-ing the yarn wigs that came with the rental. He got weirdly stubborn about his artistic vision. EJ was confident that she could get Jamie's long and wavy hair tucked away, something about a wig workshop during her dance academy days. She sectioned Jamie's hair into two parts and started braiding the left side.

"So . . . are you and Lee on the road to being official? I mean, have you talked about it? Should I get Tessa to bring it up?"

Their younger friend was putting zigzag cornrows into Lee's hair in the main common room. They both knew Tessa would and could get all the dirt, if deputized. Jamie shook her head.

"Eej, it's been under a month. No guy wants a girl pressuring him this early." Jamie gave a half shrug. "We're seeing each other plenty. We're having a good time. I don't want to wreck things by getting too serious too fast."

The world of heterosexual dating was very new and terrifying, but Jamie had one star to guide her: prior experience as the "gay best friend." Over the years, kissing turned into making out, which turned into sex, but things always fell apart the same way: with the dishonest "He thought we were just having fun," the infuriating "He said he felt too pressured," the annoying "He doesn't want to put a label on things." She was determined not to make the same mistakes, even if that meant taking things slow.

EJ paused in the middle of the second braid; the look on her face said Jamie's bestie was slightly skeptical of this approach. "You do want to be his girlfriend, though, right?" she asked, talking to Jamie's reflection.

"Definitely. Lee is amazing! He's really caring. He's a feminist. He only got hot recently so he doesn't have a huge ego." Jamie stilled EJ's hands and turned to face her. "I know how great he is; that's why I'm being so careful."

EJ started to speak, broke off briefly, then started again. "Look, my momma would say, 'A closed mouth doesn't get fed.' That's all."

It clearly *wasn't* "all" as EJ squeezed her hands and went back to braiding. She'd wrapped the hair ties about both ends of Jamie's braids and caught her eyes in the mirror.

"This is going to sound crazy, but," EJ began, "the moment you met Lee, I felt something in the air. It was this crackle, this feeling of electricity. Like the air right before a thunderstorm. I felt like I was witnessing the start of something great."

Jamie felt her eyes widen slightly.

EJ went back to braiding. She tried to continue, a little nervously. "And yes, I know I am way too invested in your relationship, but I would hate to see you two fall apart before you begin because Lee thinks you're dragging your feet. He strikes me as someone who needs a bit of reassurance."

Jamie turned and looked at her friend, not sure what to feel. It was nice that her budding relationship had at least one cheerleader, but it upped the pressure. She leaned back in her chair and sighed. "I will think on that, okay?"

EJ nodded and reached for the extra-long hairpins.

And now Lee was here. He had taken off his wig and now ran a hand over his hair. "This is so weird. Cool, but weird. No one's ever braided my hair before. I kept it short for most of my life, so I never had the chance."

That was for the best, TBH. Lee looked like the least stylish member of a boy band, or Lil Wayne's accountant trying to be down. The patchwork overalls didn't help. Lee seemed to read her thoughts. He gave her his best model pose.

"On the hot, light-skinned dude scale of Drake to Jesse Williams, how attractive am I right now?"

Jamie laughed. "Your sexual energy is too strong. I can't stand up, I'm so overwhelmed."

He gave her a squeeze in response. "You seem done, wanna go back to my place?" Lee patted Jamie's wig. Her head lolled slightly. "I don't think you're up to four flights of stairs."

"I am definitely tipsy," Jamie agreed. If she'd been sober, she'd probably be flustered or panicking now. (She hadn't spent the night before!) Instead she said an easy, "Let's get out of here."

They drifted out of the party arm in arm and walked to Lee's car in pleasant silence. Another nice thing about him was that he didn't drink, so she always had a sober ride home. They got in the car and started toward his apartment. Jamie's nerves suddenly sobered up.

I'm going to sleep over! Am I even wearing cute underwear? Jamie wasn't sure. She skimmed her IG to calm down.

"Oh cute! EJ got a photo with Jonathan Coulton. She loves him." While the rest of the campus got dressed up to dance in each other's living rooms, EJ had spent the biggest party day of Halloween weekend in Northampton at a live taping of *Ask Me Another*.

"That's cool," Lee replied. "Was that the NPR thing? I think Will was there, too. Maybe they met up?"

Jamie couldn't help her snort. There was no way EJ would hang out with Will by choice.

"Okay, that's pretty unlikely," Lee admitted. "But they could be such good friends."

She snorted again.

"You scoff, but Will lived with my fam in Cali—"

"Wait, what?" Jamie's eyebrows shot up. She knew Will and Lee were very close, but she didn't realize that they'd lived together. "When was this?"

Lee tilted his head back. "It was right after my birthday, so he was fourteen or fifteen."

This helped explain quite a bit of their dynamic; they were pretty much brothers. Once she'd processed that part of the story, she let her mind absorb the rest.

"Why'd he move in with you?" Jamie asked.

Another thoughtful pause. "Mostly to start his career. If you live anywhere near Hollywood, you've probably hosted at least one friend or family member trying to get their break. My mom's place was practically a hostel. It's more common than you think."

"Hmm." There was definitely a story behind that "mostly," but it couldn't explain everything. Will's past demons didn't talk shit about Jamie's bestie behind her back—or insult EJ to her face.

Lee seemed to tap into his psychic powers. "Look, I know Will hasn't been his best self at Longbourn, but I think he's just intimidated. Will's used to being the smartest guy in the room and on a movie set or a back lot. He usually is. Here, he's just one pretty smart guy."

"Every Longbourn student goes through that. It's a competitive school." Jamie glanced out the window at the narrow houses. "He didn't strike me as someone easily made insecure."

They were stopped at a red light. Lee turned to her. "He isn't usually. This whole thing with Carrie Dean just put him through the wringer."

Jamie usually admired Lee's desire to see the good in everyone, especially Will, but right now, she was annoyed with how easily he let his friend off the hook. He was still making the case for why Will and EJ should be friends, something about how they're both film snobs, and music snobs, and have twentieth-century habits like talking on the phone and sending long emails.

"And I think he's going to get a telescope because of that meteor shower. He brought up EJ's stargazing story like three times." He shrugged faux casually, the way her mom would shrug when introducing her to a "very progressive Jewish young man."

"Who knows what could happen?" Lee said with a small smile.

Uncanny—he sounds just like my mother, too. For many reasons, Jamie had to nip this in the bud.

"I know you like EJ and you like Will, but trust me: they will never be friends. EJ's good at being polite. Her mom is from the South."

"But—"

"And if you think your boy has a crush on Eej, you couldn't be more wrong. From what I heard, he thinks she dresses like a 'lady pimp.'"

Lee winced as the light changed. "You heard him say that?" They turned onto his street.

"Worse. EJ did."

Lee parked and sat back in the driver's seat. His hand gripped his chin. "That explains so much."

They got out of the car and walked to his place, the bottom floor of a two-story house that had been divided into apartments. "That's not who he is, though. That was one bad night."

He dug out his key and opened the door.

Jamie shrugged. She was thoroughly unpersuaded by this argument. "I can see he's good to you, but neither EJ nor I have had the benefit of years of friendship. If Will is better than that night, I'd like to see the guy you know show up, all the time."

Lee led Jamie into his apartment. They hung up their coats and gulped down tumblers of water before heading to his room. Once inside Lee sighed heavily. "Can I trust you, like seriously?"

Jamie sat on the edge of the bed and nodded, puzzled at the change in Lee's demeanor. *Did he and Will kill someone together?*

Lee sat next to her and began rapidly typing on his phone. She watched him, noting the tightness of his shoulders, his jaw. Eventually, she placed a comforting hand on his back, which he leaned into with a sigh. After what felt like an eternity, he finally stopped typing and looked at her. "I don't want Will to get between us, so I think you have to know what I know—but you can't tell anyone. Even EJ. If this got out, I'd be wrecking his life and losing my best friend."

Jamie looked down and saw that Lee's hands were trembling. She squeezed one in her own. "You don't have to tell me anything," she assured him. Jamie wasn't certain she wanted to see what was on Lee's phone if it was so life altering.

"I know. It's just . . . it would be easier for us if you had the whole story." With that Lee slid his phone into her hands. "It's Will's side of the whole Carrie drama. Once you read it, you'll understand. And you won't think ill of me where he's concerned."

Lee looked so sad that Jamie had to hug him. "Okay," she said, "I'll read it." She picked up Lee's phone and began.

- Will met Carrie (America's newest ingenue superstar) when she had a three-episode arc on *FT: Hawaii*. The actress / singer / lifestyle blogger played an actress / singer / lifestyle blogger with a crazy stalker who took a shine to the forensic team's sarcastic medical examiner. Their on-screen kiss for the winter finale episode blew up Twitter and sparked enough of something for the pair to start dating in real life.

- Carrie was clearly in love with love. She had a reputation for brief serial monogamy and perpetual heartbreak. (Her exes were the subjects of her songs. Will wasn't concerned about this because he wasn't a cheater like the guy her first single was about, or emotionally abusive, like the subject of her second album.) Carrie took Will on ultraromantic excursions that seemed to be planned by the producers of *The Bachelor*. Will, who typically dated sarcastic intellectual women who mocked these sorts of Hallmark displays, was charmed. After a whirlwind romance with hot-air balloons, horseback rides, and romantic declarations on the beach, they became exclusive. Carrie made Will love California. Carrie made Will learn to drive. Carrie made Will try new things. Carrie made Will happy. (Especially since his favorite people on the West Coast tended to be on location or away at school.)

- Soon Will and Carrie were an official Hollywood Couple, so Carrie's people started helping to raise Will's profile. His agent, Katerina, was suddenly inundated with requests. He introduced Carrie and her band on the *Today* show. He charmed on *Hollywood Game Night*; he got listed as one of the nonwhite, sexiest men alive. Will, who'd never been terribly ambitious in his career, now found himself wanting more, and Carrie had shown him it was possible. He gave up his gig with *FT: Hawaii* and shot a pilot where he'd be a romantic lead. Will was excited to help break a barrier for Asian American actors. He could do it—and all because of Carrie. He looked into moving to LA. He thought, more seriously, about proposing.

- One day, Carrie asked him to come over. At her manse in the Hills, Will did not find Carrie. He instead found her agent, momager, and several bodyguards. On top of a pile of nondisclosure agreements and other legal forms was a note from Carrie that simply said "I'm sorry." Carrie's people called his agent, Katerina, and threatened to use their considerable abilities to make Will unhirable should he refuse to go quietly. Carrie's people threw a sizable, but still insulting, pile of money at Will for his trouble. He and his agent kicked the furniture in her office, and Katerina admitted to being "no match for these sharks."

- Carrie then presented a crying face to the world and implied that Will dumped her. Implied that he's cold, snobbish, and a little boring—a romantic heartthrob no longer. His pilot (which sounded so good) went nowhere. Cast and crew blamed him. All other offers disappeared. Will was no longer interesting. Carrie's fans turned on him. There were jokes about his driving, his penis size, and his ability to speak English. Will was angry. He was also very, very sad, but no one seemed sympathetic—or they were afraid of catching his bad press. Either way, he felt very alone. Katerina told Will to take three months in Belize or Saint-Tropez, but Will felt too raw for the sun. It was his sister who suggested he go back to school: "You'll look busy and intellectual." A month later, Carrie was on the arm of a Minnesota quarterback called Johnny Storm. He's the whitest white man. She had an editorial in *W* go to print where she is dressed like a geisha. People debated if the spread is about Will rather than whether the spread is racist. Others pointed out that Will isn't Japanese. Still other people wrote think pieces about whether Will was a bad Asian for having a problematic girlfriend. Will knew the shoot was done before they met, and he started wondering if their entire relationship was PR cover. Will refused to admit that his heart was broken, but he did have the distinct sense of being played. This was close enough. He applied to Longbourn knowing that his best friend was there, and it is far from everything else.

Yikes, Jamie thought as she finished up. *This is not an excuse for his behavior, but it's a reason.* She pulled Lee closer and rubbed his back. "I'm sorry that he went through all this. And I'm sorry that you had to keep this secret. It's been wearing on you, huh?"

He nodded.

She continued. "It probably hasn't helped that I've been holding EJ's grudge for her—even when she told me not to. That stops tonight. There's only room in this relationship for the two of us." With that Jamie handed the phone back to Lee.

Lee tossed the phone onto his desk and wrapped his arms around her. "You're very wise, Miss Jamie," he began, pulling her close. "Let's just focus on you and me. Everything else will fall into place." He kissed her forehead. "Okay, Raggedy Ann?"

She nodded against his chest. "Okay, Andy. Now let's finally get out of these costumes!"

Lee's face broke out into the brightest of grins. "I just like you so much."

"What a coincidence—I like you, too!" She stroked his cheek and drew him in for a whisper of a kiss. He returned it, and then his face broke into the brightest smile.

"I just feel so close to you now," he said. "I feel like 'we' became 'us.'"

Jamie did her best to savor the bright spark of happiness that she was feeling. She could burst into confetti at this moment, and that would be a fine way to go. Lee set her back down on the ground. She stripped to her camisole and turned to see him waiting for her in bed. "Ready to get our snuggle on?" he asked.

"Oh, you bet," she replied, crawling in next to him with a smile.

EJ's November, in Text Messages

From Jamie on November 1

We're official!

So happy for you! I'm happy for me too! Lee's roommate high-fived both of us when he found out

Ha! That's awesome

I want to hear everything

Soon, I promise

Let's meet for lunch!

From EJ to Jamie on November 5

Hey girl, hey

Guess who I ran into at the Arthouse Cinema

Will

hehe, which version

Debate club Will

we were at that Wong Kar-Wai thing

Oh yeah Lee mentioned he was going to that
when we borrowed his car

I know! I had to give him a ride back to campus

He missed the bus back arguing with me about
"In the Mood for Love"

He called Tony Leung stiff!

😬 How dare he talk about your husband that
way!

ikr 😑

From Tessa on November 14

Congrats, you found a musical I liked

That was amazing!

I knew you'd enjoy the concert format

Mel was soooooo fricking good!!

See what happens when you support your fellow Bennet Women?

Haha, you got me

I'm not dreading the next event now

Anyway, how was your meeting with Stella?

Hilarious!

She wants me to apply for a Fields Fellowship

OMG

You should go for it, though

Nah

What do you mean, nah?

From Lee on November 19

We have to talk about that score line

7-2?!

My Gunners are on fire, baby!

For your sake we won't talk about Man United

Anyway, want to come over to play Settlers?

It'll be me, Jamie, Will, and You

Maybe ...

I thought I might just chill tonight

Okay

Will says he can beat you, BTW

Easily

 When and where?

⌒∽

Group text between EJ, Jamie, and Tessa on November 20

Tessa:

We're going to have an intervention when you get back

Jamie:

We may have an intervention

What's wrong with just wanting a normal job after college?!

Tessa:

This isn't about wanting a normal job

This is about passing up a Fields Fellowship

Which I have a 1% chance of getting

Jamie:

Your advisor thinks you have a good shot

I just don't understand why you're not even thinking about it

This isn't like you

Tessa:

Bennet Women try, Eej!

You preach that more than anyone

You have to try!

My train is here. Can we talk about it after Thanksgiving Break?

Please?

THANKSGIVING BREAK

EJ Goes Home

Going from a small New England town to the DC suburbs was a little like going from Kansas to Oz. Everything was a little brighter and louder—life felt like it was in Technicolor by comparison. EJ released a sigh she didn't know she was holding when the train pulled into New Carrollton Station.

The stop was in Prince George's County, one of the wealthiest majority-black counties in the country; her parents had wanted to raise her here to make sure EJ saw black doctors, black lawyers, and black school principals in her daily life. They wanted her and Maya to "dream freely." It worked—both EJ and Maya grew up to want difficult but wonderful things.

At the Hertfordshire Station, EJ had been the only black face in the place and the only person of color not behind the concessions counter. By the time her train reached Baltimore, she could see others like her: black kids coming home from their fancy Northern schools. Just in her train car, there were a bassist from the Berklee College of Music and twin first-generation Nigerian guys in Princeton sweatshirts. EJ walked briskly to the taxi stand, feeling wonderfully inconspicuous.

In the cab, EJ gave her address and asked the driver to go overland. Her parents would always offer to pick her up from the train station, but she liked having the twenty minutes of the drive to . . . exhale, to really let the feeling sink in. She was home.

Just thinking the words caused something in her shoulders to release. It was like she wasn't herself at Longbourn—and she really did love the school—but she never felt as relaxed there as she did now, especially since Jamie and Tessa would not drop the subject of the Fields Fellowship.

EJ sighed deeply and leaned back in her seat. She'd thought Tessa would understand a little since they were both women in STEM, but she ended up being more insistent than Jamie. Neither of them seemed to get how much work it took to accomplish what she did. She wasn't a genius, just a really, really *hard* worker. The Fields Fellowship wasn't for people like her.

She shook off those thoughts and put on her headphones, gazing out the window as they passed her old elementary school. It was a K–8 French immersion school and meant more to her than her high school ever would. Her only grade school friendships that survived to the present had begun while she learned to sing "Allouette."

I have to text Erica and Renata to see if they're back, too, she thought, watching the familiar scenes from the window. It was always harder to make plans over Thanksgiving Break. But there was still time.

She was listening to "Home" from *The Wiz* when the cab pulled onto her family's tree-lined street. It kept her from jumping out and running the rest of the way. The taxi pulled up to her house with a friendly honk. Everything about the scene was so comfortably familiar: the robin's-egg-blue exterior, the bright-yellow door, the tall trees that surrounded the house. Momma said the little cottage made her feel like she was living in a fairy tale.

Growing up, EJ had often felt the same way. It was built in 1923 and, for better or worse, had much of the original detail intact. She loved the wood floors, the pressed-tin ceiling in the kitchen, the character of the place. This was what gave EJ her love of old things. She couldn't wait to get inside.

She paid the driver and had just stepped out of the cab when her father swept her up in a warm hug.

"My baby girl is home!" he cried happily, spinning her around.

"Daddy!" She giggled and returned the embrace. Once she was returned to the ground, she left her dad with her suitcases and raced up the steps to her mother. Her mom beamed at EJ and gave her a squeeze.

"Welcome home, Ella." She took EJ's hands and leaned back. "Let me take a look at you." EJ bounced on her heels as her mother looked her over. "You look good, baby girl. Healthy and happy."

"Thanks, Momma!" She stepped into the house and gaped. The formerly mustard-colored walls were now a pale periwinkle—somehow making the space feel large and new. "You painted! The house looks wonderful!"

"We fixed the floors, too. It's still the original wood, but the hump everyone used to trip on is gone."

"We had to modernize just a little." Her dad laughed. By this time, he'd joined them inside with EJ's suitcases. "But don't worry, your mirrors are still safe, see?" He set the luggage by the banister.

They moved to the doorway of the long, narrow living room. One wall was covered in floor-to-ceiling mirrors, like a dance studio. EJ had been dancing in front of them since she could walk. She smiled at her parents in the mirror and then walked to the hallway closet, where she hung up her coat and talked about the noisome seatmate who rode beside her from New Haven on.

"So we're waiting at Penn Station, and I'm like, 'Finally: after the olives, the pickles, and the sardines, he's run out of stuff.' I can see all his containers are empty. Then guess who comes back with a tuna salad sub? At that point, I just put my coat over my head and pretended to sleep." She laughed, then paused, noticing that her parents made no move to the kitchen as expected. Usually, they sat around the kitchen table and traded stories until they remembered dinner. Instead, they stood and beamed at her, silently. It was weird.

"What's going on?" She tilted her head quizzically.

Her father giggled. Mom elbowed him and adjusted her glasses. They were both clearly trying not to laugh—or something. "There's a surprise for you downstairs," her mom replied. Then, with remarkable dexterity for two pleasantly plump people in their late fifties, her mom and dad darted down the steps to the TV room.

EJ followed at a measured pace, calling down, "I know marijuana is less illegal in Maryland now, so I have to ask: Have y'all been hitting the wacky tobacky?"

"Ella!" a familiar voice chastised. "Is that any way to speak to your momma and daddy?"

"Maya!" She gasped, running into the family room. EJ's older sister was waiting for her on the downstairs landing. EJ screamed happily before wrapping her sister in a hug. This was more than she could have hoped for. Her parents loved and supported her, but Maya understood her. Even with four years between them, they were an artist collective of two. EJ was a patient life model for Maya's drawings and paintings while Maya drove EJ to her many classes and critiqued her living room rehearsals. Then there was the normal big-sister stuff: Maya took EJ to her first concert, got her into anime, and did her best to prepare her for the world of guys. She also got her a vibrator for her twenty-first birthday.

Maya had been living in Hawaii since she served there in AmeriCorps two years ago. Between the six-hour time difference and their busy schedules, the sisters hadn't been able to do anything but text since September. This visit was a Thanksgiving miracle.

"You look great!" EJ exclaimed, admiring the purple ends on her sister's curly, dark hair. The Pacific sun had brought out its red highlights, too. "What are you even doing here?"

As they stood arm in arm, Maya began giving details behind her visit. "I got invited to present on the work the Ohana Center has been doing on literacy and the Hawaiian language. The conference is going to be next week, in New York, so I thought since I'm on the mainland . . ." She smiled at Momma and Daddy, then looked at EJ. "I'm going to ride up with you on Sunday—at least as far as New York." She gave EJ a squeeze. "I can't believe I've been able to keep from telling you for so long."

EJ returned the hug and gazed over at her parents. "I can't believe y'all didn't say anything. Daddy's never even been able to throw a surprise party."

It was an old family joke; everyone gave the obligatory laugh.

"That's because we didn't know," her dad replied, settling on the couch. "Sunday afternoon, we came home from church to find Maya putting a pot roast in the oven."

"Y'all know I love cooking and I love Sunday dinner. I wanted to start my trip home with the things I missed the most."

"I missed you the most," EJ said, dropping her head on her sister's shoulder.

Her mother sniffed and hugged them both. "My girls," she exclaimed. "All of us, together again. I'm just so happy."

That night over takeout, EJ told her family about her capstone progress and craziness on her floor. ("I had to tell Dia three times: no tap practice in your room!") She told them about Tessa and Colin (getting back together again, ugh) and about Jamie and her new boyfriend (with the briefest mention of Will)—all the fun stuff.

Now she had to make sure her father never heard about her getting the opportunity of a fellowship. He believed that EJ should strive for every award and go for every prize. After four years of doing things his way, she was just tired. Her big first choice for her adult life was going to be getting a nice, normal job.

But why would they talk about that when they could talk about Maya's book for the Ohana Center, or her mom directing her first musical for the city's community theater, or Dad getting "voluntold" to chaperone their church's traditional youth trip to the Great Blacks in

Wax Museum in Baltimore. With so many other things to talk about, there was no reason for the Fields Fellowship to come up.

⋘⋙

But of course it did, on the Friday after Thanksgiving. The conversation with her dad went about as well as she thought it would, ending when she stormed out of the house so angry, she forgot her coat. She'd never had such a serious fight with either of her parents. Her father had never yelled at her the way he did just then. She felt the heat rise in her cheeks as she strode over to Maya's rental car.

"Where do you want to go?" her sister asked, handing her a hoodie and a fleece hat with cat ears. EJ hadn't even noticed that she'd followed her out.

"Anywhere," she replied, pulling on the sweatshirt. "Starbucks," EJ suggested suddenly. "No—New Deal. Let's go to New Deal Cafe, it's been forever."

"Our old place. I'm glad it's still around—and a little surprised." She gave a small smile. "Get in."

The short drive over was silent. EJ stared out the window, not really seeing anything. She just didn't understand how things blew up so much. Maya didn't say anything. When they pulled into the parking lot, EJ could see figures dancing in the back room of the café. It was a live-music night.

"Live music? The day after Thanksgiving? All right, New Deal," Maya said with a touch of admiration. "Not just surviving but thriving."

EJ quirked her lips. "Yeah, but I'm not up for dancing with boomers." She got out of the car dejectedly and walked around to lean against the trunk. After a moment, Maya joined her.

The sisters leaned against Maya's rental car in the small strip-mall parking lot. Silently, they watched their breath stream and curl in the cold November air.

Maya spoke first. "That was the closest I've ever seen you come to fighting with either Mom or Dad."

"Oh God, that wasn't fighting?" EJ groaned.

"Sorry, goody-goody." Maya patted the ears on EJ's hat. "That was, at most, an impassioned disagreement. I must have worn y'all out when I left."

In the fall of her senior year of high school, Maya had told her parents that instead of applying to college, she intended to move to Oakland and become part of the art scene. To put it extremely mildly, her parents disapproved of this plan. The arguments continued for all of Maya's senior year.

EJ tilted her head in consideration. "There might have been some collective trauma. You were a fucking lot back then." They laughed, and she felt a little tension leave her shoulders. "I made a point to avoid fighting with them when you were gone. You know, be 'the good one.'"

Even though EJ agreed that her sister should be able to make her own choices, the fighting had taken almost as much of a toll on her as it had on their parents.

Maya shook her head, curls bouncing. "Eighteen is a hell of a drug." It wasn't an apology, but it was close. They both fell silent. EJ quietly remembered that awful time. Daddy took it the hardest. He'd devoted his whole life as a teacher to getting kids to college, minority children especially. Maya's decision must have seemed like a rejection of his life's work—especially given how he vented his disapproval. "What happened, anyway?" her sister asked.

"Oy." EJ scrubbed her face. "My wonderful, far-too-devoted academic advisor called me to make sure that I saw her email about the Fields Fellowship: it's like a Rhodes Scholarship for engineers. Basically, you get to do a master's program anywhere in the world, with a stipend. No teaching, and you only have to do a yearlong public service internship afterward. Anyway, there was a second call for candidates, and Stella, my advisor, thinks I should apply. She wants my decision on the first day of classes after break. Stella leaves this all on a voice mail, *on the house phone*, which Dad hears. Of course, that is where we begin."

"*Oh.*"

"Exactly. He asks if I'm applying. I say, 'No. I'm ready to work and need to focus on getting a job now.' Cut to Dad lecturing me about dreams deferred, wasting opportunity, shaming the ancestors, et cetera . . .'"

"That is a familiar tune."

"I know. I said to him, 'I don't know why you're giving me the same lecture you gave Maya for not going to college.' No offense."

Her sister waved off any further explanation.

"But I'm going to graduate," EJ continued, "on time and with honors from one of the hardest engineering programs in the country. Why isn't that enough? That's when he starts talking to me about passion."

"That's a bit ironic. Since my lectures were about responsibility and how passion is not everything."

"I know!" EJ growled. "What changed? Anyway I'm sitting there, taking it all in, when he says, 'A Fields Fellowship is every engineer's dream. If you don't want this, why do you even want to be an engineer?'" She exhaled lengthily. "I told him the truth."

Maya looked at her with interest. "Which is?"

"That engineering is not and was never my dream. It's a compromise. That I am an engineer because I couldn't be a ballerina. I told him that I wanted to be the next Michaela DePrince or Misty Copeland more than I have wanted or will want anything else. That I stuck with engineering because I could see how proud it made him. That I went to Longbourn instead of taking a near full ride to UMD because of how excited he was when we got the acceptance letter.

"That I stopped going to church because it was easier to not believe than keep the faith in a God who would give me the drive and the talent but not the money to make my dreams come true."

Maya sucked in a harsh breath. "Shit. Is that true?" The religion thing was something else that had brought Maya and Daddy closer together while pushing him and EJ apart. Her belief had been waning since grade school, but she'd remained an active member of the church, helping in the nursery and going on all the volunteer trips. She didn't even sit in the top balcony, where the teenagers were tacitly allowed to play with their smartphones during service. She sat next to her parents and tried to pay attention. She still loved the music, but the meaning had started to fall away.

"Mostly, by sixteen, Christianity had lost my head but not my heart. Once ballet went away, I don't know. It was like the part of me that was capable of believing died."

"Shit," Maya said again. "I got that giving up ballet was really, really bad for you. But I don't think I realized the extent of your feelings. You recovered so quickly."

EJ looked up sharply. Of all people, she'd thought Maya would have understood her silent sacrifice.

"I didn't recover. I swallowed my pain. I cried in my room. I didn't tell you because I didn't want it to make it back to Momma and Daddy. I thought they might feel ashamed. I felt ashamed. I had to tell my classmates, girls I'd seen almost every day since I was twelve, that I wouldn't be able to continue. It was like getting your credit card declined in public."

She shifted against the car. "That's one of the reasons I chose a branch of engineering where I can make more money and I can start working right away. I never wanted to run out of choices like that *ever again*." She rubbed her neck below the brim of the hat. "And now we're back to the Fields Fellowship." She watched the distant blink of newly hung Christmas lights decorating one of the nearby townhouses.

Maya broke the silence again. "So I'm not used to winter anymore— I'm cold! What do you say to Board and Brew? We can play Bananagrams," she said/sang enticingly. "Earl Grey lattes, on me."

The board game café was the first place EJ had gotten her sense of life beyond high school. Maya and her friends used to go there all the time. They were surprisingly cool with EJ tagging along because she was great to have around for trivia nights. It was how she got interested in her high school's quiz bowl team.

"Sure, sounds good," she replied.

Maya elbowed her playfully. "*Allons-y*, hon," she said, hopping in the driver's seat.

EJ sat in the passenger seat and buckled her seatbelt. Maya went to turn the ignition but paused.

"About what you said earlier—'being the good one.' I think you're taking the wrong lessons from my life." Maya shifted in her seat. "The problem wasn't the yelling—that was a symptom. The problem was tunnel vision."

She turned to face EJ. "Both Daddy and I saw only two paths: He saw 'college' or 'ruin.' I saw 'art school' or 'being a hack.' So I rejected the gift that Momma and Daddy had saved for me because I thought there was only one way for me to be my own artist. Now I know better. I'm an illustrator. I've designed posters and album art for local bands. I sell small sketches and paintings at the farmers market. I have an Etsy store. But I'm also a college sophomore at twenty-seven. I work with my kids, and go to school and paint, but I barely have time for a social life. I'm currently happy with my life, but it was a rough road to get here, and it didn't have to be."

EJ frowned. "Do you regret your choices?" she asked, turning toward her sister.

Maya shook her head. "Not the choices. I mean, I still have less debt than many of my peers and about as much success. I do regret how I made them. I wish I'd been clear about what I wanted, and more open to seeing what paths could get me there."

She adjusted the rearview mirror. "Looking back, I think what I really needed was a gap year and maybe to go to a state school. My four-year art degree would have cost as much as our house. I think I couldn't handle that pressure."

EJ quietly quailed. Her degree did cost more than their house.

Maya seemed to read her thoughts. "Don't. You got so many scholarships that Momma and Daddy are basically paying UMD tuition for your Longbourn education." She rubbed her forehead.

"All I'm saying is with this Fields Fellowship, don't reject it automatically because it doesn't look appealing. Ask yourself: What do you want for your life? Can this help? Forget about your ego. Forget about Daddy, forget about your advisor. Really investigate if this fellowship can give you what you want. Especially if you're thinking about going to grad school at any point. I can tell you right now, it's easier to go to school than go *back* to school."

Maya started the car. EJ marveled at her sister. She could see both who'd she been and who she was. Maya had grown up. Not that she was immature before, but she seemed more secure now, more balanced. And worth listening to. EJ considered her sister's advice as they drove to the café.

The next morning, EJ got up and made coffee. When her father came down for breakfast, they both apologized for yelling. She promised to give the Fields Fellowship strong consideration, and then she left for a hair appointment. It was enough to keep the peace until Sunday. Over the weekend, there was a round of family bowling and a big happy dinner. Maya and EJ were leaving on the early train the next day.

Will's Thanksgiving

Will had forgotten how nice it was to be back at Pemberley. Before Longbourn he'd been living in California, and before that he'd been bouncing from location to location. Pemberley was home, particularly because it was also home to his favorite person in the world: his sister. Lily, to paraphrase *Jerry Maguire*, completed him. When they were kids, he was bookish and solemn while she was athletic and energetic. They got each other through the horror show of their mother's death and their father's inability to cope with it. Then came Will's vault into semistardom; they survived that, too. There had been a brief but painful estrangement during their high school years. But in the end, they found that the only people they could truly rely on were each other. Thankfully, time had mended that breach, and the siblings were closer than ever—especially since Will and Lily were both going through their first year of the traditional college experience. Longbourn had been Lily's idea, and these days Will always listened to his sister.

Zara was joining them for their holiday meal. Usually she'd be back home in Providence, but this year she'd been in the Macy's Thanksgiving Day Parade. Her float sat between a pirate ship bearing Pentatonix and a Sonic the Hedgehog balloon. Will DVR'd the whole thing so Zara could see herself when she came over.

Around 2:00 p.m., he heard the doorbell, then his sister's joyful squeal. "Lady Z," Lily cried. Will joined them in the foyer, receiving his own hug and kiss from Zara.

"Fuck, Will, I forgot you guys live in a museum," Zara said, gazing at their surroundings.

There was a lot of art on the walls. The house itself was over a hundred years old.

"We like to think of it as a *cozy* museum," he said with a smile. "Is that wine?"

"Indeed." She looked him up and down. "Nice blazer—I hope you know there's not a job interview at the end of this."

Will shot her a look.

She gave him a conciliatory smile. "I brought red." Zara handed him the bottles. "Do you approve?"

"Of course. These are good bottles." Well, they were good but not great. Will hoped she hadn't been overcharged for them.

"That means 'try again,' right, Lily?"

His sister nodded, her teal hair swishing across her shoulders. "But don't mind him. Z, are you hungry?"

Zara's eyes widened. "Starving! I didn't realize how hungry I was until just now."

"Let's eat, then!" Will offered. "We've got dinner on 'warm' in the oven. It's mostly vegetarian, but Lily made sure there was a little turkey for you and me." The celebratory meal came from an eighty-year-old deli in the neighborhood with a name like a law firm. It was where Lily and Will had gotten their Thanksgiving dinner every year since their gran passed three years ago. Their father made no bones about preferring his new family with their stepmother and new baby. Will and Lily had spent one holiday with them since his senior year of high school, then decided not to repeat the experience. They were all happier this way. Lily sent them a Christmas card, which was more than he was willing to do.

"I also went to that place you took me to last summer and got some pigeon peas and Christmas rice," he added.

Zara squealed and kissed him on the cheek. "You know how to make a Dominican girl feel at home."

Will led the way to the kitchen. "Anything for my favorite superhero."

She elbowed him, lightly. "Hey, I don't turn into an action star until next summer."

They ate dinner and watched the parade. Once the food was put away and the dishes were done, they got ready for Will's favorite tradition: staying up late and watching his grandma's old movies. This custom grew out of Thanksgivings with his paternal grandparents, who shooed the children upstairs once the adults had started cocktail hour.

Since his gran was the movie buff of the family, he and Lily fell in love with films from the golden age of Hollywood—particularly the musicals. She and Zara stretched out on the room-filling sectional sofa while Will riffled through a highly organized cabinet of DVDs. Gran had made sure her DVD collection went to them in her will. Their father thought this was a sign of senility that her doctors had missed.

"*The Lady Eve*!" Zara shouted her request to Will, like he was a DJ at a wedding. He moved to a different shelf to oblige.

Lily, who settled comfortably on the end of the chaise lounge, sat up suddenly and shouted, "Popcorn!" before rushing off in a gunmetal streak to the kitchen.

Zara watched her go. "I watched that dress come down the runway at fashion week, and I wondered how anyone could wear it without looking like a mushroom. Then here Lily is, making that gray sack look like a million bucks."

Will leaned against Zara and smiled. "You should know by now that Lily is magic."

They could hear the slam of cupboards and the clang of pots. "You know we own a microwave, right?" Will called down the long hallway.

"Stovetop is much better!" Lily retorted. "I just have to find the popper."

"You can use a pot, too," Zara offered. "That's what we did growing up."

"Trust me on the popper, Z!" Lily called back. After a few more bangs, there was a victorious chirp. "Found it. Just give me ten minutes."

Will and Zara settled back on the couch and exchanged amused shrugs. He dug a bottle of wine from somewhere and looked around for glasses.

"Don't bother, we'll drink it from the bottle like art students in a movie." Zara laughed and handed him the corkscrew from the coffee table. "You're already halfway there with that turtleneck."

Will huffed indignantly, to his friend's amusement. "It makes more sense with the blazer, but you guys insisted we were being casual after dinner."

"It's hilarious that you think you're being casual right now." Zara was giddily wearing a unicorn onesie. She crossed her legs and sat in lotus position. She absently twirled a dark lock of hair around her finger. "Oh hey, did you ever see my dancing friend again?"

"Who?" Will frowned.

"Come on, Will—you weren't that drunk the *whole* night." She plucked the wine bottle from his hands, sipped, and then pointed it accusingly. "My girl from the diner, Miss Elizabeth Jacqueline. Black girl, sequin dress, blessed in the chest . . ."

"That's what EJ stands for?" Will sat up slightly. "How did you even know that?"

Zara smiled. "The way I knew your sister was gay before you did—I asked. I showed interest in her life. It's kind of my deal."

Will sighed and bit his lip. Zara couldn't know how much her casual words stung. He signaled for the bottle's return. "I wasn't a great brother then," he replied sadly. To this day he hadn't been able to forgive himself for how he failed Lily in high school. How he didn't realize she needed him until it was almost too late.

Zara complied with his request. "No, but you got better. Most guys are little shits at that age." She patted his knee. "You're a great brother now, so it averages out."

He took a healthy drink and returned the bottle as he raised his eyebrows. "Is that how it works?"

Zara shrugged. "I dunno, probably." She took a slug of wine. "And don't think you're getting away with anything. You said EJ's name like you say it all the time. So you must be hanging out."

Will shrugged with aggressive nonchalance. "Lee started dating her best friend. We're thrown together a lot."

"Lies!" Lily contradicted as she came around the corner. "I have popcorn with M&M's and Reese's Pieces in the green bowl, and I have baby carrots for those among us who will be playing superheroines in the near future."

Zara put the wine down and reached for the bowl. "My trainer gave me the week off, honey. He said I was getting mean." She smiled wolfishly. "Gimme the popcorn and tell me about your brother's falsehoods."

Lily settled between them. She adjusted her glasses, gave a toss of her colorful hair, and folded her hands like she was going to give a presentation to the ladies auxiliary. Will rolled his eyes and retrieved the bottle in preparation.

"My dear Zara, our Will has a crush on the very Elizabeth Jacqueline you met a few months back."

"Untrue!" he protested.

"Oh yeah?" Lily said, folding her arms. "Then why do I know that EJ hates butter pickles? That she's hardcore into astronomy? That she's deadly at Settlers and Risk but only okay at Scrabble? That she can name more operas than members of One Direction? That she has a favorite cinematographer? I could go on—" She gave her brother a pointed look.

"All that proves is that EJ has a lot of opinions—and she does—and I have a good memory."

Lily shook her head vigorously. "No! And I will tell you why." She turned to Zara. "Remember how, after Carrie, Will had a series of sex pals?"

Zara nodded. "His ho period—nothing wrong with that."

"Nothing at all," Lily agreed. "Consenting adults, blah, blah, blah. He doesn't really tell me about most of them, but there was one girl for most of the summer he called Freckles. Now, brother." She turned to Will again. "You and Freckles were on and off for at least a two-month period."

"That sounds right," Will said, feeling unfairly cross-examined.

"And," Lily continued, "you have a thing about making your paramours breakfast the morning after."

"It's the gentlemanly thing to do," he nervously affirmed.

"Okay, brother, please tell me how Freckles took her coffee." Lily and Zara looked at him in anticipation.

Will frowned and thought. *I don't think Freckles drank coffee.*

He tried to remember.

After a few more moments of silence, Lily began making suggestions. "Did she like green tea, instead? Cold-pressed juices? Yerba mate with a metal straw?"

Will squinted at Lily, who smiled sweetly. Zara looked on and snickered.

He threw up his hands. "So what if I don't remember?" he cried. "I can't notice everything."

Lily twisted toward Zara. "EJ takes her coffee with one cream and one sugar. When she's tired it's just black, and when she's stressed, it's black with three sugars. Does that sound right, brother?"

"No, it's one cream and two sugars—not one—a Dunkin' Donuts regular," Will corrected. Zara and Lily regarded him in bemused silence. Will forcefully huffed a sigh. It wasn't his fault he was observant.

Anyone who spent time with EJ would pick up on her opinions—she could be pretty witty most of the time. And she had better than average taste in music. *And she has that fantastic peachy little ass.*

Will started at this thought and set the wine bottle back down on the coffee table. Then he stood solemnly, walked to the bar cart in the corner, and poured himself a double shot of bourbon.

"So I have a crush," he said casually as he sat back down. "Can we please start the movie?"

"Okay," agreed Lily. She found the remote and pushed play.

"Okay," seconded Zara.

The movie began, but Will couldn't focus. He wasn't sure how to feel. It wasn't like she could be his girlfriend, at least not publicly. Carrie was dating an NFL quarterback. He needed, well, at least an established model. Carrie had taught him how to be famous. How to use the paparazzi. Where to go to get photographed. How to plant "leaks" in the press. Will had been embarrassingly naive about what it took to succeed in Hollywood. Only the people willing to leverage their personal lives got to move up the food chain. Carrie went from half-forgotten child star to phenomenon, and her music was only fine. She knew how to play the game, and Will learned well—even if he hated her for it. He wanted to win this breakup, and being with EJ, lovely as she was, wouldn't look like a victory.

"But do you want what Carrie wants, Will?" Dr. Marjorie's voice interrupted his thoughts. In their last session, she'd pointed out that Will started playing Carrie's game only because he felt ignored at *FT: Hawaii.*

I should be acting, not just reacting, he scolded himself.

He shouldn't be dating to beat Carrie Dean. He should date who he liked—and he was drawn to EJ. Besides, if this was going to be anything more than an embarrassing admission to Lily and Zara, he had to make a move. First things first.

Breakfast at Pemberley

On the morning of Black Friday, as Will slept off his slight hangover, Zara and Lily were in the kitchen, eating leftovers at the breakfast bar. Zara revived the subject of Will's crush. "Okay, L, now that we're not teasing Will, I have to say I think your evidence was circumstantial. You know your brother thinks he's the world's greatest detective, collecting random facts about people. Carrie hated it, so he got out of the habit, but maybe he's just back to his old self?"

Lily pushed her glasses up her nose. "You have a point, but . . ." She paused to make sure she didn't hear her brother's footsteps, then moved into whispering distance. "So I didn't say this in front of Will because I knew it would be truly embarrassing, not just 'fun embarrassing': on his first day back home for Thanksgiving Break, Will asked if I thought he could join Ballroom Club without too much hassle."

Zara started. "Wait, your brother?" She shook her head in wonder.

"I know. Mr. 'I'm not here to make friends' suddenly takes an interest in campus life. Let me tell you the whole story." Lily pushed her plate away and turned toward her friend. "We were in the kitchen doing dishes and had some music going on the Echo. This like, sixties bossa nova comes on. Will, to my surprise, starts humming along. After the song ends, Will is just standing there, kinda dreamily—plate in hand. I'm like, 'Hello!'

"He sort of wakes up and then asks me about the ballroom team. Then I'm just like, 'Explain.'

"He says, 'It's the song. The other day I was passing through the lower campus, and I hear this song coming from one of the smaller rooms. I wanna see who dug up this old chestnut, so I peek in. It's EJ with the ballroom team. She and her partner are doing some sort of demonstration dance, and, Lily, she's just. So. Good. She moved the way a summer breeze feels.'"

Zara gripped the countertop. "Oh my God, he got all poetic for her! What happened next?"

"After all that, he sighs and finally puts the plate in the dishwasher. Then he says, real quietly, 'I didn't realize—she's inspirational, Lily. I ended up watching the whole routine through the window.'"

"'Inspirational,'" Zara repeated. "Like when he heard Carrie singing a cappella during her sound check."

"Or like when stunt-lady Casey did that 'inspirational' cliff dive on the second *Wolf Pack* movie. I think we've got more than a crush, Z. I think his heart's halfway there."

They were interrupted by the sound of footsteps. Will came into the kitchen yawning. "Is there coffee?" he asked.

"No, but there's hot water, and I'll get the French press for you," Lily replied. She was a tea drinker and Zara was a weirdo who hated hot beverages.

"Thanks." Will grabbed the electric kettle. "And thanks for making me drink, like, a gallon of water last night. I do not have the hangover I deserve." He poured the hot water and then called out to their Echo, "Alexa, play 'Something Stupid,' Frank Sinatra."

The music filled the room, and Lily froze in her tracks. "This is the song!" she mouthed to Zara.

The actress's eyes widened. "Interesting choice, Will," she said mildly.

"I just woke up with it in my head," he replied casually.

"Uh-huh." Zara crossed the kitchen to where Will was making an omelet. "So, Will, why haven't you asked this girl out? It sounds like you've had this crush for a minute, which is dangerously close to pining."

Will sighed. "I've been thinking of telling her how I feel."

"Wait, what?" Lily cried. "You didn't tell me that."

"Okay, I've just been thinking of it since yesterday. The problem is she's pretty but not industry pretty, so I think it would have to be a secret relationship—definitely couldn't leave Longbourn . . ."

"*Nooooooo!*" Lily cried.

"Patience. Let me make my case to you—and her," Will said, interrupting his sister's further objections. "I've been working on something since last night. It will either be a letter or a speech. I think it captures all of my feelings." He abandoned his eggs and pulled his phone out of his pocket. "Can I read it to you?"

"Read it! Read it!" they cheered.

"Okay, okay." He leaned back against the giant fridge and began. "Dear EJ, I hope you had a lovely Thanksgiving with your family. This time away from Longbourn has given me the opportunity to reflect on what it's meant to me, and what you mean to me. I've tried—believe me, I've tried—to keep this to myself, but it's impossible. I adore you, EJ. You're probably as surprised to be reading this as I am to be writing it. Who would have thought I'd find my dream girl in the boonies of Massachusetts? A girl whose clothes are from TJ Maxx instead of Saks—"

There was an impatient squeak from his audience. Will put up a reassuring hand. "I'm building to something, I promise."

He continued. "Fortunately, I'm the kind of man who can recognize a jewel in any setting. I'm sorry to admit it took me longer than it should have. You were like Billy Joel's classical album. At first, I wasn't quite sure I even liked it, but then, as I understood its beauty, its complexity, its ambition, it became my favorite. EJ, I—"

"Ay, Dios mío!" Zara cried as she grabbed Will's phone and deleted the drafted letter with a flourish. Then she gave him a slap on the head.

"Ow!" Will rubbed his temple. "Why'd you do that?" he asked peevishly.

Zara put both hands on his shoulders and looked at him solemnly. "Because I love you and I want you to live. Finish making your breakfast."

∽

Hours later, the trio took a taxi downtown. Will and Zara were going to the Met. Lily wanted to spend some time in FIT's jewelry studio to work on a beading project. In the cab, the ladies explained to Will what he'd done wrong.

"Everything," Lily said. "That was bad, bad, very not good at all. Bad."

Zara nodded. "If she murdered you after that, all her attorney would have to do is present your letter as Exhibit A. No jury in the world would convict her. And since when did you become so class conscious? TJ Maxx—"

"She's always talking about getting stuff on sale and getting good deals," Will protested. "I thought it showed that I was paying attention."

The actress scrubbed her face. "Listen to someone who didn't grow up with money: you develop those skills because you have to. That was like saying to someone in a manual wheelchair, 'Dude, your arms are so diesel.' It's just inconsiderate."

"And talking about how reluctantly attracted you are is not helpful," Lily chimed in. "Especially if you're going to ask her to be a secret. Do you think you'd be ashamed of her?" Her voice was tinged with distress. Will had the feeling he was failing a test he hadn't signed up for.

"I didn't want to insult her intelligence by pretending there wasn't past weirdness between us." He looked out the window, too upset to enjoy watching the city go by. "She's very analytical, even in matters of the heart."

"Being smart doesn't mean you don't want romance," Zara retorted. "She probably wants it more."

The cab slowed as they arrived at the museum. Lily asked the driver to wait as Will and Zara got out. She moved to the edge of her seat and took her brother's hand through the window. "I love you most. I love you best, you know that, right?"

Will nodded, sensing he was going to dread what she said next.

"I don't think you should go after EJ. You're not ready."

"Why?" he asked softly.

"There's too much Carrie in your letter and your approach. It's selfish. It's about your image. It's not about her."

Will looked crushed. "But I like EJ, a lot. I said a bunch of good things," he insisted.

"But the nice things you said made the awful things sound even worse." Lily tugged on the ends of his scarf. "You wouldn't be good to her, not now. Until you can say how you feel in a way that's all about her, you need to say nothing at all." She blew Will a kiss and sat back down in the cab.

Will stood frozen on the steps of the museum and then turned to follow Zara inside.

EJ

At the train station Sunday night, EJ kissed her parents goodbye quickly so she and Maya could get seats together. Thanksgiving weekend was always super crowded on the ride back. Once they got to Delaware, EJ popped open a bag of Utz cheese curls and sighed happily.

"These are better than every other cheese curl. I don't know how they do it!" She lifted one with delight, then consumed it happily.

Maya gaped at her in mock shock. "I remember when you were a vegan who wouldn't eat carbs."

EJ snickered. "Going vegan just made dieting easier. No one ever offers you food." She laughed.

Maya gave a sharp intake of breath. "Oh God. First, it was morning runs. Then doing arm curls on the bus. Then the lunges across the living room and the hundred crunches before bed every night. Then once you had a little bit of body, you went all-in on dieting—hard." She sucked her teeth. "Like there was something wrong with looking like a Murphy woman."

EJ willed herself not to roll her eyes. The women on her mom's side of the family tended to be "thick as grits," to borrow a phrase from her aunt, Denise. Both Maya and her mother fit that mold. She also had their mother's medium-brown skin and "good hair." EJ took after their father with dark skin and a cotton-candy afro.

"I had to diet. Momma and Daddy wouldn't let me get a breast reduction," EJ joked. "I had the perfect Balanchine body until puberty hit like a freight train."

Maya shook her head. "It made me tired to watch you," she continued. "The daily weigh-ins, the YouTube Pilates, all that green juice. I think there was, like, a month that you didn't eat solids."

EJ shrugged. No one got it then and they still didn't now. "I did what I had to do. I was already a little too tall for some companies and—let's be real—too dark for others. Since the pool of places that would be open to hiring me was pretty small, I had to make sure I was able to compete. Some places could look past the booty, some places could look past the boobs, but there's no dance company you can get in with both—even Alvin Ailey. Believe me, I checked." EJ laughed.

Maya did not. She continued as if she had never stopped speaking. "I remember the constant tape measuring, the shrinking portions, the word *discipline* taped to your mirror like some kind of curse. You wouldn't eat anything if you didn't know its calorie count. You never stopped exercising." She took a moment to look at EJ. "You know you scared the hell out of us."

"Oh, come on, Maya. I wasn't half as bad as some of the girls in my class—the ones not blessed with thinness, that is. At least I ate every day."

Maya sucked her teeth again. "And that unhealthy culture is why Mom and Dad pulled you out of dance school."

EJ was grateful she was sitting down. She shook so violently that she thought she might fall over otherwise.

"What?" was all she could manage.

Maya looked panicked; her eyes darted around the train car. "I don't—maybe. They never said so directly, explicitly, but—"

EJ must have been looking at her sister awfully hard, because she stopped hesitating and told the story.

"Okay. I happened to be with Mom one day when she came to pick you up. It was the spring before your last recital. She wanted me to help carry your giant tutus to the car. Mom's handing over her credit card to the receptionist when your class lets out. We overheard a teacher compliment you on the obvious success of your regimen. She said you were 'about fifteen pounds from being hirable' if your technique stayed strong. I saw Momma tense all over. She held it together until we got back to the car and I saw her text Dad, saying, 'These people are trying to kill our baby.' You remember this was around the time that Cousin Gigi had been hospitalized for her bulimia."

"That's different. I didn't have an eating disorder."

"You definitely had something unhealthy going on, and it was only going to get worse with you chasing those last pounds." She shook her head, frowning. "Who says that to a teenage girl, anyway?"

EJ fell back into her seat. She could see Maya was talking to her, and getting more and more distressed, but she felt like she couldn't move. At some point, she must have started crying. She didn't realize it until Maya brushed the tears from her cheek. The woman in front of them turned around in concern, but Maya waved her away. She pulled EJ close and rocked her.

EJ couldn't respond. She just cried and let herself be held. "Why didn't they tell me the truth?" she said, her voice distorted by sobs.

For so long, EJ had made a point of being "the good one," the one her parents could talk to calmly—without yelling. Now it felt like all the effort and holding stuff in hadn't made things better.

What was the point of having discussions if—when it really counted— they just lied? Something fundamental had shifted with this new knowledge. Whatever their reasons, her parents seemed different to her now.

It took her a little while, but eventually, EJ's tears slowed. She sniffled. The train made it past Philadelphia before she could speak again.

"I don't know what to do. All I can think about is how my life would be different if they'd had a conversation with me. Maybe I would have been a dance major. Maybe I would have gotten into acting. Maybe I would have gotten back into tap—I liked tap!" She broke off with another sob. Maya looked miserable, but EJ carried on.

"When they sat me down and said, 'Baby, we can't afford this,' I listened. I acknowledged how they had given so much to get me that far, and I accepted it. I didn't scream. I didn't even cry in front of them. I thought I was sacrificing dance for them. Because I loved them."

Maya stroked EJ's hair and wiped her tears with the sleeve of her coat. "Sweetness, they could never afford the lessons. Even with your scholarships, you know you were attending a very expensive ballet school in a pretty expensive area—not to mention the summer intensives. Don't you think they might have liked to take a vacation instead?"

Even in the midst of her swirling emotions, EJ had to acknowledge the truth of this. She thought back to the improvements her parents had made in the house. They must have wanted to do them for some time.

Maya continued. "Know what I remember? Your recitals, all the other parents were defense contractors and lobbyists on their iPhones—and then there were Momma and Daddy: a public-school teacher and a guidance counselor, right there with them."

She wrapped her arms around EJ's waist. "I'm not judging you, though. They couldn't afford to keep me knee deep in really good art supplies, either. I didn't realize just how generous they were until I started buying my own. You know how it all got paid for? Dad teaching summer sessions, Mom doing extra tutoring through the year. She shops at Macy's sometimes now, not just Marshalls. Daddy golfs, for Christ's sake." Maya stroked her back. "They made it happen because it made us happy."

EJ was silent, considering.

"The world is not as altered as you think," Maya added.

BACK TO CAMPUS

EJ

On the ride back to Hertfordshire, EJ remembered that she still needed an answer for Stella. She took a deep breath and pushed everyone—her parents, Jamie, Tessa—out of her mind to focus on one question: *What do I want?* She applied it to her career and her life.

Kids? Meh.

Money? Yes, but she didn't need to be rich—she wanted something more like security.

And I'd like to do something good—at least not evil.

Maybe I could help cities adapt to climate change? Or help climate change not *kill us all?*

The train was slow, so EJ had a lot of time to think. She started with a word cloud. That turned into a list of questions. After some research on her phone, it became a list of . . . *demands* was too strong. Conditions? That was more accurate but still not quite right. It was a list of the things EJ wanted out of the Fields Fellowship. If Stella thought it was possible to get what she wanted, then she'd go for it. Still, EJ was fairly sure that Stella was expecting her effusive yes. She hated the thought of disappointing her, but she had to put her needs out there.

The best advice she got on this subject ended up coming from Will Pak, of all people. She was sitting in the school's small art gallery after lunch trying to psych herself up for this conversation when Will sat next to her on the bench. They talked about art for a minute—Will was really excited about the Turner painting on display. EJ tried to keep up her part of the conversation, but he could tell she was a little nervous. Somehow she ended up blurting everything out. Then Will told her a story from his career.

He said when he was seventeen, he was having trouble making the jump from kid TV to teen roles. Then one day his agent called him with an audition for this sitcom pilot that was pretty much a sure thing. The director and writer were both well known. It sounded like the perfect gig—except his character was a sexless, nerdy Asian stereotype. He said he avoided the conversation for as long as possible, but eventually had to tell his agent that he wouldn't accept the role, even if offered. He didn't want to play stereotypes. And if that meant that he did mostly commercials or small parts, he was fine with that. Will said his agent was mad—but not for him passing on this opportunity. She was upset that she was working so hard to give him something he didn't want.

"If someone's going to have your back, they need all the information. Telling your advisor what your goals and desires are—it's not unreasonable. If she's someone you trust, she's going to want to know."

It was precisely what EJ needed to hear. Stella had been firmly in her corner since EJ had asked her to become her advisor. She helped balance her schedule, maximize her GPA, and minimize stress. She told EJ which professors were looking for protégés among their students and which ones were looking for girlfriends. She even recommended that EJ take one of her core classes at Smith because the lecturer teaching the course at Longbourn never gave women better than an A minus. Stella also preached the gospel of work-life balance to her undergraduates.

"She'll understand," EJ said to herself, repeatedly, as she climbed the stairs to her advisor's office. When she finally reached the top floor of the Physics Building, EJ squared her shoulders and did her best to exude cool confidence as she walked through Stella's open door.

Her advisor was riffling through her bookshelves when she arrived. "EJ! Good, right on time." She turned around in her office chair.

"Would you like an apple cider doughnut? Donny brought them from his writer's retreat."

EJ loved apple cider doughnuts. This was a sign that the universe was on her side here. She was going to tell Stella all her thoughts. After the usual holiday break pleasantries, she launched right in.

"I have to be honest, Stella, while I was tremendously honored that you would consider nominating me for the Fields Fellowship, my initial instinct was to say no."

"Oh?" Stella's thin eyebrows hopped up over her large round glasses. She wobbled her head in a way that made her earrings jingle lightly. "Were you feeling burned out?"

Stella was the first person to even suggest this possibility. "Yes! After my capstone, I just felt like all my resources were depleted, but that wasn't the only thing. I'm a little weary of the life of an engineering student. I'd like to have a bit more money in my pocket—I'm at the point where, if I'm going to endure the casual racism and sexism that we have to put up with in this field, I want to be paid for it. If I were to do the fellowship, I'd like to start in January of next year so I could work for a bit and raise money for my time over there. I know it wouldn't be much, but if I could have a head start against being broke . . . Do you think that would be okay?"

Stella nodded. "They don't care when you matriculate as long as it's in the following academic year. Is that all?"

EJ gave a small, embarrassed laugh. "No. I'm also thinking about my future. I don't just want a career. I want a partner, and I want to enjoy my life when I'm not in labs. Basically, I want to live in a city, preferably in the UK. I know there's no official geographic restriction for the fellowship, but is international study discouraged?"

Stella shook her head vigorously. "Quite the opposite, in fact. The program was started as an exchange between North American and European universities. Before you go on, let me say that you can study whatever you want as well, and I mean whatever. I've seen everything from MFA in sculpture to way too many MBAs." She shook her head. "The only thing the foundation asks is a year of public service after you graduate."

EJ sat back in the creaky wooden chair. "Huh," she said aloud. "Well, that's good, because I'm interested in doing two one-year master's programs: the first in historic building preservation and a second in sustainable design. Basically, I want to create the products and materials that help maintain our beautiful old buildings and prepare them for climate change. I know it's small compared to designing the next Mars rover, but I think it's important. And while I'm all for discovery, someone's got to make sure that we keep what we have."

"Then let's do it!" Stella declared, stretching her arms wide. "It's a little unusual, but I'm confident you can make the argument for both. Is that all, now?"

EJ checked the list in her lap. That was all, and asking for it was much easier than she expected. She nodded.

"You'll apply, then?" Stella asked. At EJ's nod, she squealed. "I'm so glad!" the older woman effused, clasping her hands together.

"Thanks, Stella. I know I'm not the typical Fields Fellow genius, but I'll do my best not to let you down."

Stella crossed her arms. "Now stop that. You're a brilliant girl. You just don't see that because you compare yourself to the most brilliant person in the room. You know the old Longbourn joke: How do you know you've met the dumbest person on campus?" She paused and leaned forward. "He'll tell you he's the smartest. *Ha!*" She chuckled for a bit, then continued. "The only way you'd let me down is by not seeing this through, and I know that's not in your nature."

Stella adjusted the large-framed glasses that made her look like a friendly owl. "I nominated you for two reasons: first, because I know you would take the public-service part seriously—not take something corporate clothed as nonprofit work or blow it off completely by taking the donor option and running to the first oil field you could find."

"The donor option?"

Stella rolled her eyes. "It was introduced recently so that the fellowship 'wouldn't hold back entrepreneurs,' meaning the tech boys. Essentially, if you want out of the public service requirement, you can donate fifty grand instead of completing your service year and go off to make your millions."

EJ's face reacted before she could speak.

"See!" Stella exclaimed. "I knew that wouldn't fly with you. You have this strong sense of honor, which frankly, wouldn't serve you well in I-banking—or most of law—but is still very valuable to engineers. I know I can trust your bridges."

She went on. "The second reason I nominated you is also the reason I believe in your success: your discipline. If you get this opportunity, I know there is no force that will be able to stop you from making the most of it. I've seen how you work. That internal drive is crucial, especially for women in this field. We don't often have the boosters that the boys do. What powers us has to come from inside."

EJ simply nodded. She'd never known Stella had so much faith in her. Nor had she realized the value of her "wasted years" in ballet until this moment. Even without going pro, dance had given her a thirst for perfection and a relentlessness in pursuit of it. It had shaped her into a potentially awesome engineer.

"Stella," she said hesitantly, "I think I can do this."

"I know you can, EJ."

EJ sat quietly, reflecting on the fact that if she hadn't had that heart-to-heart with Maya, she wouldn't have even attempted to do the Fields Fellowship her own way. Hell, she was probably going to chicken out until she talked to Will in the art gallery. Because of those two conversations, she'd found the courage to ask for what she wanted. She still had to back it up with her application . . . but she was going to try. *Bennet Women try.*

Will

What a week! The Longbourn magic seemed to be happening for Will. On Tuesday, the day after he returned to his sublet, he got a call from the anthropology professor who was leasing the place to him. She wanted to come by and get her masks off the walls. Will gladly told her yes. When he got back from lunch and running errands, every single mask was gone. He didn't realize how much they were messing with his well-being before, but now his mind felt quiet. It was wonderful. He opened a good bottle of wine and put on some Thelonious Monk.

It is high time, Will thought, *that I spent the afternoon in my living room.*

The next day, he went to his 9:00 a.m. Impressionism and Post-Impressionism class with the enthusiasm of someone returning from a vacation. When their professor, Andreas, told the class about the arrival of the Turner painting, Will instantly perked up. He was kind of a Turner superfan. He had read two biographies of the painter and had made all his friends watch *Mr. Turner* at least once.

The gallery was Will's favorite space on campus. It was chronically underused by the student body, which meant it was always peaceful. Also, the school's curator did a bang-up job in putting exhibits together. The current exhibit, *On the Waterfront*, was a collection of seaside land-scapes from Whistler to Hockney. Today, though, he was interested in only one work. Will moved with elegant speed through the exhibition space until he saw the painting, on its own wall. He noticed someone sitting on the bench in front of the painting, but not looking at it. He stepped a little closer and realized it was EJ. She was wringing her hands and very focused on the notebook on her lap. Will briefly considered quietly backing out of the room. It was strange to see her so soon after he'd realized he felt something for her. He'd barely gotten comfortable with this truth himself. Besides, EJ seemed lost in her own thoughts.

As Will took his first backward step, his body betrayed him with a loud sneeze. EJ started and turned. "Oh. Hello, Will."

She'd changed her hair over the break. Instead of extensions, it was all up in a sort of cornrow French twist. Will felt like he was seeing her face for the first time. It was a lovely face.

How does her skin seem to glow on a gloomy November day?

He walked toward her, doing his best to remember what their dynamic was before.

"Hey, Eej. How was home?" He was surprised to see her shoulders sink as he joined her on the bench.

After a long silence, she replied with, "It was different," and tellingly said no more.

Will didn't want to press, so he changed the subject. "Are you here for the new Turner?" he asked, pointing forward. She glanced around, confused until she registered that he was talking about the painting in front of her.

"Oh yeah, it's lovely." She went to tuck a couple of loose twists behind her ear out of habit. "I went to Venice while I was on my junior year abroad. It was only for two days but—"

Will couldn't stop himself from speaking. "I'm sorry, that's not acceptable. We have this amazing piece of art here, and you're not seeing it." He knew, of all people, EJ could get what he loved about Turner. Someone who had opinions on the Best Cinematography Oscar would have to.

"I can see it fine," she grumbled. "It's right *there*."

Will sputtered. "No—just . . ." *In for a penny, in for a pound.* "Close your eyes." The look EJ gave him was skeptical at best. "Please, Eej, humor me."

She gave a one-shouldered shrug and finally closed her eyes.

Will moved close to her and spoke low.

"Picture it: Venice, eighteen hundreds." He paused at her giggle. *So she does know* The Golden Girls. "You've spent the morning selling bread in the piazza, where you were caught in a crush of people and surrounded by tall—three-story—buildings. Now that you've sold everything, you're going back home for lunch and to finish the day's chores, but you crave fresh air. You dodge puddles of water and weave around the wooden carts of fruit sellers and fishmongers."

He slid closer to her, and their knees brushed—just for a moment. EJ didn't seem to notice.

"Go on," she said. Her eyes were still closed.

Will continued. "You finally free yourself from the market and make your way through a series of narrow alleys. Anyone else would lose themselves, but you're a true Venetian. You know exactly where you're going. At last, you're back on one of the wide thoroughfares with plenty of space. The air is fresher here, and it ripples the hem of your skirt. Now you retrieve an apple from your pocket and take a leisurely walk by the canal. You walk over a bridge. The sun is so bright, and the sky is beautifully clear. The basilica gleams in the distance like a pearl. It is the most beautiful day.

"You walk to the center of the bridge, and the men in boats are going toward the main square. There are too many men in the dinghy. They are singing and sweating. One notices you and almost tips the boat over trying to wave. You hear the staccato splashes of oars hitting the water from all sides. A man in a gondola shouts a marriage proposal, but you ignore him. Your eyes are drawn upward, to the bright blue sky. Only the faintest whisper of clouds. At this brief moment in your busy life, you feel peace. Now, open your eyes."

EJ blinked as if waking from a dream. She stood and thoughtfully approached the Turner. After a few moments she took a couple of steps back and, still looking at the painting, unconsciously drew a curve in the air between the basilica and the sky. Then she turned to him, eyes sparkling.

"It's like magic: then I didn't see it, now I do," she said brightly. She walked back to their bench. "That was amazing. I felt like I really understood what capturing that moment meant. You should do, like, a *Reading Rainbow* for art. If people could see paintings as moments in a story, maybe they would be more interested."

They ended up having a really nice conversation. EJ, who was clearly stressed out about something, unburdened herself to him. He listened and gave her some hopefully helpful advice. She hugged him when she left. Will felt warm all day.

READING PERIOD

EJ

It was the last salsa night at the Tropicana before finals, so most of the Longbourn ballroom team piled into cars and took the one-hour drive over. Since there were enough sober drivers, EJ squished herself in the back of a Jetta with Franz. She intended to have at least one of the club's embarrassingly ornate drinks tonight. EJ vaguely remembered drinking something blue out of a top hat with four other people the last time they made the trip.

Aside from the booze, the Tropicana drew people in with the best salsa night within thirty miles and the only social dancing outside of competitions. The best and worst part of going out salsa dancing was salsa culture. On the plus side, it was super open and inclusive, which meant it was considered a faux pas to reject partners when asked to dance. This created a dance-floor meritocracy: the most skilled partners were the most popular regardless of size, age, or height. Unfortunately, this meant that salsa nights attracted a certain kind of sketchy middle-aged guy who reveled in getting close to young women.

Once the lessons were over and the Longbourn contingent was scattered throughout the dance floor, EJ found that she was the target of one of these sketchy dudes. She'd given him one obligatory dance, on the off chance he had any skill. He did not. In fact, the guy was the worst kind of bad dancer. His palms were sweaty, and he wore way too much cologne. Plus, he counted all his steps aloud and clamped down on both EJ's wrist and any of her gentle attempts to back-lead.

She thought she'd done her duty after the first dance, but he just wouldn't leave her alone—even after she excused herself once to the bathroom and twice to the bar. Everywhere she went, there he was. Franz found the whole thing funny in a way that made EJ want to punch him—but he also helpfully swept her onto the dance floor every time the guy got close enough to tap her on the shoulder.

They were doing a highly unskilled bachata when the song trailed off. EJ spotted her eager suitor over Franz's shoulder and asked her friend if he wanted to step outside for a cigarette.

"I quit, remember? That's why I was so angry for most of September," he said with a light laugh. "Do you smoke now?"

She shook her head. "No, but I'm thinking I should start." Her shoulders dropped as the floor began to clear and she resigned herself to either getting a ride home, or dancing with the gross guy again so she could get thirty minutes of peace. Leaning against a column, EJ looked in his direction. Captain Sketch spotted her and began making his way over. Just as she was preparing to receive his clammy embrace, EJ was swept into a much more pleasant hug.

"There you are, sweetheart! Sorry I'm late." She found herself held by a stranger who happened to look like a matinee idol. He had wavy blond hair and cheekbones to cut glass, with a muscular frame that was just shy of burly. She beamed up at him, affecting familiarity.

"That's all right, sugar dumpling. I'm glad you could get out of your MMA training tonight. Let's get you a drink."

They made their way to the bar with his arm around her waist. She risked a look back, and Captain Sketch was gone, on the hunt for someone else. EJ shook her head.

The things you have to do so some creep doesn't follow you to your car.

At the bar EJ discreetly shook the hand of her rescuer. "Thank you and I'm buying," she said with a smile. "My name is EJ, by the way."

"Jordan Walker, milady." He kissed her hand with a courtly bow.

EJ suppressed a flutter. Just that little interaction was a reminder that she hadn't gotten laid in a long time. "You, Sir Knight, are very smooth, and it may be effective. What are you drinking?"

Usually, she wasn't attracted to blond guys, but Jordan looked like if James Dean and Nureyev had a hot son who wrote poetry.

"Sex on the beach. I'm sorry—that's what I'm thinking, looking at that dress." He gave a comic wiggle of his eyebrows. "I'll have a whiskey sour, thanks," he finished.

She giggled and hailed the bartender. "What do you do when not rescuing girls at bars?" she asked, launching the small talk.

"I'm doing drama at UMass," he replied.

"Are you local?"

"Nah, I'm from Philly. I came here because UMass is in the consortium with Longbourn, and I desperately want to take the drama seminar with Sir Titus Allen-Henry."

"Wow, the master himself," she said reverently.

"I hear he plays checkers with his Tonys and his Oscars," Jordan joked. "I'd love to be in the presence of that much talent."

EJ certainly agreed. Sir Titus's presence had helped draw her to Longbourn—and she was an engineer. He directed a production of *The Tempest* that EJ saw more than five years ago and still thought about from time to time. "I get it. I helped build sets for the Drama department's showcase my sophomore year so he would wave to me. *He did*," she added in a whisper.

Jordan shot her a sideways smile. "I had my audition yesterday, just waiting now. They usually don't let kids from the consortium in—or underclassmen—but I'm pretty sure I nailed it."

"Cheers to you!" They clinked their glasses. Then EJ furrowed her brow. "Wait, 'underclassmen'? Did I commit a crime?"

Jordan laughed. "No, you're fine. I'm twenty-two. I had to take some time off between high school and college . . . not by choice, but that's a sadder story for another time." He looked at her with a wicked smile. "Maybe breakfast?"

"I'm generally not in the habit of hooking up with strange boys, but let's see how you dance."

EJ didn't change partners again that night. When they weren't dancing together—and God he could move—she and Jordan were huddled at a back table sitting really, *really* close to each other. Jordan was a great storyteller, and even in the noisy club, she liked listening to him talk. He told her about making cheesesteaks for the Roots at a summer job and falling in love with musicals by catching *On the Town* on Turner Classic Movies. It was at this point that EJ decided she was definitely going home with him. She made a point to introduce Jordan to Franz, who kissed her on the cheek and said, "Look at you, moving up in the world." Then Jordan hailed an Uber for his place, and they made out in the car.

By the time they arrived at his apartment, EJ wanted to do everything to and with Jordan. She couldn't remember the last time she'd felt this turned on while still fully clothed. Jordan surely felt the same. His eyes seemed to sear her skin.

If looks could strip, EJ thought, *I'd be naked right now.*

They'd barely closed the door to his apartment before they were exchanging frenzied orgasms in his living room. Then they drank water—a lot of it—and flirted and somehow got onto the topic of Kris Jenner: Jordan called her his role model. EJ didn't know who she was and suggested going to bed so she wouldn't have to admit it. They slept, loosely tangled in each other. The next morning EJ woke up to kisses on the back of her neck, then moving along the curve of her shoulder.

"Good morning," she said with a sleepy smile. It took her a moment to remember that she'd gone to bed in her underwear. *Thank God I wore cute undies,* she thought as Jordan leaned in for a kiss. They made out at a more leisurely pace but put the brakes on actual sex once they realized neither of them had another condom. "Didn't I promise you breakfast, anyway?" He offered EJ his hand and helped her out of bed.

They showered together, then returned to his bedroom to get dressed. Facing the mirror on the back of the door, EJ slid on her dress from the previous night. Jordan came up behind her and grunted lustily. "That dress."

EJ raised her eyebrows in the mirror. It was cute but distinctly, purposely *not* a sexy dress. Perhaps a little on the short side, but it was a baby-doll dress with a solar-system print and a bit of swing in the skirt. "Do you have a Miss Frizzle fetish I should know about?"

"Maybe." He looped an arm around her waist and lightly bit the shell of her ear. EJ suppressed a shudder.

"Sure I can't convince you to get back in bed?" he asked too sweetly. "It wouldn't be too risky. I mean, I couldn't help staring at this in the shower"—he squeezed her ass—"and I noticed that you're on the patch." He began planting kisses on her neck while sliding his hand up her dress.

There's nothing less sexy than gonorrhea, EJ thought to herself, repeatedly. It was a helpful hint from a former Bennet RA. *"When a truly yummy dude is trying to tempt you into unsafe sex, just imagine telling future partners about your STI."*

She deftly slid away from him, humming "Some Other Time," from *On the Town.*

"That's not fair," he pouted. "You can't use my favorite song from my favorite show against me."

EJ raised her eyebrows at him again. "You're the one talking about 'unfair'?"

Jordan gave another one of his wicked half smiles. "I had to try," he said sheepishly.

Did you? EJ thought with a prick of irritation. *Really?* But everything up to this point had been quite lovely, so she let it go. "I'll find my leggings, and we can get out of here."

Jordan was pulling on his jeans. "Pretty sure they landed on the ceiling fan," he replied. He was smirking, just a little.

EJ was stuck halfway between smiling and rolling her eyes. "Thanks, I'll be ready in a sec." With that she went into the living room.

They had breakfast—well, brunch—at a full-service deli near his place. Over the meal Jordan talked about life as the oldest sophomore in his class, and EJ talked about Longbourn and its many quirks. He was especially interested in Bennet House.

"That would make a *great* TV show," he said, sipping his coffee. "All that sisterhood, and solidarity, and pants-off dance-offs."

"Hey! There was only the one," EJ objected. They moved on to their favorite books and music preferences until there was a natural lull. She put her plate to the side and asked a question lingering from the night before. "I understand if you're not comfortable sharing, but what caused your 'gap year' so to speak?"

"Where to begin?" Jordan sighed. "Well you've probably gotten this going to Longbourn, but everything Fitzgerald said about the rich is still true. What happened to me? Basically, I pissed off the wrong rich kid, and paid for it. There was this guy—he's a TV actor now, Will Pak . . ."

Jordan seemed to check her face for any recognition. EJ shrugged blankly as her stomach dropped. Over the next several minutes, EJ listened as Jordan told her how Will Pak had ruined his young life.

Jamie

Don't laugh. Don't laugh, Jamie told herself as she watched Tessa's jaw drop. Because of her very open and sex-positive sister, EJ had a frankness about these things that shocked people. Especially since somehow they got the impression that butter didn't melt in her mouth. EJ wasn't the Queen of Slutsville by any means, but her girl did like sex and talked about the mechanics of her encounters like other people talked about impressive plays at a baseball game.

Jamie couldn't hide her smile of amusement as she watched Tessa listen to EJ finish her hookup story. "But we used the condoms I brought for round one and the"—tongue pop—"the night before. He didn't have anything, so we got each other off with our hands. I was disappointed, but no matter how good it would have been, I literally don't fuck with unwrapped dick."

Tessa dropped her fork, still loaded with waffle and whipped cream. "Elizabeth Jacqueline Davis!" she cried.

Jamie choked out a laugh. Tessa shot her a look.

"I can't believe any of this. Especially you going off with a strange man. You could have been kidnapped. Or killed!"

"Ever since you watched *Looking for Mr. Goodbar* in that seventies film class, you've been worse than my mother," EJ huffed. "I was not only safe—I was Bennet safe. I had my own condoms and wouldn't fuck without one. My birth control is up to date, and I went in with realistic expectations."

Oy, Eej loved passing down the wisdom of "Bennet safe." It had become part of house programming in the '90s. The way EJ told it, back then one of the Bennet House RAs noticed how woefully unprepared Bennet Women were for the world of casual sex. She developed the concept of "Bennet safe" and reworked her orientation talks, making sure that her dormmates knew how to use condoms and dental dams, where to get contraception, and that sex does not equal love. According to the alumni magazine, that RA had since gone on to a successful career in public health.

"She even texted me his address and a picture," Jamie chimed in, pulling up the grainy paparazzi-style photo. Even in the dim light, it looked like EJ had bagged one of the better Hemsworths. Jamie showed the photo to Tessa, who nodded appreciatively.

"Well, damn," Tessa said, sitting back in her chair. "I have nothing further."

Jamie giggled and then looked at EJ. On campus, hookups were one thing, but this—it was something different from her little engineer. Really, truly out of character for her. "I can't believe you hooked up with some rando," Jamie said, elbowing her friend in the side. "You swore off complete strangers after the incident with the French dude on the ferry to Mykonos."

"He was that regrettable," EJ agreed.

"What made this guy the exception?" asked Tessa. "Besides the obvious."

"The obvious was a big factor. I think the only person with a better body in like three towns is our resident celebrity—and he's attractive for a living. Also, Jordan was charming, a good dancer, and I guess I needed a little fun."

"And was it *fun*?" Jamie inquired.

EJ couldn't help her wicked smile. "Yes, surprisingly so. In my limited experience with the very, very good-looking, i.e., Monsieur Mykonos, they tend to expect worship and don't do much to ensure your good time. Jordan was a gentleman in all things: ladies first."

Jamie could tell that EJ wanted to wink but thought better of it.

"Soooooooo are you going to see him again?" asked Tessa.

"I don't expect to. We didn't exchange numbers or anything. I'm content to let it be a sunset—beautiful and then gone."

Again, out of character. Eej would usually text back and forth with her hookups before they disappointed her. Even Mykonos hung around for an extra half a day.

Jamie demurred. "I dunno. I saw the way that very hot man kissed your hand when he dropped you off. There might be something there."

EJ shook her head definitively. "He's also two towns away and two years behind me—"

"Cradle robber! He's nineteen?" Tessa cried laughingly.

"No, he's twenty-two, but a sophomore. It's a long story and not mine to tell." EJ shrugged. "I don't want to start something I can't finish, and I know I don't want to be in Massachusetts in a year."

"But you have such a great story!" Tessa protested. "The dance-floor rescue is just so romantic. I could totally see it shot in black and white with some sexy jazz music. I'm convinced great couples come from great stories. My parents met in a laundromat, and they divorced when I was five."

"Even so, T, I'm gonna stick with the sunset." EJ spread her hands across an invisible horizon and let that be the final word.

They got onto the subject of Jamie's attempt to change advisors as she revealed that hers was unequivocally sexist *and* transphobic— something Jamie had learned only after her transition. EJ suggested dropping the phrase *my friend at the ACLU* into her next conversation with the dean.

Brunch ended on the subject of what Tessa should do with her hair. Tessa was on Team Cut It. Jamie was on Team Dye It. Eej was on Team Why Not Both? The friends talked until the dining hall began closing to prep for dinner, when they ended their time together reluctantly.

"Hey, EJ," Jamie said as they walked out the cafeteria doors. "Still up for Scrabble at Will's tonight? It's the final game night while we're all still here."

"I completely forgot," she replied. "I think I promised Dia I would have dinner with her and her sister. She's a civil engineer in New York."

Look at Tinkerbelle networking! Jamie thought, giving her friend a small smile. Then she stopped short. "Hold the phone, Joan. You and Dia were talking about this in the hallway yesterday. You told her you couldn't make it because of game night."

EJ squirmed uncomfortably. She was such a terrible liar that she attempted it only when panicked. But why?

"What's going on, Eej?" Jamie asked with a troubled frown. "You don't usually lie to me, even tiny ones."

EJ sighed. "Look, I didn't want to put you in a bad position, but I can't hang out with Will anymore."

Jamie wanted to scream. This was the worst possible moment for EJ to turn cold on Will. "Why?" she exclaimed. "I mean, I thought you guys were doing okay now."

EJ's arms were folded, and she couldn't look Jamie in the eye. "We were. It's just, I found out some things, and . . . I can't keep his company." She tried to walk away, but Jamie stopped her.

"What things?" she asked earnestly. "If it's that bad, why won't you tell me? Does Lee know?"

She shook her head. "I can't say—about anything, really. It's not my story to tell, and I was asked not to tell it." She looked around helplessly. "I don't know what Lee knows, and I don't think I could prove what I heard. It's too complicated. The best thing for me to do is stay away."

EJ patted her arm. "I will do my best not to make things awkward for you and Lee."

"But!" It was all Jamie could get out. This was bad. But how could she explain without breaking Lee's trust or spoiling Will's surprise? Her mind whirred, trying to think of something to say.

"I wish things were different. Sorry, honey bun." With that, EJ headed to the library, leaving a puzzled Jamie in her wake. Quickly, she dug out her phone and sent a text to Lee.

EJ

Bennet House was quiet and still. Only those unlucky underclassmen still waiting to take exams remained, along with their RAs—who were obliged to stay until their residents were gone or the dorms were closed. There was at least one who didn't mind. EJ was watching a gentle snowfall from the window seat in the common room. She was near weightless with relief. Her coursework was completed. Her capstone was defended. Her presentation prospectus had been submitted to the National Society of Black Engineers. In short, everything was done.

Next semester would be the first time in her academic life she'd be taking it easy. She was also looking forward to competing in ballroom again, not just teaching. EJ had enjoyed coaching the newbies in the fall, but it had been hard for her to stay on the sidelines. The spring offered two big competitions, and she'd have January and some of February to get herself back up to gold standard. She couldn't wait to start.

EJ gazed out the window, immersed in her happy thoughts until she registered the *hiss-thwomp* of a large suitcase being dragged down the stairs. Dia emerged from the landing. She spotted EJ and waved happily. "There you are! I have something for you."

The younger woman jogged over with a sparkly oblong package in her hand. "I finished it last night." She rocked on her heels as EJ carefully unsealed the tape from either end to reveal a long, wide scarf, made with more love than skill.

"Oh wow!"

"I did the knitting workshop in October and haven't been able to stop."

Clearly, EJ thought with a soft chuckle. She was wearing a hand-knit scarf, and her curls were mostly hidden by a hand-knit hat that was slightly too big. She was sure Dia's whole family was getting scarves this year.

"Do you like it?" Dia asked hopefully.

"Yes, I really do. It's so soft. And in Longbourn colors! I love it." EJ was especially partial to homemade gifts, which her friends either loved or hated about her, depending on the skills they possessed.

"I know how much you love Longbourn, and I feel like you helped me love this place, too." With a small jump, Dia embraced her RA. "Thanks for everything. Merry Christmas." As Dia let go, her phone rang.

"That'll be my big sister Dylann." Dia dropped her voice. "The one from *New York.* We're flying home together," she added brightly. She wheeled her suitcase toward the door. EJ could see Dia's sister in the car with their cabdriver. "You two should definitely get coffee next time she comes this way. She's an engineer, too. I think I mentioned that. Hold on." Dia turned and screamed out the door, "Dylann, come give EJ your business card." The petite freshman turned back to EJ and beamed. "I make things happen."

Moments later, a tall woman with ash-blonde hair and Dia's face came to the door. She shot a crooked smile at her sister. "Apparently I should give you my business card," she began, offering it to EJ, who crossed the room and took it with mild apprehension.

Dylann continued. "Women need each other in this field. I would love to talk with you—in person or remotely—sometime next year. Don't hesitate to call."

"Thanks, I will get in touch."

"Good," Dylann said as she walked a beaming Dia to their waiting cab. On the way out Dylann paused, holding the cab's door, silently asking how her sister had done with the international thumbs-up or thumbs-down sign. EJ responded with a three-fingered "A-okay." Dylann nodded as if to say, "I'll take it."

✑

After a goodbye lunch with Tessa, EJ finally started packing. She waited until after her residents were gone so she could blast her music with the door open. Dropping the needle on her vinyl of *Back to Black*, she vowed to be finished by the end of the album. She was retrieving her favorite sneakers from beneath her bed when she noticed some awkward percussion interfering with the horns. Sitting up, she saw Will leaning against her doorjamb, hand raised to knock again. Despite his gentle approach, she was surprised.

"Jesus Christ!"

"We've got to stop meeting like this." He laughed.

"What are you doing here?" she asked, not quite coldly. She stood and turned off the music a little resentfully.

"We missed you at game night. Jamie said something came up at the last minute," Will began.

"I thought you were driving home today. Traffic is going to be bad now." She glanced at her watch. She'd thought she'd be safe from Will until January.

"Native New Yorker, remember? I don't drive at home. That's why God invented taxis." He stood in the doorway a bit awkwardly before asking, "Can I come in?"

EJ hesitated but eventually stood aside. Wanting more distance than her love seat provided, she directed Will to her desk chair and sat at the far end of her bed. "When's your flight?"

"Don't worry, Eej; I'm on my way to the airport. I promise I won't take long." He leaned over and elbowed her lightly. "You sure seem eager to get rid of me." He laughed. She did not. He did not appear to notice.

"Anyway, I wanted to thank you." Will coughed. "Remember when we were in the school gallery, and you said I should host a *Reading Rainbow* for art? Well, you kind of sparked something, and it's going to be the basis of my independent study next semester. I'm going to create a web series on art for it. If everything goes well, it could be more than my degree—it could be my next project. There's a lot, *a lot*, still to do, but I wanted to say thanks." He stood and proffered a coolly elegant gift bag in a holiday-neutral ecru.

Oh God. This was so much easier when he didn't like me. EJ looked at the bag—then at Will. "I can't accept this," she said.

Will pressed the bag into her hands. "Oh, I promise you it's nothing expensive. Jamie told me—"

"I can't accept this, Will," she said emphatically, returning the bag to him. "I can't accept anything from you, and I can't be your friend."

Will sat down slowly, cradling the bag in his lap. "I don't understand."

EJ squeezed her hands together anxiously. "Recently, I learned about some events in your past that prevent me from continuing to associate with you. The victim asked me not to share this story, so I'm keeping it to myself. But now that I know the truth about you, I will be civil with you in social situations, but morally, I—"

"I'm sorry, 'victim'?" Will choked out. "Morally—what? Who?"

"Jordan," EJ intoned. "I know what you did to him, Will."

The actor staggered slightly. "Jordan"—he took a steadying breath—"Walker?"

Oh God, his actor is showing, EJ thought impatiently.

"Yes, Jordan Walker. Were there any other scholarship kids you got kicked out of school for dating your sister?" she said in an acidic tone.

"What?" Will cried.

"I know everything, Will," EJ continued. "How you punched him and threw a wad of money at him so he'd leave Lily alone. How you didn't stop there." She watched the color drain from his face.

"How did you hear about this?" he asked crisply, sliding into cool-patrician mode as easily as a duck slid into water.

So it's true! Part of EJ hadn't fully believed it until now. "He told me. Jordan and I . . ." She paused. "We, um, met a couple of weeks back. He just—"

"He's here?" Will gripped the edge of her desk. He seemed ready to leap into some sort of action.

EJ paused warily. "I don't think I should say more. He's finally gotten his life back together. I couldn't be responsible for you taking it all away again. Leave him alone, Will. You've done enough."

"Fucking hell! *I've* done enough—" Will dropped the gift on her desk and shoved himself out of his seat, pacing the length of her single.

EJ thought he'd forgotten she was there when he stopped and turned to her. "Can I just ask," he began with some agitation, "why'd you believe this horrifying rumor about me from some guy you just 'met'?"

How did Will make finger quotes so damn sarcastic? She knew he would find a way to be horrible about the circumstances. Whatever. Sarcasm didn't change the fact that he hadn't denied anything.

"You didn't punch him and throw money in his face?" she shot back hotly.

Will dodged the question. "Did Jordan fuck you stupid? Or are you always so trusting of your one-night stands?"

EJ gripped her quilt tightly with both hands. "This"—she lifted her clenched fists—"is me not slapping the hell out of you because I don't want to explain your bruises." She pushed herself to the edge of the bed.

"I believe Jordan because, number one, there's no way he knew that we knew each other, and there was no advantage for him in inventing such an elaborate lie about some random TV actor. Two, he said you called him a 'grease-stained nobody.' That detail was particularly convincing because it isn't too far from what you called me at the Fall Formal: a lady pimp in a cheap sequin dress, right?" EJ looked up sharply, silencing any justifications.

The actor tensed and swallowed. "I think we've gotten to know each other better since then."

She crossed her arms. "Have we, Will? Really? We've watched a movie, played some board games, and had a few polite conversations, but that's it. If I add it up, I've probably spent as much time in your company as Jordan's. And *he* never insulted me."

She sat up with all the dignity she could muster. "I think a better question is why should I believe you? Like Maya Angelou said, when someone shows you who they are, believe them the first time."

"And who am I to argue with the great Maya Angelou?" he said sardonically. Will ran his hands through his hair in a gesture of frustration. "And that's your final word on things."

"That's how I feel." EJ folded her arms as she watched him cross the room.

Will made his way to the door angrily.

"What I don't understand is why you care. I've already said I won't tell anyone, especially Tessa, Jamie, or Lee. You're getting away with it."

He turned back to her, nearly shouting, "I did nothing wrong. I was protecting her! I did what I had to do."

People do love protecting young women from their own choices, she thought. "I don't understand why we're still having this conversation."

"I want you to hear my side!" he cried.

EJ scrubbed her face with her hands. "Again, why?" she shot back. "Until a couple weeks ago, I was just the girl you had to fake politeness to so Lee wouldn't be mad. Congratulations, you don't have to pretend anymore. I'm the one removing myself."

Will laughed bitterly in response and turned toward the door. "You're right. Lee and Jamie are doing great. We don't need to be anything to each other." He threw on his coat and hastily tugged on his gloves.

EJ looked back to the desk and noticed that the present was still there. "Will, please take your gift," she said to his stiff back.

"No. It's not a gift anymore. It's a bet." Will looked at her over his shoulder. "If I know Jordan Walker at all, you're going to find out just how wrong you are before the spring semester ends. On that day, I want you to open that bag and know just what you gave up for him." With that, Will thundered down the stairs and into the cold December night.

EJ remained at the edge of her bed for some time, staring at the linoleum floor. Nothing about the exchange felt victorious. And Will looked so hurt—not guilty, not just angry, but hurt. She found that wholly bewildering. Lifting the gift, for the first time EJ noticed that the bag was patterned with shimmering stars. She was confused by this thoughtfulness. Frankly, she was confused by everything. She stuffed the bag into her bottom desk drawer and closed it with a slam.

"Since when does he care what I think?" EJ demanded of her empty room. In the responding silence, she went back to packing. She couldn't wait to be gone; the dorm felt like a crime scene.

CHRISTMAS BREAK

Will

Though he'd never been a big fan of the show, today Will was intensely grateful for *Saturday Night Live*. It was the reason Zara hadn't left for Providence as planned. The original host had caught the flu, and now she was going to be hosting the Christmas episode. It was great for Zara and good for Will. He needed to talk with someone who knew the whole truth about Jordan and wasn't Lily. After texting her from the runway, Will hopped a cab from JFK straight over to 30 Rockefeller. He dropped into her dressing room to vent—and, embarrassingly, cry.

Zara hugged him for a full three minutes, then listened, taking off her stage makeup as he raged. Once she had a clean face, she told Will that they were hitting up the new Austrian bakery four blocks over to talk things through. Before long he was eating a very good Sacher-Torte with an even better espresso. Zara was rehashing his fight with EJ to see if she'd missed anything.

"So EJ hit you with vague accusations from Jordan. Did she say what they were?"

"No, she clammed up after she mentioned his name. I think she's worried about violating his privacy. The poor fool. Jordan's smart. He's using EJ's high-and-mighty sense of honor against her." Will took another large bite of his dessert. It was fantastic, though he couldn't say he was enjoying it.

Zara shook her head. "I don't understand why she still believed him after you told her about Lily?"

Will swallowed his mouthful. "I didn't tell her anything," he replied bitterly. "She's not entitled to my sister's story after the way she treated me. She'll find out the hard way."

He glanced over at his friend. She sat up stiffly and folded her arms. He must have failed some sort of test, again.

"You would let her fall into one of his traps because she wouldn't go out with you?" Zara's voice rose. "You know what kind of man he is. You know what he's capable of!"

Will looked around. Thankfully the bakery was empty. He couldn't look at Zara right now.

Zara pursed her lips. "Let me ask you. If there had been a guy in Lily's class at Hanover Academy who knew about Jordan but also had the sweetest crush on her . . . if that guy decided not to warn Lily out of spite—for any reason—would you ever forgive him? Think a moment before you respond."

Will felt his face flush but remained mutinously silent. After all, they both knew the answer.

"I just don't understand why she believed him about me!" he cried.

Zara rubbed her forehead. "Okay, take me back. What did you do for EJ after the Fall Formal?"

Will tilted his head in confusion. "What do you mean?"

Zara dropped her head back. "Remember when you were a mean, snotty asshole to everyone for a night, including a bunch of people you just met? It's the same night you got drunk and passed out in public."

Will bit his lip and frowned. He didn't remember that night, but both Zara and Lee had brought it up since then. "I sent you flowers, right?" he replied.

"And you sent chocolates to my mom for her birthday, which she loved. But how did you apologize to EJ? What did you do for her?" Zara leaned in with a slight edge to her voice.

Will was silent. He felt his shame growing.

Zara threw up her hands. "Okay. So you don't apologize for talking shit behind EJ's back and then being an asshole in what you now know is her favorite place."

"I didn't know she heard me," he almost whispered.

"But you damn well know what you said. And what you did after." She leaned forward like a movie detective in an interrogation. "Because if I'm EJ, I'm noticing a pattern. I'm not even worth a verbal apology from you until my best friend is dating your best friend. That's why she doesn't trust you."

Will groaned. "Why can't you be on my side here? You know everything that Lily *and* I went through with Jordan."

Zara gave him a long look. "Who are you talking to? Do I look like Lee? Because that's who you call if you need someone to listen and pretend you did nothing wrong. I'm the one who calls you on your bullshit. And don't ask me to wait for a 'good time.' You are the biggest asshole when you're hurting, and you need to hear this before you cut another person out of your life."

She drained the last of her coffee and shifted in her chair. "So we both know that EJ is wrong *now*. But isn't it mostly because you were wrong in the past?"

Will made a noise of protest, but Zara cut him off with a look. "Stay with me: In a world where you roll up to Longbourn still dating Carrie and not lashing out, maybe EJ hears Jordan's story and thinks, 'That's far fetched.' Instead, you gave her all the reason in the world to believe the worst of you that first night. By your own account, you've only been nice to her since October."

Will knew she was right, but also knew there was no way he was apologizing. "If I promise to warn her off, can we never talk about EJ again?"

Zara held her hands up mollifyingly. "If that's the way you want to play it. I won't mention her name." She glanced across the table at him.

He must have looked pretty pitiful, because her expression instantly softened. "I'm sorry things went down the way they did."

Will bit his bottom lip. "You and me both."

They were silent for a little while; then Zara spoke again. "Are you mad?"

Will sighed and shook his head. *Mad* wasn't the right word. "I just feel down. It sucks," he said wearily.

"Do you and Lily still want to do Christmas in Providence? Sean will be there, too."

He brightened. "We'll be there with bells on."

Will had it on good authority that Zara's boyfriend was going to propose at Christmas. He wouldn't miss it for the world, even if she had just spent the last twenty minutes reading him the riot act. "You know you're the best big sister a guy could have, right?"

Zara wrinkled her nose in a charming way, then checked the time on her phone and put on her coat. "I'd better get back to our rehearsal." They gathered their dishes and put them in the bus bin. "You got anything going this week?"

He wrapped his scarf around his neck and paused thoughtfully. "I'm meeting with Katerina, and then Lily and I have meetings with our accountants, and I'm getting lunch with my property manager, getting new tenants for my condo."

Will's maternal side of the family didn't believe in renting. If a Chiu went to New York for college, like his mom, or took a job in Melbourne, like his (also deceased) uncle, they received an apartment as a gift. They were then encouraged to get roommates and live off the rent. Through this practice and too many family deaths, Will and his sister owned a lot of property. He inherited the places in North America while Lily received the houses in the UK and Australia. They kept up the family tradition and rented out the property, though, because he was a little more conscious about the damages of gentrification than his predecessors. He charged about half as much as he could and asked his trust to give preference to artists and academics.

Zara tilted her head thoughtfully. "If you're really wanting work, hang out for the rest of today's rehearsal, and we'll see if we can get you into a sketch. Just make sure to avoid anyone with a nasty-sounding cough. The flu has been taking cast members out left and right."

"Are you serious?" Will asked hopefully.

Zara nodded. "I'll try and use whatever sway I have. I think they like me." She smiled at him.

He paused at the door to the street. "Let me sweeten the deal with a couple of boxes of pastries," he said, returning to the bakery's counter. "If I know comedians, this should make us friends for life."

On Christmas Day, Zara's family gathered in the living room in matching pajamas. They'd just finished unwrapping gifts when her boyfriend, Sean, asked everyone to help him find one last present. After some theatrical searching, he located the gift he was after. To Will's enormous satisfaction, Zara was genuinely surprised when it turned out to be a vintage engagement ring with a sapphire stone. Sean teared up as he took Zara's hand.

"It's hard to believe that four years ago we couldn't stand each other," he began.

"I thought you were a prick." Zara sniffed. There was a shared ripple of laughter. Lily found Will in the small crowd and slid her arm through his. They smiled at each other. It was exciting to be here for this moment.

"You weren't wrong. Back then I'd never been challenged the way you challenged me. I also never had someone who believed in me the way you believe in me. You make me better: a better man, a better writer, a better son, and a better friend. And if you think it's a fair trade, in exchange, I'd like to spend the rest of my life making you happy."

He dropped to one knee, and Will surprised himself by cheering with everyone else.

"Zara Selena Hernandez Castillo, will you marry me?"

Will didn't hear her say yes, but that was because she seemed to be beyond words. Zara had started bawling about a third of the way through Sean's proposal. He'd barely gotten the ring on her finger before she was pulling him into a kiss. He looked at her family. Mom and stepdad, father and girlfriend, her elder sisters and their kids. Everyone who cared for her rooting for them at this moment. There was just so much love in the room.

As he discreetly wiped a tear from his eye, Will felt Lily give him a warm squeeze.

"Don't be ashamed of your tears, big brother," she said quietly. "This is a beautiful moment that they both fought for. It's okay to recognize that."

He swallowed hard and said something he'd never thought he would say out loud. "I want this so damn bad, Lily. I want to love someone wholly and for them to love me."

"I know you'll find her, Will. The same way I know I'm going to have my version of a normal life again."

It was the most hopeful Lily had sounded since their gran died. She'd been living with their gran since returning from two successive stints of rehab, running errands and eventually managing the household. Lily thrived.

They had just celebrated Lily's graduation from high school when the older lady suffered a massive stroke. Three days later she died. For months, Will had watched his sister carefully, worrying about her sobriety, until she told him that caring for Gran made her the strongest she'd ever been. Soon after, she got back into the world, slowly. First with a job at a bookstore near Gran's place in the Hudson Valley. Then moving back to New York. Gran had left Lily her house in the will, but their dad contested it and was happy to fight his daughter in court until the end of time.

Tonight, all these years later, Lily had settled with their father and started fashion school. She'd reentered the world. Will looked at his sister with admiration. *When did she become the strong one?*

She kept going in a firm voice. "We're going to be honest, we're going to put the work in, and we're going to make it happen." It was a mantra she picked up during recovery. Usually, it didn't have an effect on Will, but today he felt a tiny prick of his conscience. If he was going to be honest, then he should probably tell his sister about how things had gone down with EJ, and why. He sighed at the thought. *But not today. No need to ruin Christmas.*

Instead, as Sean and Zara took pictures and called their publicists, Will and Lily went back to the guest bedroom to read. "Hey, big bro, you got a couple of think pieces," Lily reported, glancing up from her phone. "It's about your *SNL* cameo."

Will raised his eyebrows in disbelief. "I was in a sketch and a half."

"It was enough to remind this lady that you're funny and that the show only just got an East Asian male cast member. Also, you're a GIF." She scrolled down that article and handed her brother the phone. Will looked at himself. He would be ripping open his shirt on the internet forever.

"At least I spent last semester getting abs," he commented.

"The second article is an open letter to *SNL*, thanking them for acknowledging your hotness." Lily made a face. "The one thing I really dislike about you being famous is having to hear people talk about how sexy you are—it's uncomfortable."

Will socked her with a pillow. She found one and socked him back. By the time Zara came upstairs to get them, the siblings were lodged in a full-on pillow battle.

"As much as it touches me to see you two engaged in some old-fashioned nonsense, knock it off! You almost took out my Girl Scout troop picture from sixth grade."

Lily and Will dropped their pillows remorsefully. "Sorry, Zara," they said in unison.

She rolled her eyes. "Anyway, I came up to ask if you wanted to watch our *SNL* episode again. Sean hasn't seen it yet."

"Sounds good," Will replied. "Though I don't know if Lily can take my sexy abs on your stepdad's shiny new TV." He dodged the pillow Lily launched at his head and ran down the stairs laughing. *This is a merry Christmas,* he thought. *How about that?*

EJ

By the time EJ parked in her parents' driveway, she'd put the whole thing with Will/Jordan out of her mind. Frankly, she had bigger problems. The awkwardness from Thanksgiving still lingered. Though she was still happy to be home, everything had a sort of heaviness. EJ wondered when she'd have the courage to talk with her mom. It had to be her mom; her dad would find a way to turn it into an argument. She just needed to say her piece.

A few days later, on Christmas Eve-Eve, EJ woke to find herself alone in the house. She had no dogs to walk, no people to visit or children to babysit, so she did an unhurried stretch and resolved to remain in her pajamas all day. "This is a Lord of the Rings trilogy kind of day," she said before heading to the kitchen to make popcorn.

Many hours later EJ was cheering as the warning beacons of Gondor were lit, when the front door opened with a creak.

"Hello," her mom called into the house. "Is anyone home?"

"I'm in the basement, Momma," EJ called up.

Ordinarily, EJ would have rushed up the stairs to hear about her mother's day, but after her sister's recent revelations, she quelled that urge mutinously.

"Ella? Would you come upstairs, darlin'?"

As she climbed, EJ acknowledged she was no good at rebellion. It was uncomfortable—as was sustained anger at her parents. "I'm definitely going to have to have a difficult conversation before I head back to Longbourn," she mumbled to herself.

When she reached the foyer, EJ saw that her mother was still wearing her winter coat and pulling her boots on.

"Still in your pj's, baby girl? Come on, get dressed and take a walk with me up the trail."

The trail was one of the main reasons EJ's parents had settled on this house. It started a couple of blocks down from where their street stopped in a dead end. When you started walking, it didn't take more than ten minutes to be completely surrounded by trees. Though it was owned by the parks and planning department, the trail was wilder than most, either through neglect or design. That suited her mom fine. She was a nature lover and former Girl Scout. EJ and her mom both loved the trail and had several important life conversations on these walks through the woods. It looked like they were about to have another one.

"Where is Daddy?"

"Out last-minute shopping," she responded too casually.

"Okay, I'm gonna go get changed."

EJ got dressed, and before long, they'd passed the neighbors' houses, with their Christmas wreaths on the doors and deflated Santa Clauses on the front yards. It was late afternoon, but not yet dark, so none of the electronic displays were active.

On the trail, they made their way to the woods in pregnant silence. She knew Maya had called home and told them about everything on the train. She knew that she'd been more distant in her calls home since then, when she remembered to call. She knew that her mom had noticed. But as much as she wanted to find out the real reason her parents had taken her out of dance school, she didn't know where to begin.

Thankfully, her mother had no problem starting the conversation. "Maya told me that we need to talk—your father said the same thing. Where should we begin, Ella?"

EJ thought before speaking.

"Okay, on the train ride up to Boston, Maya presented an interesting theory on why I had to leave the Capitol Ballet School." It was the only opening she could think of that wasn't an accusation, which she wasn't ready for.

Her mother hummed thoughtfully. "Parents don't like to acknowledge this, but often when families are equally matched two-to-two like we are, I think each parent tends to get their stamp on one child. Maya and your daddy are the exact opposite in interests, but they both see the world the same way: in black and white. You and I see the gray, the nuances. I know you understand how . . . multifaceted something can be. You, better than your sister, will understand when I say that there wasn't *a* reason we had to stop; there were reasons." She let that lie between them and turned her eyes back to the path. EJ wondered if that was all her mother had to say on the matter.

"Reasons?" she dared, hoping for more of an answer.

"Our priorities were out of whack, baby girl. We righted them. Money was tight, our lovely old house needed several repairs we'd been putting off—that was the summer of buckets, remember? The school's fees were rising, and we didn't trust the staff as much as we used to. We had to be responsible parents. The money we saved on dance went right into your college fund. We didn't need to take out a loan for your tuition until this year."

"I didn't realize you needed to," she said softly. "I thought my college fund was covering your contribution."

Her mom gave a dry laugh. "I wish. The tuition goes up every year. Cost of living goes up every year. Grants stay the same—or shrink. So we pay a little more."

"Oh." EJ felt foolish. She'd quietly prided herself on not taking her parents for granted, and yet she hadn't even noticed everything they were doing for her, without complaint. She was the only one of her smart/nerdy circle of friends who went away to school. It wasn't because her friends were any less intelligent—Kayla was more talented with computers—it was because her parents were both willing and able to let her go.

"That is the whole truth. Do with it as you will." They walked for a bit longer. EJ gazed at the bare-limbed trees. They were passing a smaller copse of ghostly birches when her mother spoke again, softly but firmly.

"But know this, Ella Bella: I am your mother first, last, and always. That means I want you healthy *and* happy. I will not compromise one for the other. You're grown now, so you get to decide how you feel about our methods, but it changes not a thing for me. When I saw how you wouldn't go near ballet again, I knew we had gotten you out just in time. Remember how we offered to pay for a smaller studio a year later? You said no. I guess you didn't want anything but the best pro-track studio."

Her mother sighed. "That was what really made me sad. I didn't realize your ambition had overwhelmed your love of ballet itself. But once you were out of training mode, you didn't even want to see *The Nutcracker* anymore."

EJ felt like she'd just been slapped. Her face flushed with astonished heat. "That wasn't it! That wasn't why, at all. It just hurt too much; it still hurts."

She stopped their progress on the path. "Putting ballet to the side meant imagining a whole new future for myself. Since I chose engineering, it meant changing gears entirely. I needed a plan to get into a good college. That meant switching to all AP classes and the right extracurriculars. It meant strong SAT scores and a whole lot of work. And since money was an issue, I didn't feel comfortable going for anything that wasn't free." She sniffed. "I don't know, maybe I *could* have gone back to dance, changed styles—tried out for poms. I don't know! The point is that I'll never know!"

Suddenly she realized she'd been shouting. EJ stopped short and wrapped her arms around herself. "I just wish you'd trusted me enough to tell me everything," she finished softly. "I wanted to be the one you could talk to."

Her mother looked at her sadly. After a moment, she closed the space between them and held her close. EJ could just hear the sound of her own noisy breathing. When Momma went to speak, again, her voice was raspy and low.

"I'm sorry, baby girl, that was our mistake. We should have been paying more attention. I honestly thought you'd moved on, fed your competitive side with the robotics and your creative side with the school musicals and practicing your piano. They were things you loved—"

"But they weren't ballet!" EJ softly interjected.

"No," her mom conceded. "They weren't." Her sigh was a small cloud just beyond her lips. "Losing a dream that young must have felt like losing the love of your life."

EJ nodded and sniffled. She could feel her eyes sting with unshed tears. Her mother drew her close again, and she let her head fall on her mother's shoulder.

"Go on, my sweet baby Ella. You've got to mourn it to let it go. That's where we went wrong the first time. We didn't notice you keeping it all inside."

EJ hated this. She didn't want to cry, but after the first sob escaped, she couldn't keep them back. She stood among the trees and cried while her mother held her.

On the walk back to the house, EJ turned over her mother's words and tried to smooth them like a salve over the lingering feeling of betrayal. *Is this,* she wondered, *one of those quiet moments where you can choose the way your life will go?* Maybe because it was senior year, and everything felt so important and so final, EJ saw two choices before her, like alternate paths through a wood: she could forgive but draw away from her parents, or work on understanding and accepting the steps that led to her life now, including the decisions her parents made back then.

Momma stopped their progress again. "Would you look at that sky," she said in wonder.

EJ looked through a break in the trees. The clouds were tinted with pink and purple as a blood-orange sun sank toward the horizon. EJ thought of the first time she and her mother watched the sunset from that very spot. How her mother gave her a love of the outdoors and made her unafraid of dirt or bees. She thought of her father's gifts: his gentleness and wanderlust. She thought of the many ways her parents supported her. Memory after memory bubbled up, making EJ consider all that her parents meant, beyond this single incident. She knew she wouldn't trade the dance career that might have been for everything her parents were to her.

At the end of the trail, EJ stood with her mother and watched the sunset. Then, arm in arm, they walked back to the house. When they got inside, Daddy was putting away groceries. As her father stretched to reach a high shelf, EJ sidled up to him and wrapped him in a hug. The tension from his back released, and he kissed her on the forehead.

After the reconciliation in the woods, EJ wasted no time reconnecting with her parents. Over the break, she brought her mom and dad up to speed on the Fields Fellowship and the meeting she'd had with her advisor. Her dad was extremely pleased that she was going for the prestigious prize. Her mom, on the other hand, seemed prouder that EJ figured out what she wanted from the fellowship first.

"The difference between finishing a postgraduate program and dropping out is often knowing what you want to do afterward," she said. Her mom was a guidance counselor and kept in touch with many of her former students. Several of them still asked her for advice.

EJ spent the rest of her break doing the things she loved: she got together with her friends from grade school and, for the first time in years, reached out to some of her old friends from ballet. Emotionally, she still wasn't up for seeing *The Nutcracker*; instead her mom took her to *A Midsummer Night's Dream* at the Shakespeare Theatre.

Sitting in the familiar space, EJ thought back to Maya's words: "The world is not as altered as you think." Then the house lights dimmed, and a hush fell over the audience. EJ felt that wonderful shiver of anticipation that she felt before every show. She squeezed her mom's hand and smiled; she couldn't wait to see what happened next.

SPRING SEMESTER

Jamie

As much as college was supposed to be about sharpening intellect and the like, what most people remembered were the rituals. Sure, they were often lumped in with the more rational term of *tradition*, but sophomores painting the statue of Wally for good luck before exams or seniors standing on the quad with candles were all tapping into something primal. Something humans had done for centuries, without a degree. These small but meaningful actions that somehow helped ground you and get you through to the next thing. Two of Jamie's favorite rituals were happening today: waffles at the dining hall in the morning, and in the evening, there was Hearth Night, her favorite Bennet House tradition. She found them both very cleansing.

At the first weekly waffles of the new semester, Jamie, EJ, and Tessa grabbed a table by the window. EJ was telling them about the trouble getting vegan marshmallows in town when Tessa's phone began to ring. T glared at the screen and angrily declined the call.

"What was that about, hon?" EJ asked with concern.

"Colin's been texting me all morning, like it's going to make a difference. We are so very done."

They were sitting around a hexagonal table on the second floor of the dining hall. A light snow was falling outside. Tessa pushed her tray away and slumped forward on the table. "I haven't been in a relationship for the past few months—I've been on a roller coaster." She sat up with a groan.

"First we had that fight at the Fall Formal. Then we made up. Then we had another fight, and it was radio silence since Halloween. Then he wrote that very sweet Christmas card over Winter Break. I let him call me, and he says things will be different this semester: that he'll listen more, be more considerate. And today he FaceChats me and tells me he's in Sydney."

"He's in Australia?" EJ exclaimed. Tessa nodded miserably, tracing patterns in the remaining syrup on her plate.

She went on. "Apparently, he found a study-abroad program there, applied in November, and got in over Winter Break. He said nothing of this to me until this morning but seemed surprised when I told him this meant that we're definitely over."

"Asshole!" Jamie spat. "How was he surprised that this wouldn't go over well?" she asked incredulously.

"That's what kills me." Tessa sniffed. "This is just more proof that he doesn't listen to me. If there's one thing I've been crystal clear about, it's that I am not interested in doing a long-distance relationship."

EJ patted her shoulder. "I'm so sorry, honey bear. I know how much you wanted things to work out with him."

Jamie snorted. She couldn't help it.

Tessa smiled a little. "I thought you didn't like Colin."

"Oh I couldn't stand him, no way," EJ responded. "But you saw something in him, so I was willing to keep my mouth shut."

Jamie expanded on this theme. "Aside from not liking Colin as a person—I never knew anyone so boring, yet so self-absorbed—I didn't think he was good for you. He wasn't supportive of your goals and treated you like his accessory. You can do so much better. You *deserve* so much better."

EJ nodded in agreement.

"In a way, I think this is for the best." Tessa gave a half-hearted shrug. "But it'll be hard for me to find someone as compatible as Colin."

Jamie shot EJ a confused look. Then she frowned and put down her fork. "Tessa, please. Explain."

She sighed and obliged. "Well, for one, I'm a plus-size person and not proportioned like Ashley Graham." She gestured to her round figure. "Colin was the first guy to like me because of my body, not despite it. Also, we're both actively Christian and liberal, which can be a hard combo to find. We both love to sing. I'm really gonna miss singing with him . . . We met on the worship team." Tessa sighed and tried to think of something else. "We're both birders," she added sheepishly.

"And he's waiting for marriage, which is big. I'm still waiting until I fall in love. Very few guys, even good Christian boys, are willing to stick around if sex is not on the table immediately. It meant a lot to have a boyfriend who wasn't constantly pressuring me." She dragged a bit of waffle across her plate sadly.

This drove Jamie nuts. Tessa always forgot Colin's faults when they spent enough time apart.

"That all sounds good for a dating profile, but what about the reality?" Jamie blurted out. "Colin was only a good boyfriend like fifty percent of the time. The rest of the time he was being condescending or ignoring your needs, then trying to make up for it with a big stupid gesture. You were on your third 'break' for a reason." Tessa's face crumpled, and Jamie was instantly remorseful. "I'm sorry—that was too much, too soon."

Tessa sat up straight and shook her head. "No, I need the tough love. I need to let him go," she admitted. "I can't believe I was contemplating the prospect of marriage with someone who'd leave the country without telling me."

She released a long, low groan and dropped her head on the table, letting her arms go limp. "I'm sick of this subject. Let's talk about happy things, happy people. Jamie, you and Lee seem to be doing well."

Is there such a thing as too well? "Things are good—I think," Jamie said. "Possibly weird?" She shifted uncomfortably. "It's so . . . he met my mom!"

"Whoa," EJ responded. Both she and Tessa leaned back as if blown by a strong wind.

"How did that happen?" Tessa asked.

"Okay, so when Lee was set to fly back to LA for Winter Break, there was a huge dump of snow that shut down the airport. Lee's stranded, and he hates hotels, so he turns up on my doorstep."

"Couldn't he have stayed with Will?" EJ asked.

"Will had already left for New York. I was the best option."

"How'd it go?" asked Tessa.

"Great! He's such a sweetie—any mother is going to love him. The strange thing is how *not* weird he found any of it. Like, the next morning, I wake up and find him and Ma doing the crossword together. He was all, 'NBD, your mom is awesome.' But it *is* a big deal, right?" EJ and Tessa nodded.

Jamie relaxed in her seat. "Good. I was starting to feel a little nuts." She sighed. "It feels wrong to complain when he's so great and things are going so well, and it was all so unexpected . . . but things are starting to feel like they're happening too fast."

"Have you told him that?" EJ asked. "He probably thinks he's giving you what you want."

"No. I guess I've been okay to float along and see how this goes."

Tessa lifted her head and sat up slowly. "That's how Colin and I started," she said absently. "Easy and fun. We never had any serious conversations, never really asked any questions . . ." She turned to Jamie and put an urgent hand on her arm. "Talk to him, Jamie. Or else you might wake up one day and find him in Australia."

∽

Jamie thought about Tessa's words for most of the day. Then it was time for her second-favorite ritual: Hearth Night. On the first Sunday evening of the spring term, the Bennet Women lit a roaring fire in the house fireplace, and after a round of cocoa or tea, they had the Burning of Sorrows. Everyone wrote down a regret or disappointment from the last term on a slip of paper. At an appointed time, they threw their sorrows into the fire. This helped even the most skeptical of them start the semester with a touch of optimism.

Next came a round of cookies and the Consumption of Hopes, which Jamie knew was a knockoff of a Russian New Year's tradition. It was still nice, though. For this rite, they wrote a desire for the next semester on a marshmallow with a food marker, put the marshmallow in their cocoa, and toasted the new term. This took a bit longer because many people would make their toast out loud. Like declaring your New Year's resolution.

The best part was after you got up and said, "I will [blah, blah important thing]," everyone else raised a mug to you and shouted, "And so you will!" in response. Jamie had never missed a ceremony. She'd even made a point to visit before she flew out for her semester abroad in Paris. (She was Jewish—God knew she loved a ritual.)

Tonight, Jamie pledged that she would stop avoiding difficult conversations with her boyfriend.

"And so you will!" her housemates chorused back.

God, I love being a Bennet Woman, Jamie thought. She was arm in arm with EJ, leaning against the wall closest to the fireplace. Jamie tried to ignore any creeping sense of finality.

"Nothing will ever be like this again," she murmured, with the smallest touch of alarm.

EJ wasn't quite listening, though. Jamie knew she was looking for people who seemed particularly upset. Hearth Night brought a lot of suppressed emotions to the surface. She watched her friend frown slightly and followed her gaze to a very verklempt Tinkerbelle. She had kicked off the declarations by saying, "I will pursue acting no matter who supports me because I have the talent, and it is my dream."

When her fellow Bennet Women replied, "And so you will!" Dia burst into tears. Now she clung to her roommate, who bore the attachment with unexpected tenderness.

"Graciela is not a hugger," EJ murmured. "Dia must be going through it. I'll have to check on her later."

Jamie looked on sympathetically. Dia was wacky, but she was sweet; Jamie hoped she was okay.

Dia

"Why are you here at this ungodly hour?" Sir Titus asked the bleary-eyed undergraduates as they tried to hide their yawns. Everything about the seminar seemed designed to challenge the students' commitment, especially the 8:00 a.m. start time on Monday mornings. Yet, despite seeing an hour that Dia had forgotten since praying at the flagpole in high school, everyone was captivated as Sir Titus addressed them from the stage in a gravelly English accent.

"You are here because you want to be artists in the acting profession. You are here at this ungodly hour because this is when we could secure the auditorium for a solid four-hour block all semester. Why must we be in the auditorium? Because, as actors, the stage is our home. You'll note that I said that you *are* actors. You're not 'studying to be' or 'becoming.' You are actors from the day you start to dedicate yourself to the perfection of your craft. There are actors who wait tables between auditions that are on no one's stage but remain artists. Conversely there are people who have fallen into TV or film roles whom one could only call 'film professionals.'" He chuckled sardonically and turned slightly left, treating the undergrads to his still impressive profile.

"The core of acting is showing up, doing the work, and being fully invested in that work. In this class you are professionals. The eight o'clock start time is your call time. We have a fifteen-minute break at ten, and we will never finish early.

"You have three unexcused absences. Any more than that will require a conversation between me, you, and your academic advisor." Sir Titus placed both hands on his cane and leaned forward, fixing his students with the same steely look that may have once made Meryl Streep burst into tears.

"If you need this class to graduate this year, we will find a way for you to walk, but you will not remain with us. If there are extenuating circumstances, please talk to me. I'm a teacher, not a monster, so I won't punish you for an unavoidable crisis. However, if you are not prepared to deal with the petty tyrannies of creative types, this would be the time to consider a different vocation." Another dry laugh, then Sir Titus tossed his mane of white hair and switched from stern headmaster back to charming grandfather.

"You will be on the stage every week in monologues, scenes, or for exercises. Everything you need to know is in that magazine-size document I call a syllabus. As you know, at the end of this seminar, we'll have a showcase of dramatic scenes. This is to incentivize collaboration; actors need each other. I encourage you to get acquainted quickly, as I'll want to know your scene partners by mid-February.

"The showcase will be in April. Thereafter, this course will focus on the business of show: reading contracts, finding agents, how to audition, and understanding rejection. I hope that what you learn here will prepare you for the acting world." He breathed a deep sigh. "But enough preliminaries, everyone onstage. Come up! Come home."

The students quickly joined the venerable man onstage and arranged themselves into a circle.

"Introductions!" he commanded from its center. "I want to hear your name, where you're from, and when you knew, to your core, that you wanted to be an actor—oh, and please, I want this to be an honest answer. Don't try to impress me with your cleverness. These things become so exhausting when everyone is trying to be Oscar Wilde." He pounded his cane on the stage. "This is a sacred space—a safe space.

And the best work happens when we can be a little vulnerable. Let's start with our youngest." He turned to Dia. "Please."

She was caught off guard. Her patented introduction was precisely the opposite of what Sir Titus wanted, and she didn't have time to think of something new. She decided to start talking and hope for the best.

"Hi. I'm Dia Shumway. I'm from Spring Valley, Utah, and I knew I was serious about becoming an actor when . . ." Her eyes filled, but the tears did not fall. "I learned that my parents were pretending to support me while expecting me to fail." Collecting herself, she gave a small but defiant toss of her curls. "When they told me, I think they wanted to crush me, but instead it made me more determined. I plan to succeed despite them." This was met with sympathetic applause; someone in the circle gave her an encouraging squeeze of the arm. She smiled ruefully.

"I take it this all transpired recently?" Sir Titus asked.

"A couple of days before Christmas."

He nodded sagely. "I'm sorry, Dia. But this sort of thing is fairly common." He addressed the circle. "At some point in your career, whether it's a parent, a partner, or a very close friend, there'll be someone whose dreams for you are quite different from the ones you have for yourself. Like Dia, you'll have to learn to move despite them or without them." He turned back to the freshman. "It's quite painful, but the earlier you learn this kind of lesson, the better you are for it. Let us carry on . . . going left."

Dia's introduction was like a dam breaking, and Sir Titus got all the honesty he could hope for. It was like *A Chorus Line* without the leotards or heavy brass instrumentation. The students talked of school plays, caring teachers, and moments of transcendent inspiration in dark theaters. By break time the group was emotionally exhausted, but by the end of the first class, the actors were already quite attached to each other. Afterward, as she was gathering her things, Dia noticed a shadow in her peripheral vision.

"Hey, Dia?"

She looked up. It was the ridiculously gorgeous guy she'd run into at callbacks.

"Hi. Jordan, right?"

"That's me." He gave a brief wave. "I wanted to thank you for your honesty. It was so brave. I think it really set a good tone for the class. Removed the cynicism, you know?"

"It definitely wasn't all me," Dia replied with uncharacteristic shyness. "Everyone else had to keep it going. Besides, I didn't even mean to be brave."

"I guess you have a brave heart, then. I should call you William Wallace—no, just Wallace. Can I?"

"Sure," she giggled. Then, living up to her new name, she said, "You mentioned you had a similar issue with your uncle. Would you mind talking more about how you push past it? Maybe over lunch? I'm buying—well, my meal plan is. My parents couldn't cut that off; they already paid for it."

"Yikes, sorry."

Dia shrugged ruefully. "It's only my spending money, for now. At least they're not pulling me out of school. I'm thinking of this as practice for living as an actor in New York. I—sorry. Way oversharing."

Jordan slung an arm around her. "Don't worry, Wallace. I can spot a survivor when I see one, and you're gonna be fine."

"Thanks, Jordan. Let's go. I could eat a horse. Four hours straight is a lot of class."

EJ

When EJ returned to campus, her mom seemed to be making up for their brief period of estrangement by emailing her something nearly every single day. First, there was an article about a woman in Baltimore who was helping sexual-assault survivors through ballet. While EJ was impressed by this woman's work, what piqued her interest in the story was the accompanying photo. "The Curvy Ballerina" had a body very much like hers—thickish thighs, substantial booty—but there she was, *en pointe*, in flowing white, looking beautiful. This got EJ wondering. She started following her on Instagram.

Then her mom sent her an old profile about astronaut Mae Jemison, who also planned to pursue a dance career as a teenager and took classes at Alvin Ailey while she was in med school.

She built a dance studio in the basement of her house, Ella! her mom wrote in the email.

This made EJ think, *Why not?* She checked the school calendar; they were still in the add/drop period. Then she went to the dance department's website. There were still open slots in Advanced Ballet, no pointe shoes required. Perhaps this was the time to go back? Avoiding it these past six years hadn't helped her get over things. Maybe she needed to find a new way to love ballet. EJ sent a quick email to her advisor. Stella responded with Go for it! You're only taking two other classes.

She took a breath and registered for her first ballet class in six years. "Let's just see what happens," she said to herself. Then she called her mom.

∽

EJ didn't tell her mother everything, though. Since she couldn't get into the whole Will/Jordan situation without talking with her mom about her sex life, she called Maya instead. Over FaceChat, she gave Maya the short version of all that happened: from the Fall Formal through her last conversation with Will. (She didn't share Jordan's whole story—but she included enough to preserve his privacy and inspire outrage.) After she finished, EJ watched her sister frown thoughtfully.

"I'm surprised that you forgave him the first time. But then you don't stay mad at people on your own behalf—even when you should. I still don't understand the whole Jordan thing, though."

"He asked me not to say anything."

Maya shot her a look of disbelief through the screen. "Can't help you if I don't know the whole story. BT dubs, that may be exactly what Jordan is counting on."

Okay, that rattled her. If Jordan was trying to play her, swearing her to secrecy was probably the smartest thing he could do. She took a breath and told her sister the whole of Jordan's story as she remembered it: Jordan's loneliness among the rich kids at his prep school, Lily's going from his only friend to girlfriend, how Will disapproved and tried to bribe Jordan to leave Lily alone. How Will got Jordan kicked out of school. As she talked, EJ watched her sister's expression. Maya's frown deepened with every sentence.

"That sounds like a soap opera," she said when EJ had finished.

EJ felt a breath of relief. Maya believed it, too. "I know! It's the craziest thing I ever heard!"

On the screen Maya was waving her hands wildly, signaling for EJ to stop.

"No, I mean this sounds like the plot of a literal soap opera. Hold on." Maya turned away from the screen; EJ was nervous as she heard her sister typing on her phone.

She turned back to the screen. "Yeah, this is the plot from the first season of *The Golden Ones*, a Korean soap opera. It was really popular with my kids at the Ohana Center. I thought it was a blatant rip-off of *Boys Over Flowers*, but that didn't bother anyone else."

A link popped up in her chat window. EJ clicked on it hesitantly. The show was on Netflix. As she scanned the episode summaries, her stomach dropped. Episode 1: "Dong Jo's family runs a Donut Man in a poor neighborhood of Seoul. After saving a businessman's life, he gets the chance to attend the prestigious Yong Academy."

Episode 3: "Dong feels out of place at the academy until he meets the beautiful Jin-Hyun. She becomes his first friend."

Oh dear. She felt her stomach drop but kept reading. Dong's only other friend was Avi from India, the school's cricket star.

Jordan told me his only other friend was the school's black lacrosse captain. He made the friend black for me! EJ quailed internally.

She turned back to face her sister. "I feel sick," she groaned. "But it still doesn't make any sense. Why blame Will? How did he even know I knew Will?"

"Maybe he just knew that Will was at Longbourn and took a wide swing. Or"—Maya paused thoughtfully—"maybe you should start locking your phone better."

"But he hasn't contacted me since. Why do this at all?"

Maya looked sympathetic. "I don't know, sweetie. But there is someone you can ask."

Please. No. She scrubbed her face with her hands. EJ shrugged sadly. "I think I'd rather never know why than admit any of this to him."

"I know how attached you can be to being right, but sometimes other things are bigger."

EJ then gave her sister some more specifics about the fight with Will, like how he'd accused her of believing Jordan because she'd been "fucked stupid."

Maya was *not* pleased, to say the least. After she expounded on where Will could go and how he could get there, she took a breath. "Ella, I need you to do me a favor: get your degree and leave that place before I have to come up there and start slapping people."

EJ laughed and nodded in response. "You see my problem: How do I talk to Will about Jordan again without looking like Boo Boo the Fool?"

On the screen, Maya worried her bottom lip thoughtfully. "Here's what you do: blame me," she began. "Tell him your big sister made you. Once you know what Jordan's motives may be, you can say a hearty 'fuck you' to both him and Will."

Even though she felt about as low as could be, EJ laughed. "I like your plan. It has a lot going for it."

And so EJ carried on. She counseled her residents. Dia came by pretty much every day for two weeks. She worked steadily on her Fields Fellowship application and practiced new ballroom routines with Franz. She fielded a surprising number of requests to rehearse in the "big common room" at Bennet House. She started ballet again, and it was wonderful.

She'd forgotten how much she liked the ritual of class. Stretching and chatting while rolling off her leg warmers, tendus and battements at the barre, the sound of eleven women jumping at once. She'd missed all this. Her fellow students were a delight as well. While there was one dance minor who was still pursuing a career, most of the other women had a story like EJ's: one was too short, another way too tall at five feet, eleven inches. One didn't have the turnout; another's family wasn't willing to support her through her apprentice years.

The person EJ felt the most for was the woman who'd realized that she just wasn't talented enough to go pro. She was a good technical dancer but didn't have the extra thing you needed to make a career. EJ was honest with her new friends in a way she couldn't be with anyone else. There was an instant level of understanding.

About three weeks into the semester, EJ and her new friend, Yuna, were waiting their turn to go across the floor. She was marking the combination when she noticed Yuna glaring out the window in the door.

"One of the tappers keeps looking in here," she explained. "It's so rude." They moved into parallel position, and for thirty seconds, EJ's focus was on her steps as she crossed the floor, dancing the combination.

And balancé, balancé, *prepare, then leap.*

Though she still watched her arms in the mirror and thought of ways to improve, dancing as an engineer with a hobby was much less stressful than as a sixteen-year-old trying to break into the ballet world. She felt so much freer—and there were no toe shoes! It was nice.

They finished with a double pirouette and got back in line to wait for their next turn. Yuna checked the door again. "He's still staring at us!" she growled. "Go!" she mouthed to the door, making a shooing motion.

EJ glanced over in time to see the peeping tapper look stricken and turn away. It was Will.

"Oh!" she cried out.

Yuna turned to her. "*Oh* indeed?" She looked from EJ to the door and then to EJ again. "Was he the guy who complicated your Winter Break?"

EJ was purposely silent. She'd accidentally let a small bit of her whole thing with Will slip, and Yuna was, well, nosy.

"I'm going to call him back, then." Yuna smiled wickedly. "I'm getting the whole thing out of one of you."

"You wouldn't dare!" she gasped.

"Oh, EJ, you should know by now that I dare, all the time."

She did not care for the gleam in Yuna's eye. Thankfully, they were called to center for the end of class.

Once they were done, EJ hastily threw on her winter coat, scarf, and boots. Yuna would take her time putting on her many layers; she was a sophomore from Lebanon and still not yet used to the cold. With a wave to their dance instructor, EJ rushed into the hall and ran straight into Will.

"Jesus Christ!" he exclaimed.

"That's my line," she replied.

Will gave an odd small smile. "Would you mind stepping in here with me? This will only take a second."

EJ followed him into the small, empty classroom without comment. This felt like destiny. She had seen neither hide nor hair of Will for a month—besides that *SNL* GIF. Then she talked about him to Maya and *voilà!* He appeared the next day. She decided to just go with whatever happened in this moment. It was probably going to be their last interaction.

"My sister said I should talk with you," she offered, shifting her dance duffel to the other shoulder.

He was unzipping his messenger bag. "Really?" he said, looking up. "My sister and one of my best friends said the same thing. Funny old world." He gave a short laugh.

You're telling me, thought EJ. She bit her lip and was trying to think of how to begin when Will produced a thick envelope with her name written on the front in neat handwriting.

"This is what I owe you." He hesitated before handing it over. "Okay, I've gotta go tap."

Will rushed out of the room. EJ looked after him, amazed.

"And we're back to weird Will," she said aloud. She looked at the letter in her hand, then shoved it into her dance duffel. She had a meeting with her advisor in an hour, class in the afternoon, and then ballroom practice tonight. She knew from Jamie that Will was going Cosmic Bowling with Lee and a few of his friends, so they weren't going to have the chance to talk things out tonight anyway.

He could wait until she was good and ready.

EJ stepped outside the classroom and took a breath. She felt like her duffel weighed an extra five pounds. Now to pretend like it was an ordinary day until at least nine tonight.

THE LETTER AND AFTER

Dear EJ,

You're probably surprised to be receiving this letter—or any letter since it's the twenty-first century, and I'm not a mortgage company. But after my first stalker, I learned that there are no secrets on the internet, so I couldn't risk emailing this or even saving it electronically since most of the secrets within aren't my own.

Let me start at last December. After our argument, I had every intention of ignoring you for the rest of the semester and then forgetting you after graduation. That was the case until I vented about you to Zara. (She says hi, BTW.) She reminded me of how appallingly I behaved to you, your friends, and the staff at Cousin Nicky's—who I now know are very dear to you. Then she asked what I had done to apologize, and like a cold slap, I realized that I had done nothing. Despite being, by all accounts, the entitled terror that made Jordan's story believable, the thought hadn't even occurred to me.

Although it's very, very late in the game, I'd like to do so, now. (With an additional apology for the one-night-stand comment. That was uncalled for.) For my behavior then and my subsequent arrogance, I can only say I'm sorry, EJ.

Now to answer why I cared so much about setting the record straight: Jordan is at the center of how I almost lost my sister and how I got her back again. She is the person I love most in the world and the reason I cannot let whatever he said stand. Please read patiently; this is a long story.

Jordan and I became friends at a crucial time in my life, during my parents' separation and divorce. His mother was my mother's best friend, and she rushed to my mother's side after my father moved out. Their family stayed with us, Jordan's mom supported mine, and he supported me. I'd become increasingly withdrawn as the reality of the divorce dawned on me, but he was one of the very few people who could get me to put down my books and play. Lily would have been jealous of anyone else hogging her big brother, but she loved Jordan, too. Everyone did. I even owe him my acting career. Before the final legal proceedings, my mom offered to send me anywhere I wanted to go. I chose drama camp because Jordan was going.

Sadly, we both lost our mothers in different ways. My mom was killed in a car accident and his died of an aneurysm. We tried to keep in touch for a while, brothers in grief, but I lost track of him after he went to live with his uncle. I didn't know what happened to him until Lily told me he was at her high school, Hanover. I've provided all this history to say that no one would have been happier than me for Jordan and Lily to get together if she were interested in men. This is the part of Jordan's lie that was most maddening. It was so blatantly false. If Lily had public socials, it could have been disproven in seconds. She's been out and proud since ninth grade—another source of tension with my father. Jordan was just her friend . . . and then her dealer. Lily's freshman year at Hanover was miserable. Before she died, Mom had sole custody of us, and my father hadn't exerted himself terrifically to be involved. After Mom's accident he packed Lily off to boarding school as soon as he could. Having his teenage daughter around made him look a little creaky to his new trophy fiancée. Making things worse, she struggled academically and was very frustrated. Lily had always been an effortlessly smart kid, so it shocked her to have to work so hard for just okay grades. She thrived on the tennis team (the sport was her true passion), but this didn't matter to our father. He was almost solely interested in her academic performance.

During this time, I was in LA. Dad and I had parted by mutual agreement. I'd landed my first TV show and was living with Lee and his family. I'm sorry to say I was not the best brother then: not very accessible and unconsciously selfish in a way teenage boys often are. My sister told me of her loneliness and her sadness, and I listened, but not enough. I was having too good a time in California. When I heard Jordan was at Hanover, I was relieved. By some miracle, here was a trusted family friend who could help Lily through things. My guilt for abandoning her in this hard time will stay with me for the rest of my life.

I thought Jordan was a friend to her, at first. Lily sounded happier, she said she was more focused in class, and she was making new friends. Later I found out the focus was from the Adderall he sold her, and the friends were . . . not good. I don't know what happened in the year in between, but when I got there for my senior year (part of the deal with my father was that I graduate from Hanover), she'd moved on from Adderall to coke, and had tried oxy. I could see something was up with her, but she chalked up her agitation to our dad's pending remarriage and missing Mom. I believed her. Hell, I was not looking forward to having a twenty-year-old stepmom, either.

All this time Lily was getting way into debt. Once Lily realized how much she owed, she came to me with the truth. She knew that our father would make her life miserable if he found out. She promised to go into drug counseling if I paid Jordan off. Of course I did—I would have done anything. That's where the money throwing / punching comes in. It was petty, but it felt good at the time. I hate that he was able to use that against me, too.

I graduated that year and hoped that would be the end of things. Jordan must have worked out how much this secret was worth to Lily, because he started blackmailing her that summer.

He'd kept some incriminating texts and photos and threatened to publicize them unless she gave him $10,000 by the first day of school. Lily knew that if word got out about her addiction, Father would at least disinherit her. At worst he'd kick her out and cut her off from our paternal grandmother, who was the only other family we had left. The worst thing Jordan did was take the locket my mother gave her as collateral. He knew exactly how much that locket meant to her. I would have paid again, but I was in Croatia for the *Wolf Pack* sequel and not really accessible. I think losing it, in that way, is what broke her.

When I got back from filming in August, Lily was in the hospital. She couldn't get the funds from her trust without going through our father and couldn't raise it on her own without arousing suspicion. It was a month before school started again, and she knew she couldn't pay. Overwhelmed with shame, she slit her wrists.

Once I'd gotten the story from her, I wanted to make Jordan pay, so I started asking around. I found out this was a pattern. He'd get a girl hooked on drugs, usually a freshman or sophomore. If she stopped using, he'd blackmail her: either for cash or into working for him. In one case he even tricked a shy freshman into being his drug mule. No one spoke up out of fear of expulsion or something even worse at home. The few girls with little to lose were too embarrassed about living some horrible after-school special to come forward.

Since I couldn't see a way to expose Jordan, I wanted to at least recover the necklace. I called the school, reported her necklace stolen, and offered a reward. Jordan wasn't particularly careful, so his roommate saw it and told the house proctor. They searched his room and not only found the locket but enough drugs to get him expelled. I wish I had done it sooner. Lily hasn't been the same since. She used to be this fun, outgoing girl. Always the first, always the bravest, daring. After everything with Jordan, she became really withdrawn, barely leaving the house. She's just started getting back into life again, though she says tennis hurts too much to play now, something about the damaged nerves in her arm.

Enclosed you'll find a list of contacts you may reach to verify my story as well as a photocopy from my sister's recovery journal in which she describes Jordan introducing her to drugs. I want you to know who I am, EJ. I fully trust in your discretion and await your reply.

Sincerely,

Will Pak

PS: If you believe me, please open your Christmas present, if you still have it. I hope my anger that night didn't cause you to throw it away. I can only assure you that the gift, itself, was created and offered in the purest spirit of my admiration.

EJ

She was sitting up in bed. She leaned back against the wall and squeezed her comforter with both hands before instinctively reaching for her phone to text Jamie. Then she remembered that it was 2:23 a.m. Instead she read the letter again, for, like, the twentieth time. Will's apology had truly touched her. And it had convinced her. Of one thing she was certain: he was telling the truth.

After the first reading, EJ had created a timeline of Will's story and Jordan's story. Now that she knew that Jordan's story was a rip-off of a Korean drama, she could clearly see how he spun his lies out of what had occurred in real life. He was distressingly cunning and seemed to know the very details to include to make her too angry to question him. Now everything she didn't ask came in a flood.

Why was I so trusting of a guy who tried to pressure me into having sex without a condom? Who divulges that much personal history to someone they just met? Over brunch? Why did he leave to take three calls during one meal?

She could see it all now: the shiftiness, the circles beneath his eyes, the morning-after Jordan who was a little seedier than her gallant rescuer from the night before.

Why did I let him drop me off? That's one thing I never do with hookups . . . but he was so insistent. Why was he so interested in Bennet House anyway?

Her breath caught in realization. Jordan must have been looking for a new market. After all, Jordan was especially interested in Bennet House after she'd mentioned it was a women's dorm. It made sense, since Will said he particularly targeted women to blackmail, trick, or use. She groaned. It pained EJ to think that she might bring danger to their doors. But since she had an idea of Jordan's modus operandi, she'd do what she could to prevent any damage.

The next morning, EJ awoke around ten and got the unpleasant business out of the way first. She made three increasingly awkward phone calls conveying the message that Jordan Walker should not be welcomed to Bennet House on her account and that she could not vouch for his character. Then she sent Will a text. EJ knew she needed to do some apologizing of her own. Whatever her reasons, she had harshly misjudged him. Even though she hadn't made her claims public, EJ knew the accusation had to hurt. She also knew any amends would have to wait, after the night out he'd likely had. Jamie had messaged her after midnight saying that Lee's cosmic bowling thing had turned into margaritas and karaoke. She knew Lee's a cappella friends didn't leave a karaoke bar until it closed. Will probably stayed up until three—and may have needed his own pitcher of drinks to get him through it.

Folding the letter up for a final time, she remembered the postscript.

"I should open his Christmas gift," she decided. Freeing herself from her cocoon of blankets, EJ put on her slipper-socks and padded across the room, removing the gift from her closet. Somehow, EJ had never had the heart to throw it away.

She set the gift on her bed and fished through the delicate paper until she felt the smooth wooden edge of a rectangle. It was a simple five-by-seven desk frame protecting a vibrantly rendered drawing of a young black woman. EJ looked it over appreciatively, then squinted. Something about the scene looked familiar.

"It's me," she gasped, recognizing herself in her favorite booth at Cousin Nicky's. She was studying, one hand supporting her chin while the other held a highlighter right above the page. A mug of coffee steamed near her stack of textbooks. Light from the window cast the whole scene in a warm glow. In the right corner, small but distinct, EJ spotted Will's signature. "I didn't know he could draw," she said, surprised. "I didn't know he—" She stopped herself, not able to accept the most logical implications of being drawn with such care. "I didn't know he was looking."

EJ sent Will a follow-up email, to ask if they could meet, then sent a text to Jamie. It was a little on the early side for Saturday, but she thought she'd take a chance.

> Hey, gingerbread, can you come over when you get this?

> I need to talk.

Almost immediately, EJ heard the following sounds: a door closing, hurried footsteps, and a knock on her door.

"Come in!"

"Hey, Eej! What's up?"

"Wow, you are bright eyed and bushy tailed. Didn't expect that."

Jamie nodded a little manically. "I stopped drinking the very weak margaritas after Lee asked me to stay over and stay sober. He wanted to make sure no one drew a dick on his face." She paused. "I think there's a story there. Then this morning, I thought I was grabbing a can of sparkling water from his fridge and realized halfway through it was a Red Bull." She walk-hopped to EJ and joined her on the bed. "Anyway, what's going on?"

EJ smiled at her friend and took a deep breath. "So basically . . ."

She brought Jamie up to speed: what Jordan said about Will, what happened with Will before Winter Break, the letter (in broad strokes to protect Lily's privacy), and finally the present.

After she'd heard all, Jamie had one question: "Why are you sitting here talking to me and not smooching the face off Will?"

"What?"

"Go kiss Will's face off," Jamie repeated emphatically, waving away EJ's shocked expression. "Let me give you my perspective. First, on Halloween Lee gives me the whole of Will's tragic backstory with Carrie, so I actually understand why he's being such an asshole."

"*That's* why you stopped hating him!" EJ interjected. It usually took Jamie a good three months to stop holding a grudge.

"Exactly, now we're all pals. Anyway, right after Thanksgiving, I run into Will at the campus center, and he asks me about some of your favorite things. He wants my opinion on what he's giving you for Christmas. I ask him why, and I can barely hear his response because I'm watching him light up while he talks about you. 'Finally!' I think. 'There's a guy on this campus smart enough to truly appreciate my Ella.'

"Once he's finished talking about how perceptive you are, and intelligent, et cetera, I tell him how *impossible* you are to shop for and about your preference for handmade things. He then digs out his sketchbook and shows me this." She taps the framed drawing.

"He's all, 'I was inspired by this show at the Met . . . I think this is my best one, the colors . . .' All I'm thinking is 'He loves my Ella!' I tell him it's perfect. From then, I've been waiting to hear about this super-romantic gift and how you guys are going to get married and have Blasian babies. The next thing I know, you aren't speaking to him, you're lying to me, and God knows why."

Jamie grabbed EJ's hands. "Do you understand how I have been dying for the last couple of months? I have to be honest, I'm not so interested in our journey to this moment right now. You know he's a good person now, who happens to be crazy about you. Go kiss him, *bubbeleh!*"

EJ looked at her friend skeptically. "I am sure of the former and know nothing of the latter," she corrected. "The only thing that's clear is that Will is talented. Artists don't need to be enamored of a person to draw them well." She dropped Jamie's hands. "Also, 'bubbeleh'? Really? Schnitzel, we're the same age!"

Jamie gave her friend a long look, then shifted her gaze to the drawing. "Ella, this was not done by a disinterested person. It's a declaration, and if it's too subtle for you, don't be surprised if you get something more direct soon."

EJ pursed her lips. "Well, first he'd have to text me back. I sent him two texts and an email, which I think is the absolute limit before—" Both women started as EJ's phone began vibrating aggressively and playing "9 to 5."

"Answer it already," Jamie said, smiling. "You know who it is."

EJ rolled her eyes but picked up the phone. "Hello? Oh, hi, Will." She shooed a smirking Jamie out of the room.

"Hey, yeah. I'm on Lee's phone, just got your email. We've been drying out mine all morning. I crashed at Lee's place after karaoke. Stu and his other aca-friends stayed up watching reruns of *The Office*, and they thought it would be a great prank to put his phone in Jell-O." There was a telling silence. "Our phones look a lot alike."

EJ shook her head. "That sucks. That show has a lot to answer for."

"It made things awkward over breakfast, but the phone turned on briefly about an hour ago, which means it's not completely dead. My people do good work."

"Which side: Korean or Chinese?" EJ asked.

"It's a Samsung, but most phones are made in China, so . . . both?" She giggled, then spoke. "I read your letter, several times."

"And?" he pressed.

"I believe you, Will. I do and I'm sorry." She breathed a sigh. "If you have time, I feel like we should talk in person."

There was a long pause. EJ hoped it wasn't too late to make things right.

"I'd like that. When are you free?"

"I don't have much going on today. Wanna come by Bennet House a little later, like three?"

"Would you mind coming over to my place? I know there's little chance anyone will make a fuss . . . but I could really use a quiet night at home after the last one."

"Can do—and Will, I loved my gift. Thank you." She disconnected the call and texted Jamie.

> J, I've got a couple of hours to prepare some sort of conciliatory gesture.

> Let's go shopping.

⁓

That afternoon EJ turned up at Will's place bearing her own gift, less elegantly wrapped in aluminum foil. Shifting her parcel to one arm, she pressed his buzzer. The lock released, and she hurried up the short set of stairs.

"Hey," Will said. He looked at her full arms and held the door wide. "Is this for me?"

"Yup," she said, following him into the apartment. "It's an apology pie. Apple seems like the sincerest fruit."

Will gave a light chuckle and walked the dessert over to his kitchen counter. "You baked me a pie?"

"It's more of a collaboration between me and frozen-food *pâtissière* Mrs. Smith. But I got the fanciest one. It came in a black box with a cursive font. All the hallmarks of quality," she added with bright strain.

Will gave a half smile that was neither reassuring nor dismissive. "Well, I'm a sucker for apple pie, especially with—"

"Whipped cream! I know! I've done a little research." She produced a canister from her duffel bag. Handing it over, EJ turned serious. "Will, I know I apologized in my email, and my texts, but I have to say it again: I have been a complete asshole. I'm so sorry for misjudging you and for being so cold. Hell, I should have at least listened to your side, but—"

EJ thought better of explaining further; there was a thin line between offering reasons and rationalizing her actions. "I was wrong, Will, and I'd like to start over."

The actor was silent, absently twisting a long corner of the foil as he considered his response. EJ took long, deep breaths, awaiting Will's verdict. She glanced around at the now-blank walls. *Where'd the masks go?*

"You any good at chess?" he asked, finally looking at her.

She tilted her head slightly. "I'm not terrible, but I'm not great."

"Good. I'll heat up this pie, and we can each have a slice while I kick your ass."

EJ struggled to maintain her solemnity but couldn't let this pass. "I'm apologizing, Will, but I'm not sorry enough to let you beat me."

"I would expect nothing but your best efforts. But we haven't played anything against each other since November. Since you're apologizing, I should get a decent shot at a win." He smiled, genuinely, and EJ had never been happier at the prospect of losing.

Will

It was Super Bowl Sunday, and Will was waiting for his friends to come over for his "What's a Super Bowl?" party. Johnny Storm's team had crashed out in the playoffs, but Carrie Dean had been asked to do the national anthem. Will thought this was the perfect time to pretend that football didn't exist. It wasn't hard at Longbourn since they seemed to have champions in only women's soccer and Quidditch, but even the most football-averse people seemed to feel obligated to watch the broadcast so they could talk about the commercials. Will was glad to have some people over to eat junk food and watch movies. He was really happy that he could now include EJ on that short list of friends.

It had started with the day she brought over the pie and he demolished her at chess. They'd hung out in his living room and gone through his traveling record collection.

∾

"Some classical and a whole lot of jazz with an emphasis on Thelonious Monk," EJ observed. "In fact, the only popular music you have is from Stevie Wonder, Billy Joel, and Ben Folds. Where's your practice keyboard?"

"Well deduced, Holmes," Will replied. "It's in my room. I practice every morning after working out but before my vocal exercises. You play, too, right? I noticed your keyboard . . . the last time I was in your single," he trailed off awkwardly, trying not to resurrect the recently buried past.

EJ responded cheerfully. "You're right. My keyboard is the main reason I brought my car to campus. Had to make sure she traveled comfortably." They traded stories about the tribulations of travel with a keyboard until Will suggested playing duets.

Since then, EJ rejoined their regular game nights and met Will for coffee in the campus center after their dance classes. She got him into her movie / TV adaptation book club; he took her on a day trip to the Peabody Museum. They were very different but liked many of the same things—or they liked different things for the same reasons. And she was so kind. She asked him about Lily in the gentlest way possible and listened patiently when he revealed his fears for his sister.

"Life is long," she said. "You're supporting her now, just keep it up." In the back of his mind (heart?), Will could feel his crush starting to bubble up again.

The door buzzed. EJ arrived about an hour before game time with a small pan of seven-layer dip and a bag of tortilla chips. "I think this is the best part of a Super Bowl Sunday," she said, proffering the dish.

"Thanks, Sara Lee," Will said, bringing the dip into the small kitchen. "You know, since you seem to have a habit of bringing food every time you come over, you've got an open invitation."

She laughed and hung her coat on the back of a chair near the breakfast bar. "When are Jamie and Lee getting here?" she asked.

"I'm surprised they're not here already," Will said as he poured tortilla chips into a bowl. Just then both their phones chirped, as if in response. There was a text from Lee.

> Disaster! Major roof leaks. Calling maintenance.

"Jesus Christ!" EJ exclaimed. She must have been reading the same text.

Need help? Will wrote back.

> Jamie's here with all the towels.

> Watch the movie

> We'll come after maintenance man gets here

Will read the messages aloud. "Well, that'll be half past never," he commented. "Lee's super is useless."

"Is anyone else coming over?" she asked hesitantly.

"Unfortunately, I didn't invite anyone else. I was keeping this pity party pretty small, a pity gathering, really."

He scrubbed his face with his hands in a slightly helpless gesture. Will didn't know if he could keep a lid on his feelings if they were alone: the good ones or the sad ones. He didn't know if their new friendship could survive if he kissed her tonight. "You don't have to stay, Eej. I'll be okay on my own."

EJ ran a hand over her braided extensions, tucked up in their usual bun. She always played with her hair when she was nervous. Then she crossed the room and wrapped him in a hug.

"I hope this is okay. I'm a hugger, and you just looked so blue." She released him and gave a sympathetic smile. "You shouldn't have to avoid your ex alone," she said. "Even if she's just on television. I never thought about how much that must suck."

She grabbed the dip and chips from the counter and brought them over to the coffee table.

"At least at Longbourn, if your romantic past walks into the library, you can pretend to drop a pencil and crawl under a table until they go away," she said with curious specificity. "You don't have to see their stupid faces on television."

"Or on magazines, or on pop-up ads on my phone," Will added. "It's pretty unpleasant, but that's all part of the business. But we should be able to avoid the whole thing with this," he said, holding up a DVD. "Please don't laugh at my choice."

"Of course not," EJ replied brightly.

Will inserted the DVD and returned to the couch. "I borrowed it from the school's video library. It was the only way not to get one of those digitally remastered versions that makes everyone look like puppets."

He heard EJ audibly breathe a sigh of relief as a panoramic view of Austrian mountains appeared on the screen.

"*The Sound of Music?*" she cried. "Thank God. I thought you were going to make me watch a stupid boy movie like *The Boondock Saints* or *The Hangover*." She settled back on the couch. "Are you okay if I sing along?"

"I'm pretty sure it's required," Will said, smiling.

Later, as the off-screen chorus vocally climbed into the stratosphere for "Climb Ev'ry Mountain," Will discreetly dabbed at his right eye. EJ noticed, of course, but she just squeezed his arm and gave him a small smile.

"A lot of people think this movie is a cheese sandwich, but the ending gets me every time." Will turned to her. "I mean, they've just escaped from the Nazis, they have nothing but the coats on their backs, and they're literally climbing this mountain to safety, all so that Hitler doesn't make them his poster family."

"I've never thought of it that way," she said, shifting toward him.

Will shrugged. "To be honest, I had help. My mom loved this movie. She said the ending reminded her of my Lao Lao—my grandmother. She got to Hong Kong right before the border closed during the Chinese Civil War. She and my great-grandmother had traveled to visit a cousin. Lao Lao was just a little girl. When they arrived, my great-grandmother received a telegram. It began 'Don't try to come home.'"

Her eyes widened. "Oh my God!"

Will continued. "The family's factory was seized, and so was their beautiful house in Shenzhen. Mom said Great-Grandmother fainted in the station. In that moment all they had in the world was in their suitcases. We never learned exactly what happened to my great-grandfather, but he would have been considered a landlord and so probably executed."

"Holy shit!" EJ gasped. "I'm so sorry." She placed a hand on his shoulder.

"Thanks." Will turned to face her fully, and she shifted to do the same. He tried not to notice their knees touching. "There are lots of stories like ours from that time. Hardly any got officially recorded. The best we can hope for is that they get passed down."

"That's so true." EJ dropped her hand back onto her lap. He was sorry to lose its warmth. "On the flip side," she continued, "there are good stories that get forgotten entirely. Like my great-great-aunt Marjorie was a barnstorming pilot, did air shows like Bessie Coleman, but we only have one poster with her name at third billing as any proof. At least I hope Aunt Karen still has it."

They were interrupted by a loud pop as the TV switched over to the nightly news. Will winced as Carrie's face flashed across the screen and reached for the remote.

"Wait," EJ said. "Carrie's anthem wouldn't be a top news story if it had gone well. Turn it up."

As Will and EJ saw, hours after most of the US, Carrie Dean's Super Bowl performance had been a remarkable disaster. Not entirely sure of her singing, the star had recorded a lip-sync track. Unfortunately, an ill-timed sneezing fit put her out of sync with her own voice. The track was quickly cut, and she attempted to sing live but apparently forgot the words.

"Did she just sing *the dawn's gleaming twilight?*" EJ crowed at the screen. "There's a teleprompter! Find it, woman!"

Will gaped at the screen during the entirety of the brief performance, then howled with laughter. "That was terrible!" He grinned. "It was one of the worst performances of the national anthem I've ever seen—"

"I think that was grounds for treason," EJ added.

The landline rang, surprising them both.

"You have a landline, Gramps?" she asked laughingly.

"The lady I'm subletting from does," Will explained, looking for the phone. "But I've only given the number to my sister and my agent." He answered warily. "Hello?"

"Will! Finally! I need you in New York, yesterday." It was Katerina, and she was all business. "You're booked on *Kelly Ripa and Whoever* tomorrow, and *Wendy Williams* Thursday—she's not your favorite, but she hates Carrie. Also, Friday, I'm trying one of those midday shows on CNN to put your face in airports."

"What?"

"Your 'ex' angle is super juicy, perfect for the morning shows. They like the tabloidy stuff. Which reminds me: I can get you on *GMA* Tuesday with Michael Strahan and Sara. She *hates* Carrie, so she'll love you. You can promote the *GQ* thing."

After his minor success on *SNL*, Will had filmed a video on fashion for the everyday guy for the *GQ* Canada website / YouTube channel. He was a slightly bigger star there.

"We've only filmed the one."

"And it's going live tomorrow—not just in Canada anymore but on the US site, too. They want some more in the bank, by the way, so that's your Wednesday, okay, darling?"

He was still confused. "Because of Carrie? But—"

"Have you gotten any of my texts?" Katerina interrupted.

"No, sorry, my phone's been temperamental since—"

"Never mind. Just get down here. Don't even pack. I spoke with Lily, and she said she'd pick out some things from your closet at the Pemberley house. You're booked on a flight that leaves at midnight. Get yourself to Logan now and call me when you get to New York." She hung up.

Blinking, Will turned to EJ. "That was my agent. She's got some crazy stuff lined up for me in New York. I've got to go to the airport, like now."

"Wow, okay. Well, let me get out of your hair," EJ said, getting up quickly.

They cleared the food away and grabbed his coat. "I can at least drive you back to Bennet," he offered. "It's on the way out of town."

They rode in pleasant silence to EJ's dorm. Will's mind was churning. *Could this be the start of something big?* he wondered.

It would be some kind of karmic justice if Will rose from the ashes of Carrie's career. Now that he thought he could get his old life back, he wanted it. Will looked over at EJ, who found a way to look adorable even in a giant winter coat with that unwieldy scarf.

Well, I don't want everything back.

He didn't want Carrie anymore. EJ had cured him of that. But he did want to see how far he could take his screen career. Now that people were noticing him, he wanted to see exactly how talented he was. What he could really bring to the screen. He wanted to try.

At Bennet House, Will walked EJ to the door. They stood on the covered porch for a moment, looking at each other. Neither of them seemed to want to rush goodbye.

"Good luck with everything in New York," EJ offered a little awkwardly. "I hope you can make the most of things."

"Thanks," he said, running his hand over his hair. "I'm nervous, but kind of excited. I hope my interview skills aren't too rusty."

"Pssh, you're so telegenic, people will just be happy to look at you."

His responding grin had a hint of bashfulness.

"Don't give me that shy act," EJ continued. "The sky's blue, grass is green, you're hot, and you dress well. Those are just facts."

She thinks I'm hot. Will could have done cartwheels. "It's still nice to hear." He checked his phone for the time. And just like that he realized that he didn't know when he'd see EJ again.

What the hell, he thought. *This could be my lucky night.*

"I should go, but let me put this out there: if it wasn't clear from the drawing, I like you, EJ Davis. You're smart, pretty, and interesting. Those are also just facts. I know this is all kind of weirdly fast since we're in this rebuilding phase, but when I get back, I would very much like to take you on a date."

Was she blushing? It was too dark to tell. She was smiling, though. "I would like that very much."

"Great!" He kissed her on the cheek. *She is definitely blushing.* "I'll see you soon, and we'll be in touch."

With great determination, Will walked calmly to the car and did not click his heels or punch the air. She waved as he drove away.

Jamie

Now that she didn't have to deal with EJ and Will's cold war, Jamie was finally able to focus on her own relationship. She and Lee had been getting closer now that they'd stopped being polite and started being real. They began small: she no longer feigned interest in soccer. "It's just complicated running," she complained. He stopped pretending to appreciate *Citizen Kane*.

"It's like, I get it, but I don't care," he grumbled as the credits rolled.

The honesty helped them find new common ground, like their shared love of foreign films and Indian food. It also made it easy to enjoy each other's company. Like now: they were studying together at Lee's off-campus apartment. They sat together with their backs pressed to the opposite ends of the couch so that their legs could tangle in the middle.

She was reading over her feminist critique of Godard's heroines on her laptop. It was in French, so Jamie was more worried about grammar than the strength of her arguments. Lee was booking flights for the Gordon Campbell Society's Spring Break service trip. With the extra funds, they'd planned four projects this year: one near campus, one in New Orleans, and two in Puerto Rico.

Between bookings, he stretched, then hummed thoughtfully. "What do you think of Brooklyn?"

"I think it was a perfectly fine place ruined by kids who think a neighborhood can give them a personality."

"Okay, so no Brooklyn."

"Not if I can help it. If I were to live in New York, I'd want to be in the Village, Harlem, or Washington Heights."

Lee stretched against his arm of the couch. "Here's the thing: Will has this killer condo in Prospect Park, and his tenants should be out by the summer. He likes to rent to artists, and he's not looking to make a mint on it. I'm sure we could get it for a song—not literally, but you know."

"Wait, what?" Jamie said. She looked up sharply from the screen. "Since when are we moving in together?"

He shrugged. "We both have New York as our top post-grad destination, and it's a very expensive city. I had *a* thought about how it could be less expensive. No big deal."

Jamie glared, then took a deep breath. "Lee," she began tersely, closing her laptop with a snap, "when you say *no big deal* while moving us breezily past a relationship milestone, I feel like you are pushing me—pushing us—too fast."

Both Jamie and Lee had been going to therapy before they started puberty. She noticed that they were shaped by all that time spent in offices discussing their feelings. She was conscientious about using "I" statements. He switched entirely into "therapy mode" and leaned hard into his empathetic listening.

There was a long silence as Lee moved his laptop to the coffee table and tented his hands under his chin. "What I hear you saying is that my approach to the big steps in our relationship has caused you to feel pressured," he restated. "Jamie, I would never intend to push you into anything you don't want, but I feel like I have to initiate all the movement in our relationship. I mean, I asked you out. *I* suggested becoming exclusive. Hell, it was me who started us discussing our plans after graduation."

Lee ran his hands through his unruly brown hair before finishing his thought. "I have to say, *I* feel blindsided when you say you're feeling pressured, because this has been the pattern of our relationship—and while we're on the subject, I'd like some help. I don't want to feel like I'm in charge here."

"You're the guy! I'm going at your pace," Jamie cried.

Lee raised an eyebrow. "That sounds both antifeminist and a little lazy."

"Antifeminist?" Jamie exclaimed.

"And lazy," Lee repeated, not backing down.

She huffed, untangled their legs, and stomped off to the kitchen. Suddenly she badly wanted a cup of tea. Setting down her mug with more force than strictly necessary, she turned on the electric kettle and began the hunt for something suitable. She was even willing to drink *Lipton*. After some fruitless searching, she opened Lee's coffee cupboard and immediately softened. The first shelf now contained not only her favorite teas (Earl Grey, chai, and rooibos) but also had cube sugar and cans of evaporated milk, which she preferred to cream. She remembered then that even when Lee was pedantic and slightly presumptuous, he was still a sweetheart.

Jamie prepared tea and returned to the couch, picking up where they left off.

"I don't think I am being old-fashioned," she said softly into the hostile silence. "I was just following the culture of dating at Longbourn. Gay or straight, I've seen guys drop really nice people at the slightest hint of feeling tied down. They don't like that kind of thing."

Lee groaned. "Okay, this—this is a thing you do that drives me nuts," he said with audible frustration. "You're not dating some member of a mysterious masculine horde. You're dating me, Lee Gregory. Lee, who you know craves stability, who appreciates being able to be open about his feelings. Usually, you remember that—" He paused and wrinkled his brow. Then with a perceptiveness that would one day make him a great therapist, he said, "You don't start speaking in generalities unless you're hedging. What aren't you saying?"

Jamie was quiet for some time. "Okay, this—us—has been so amazing, and you've been wonderful. But everything has happened in a pretty darn inclusive space, and . . . I know the rest of the world isn't like that." She shifted closer to him. "I'm afraid when you're making these leaps in our relationship, you're making promises you can't keep. And that expecting you to keep them, especially after graduation, would be expecting too much." A tear escaped and rolled down her cheek. Lee moved quickly to her side to brush it away. She took his hand and kissed it.

"Jamie, I know that I can't understand everything that goes into being trans, but remember I'm mixed, and my mom is black. Hollywood, especially at her level, is still very much ruled by the old guard, so I have a sense of the many ways people can be hostile about who you are or who you love. Fighting against that was one of the few things that held my parents together for so long. And Longbourn isn't immune. I've gotten hostility about us from some unexpected corners." Lee gave a one-shouldered shrug. "It sucks, but it simplifies things: I know who my true friends are—or at least, I know who is worthy of my time." He squeezed her hand.

"The point is you have to trust me to know my own mind. We can't have a relationship if you're walking on secret eggshells."

"I know," she said, resting her head on his shoulder. The real issue was how the strained relationship with her mom really rattled her. Though they were on good terms now, not having her support after coming out was like crashing through the ice of a favorite skating pond. Even if something like that never happened again, she'd never forget how it felt to fall into that freezing water.

But that wasn't Lee's problem. It just meant that Jamie had to be brave. "Okay, I'm going to work on my trust and on actively directing our relationship." She sat up and looked at Lee. "Let me start now. I would like more baby steps. I mean, I'm really looking forward to meeting your mother at graduation, but I don't want to stay with you guys for the summer, and I definitely don't want her to pull strings to land me that internship with L.A. Theatre Works."

Jamie looked deeply into his hazel eyes. "I want to be young with you, to enjoy the fun, silly part of our relationship. I want us to live in the same city and meet for dinner and complain about our roommates, but I'm not ready for full-on domesticity. We have our whole lives for that."

"Oh?" he said, putting his arm around her.

"Yeah. I could see us together for some time." Jamie leaned over and kissed him sweetly. "I love you, Lee. It's true. I do." Lee's face broke into the most radiant of grins.

"I love you, too! I was going to tell you this weekend, for Valentine's Day. I had a whole thing." He broke off suddenly and just looked at her. Then he kissed Jamie emphatically. No more studying occurred that evening. When they left for class the next day, they floated away from each other like parting clouds, held aloft by their newly discovered love.

EJ

She was squealing, loudly. "You're in love!" EJ exclaimed after Jamie came over to tell her the story. "Oh, I'm so happy for you both!" She gave her friend a big squeeze and practically bounced off the bed. "We should celebrate! Ice cream?"

"Let's do lunch at Cousin Nicky's," Jamie countered.

"Where it all began. I'm so in."

They hopped in EJ's car and were seated in the special rear booth. By the time their food came, the conversation had moved from Jamie and Lee to EJ and Will, much to EJ's chagrin. There was everything and nothing to talk about.

"So what's going on with you two?" Jamie asked.

EJ shrugged. "Not much to tell: he asked me out the night before he left, and now, we talk on the phone sometimes."

"Lee says it's every day."

EJ frowned. *Has it been every day?*

That wasn't good. She'd been doing her best to be cool about the whole thing. After Will left, EJ allowed herself no outward signs of giddiness. There was no dreamy strolling Disney-princess-like through the quad. No stalkerish googling pictures of Will in formal wear. No doodles of hearts crowding the corners of her notebooks. EJ's margins were pristine. Admittedly, she may have lit up at every text from Will or stroked the place where he'd kissed her with a faint smile—but that was the limit. EJ had learned to be practical in these matters. She was determined to keep expectations low and excitement reasonable.

"All I can say now is that I like him, and he likes me. We'll see where this goes," EJ said before tucking into her gyro.

Jamie leaned back into the leatherette booth and sighed in exasperation. "That's it? I'm going to need some more enthusiasm here. Like with Jordan."

EJ gave a slight wince. "Jordan was a hookup. Will is something more. There's no comparing the two situations."

"'Something more'?" Jamie echoed with a smile. "Let's explore that."

EJ took another bite to gather her thoughts. "Since we made up, I've gotten to see that he's a good guy: smart, loyal, and a really honorable person—in addition to being intimidatingly hot. And he's interested in an actual relationship, which I am, too."

Jamie took a sip of her soda. "All this sounds like reasons to get excited."

"Except I barely remember how to be in a relationship, and I know that whatever we get to have is going to be over by graduation, which is right around the corner. Cautious optimism seems to make the most sense here. There's no sense in breaking your own heart."

It was a phrase EJ used often, whenever she or someone she knew seemed in danger of letting their fantasies get the better of their common sense. She'd said it so much during her first year as an RA that she received a pillow embroidered with the expression as an anonymous present. Any sarcastic intent on the part of the giver(s) was overpowered by the remarkably high quality of the needlework.

"Who says everything has to be over by graduation?" Jamie asked.

EJ took a sip of her Diet Coke before responding. "Seriously, J, we haven't even kissed yet. I doubt we'd be willing to change our lives for each other three months from now. Especially since he already has a career, and I'm building mine."

Jamie sucked her teeth. "Always so sensible."

EJ sat back in the booth. "I just learned that I should be a teensy bit less sensible—career-wise, anyway. I had a long conversation with Dia's sister that really helped shift my perspective. She's a civil engineer for the city of New York and had a lot of good advice."

EJ had reached out to Dylann after an unsatisfactory speed-networking event from her department; only one woman turned up, and she'd graduated in the mid-1990s. Fortunately for EJ, Dylann had a similarly miserable time with her school's career prep, and was happy to video chat about her experience.

"Thanks for taking the time to talk with me. I only get to talk with young women in the field at conferences, and even then, it's hard to have in-depth conversations because there's so much going on."

Dylann nodded while adjusting her lighting. "It's so true, and when you exchange information, it's never the same over email or phone. Anyway, I'm glad to support another lady engineer—especially since you've been so great with Dia. She told me about how you helped her get that small scholarship to cover her books."

EJ had nominated Dia for the Bennet House fund after talking with her on Hearth Night. Her parents had cut her off financially after Winter Break. They wanted her to quit the drama program, where she was thriving, and change her major to child development. Luckily for Dia, Dorothea Bennet had endowed a small fund to provide cash for Bennet House residents' urgent needs.

"It was my pleasure. Bennet Women support each other," EJ replied. "So I have two questions, one general and one specific." She could see Dylann's angle change on-screen as she leaned back in her seat.

"Got you. Fire away," she said with a short nod.

"Okay, first, what is the most important thing someone can do after graduation to be ready for the engineering world?" EJ asked, discreetly breaking out a notepad and pen.

"If you haven't had one, get a regular job. Office, nonoffice, it doesn't matter as long as it helps you understand having multiple supervisors and that there is no one holding your hand—this is why it can't be an internship. One thing I often see with new grad students or new hires is they don't understand the working world. This is true of a lot of our newbies; the girls are judged more harshly."

"I spent last summer temping, so I should be fine there," EJ responded.

"Then take the summer off." EJ frowned, but Dylann insisted. "I'm serious. Whatever offer you get, tell them you can start in September."

"What do I do during the summer?"

"Travel. Go someplace you've never been. Try something new. Spend time with your family and friends. If you need a job for money, get something really part-time. Once you start working, it takes over. You won't be able to take a real vacation for at least a year. And I think it's important to hit a reset button and get out of the undergrad mindset. I can think of at least three newish members of staff who are looking for someone to grade them."

"The main thing Dylann said is to take the summer off before you start working, because once you start, you probably won't stop for a while. Also, doing something cool now helps prevent burnout later."

Jamie shoved her hair over her shoulder and then nibbled at her hummus platter. "Well, I'm in favor of anything that makes you stop and smell the roses. Do you have any ideas for what you might want to do this summer?"

EJ sat back thoughtfully, lightly squeaking against the leatherette booth. "I didn't really have anything until this morning. I was listening to *Bookends*—Simon and Garfunkel—and "America" came on. It made me realize that I'd been to Spain and France, I've lived in Scotland, but I've never been farther west than Chicago. I'd still love to do a big road trip."

Jamie raised an eyebrow. "A big *American* road trip?"

"Maybe a North American road trip? Mostly in Canada?" she offered.

Her friend laughed. The subject had become a sort of ongoing joke between them. EJ would suggest a road trip, they'd start planning, and then something would remind them that driving while black and trans meant they could only travel from Boston to Nashville (stopping only at major cities, of course) before running out of stores where EJ wouldn't get followed, bars where Jamie felt safe, or restaurants that would happily serve them both—without the complimentary side eye. Jamie said they should give up the idea "until we get more cis, white friends," but EJ couldn't let it go. She knew that such a trip was possible, even probable with an RV. Her grandma Jackie had been big into RV camping; they went everywhere from the Smokies to the sequoias. Unfortunately, car camping was not *at all* Jamie's style—even if they could afford to rent something comfortable.

EJ was investigating alternatives. "I've been looking at traveling by train. We did a solid three weeks on our Eurail Passes, after JYA."

"The train, like all public transit in the US, is more expensive and less . . . good," Jamie replied. "Besides, even if I had train time or train money, I have to count myself out. I've already promised camp I'd be back for one last year." Jamie had been going to Camp Lightbulb in Provincetown since she was fourteen and had been a counselor since she was nineteen. When they met freshman year, Jamie had talked about camp the way that EJ now talked about Bennet House.

"Oh fine, I know how much it means to you."

"Tessa could go," Jamie suggested.

EJ shook her head. "Tessa's probably going to get that internship at Bryce Canyon. I don't think our summer plans will line up." She shrugged. "I just thought it would be nice to see California before I maybe, possibly, leave the country for the next couple of years."

The main reason EJ had applied to be a Fields Fellow was so she could do grad school internationally without going into an unreasonable amount of debt. Since she wanted to do two back-to-back masters, she looked only at schools with historic building conservation and sustainable design programs. After all that, her top two schools were University of Auckland in New Zealand and the University of Edinburgh, which she already knew and loved from her year abroad.

Jamie patted her arm. "For what it's worth, I'm as sure about you and this fellowship as you are about Tessa and her internship. I've never seen you have so much fun doing engineering stuff."

EJ gave a small smile. She'd really been enjoying the research for the fellowship presentation. She'd gone back to her initial capstone idea of preserving and restoring the Old Stone Mill and added in a focus on climate change. The work felt easier just because it was so interesting.

"I kind of hate how much I want it now," she admitted. "I haven't worked this hard on something since my ballet days." She felt a shudder run through her body.

"Hey, at least there's the Girly Show," Jamie offered. "That will keep you nice and distracted until the short list comes out."

EJ groaned. The Girly Show was Bennet House's annual fundraiser: a night of third-wave feminism, off-color sketch comedy, and often at least one amateur burlesque act. The whole house got involved. Those who weren't performing sold snacks or put up decorations—and everyone got friends to buy tickets and hoot from the audience. The fundraiser covered all the Bennet House activities and big, big purchases, like this year's dream item: a dance studio in the basement of the house. There was a good deal of demand, and the school was willing to support the project if the House raised 30 percent of the funding. Ever since she got the idea, EJ thought of the dance studio as her Bennet House legacy. That meant the Girly Show had to be an extra-big success.

"That reminds me, I'm gonna have to go soon. Dia asked me to help her and Graciela rehearse."

Jamie's eyebrows shot up to her hairline. "She got Goth Gracie to sing? How?"

EJ shrugged. "They bonded over *Wicked*; they're going to sing 'For Good' at the show. I'm going to accompany them."

"No rest for the wicked, eh?"

"I see what you did there." EJ laughed. "No rest, but maybe half a milkshake if you feel like splitting? This is a celebration, after all."

Will

Will was killing it in New York. Spending the previous months with contentious intellectuals had turned out to be great preparation for this particular media circus. He remembered the importance of being kind to support staff from EJ's horror stories of residents who liked to treat RAs like servants, or their parents who treated them like nannies. With this in mind, he charmed all the makeup and hair stylists and, as a result, looked particularly dashing and well rested at all his on-camera interviews. On CNN, he discussed his art history studies without seeming pompous by balancing every potentially pretentious-sounding statement with a self-effacing one: something he picked up from a well-liked professor. Finally, when asked about Carrie, he emulated a kind classmate's sympathy for fellow students who've embarrassed themselves in discussions: "Truly, I feel for Carrie as a fellow professional. All performers have bad days—hers just came at an incredibly bad time."

After the world and news cycle moved on, Will had emerged as a model of the modern gentleman: thoughtful, compassionate, and with the *Today* appearance and the *GQ* videos, a sharp dresser. As success breeds success, by the end of the month, Will was constantly off shooting: one day, a magazine spread for high-end watches; another, a PSA for the New York Transit Authority against "manspreading" with the tagline "A gentleman makes room."

Through all this, Will kept in touch with EJ. Now that he knew she liked him back, he frankly couldn't help himself. They sent each other silly photos and chatted online during idle moments. After a couple of weeks, they fell into the mutual habit of calling every day, between five and five thirty. Today, EJ caught him taking a taxi back to Pemberley.

"I saw the video of that Asian Actors Roundtable from the *Hollywood Reporter*," EJ said during one such call. "You were so thoughtful and honest."

"Thanks. It went much better than I was expecting. Katerina had to push me to do it, but as usual, she was right. She was even right about Carrie."

"I had this impression that Hollywood agents were super exploitative," EJ said. "But Katerina just sounds like a cool aunt who gets you jobs."

"Most agents are working for themselves, but Katerina is different. Her fees are hugely expensive, but she's extremely protective of her clients and their interests. If I didn't have her in my corner, I'd either have spent my career playing nerdy friends with broken English or, more likely, would have left the business altogether," Will said.

"Ugh."

"Yeah, I know," he agreed. "The industry is often gross."

"What about it keeps you?" EJ asked. "You're one of few people who could do literally whatever you want."

"At first it was an escape, then it was fun. Now if I'm honest, part of why I want to stay in the industry is that I'm a known Asian entity, and I can afford to avoid stereotypical roles. People may cast with me in mind, write for me, even. It sounds slightly nuts, but I feel like my presence makes it easier for the younger Asian guys to come."

"Not crazy—I get it. Working against the stereotypes is half the fun, especially when you can shove it in the haters' faces." EJ gave a wicked little laugh. "I remember once at this all-day robotics tournament, I'm walking in with my team—we've got these matching button-up shirts with our school logo on them, and mine is a little tight in obvious places. Anyway, this private-school jerk says, 'Hey, sugar tits, is that your boyfriend's shirt?' I did nothing but give him a long look at the time. But later, when my team was brought up to receive our trophy, I found that polo-shirted asshole in the crowd and blew him a kiss. His team didn't even win the sportsmanship ribbon because one of the parents heard what he said to me."

They both laughed, though later Will would wonder if EJ's preference for giant sweaters was more deeply rooted than he'd previously considered. He moved on to some welcome news: "I'll be in town next week. We can finally have that date."

"Ooh la la!" EJ responded. "I don't think I've ever been on a real date. I'm looking forward to it—as a cultural experience."

"Gee, thanks," Will said sarcastically.

"Oh shush," EJ retorted. "No one's bruising your ego. You know what I meant."

"Okay, okay. When are you free next weekend?" he asked, switching the phone to his other ear.

She hummed in consideration. "I have to be at the house on Friday; I'm on duty. But . . . I'm free Thursday, Saturday, and Sunday."

"Let's say Thursday then," Will said. "But keep your weekend open. Maybe we can get dates two and three in there as well. Unfortunately, I have to fly back Monday, but I intend to make the most of the time we have." He paused. "Oh! And if you don't mind, I'd like to kick this old school—plan the whole thing. All you have to do is show up."

Will could hear her smile into the phone. "Sounds good. I can't wait."

The Date

A few days later, Will was standing in the Bennet House common room, feeling his breath catch a little as he watched EJ descend the stairs. She wore a pink tea-length dress with a swirling circle skirt and ankle-strap heels that made her legs look a mile long. He met her at the landing, where she did a little twirl. "You look absolutely lovely," he said with admiration.

"Thank you," she replied. "You're not bad on the eyes yourself."

Will hadn't stopped staring, so he tried to make that less weird. "I don't think I've ever seen you in heels."

"I don't usually wear them, living up a steep hill and all." EJ shrugged casually. "You're driving tonight, so I can just focus on looking cute—now tell me all about my first real date."

Will helped EJ into her winter coat. "I remembered that we both talked about missing out on concerts. There's a bar in the square doing live music tonight: original music at six and a cover band at nine. I was thinking we could catch the earlier show and then do dinner at the Brazilian place next door."

"That all sounds like fun stuff I haven't done before," EJ said approvingly. "If the acting or the art don't work out, you should consider getting into event planning."

Later, EJ and Will applauded enthusiastically as the Kincaid Brothers finished their encore, an obligatory Irish folk cover of "Sweet Caroline."

"That shouldn't have worked as well as it did," Will commented, "but I really enjoyed it."

"I think every band in Red Sox country is required by law to cover that song. Even if they're Irish fiddle players." EJ looked around. "Speaking of the Red Sox, was there a special on green caps? I feel like half the people in this bar are wearing them."

"Well, three-quarters of them are pretty drunk, and it's only seven, so who knows—" Will broke off as EJ grabbed his arm.

"Oh no," she groaned. "That's what the band meant by an 'obligatory' cover. How could I forget?" She quickly began putting on her coat. "Cancel our reservation, Will; we've got to get out of the square—and at least a twenty-minute walk away. The sooner, the better." She sucked her teeth despairingly. "I should have known, all that U2 from the jukebox . . ."

"What? Why?"

"It's Saint Patrick's Day. More than that, it's Saint Patty's in a small college town in Massachusetts. Trust me, this delightful little square is going to be a complete garbage fire"—she checked the time—"in twenty to thirty-five minutes."

"I see," Will said gravely. "What should we do?"

EJ drummed her fingers on her bottom lip as she thought. "I know! We can do dinner at Dona Carlotta's. It's not far, but just around the traffic circle of death. No one's going to venture there drunk," she suggested.

Will put on his coat. "That could work," he agreed. "How would you feel about a little bowling afterward? It's right next door, and I've always wanted to get dressed up and go bowling—weirdly." He had even purchased socks on the off chance EJ wasn't in her usual colorful tights.

EJ pointed at him with a reproachful finger. "You're the reason that bowling alleys have gotten so weirdly posh now, with craft whiskey and Edison bulbs."

Will shrugged. "Probably. But even gentrified bowling is fun, right?"

EJ rolled her eyes and was going to say something else when he took her hand. Instead she smiled at him sweetly. "You'll just have to convince me."

It seemed like most people in town had stayed home to avoid the Celtic bacchanal; Dona's was fairly empty. Their dinner came quickly, and conversation flowed from their last phone call to their sisters to the weird-ass production of *Carmen* that was on *Great Performances*. After the dinner plates were cleared, EJ and Will lingered over their coffee and fruit plate. She nibbled a piece of papaya thoughtfully.

"I feel like we spend so much time on the phone that most of this date has just been catching up from our last conversation." She sat up straight, laughter in her eyes. "I need to treat you like a regular date . . . by asking you some official First-Date Questions *TM*."

"First-Date Questions TM?" Will echoed, mirthfully. "That sounds ominous."

She sipped her piña colada and tilted her head, considering. "How about: Any hidden talents?"

"Accents," he replied with surprising certainty. "I'm very good at accents—especially British and southern. I've got those down to regions. I can also do a passable Russian, but it tends to get vaguely Eastern European after a while."

She looked at Will skeptically. "Specific British and southern accents?"

"Yes," he said definitively.

"You realize I have to test you now." With that she began shouting out the region she wanted to hear (Welsh! Cajun! East Tennessean!) and Will performed them, delighted with this chance to show off. She relented after Will's Glaswegian rendition of "Mary Had a Little Lamb" reduced her to hiccuping tears of laughter.

"All right, you'll do," she said admiringly.

"The Scottish one really did you in," Will said with not a little pride.

"Remember how I said I'd move to Edinburgh tomorrow? I did my semester abroad and just loved everything about it. Including the accents. That was Glasgow, right?"

Will nodded.

"Forget the film career and the abs, you should just do voice acting—forever. That was fantastic."

"Thank you," he said with a wink. "Have I charmed you enough to go bowling? It's right next door and not fancy at all."

EJ drummed her fingers on her bottom lip again, but this time something felt off. Her lip was slightly numb.

"Weird!" She paused and repeated the action. "Still weird . . . Hey, Will, is there anything wrong with my mouth?"

The actor leaned for a closer inspection and then slightly recoiled. "Umm, you look like you got too much collagen."

EJ looked at him in pained confusion.

"I think your lips are swollen. Looks like an allergic reaction of some sort."

"But why?" EJ was poking her lips more forcefully. "I've eaten here at least a dozen times. Nothing's happened before."

"Did you try anything new?" he asked, looking at her mouth. Will felt guilty that he'd been watching her nurse her drink that whole time and he hadn't noticed anything wrong.

She shook her head. "I've had everything before except the fruit plate—I mean, that was complimentary because we're, like, the only people here—"

"The papaya!" Will cried. "You said you'd never had papaya before."

Her eyes widened. She'd been eating it for a solid half an hour. The fruit plate was very papaya heavy.

"It's true! Oh, papaya, why?" She sighed heavily. "I guess I'd better get home and figure this out."

Well, this sucked. They were having such a great time—what a crappy way to end things. EJ looked similarly deflated.

"All right," Will agreed. "Let me drive you back to Bennet."

The ride back to campus was a little subdued. EJ spent most of it googling her condition and reassuring him that she had a really lovely time. Will couldn't be cheered, though—especially when they turned on the radio to be greeted by the aggressive wailing of Celine Dion's "Taking Chances." He groaned and moved to switch the radio off.

"No!" EJ cried. "I love this song."

Will stopped short of slamming on the brakes. "Why?" he croaked, turning the volume down as a compromise.

"Come off it, you know why!" EJ protested. "We're the exact right age to have been obsessed with *Glee*. This song was in the first episode."

He grunted. "I was not a fan."

Will had a personal vendetta against *Glee*. His first TV show was a summer series called *Band Camp*, and it was his *Living Single* to *Friends*: more interesting, more diverse, and first of its kind. Unfortunately, *Band Camp* lasted only one summer season, while the inferior *Glee* became a cultural phenomenon—not that Will was bitter.

"Fine, be a contrarian," EJ shot back. "But you can't fault her singing. Celine can blow!" She turned up the radio as she hit the key change.

"Celine *is* great," he admitted. "But this song is so much! I think there are, like, lasers in the background," Will whined.

EJ tilted her head and listened thoughtfully. "I'll admit, the production leaves a lot to be desired, but you can find a hundred lovely acoustic versions on YouTube. When it's stripped down, the song is really good." She chuckled. "Which is not always the case. My sister was an arty emo girl in high school, so she dragged me to a lot of open-mic nights. I've heard misguided acoustic versions of pretty much every pop song you can imagine. Let me tell you right now, somewhere in America there's a skinny kid in ripped jeans earnestly singing an acoustic version of 'All Star.'"

Will paused to imagine this and then burst out laughing. "I'll take your word for it," he said.

EJ chuckled and looked out the window. "I don't think I've been down this street before," she commented.

"Neither have I. There was some detour after we left the restaurant, maybe to ensure none of the drunks get run over." He chuckled a little bitterly.

EJ wasn't listening, though—something had caught her attention. "Is that a pond? And a gazebo? Will, pull over."

He looked at her skeptically but obliged. "What are you thinking?"

"I'm thinking we can salvage this date with a little stroll. The internet says all my lips need are ice and time. It's kind of warm for March . . . could be romantic. Whaddya say?"

"Are you quoting the song?" he asked warily.

"No, never that." Her eyes sparkled with mischief.

Will answered by hopping out of the driver's side and opening EJ's door. "My lady," he said, offering his hand.

It was a pleasant night, and the moon over the tree-lined pond created a tranquil mood. They walked close together and soon were holding hands and talking softly. But just as they both seemed to be back in good spirits, EJ felt one raindrop, then another. They started walking more quickly, but when they were halfway around the pond, it began to rain *buckets*. EJ shrieked and ran for shelter. By the time they reached the gazebo, both their coats were soaked.

"I'm not a superstitious person," Will said as they caught their breath out of the rain, "but this date is starting to feel a tiny bit cursed." He shook the water out of his hair.

EJ was on the other side of the gazebo trying to hang her coat from one of the gables. They both watched it fall to the ground with a wet slap. She looked at the coat, then looked at him.

"I think the universe is telling me to stop suggesting things."

Will laughed as he took off his rain-sodden coat. EJ settled next to him and started humming "Sixteen Going on Seventeen." They caught each other's eyes and laughed. "This part seemed so romantic in the movie." He draped her coat over the side of the gazebo as she moved closer. "Hey, at least you don't turn out to be a Nazi. That would totally ruin our next date."

"So there'll be a next time?" he asked. They were close enough that their hands brushed.

"Oh, definitely." She dropped her voice, and her eyes seemed to drink him in. "I mean, have you seen you in the moonlight?"

Will exhaled deeply. He'd been too busy watching water droplets streak down her neck to think of a response that was adequately witty or romantic. Instead, he turned and took EJ in his arms.

"I have a confession," he whispered. He could feel EJ shiver in a way that was hopefully unrelated to her wet shoes. "Right now, it's all I can do not to kiss you. You're so gorgeous, and I know it would feel just perfect, but . . ." He delicately traced her bottom lip with his thumb. "I'm a little afraid of hurting you in your delicate papaya-induced condition."

EJ laughed into his shoulder. "How about you let me worry about that. I like living dangerously."

Will drew her close and kissed her in a way that conveyed all things.

Over the years, when EJ thought of this night, she'd remember the strength of Will's arm around her waist, the way he stroked the shell of her ear just before their lips touched. How she could feel his heat as their bodies pressed together, how she craved it. She would recall the steady drum of the rain as they kissed and how it felt like they were the only people in the world. Hands down, best date ever.

SPRING BREAK

EJ

It wasn't long after their amazing "Saint Patrick's Date" that EJ and Will decided to become quietly official. They didn't broadcast their relationship, but they agreed to be "all-in, for as long as this lasts." Though they didn't talk about it, EJ knew that this lovely thing between them would, if they had any sense, be over by graduation.

Maybe that was why she found herself spending much of her spare time with Will, too—and not just at his game nights, or on dates. She told herself it was because Jamie and Tessa had gotten much busier with their coursework, but if she was honest, she just really liked being with him. He was the only person who'd go with her to support Bennet Women at poetry readings or chamber music concerts without complaint. He was always sweet to the performers afterward, too.

It wasn't just when they went out. EJ liked being alone with Will. Sometimes they'd just hang out in the big common room, sharing the window seat and watching the trees. Other times, they listened to her records. Even though they teased each other about their esoteric tastes, Will never made her feel woefully out of touch. In the last week, they'd started spending time at his apartment watching international reality shows or black-and-white screwball comedies. He even liked her Katharine Hepburn impression.

Will was funny, too. That was the thing that surprised her most. And then there was the way he looked at her: like she was something precious, something magical. She'd never had a guy look at her like that. And there was the way he kissed, my God. And the way he touched her, and the way he could make her forget her own name.

"EJ!"

She blinked. Oh God, how long had Jamie been talking to her? Her friend was smirking, so her daydreaming must have become pretty obvious.

"I know that smile," she began teasingly. "You were thinking about your man."

EJ just gave a small self-conscious shrug in response. Jamie seemed like she was happier than Will or EJ about the two of them getting together. EJ couldn't complain, though, since she'd been exactly the same way about Lee.

She was keeping J company while her friend packed for Spring Break. Lee's Fall Formal fundraiser had paid off handsomely. While most of the students were still fleeing Massachusetts for warmer climes, about 10 percent of the student body was going on one of Lee's projects. The Gordon Campbell Society had partnered with Habitat for Humanity and was sending almost two hundred Longbourn students to volunteer across the country. GCS was even able to partially cover transportation for students who wanted to participate but didn't have the funds. Lee and Jamie were going to New Orleans, while Tessa was leading a large contingent of students cleaning up beaches in Puerto Rico.

"Longbourn is gonna be a ghost town," EJ said admiringly. "Your guy did well."

Since someone had to be on duty at Bennet House, EJ had volunteered to stay on campus. Stella had given her a couple of notes on her Fields Fellowship presentation that she wanted to address. With everyone gone, she'd have plenty of time to work on it. Still, Tessa and Lee had been thoughtful enough to organize a project for the folks who couldn't leave campus in nearby Seneca Falls, a former mill town that had fallen on hard times. It was only a twenty-minute drive from campus but felt worlds away.

Jamie zipped up her wheeled suitcase and stood. "Finally, done!" She stood victoriously in the middle of her room. "Where is Will, anyway?"

EJ nodded. "He's getting his house ready. Will's going to be part of an Asian American–themed episode of *Finding Your Roots*. He's excited. Will's pretty into family history but can't do the research because he doesn't speak Mandarin or Korean."

"How cool!" Jamie exclaimed. Her phone alarm went off. "Gotta go, babes. I should be leaving for the coach now."

EJ hopped up and crossed to her friend. "Okay, love. Have fun, be safe."

Jamie gave her an extra squeeze. "You too." She sighed. "Are you starting to feel it? Graduation? The end of everything?"

"J, don't. I can't." EJ shook her head furiously. It was too hard, thinking about the end of things. "You know I'm terrible with goodbyes."

Jamie pursed her lips, then shrugged. "Okay, I'll let you psychologically stall. Now get out of my room."

EJ kissed her friend on the cheek and did just that.

∽

On the night before the Seneca Falls build, Will called EJ with something clearly on his mind. "Eej, I—" he began. "Ella, I have to bring up something intensely awkward."

She sat up on her bed. "'Ella'?" she echoed questioningly. "You only use my home name when you're being super sweet or super serious. What's up?"

"It's about the build. I wanted to ask—since I'm a bit higher profile than I was even a couple of months ago, I have fewer guarantees on my privacy and so—"

"Spill!"

"I need us to be strictly platonic at the build. We're going to be off-campus and—"

"You're ashamed of me!" EJ wailed dramatically. "You're so famous now you don't want the world to know you're dating some weird black girl."

"No! No! I swear—" Will's protestations were overtaken by EJ's laughter.

"I'm sorry, had to mess with you a little. I don't want to be in the news, especially for being your girlfriend and not, like, inventing something. It won't help me in my field." She knew that celebrities managed this somehow. Dolly Parton had been married for, like, forty years, and EJ didn't even know what the guy looked like.

There was a long silence. A petulant silence, even. "I'm glad you're not upset about the need for discretion, but"—a pause—"you're mean," Will pouted.

"That's true, but I'm funny." Will was still sulking. "And I promise to make it up to you?" she offered.

"How?" he demanded.

"Well," EJ began thoughtfully. "I am young, remarkably flexible, and as you know, sexually adventurous, so I dunno . . . cookies?"

"Now I'm really looking forward to seeing you," Will rumbled.

"You'd better. See you soon." EJ disconnected the call and smiled to herself. She was happy to be Will's friend at the build, but she didn't have to be nice about it.

Will

Work kept Will in New York longer than originally planned. In the end, he was able to turn up for only the last day of volunteering. The team of students from Longbourn had shrunk steadily over the week, as the most interesting work, with drills and power tools, got completed. Will graciously accepted the lightly monotonous task of nailing shingles to the roof. He'd been at it for an hour when he realized he hadn't seen EJ yet. He asked the project manager if she knew where she was.

"I asked her to bring supplies today since she drives around here pretty often," she responded. "On the first day one of the other kids from Longbourn did a Dunkin' run and got stuck in the roundabout so long the coffee got cold."

Just then a white pickup pulled into the gravel lot. EJ hopped out of the driver's seat, and Will swallowed as she approached. She had obviously dressed to drive him insane. EJ was wearing a threadbare yellow T-shirt that clung to her like an old friend. She paired that with denim shorts that had the appearance of decency but closely traced the curve of her perfect ass. Her spring braids, as she liked to call them, were gathered in a high bun that showed off her long neck and the necklace he got her for her birthday.

After some prolonged gaping, Will scrambled down the ladder to— he wasn't quite sure what he was going to do. As EJ's friend he couldn't publicly criticize her without looking like a sexist pig or honestly discuss the effect of her outfit without sounding like a regular pig. This was probably what she had in mind.

Well played, Will thought as he walked over to the table.

"Crazy weather," EJ called. She was carrying two trays of coffee cups, each labeled with a different name. She reached the project manager and set the trays down on a nearby folding table. "Supposed to be seventy today. Climate change is going to kill us all, but this is nice for now."

She turned to Will with a wicked gleam in her eye. "Would you be a love and grab the Munchkins? They're in the passenger seat."

He looked around. No one else seemed to notice that EJ was dressed like the sexy Halloween version of a construction worker. They thanked her and took their coffee without a second glance. EJ knew he was paying attention, though. He wasn't certain until she "accidentally" dropped her clipboard when she knew he was coming back with the doughnut holes. Will was watching the denim inch up her thighs so intently that he walked into one of the parked cars.

When he returned to the folding table, EJ was alone. She looked up from her clipboard and said, "Hi, buddy!" with a merry wave.

He glowered in response. "You said you weren't mad," he half whispered.

EJ released a laugh that was high, sweet, and false. "I'm not angry, but I don't see why I should make it easy for you." Her smile was maddening.

"Fine," he said. "But remember, you brought this on yourself."

As the sun crept toward the sky, EJ and Will engaged in covert taunting. Will contrived to be in various stages of shirtlessness in her presence or was surreptitiously lifting and flexing. EJ countered by stretching languorously against the truck's body whenever she caught Will's eye and bending over more than was strictly necessary for her tasks.

At the end of the day, after the group pictures had been taken and all the high fives exchanged, Will watched her return the pickup's keys to the very chatty project manager.

When EJ returned, Will stood alone next to his car. "Hi, buddy," he said faux sweetly.

"Where'd everybody go?" Her eyes swept the empty lot. "Where's Marcia?"

"You were taking so long she worried about being late for babysitting," Will explained. "I told her I'd give you a ride back." He smiled dangerously as he held the passenger door open. EJ rolled her eyes and got into the car.

"You teased me just as much, you know, Mr. I Can't Drill With My Shirt On."

Will slowly walked around to the driver's seat and got in.

"Besides"—EJ looked at him from under her eyelashes—"it's only teasing if you have no intention of following through." And there went that rush of blood.

He looked around the empty lot, then pulled EJ into a searing kiss. He crushed her body against his and slid his hand over her enticing posterior. Her breath caught when he grazed his teeth down her perfect neck.

"*Fuck,*" she swore, clutching at his waist.

Will sat back in his seat, hoping he looked a bit suaver than he felt. "So," he began, allowing EJ to catch her breath, "how do you feel about coming over to my place, hanging out?"

"Please and thank you," she replied.

Will wasted no time in peeling out of the parking lot. *God, I adore this woman.*

That night EJ and Will cuddled on the couch looking for something they could agree on from Netflix.

"Ooh!" EJ exclaimed. "They have that production of *Company* where everyone plays their own instruments."

"Nice! Let's watch. I missed that production by one month when it was on Broadway. Lily saw it, though, and raved. 'Being Alive' is my favorite audition song."

"Sondheim at an audition? Brave man."

Just after the Netflix logo flashed across the screen, EJ's phone vibrated on the coffee table. "Hi, Dylann," she answered, moving out of earshot. She was careful with the privacy of her residents. She was gone for only a couple of minutes, but when she returned, her face was grave.

"What's wrong?" Will asked.

She sat next to him on the couch and curled into his side. "You remember the perky freshman who made my scarf, Dia?"

Will didn't, but he nodded anyway.

EJ went to speak but hesitated. After taking a breath, she finally said, "That was her sister—it sounds like Jordan Walker is making her his next target."

Will ruefully shook his head. It was infuriating after all this time that Jordan was still up to his old tricks: exploiting women and then playing on their shame.

She wrung her hands. They both felt the urgency. "I'll talk to her," she said quietly. Will could sense her uncertainty warring with her distress. "If I can get her to see . . ." She trailed off.

He took her hand and kissed it. "Hey, I will do everything in my power to stop Jordan from disrupting your friend's life. You try things your way, but if you need reinforcements, I'm here."

EJ dropped her head to his chest. "Thank you. I'll try and talk to her first."

EJ

That night EJ tossed and turned in bed. She couldn't get her conversation with Dylann out of her mind.

❧

"EJ, I hate to come with you with more Dia trouble after all you've done," Dylann had begun as EJ made her way to Will's bedroom. "But I'm just so worried about Dia."

EJ frowned. The perky freshman had seemed fine the last time she saw her—better than fine, actually. She was growing confident from her work for Sir Titus. "I can tell you that she's not missing or anything, if you've been trying to get in touch. She's been babysitting all week for a family in town."

Dylann sighed. She sounded frazzled. "It's nothing like that, just—the last few times we've chatted, all she's done is talk about some guy named Jordan Walker. 'Jordan's the best actor in our class.' 'Jordan's going to cover my entry fee for Drama Scholars.' 'Jordan thinks I should move to LA after graduation.'"

EJ gaped. "LA! Dia's always been obsessed with Broadway. With *theater*." Jamie made fun of her for being a culture snob, but EJ had nothing on Dia when she was ranting about bad acting in movies.

"Thank you!" Dylann sighed. "And yes, she might just be growing and changing. That's what college is for. I know that better than anyone." She was clearly trying to convince herself now. "I want to let her make her own decisions and everything, but the way she talks . . . it's like he's Charles Manson. I'm afraid she'll follow him anywhere." She sighed again. "Please just tell me I'm overreacting."

EJ rubbed the back of her neck anxiously. "I wish I could. I really do." She then told Dylann what she could about Jordan's past with younger women.

EJ shuddered at the memory and sat up in bed. She picked up her phone and drafted an email inviting Dia to lunch. She didn't quite know what to say, but Dia had listened to her advice before.

EJ's Lunch with Dia

They were sitting in a quiet, slightly drafty corner of the dining hall near a large window. EJ glanced out at the dangerous-looking icicles melting from the roof. She had her typical lunch: fries and a bowl of cucumbers. Dia was having the day's special, an ambitious pasta dish. After making a dent in her meal, EJ dove in.

"Dia, I brought you here because I heard that you've been hanging out with a guy named Jordan Walker. There are some things that I think you should know—"

"Say no more." The younger woman dabbed her mouth with a paper napkin, then placed a reassuring hand on her arm. "Jordan confessed to me about how shoddily he treated you—about hooking up with you and never calling."

Fuck! EJ thought as her eyebrows shot up to her hairline. "What? Oh wow. I wasn't planning on talking about that. It's, um, not the issue here."

"Are you saying you *didn't* hook up?" Dia put her fork down and folded her arms. Their chat had turned into a cross-examination.

"Yes, Dia, we did, and a good time was had by all, but that's not—"

The freshman pressed her point. "And did he call, or get in touch?"

EJ sighed. "He didn't call, but I wasn't waiting by the phone. I wasn't looking for anything more."

Dia looked at her piteously. "Eej, I know you try to be this modern woman, but you don't have to be strong with me. Jordan would be hard for anyone to get over. You should know that he does feel terrible about the whole thing."

EJ weighed the damage to her credibility against the stakes and decided to try again. "Dia, let me be clear: separate and apart from my hooking up with Jordan, I learned some things about him that give me concern. I met someone who went to high school with him. This person said Jordan had a reputation for taking advantage of younger girls"— she paused meaningfully—"and getting them into serious trouble with drugs. I don't know if I can emphasize this enough: it is not about me. I would not be having this super-awkward conversation if I wasn't actively worried about you."

Dia leaned back in her seat and considered, absently drumming her fingers on the cafeteria tray. EJ thought she might have gotten through to the young woman, a little. However, when Dia spoke, she was clearly back in cross-examination mode. "Did your friend, with this dirt on Jordan, did they go to Hanover?"

"Yes, actually. That's where everything I heard about happened," EJ said.

Dia nodded. "Jordan said a bunch of rich kids conspired to ruin his reputation at the school. It worked so well they got him expelled."

EJ groaned internally. She moved her tray out of the way and shifted her arms onto the table. "They showed me evidence, Dia, a lot of it, actually. I can't show it to you but—"

"I wouldn't want to see it, anyway," Dia interrupted. "Jordan told me about how far those Hanover kids went to get him kicked out." She looked around and lowered her voice. "You know that 'film professional' who's been on campus, Will Pak? He's one of Carrie Dean's crappy exes. Jordan says he was the ringleader, that the guy's got some crazy grudge. And I've seen what a judgmental snob he can be; we had a run-in at the Fall Formal."

EJ's shoulders fell. She'd forgotten that it was Dia who came to her defense that night. The freshman was a ride-or-die friend: to EJ then, and to Jordan now.

Dia continued. "I know Jordan, Eej. He's been nothing but kind to me, especially since my parents cut me off. Plus, he's always treated me like his baby sister. He likes how 'good' I am," she added with a touch of bitterness.

The RA sighed in defeat and took a long sip from her bottled water. "Okay, Dia, let's just drop it. I've shared my concerns; you've heard me as much as you can." EJ checked the time on her phone. "Didn't you say you wanted to get to the bio lab early? You probably should head out now since the Langston Building is pretty far from here."

Dia gave a small smile across the table. "It's sweet, Eej, it really is, how you reflexively try and look out for me. And I appreciate it." The younger woman stood and put on her pastel-blue raincoat and matching backpack. She looked like a marshmallow PEEP. "It's just . . . you're wrong here." With that, Dia picked up her tray and left.

EJ watched her walk away, almost resigned to let the freshman learn about Jordan the hard way. But as she tugged on her scarf, EJ noticed it happened to be the one Dia gave her for Christmas. Despite its odd shape, the scarf was very warm. EJ also had learned that it was made from particularly nice wool that probably cost way too much. It was sort of Dia in a nutshell: her enthusiasm, her kindness, her unconscious generosity. She ran a hand down it and said, "I can't let Jordan change her." She would have to find another way to get her to listen.

She whipped out her phone and sent a text to Will.

> I don't know how ethical this is.

> But I need your help to stop Jordan from wrecking another life.

Will responded in a flash.

> I'll do whatever you need me to do.

The Chat

The following Friday, Will's charity build was the subject of discussion on *The Chat*, a talk show in the model of *The View*, which traditionally featured women sitting around a coffee table bantering for a studio audience. *The Chat* shook up the usual formula with a gay man, a feisty Australian woman, and three ladies of color. (The show was shooting for a younger demographic.)

On-screen, they showed Will's picture, cropped from the Greater Boston Habitat for Humanity group photo at the Seneca Falls build. After the panelists openly lusted over his visibly impressive arms, they contrasted Will with his more famous ex.

"You know what I think?" the Asian American beauty blogger said with practiced folksiness. "I think Will's moved on. There are a bunch of cute girls in that photo who are future doctors, teachers, CEOs, et cetera. Pretty, smart, accomplished young women. I bet it didn't take him long to forget Carrie there."

"You bet he did!" interjected the gay comedian. "Look at their breakup. She hooks up with a racist and embarrasses herself at the Super Bowl, while he goes to one of the best schools in the country."

"She's too shallow for him now," agreed the black former child star.

The Australian interrupted. "Don't be polite, luv—you mean too dumb!" The audience cackled appreciatively.

"Hey, you said it," the Latina pop/fitness star agreed. "And don't forget all the low-key racist stuff she said about him when she was with Johnny Storm. Carrie is canceled for Will. She couldn't get him back now if she tried."

Another wave of laughter came from the audience. It was the kind of laughter that, if one had a cavernous theater room in a Los Angeles mansion, would echo off the tastefully decorated walls. The kind of laughter that could penetrate through the substance-addled mind of a disgraced celebrity and shake that person into flickering awareness. In that laughter Carrie Dean, who was halfway through her afternoon bottle of wine, heard a challenge. Blearily she reached for the phone.

Katerina

Katerina eyed her phone with irritation. Every day this week it had buzzed with messages from Carrie Dean and her people. At first, she relished Carrie's obvious desperation, but now the constant contact had become obnoxious. When all her devices buzzed at the same time, Katerina decided to respond.

"Andre!" she shouted to her assistant, her lilting accent lethally sharp. He bolted into her office. "Send these absurd people this ridiculous number." She scribbled something on a sticky note.

"That is the price for me to even speak Carrie's name to my client. Take that number, double it, and add a zero: that is the price for her to meet with Will. I want both amounts in cashier's checks before I even talk to him. Even then, I cannot promise that he won't spit in her face. If these numbers and conditions do not discourage her, then nothing will. She wants to hound me to my grave, then she can pay for the privilege." Katerina and her assistant shared a wry smile before he went to send the message.

Half an hour before the end of the workday, a shaking Andre brought in a plain white envelope. It had been hand delivered by a confused teller from the bank on the ground floor of their building. He placed the envelope on Katerina's desk. Two cashier's checks for the requested ridiculous amounts, and then some, slipped out of the envelope. "This bitch," Katerina muttered before picking up the phone to call Will at Longbourn.

To put it mildly, Will was not pleased. Katerina let him vent his outrage. But as he started moving to accusations of betrayal, she interrupted.

"Will, you and I have a long history together. Your mother brought you to me so you could act professionally without getting damaged by the industry. She chose me because she knew I would not let you be degraded or abused, that I would not force you into anything that you didn't want.

"And it has been true, yes? You have a career, yes? But no nerds, no stereotypes, no terrible accents. And when I have insisted, it has been for the best, yes? Take a breath and remember."

Will inhaled long and exhaled deeply. "Okay, I'm sorry. I know you must have a very good reason to propose bringing that person back into my life now that I'm finally happy again. I am prepared to hear it, though I can't imagine what it could be."

"Carrie Dean is now fixated on you, darling. You are a positive memento of her past, and she is desperate to recover what you represent: a time when everyone believed her hype. She will give you no peace. You must tell her yourself that this pursuit will only end in pain and humiliation. If you don't make this clear, set your terms, her public tantrum will suck everyone in: you and your new lady friend. You have met someone, yes?"

Will choked a bit before answering. "Yes, it's pretty new, but I like her very much."

Katerina smiled. "I thought so. You've been calm and pleasant, genuinely happy. Not like the all-consuming mania with Carrie. This one makes you better." The older woman paused.

"Now imagine how Carrie would try to torpedo your new relationship: staging scenes in restaurants or siccing the paparazzi on your lady friend outside her home—even leaking her photos for public ridicule—"

"But she's a private citizen! How could that even be legal?"

"Legal, bah! The point is, you know Carrie, and you know what she is capable of. If you meet with her, you can convince her that the best thing for all is to move on—especially if you can help her save face from all this. All she really wants is her career back."

Will heaved a sigh of frustration. "Is this the only way?"

"This or retirement, darling. At present Carrie is an obstacle that we must work around, not one that we can knock over."

"Can this wait until after graduation? I have stuff I need to work on until then."

"I can try. I will definitely put her off until May."

"All right," Will relented. "Let's talk tomorrow to strategize."

"Good." Katerina disconnected the call and frowned. That had gone too well; there was no way that was Will's final word on the subject.

Her phone rang again, and she knew it was him. "Carrie Dean gets no more control of my life," Will decided. "Set up a meeting for Monday at noon. Your office. It's Patriot's Day weekend. That's a holiday here, so I'll fly down. We give Carrie Dean my terms. If she accepts them, great. If not, I quit the business."

She audibly gasped. It was her most severe loss of cool in a decade. "What? Will, be calm. Let me come talk with you this weekend."

Katerina was not prepared to lose one of her most successful and loyal clients this way, but Will sounded more certain than she had ever heard him.

"Okay, Katerina. We can meet on Saturday morning; I owe you that."

She dropped her shoulders in relief, but only for a moment.

"But I won't live another day of my life in fear of her. Nothing is worth that, not even my career." He disconnected the call, and Katerina stared at the phone. She was rattled, and she rarely got rattled.

"Andre!" she shouted to her assistant. "Get me on the next plane to Boston! We have a crisis."

THE GIRLY SHOW

EJ

Looking on as the final row of chairs was arranged in the common room, EJ strongly considered putting the Girly Show on her résumé. Organizing the talent show had required attention to detail, team management, and project evaluation: all skills employers looked for, according to the career center workshop she'd recently attended. And just a few hours before the event, everything was going to plan.

Tickets had sold out ahead of time, likely because Jamie got Lee and the BournTones to close the show. Dress rehearsal had flowed smoothly: everybody showed up, and no one had ridiculous lighting demands this year. EJ tasted everything going into the bake sale and made sure the less tasty items went out last. The Longbourn events staff had set up the risers and mics for the performance the day before, and EJ had created a backstage / green room for the performers behind the double doors of the Bennet west hallway. She really wanted the show to go well; it was going to be the last big thing she did for Bennet House. After avoiding it for as long as she could, EJ was coming to terms with the fact that life as she knew it would be over in exactly one month. She'd expected to feel more ready by now.

It didn't help that she didn't know if she was going to be working next or headed to grad school. EJ had been busily trying to prepare for all scenarios. At Stella's suggestion, she reached out to the companies she would have been checking out at the NSBE conference. She also made her fellow engineers Franz and Vanessa sit through a dry run of her Fields Fellowship presentation. Still, after all the prep, EJ just had to make peace with an uncertain future. She shuddered. Living in uncertainty was not her forte.

Then there was Will. Never in a million years had she expected to feel so much for him so quickly. Sometimes after a long kiss, or when she was feeling the supreme joy of being the little spoon, a certain four-letter word had floated to the surface of her mind. EJ swatted it down, of course—it was way too soon—but she could admit that she was very attached to Will.

"Breaking up is going to suuuuuuck," she groaned to herself. It was the only sensible way, though. Will was rapidly rebuilding his career, and EJ had to get hers started. She only hoped she'd be strong enough to end things when the time came.

The Star

"Hey, watch it!" Carrie Dean snapped at a pair of twirlers in silver lamé as they rushed past. The singer was close to unrecognizable tonight with her auburn bob and minimal makeup. She planned to pass herself off as someone's best friend from Harvard, if asked. If she was recognized, she planned to tell folks she was doing research for a new show. No one could know that *the* Carrie Dean had come to this pathetic backwater of a college town to get her boyfriend back. But she wanted Will again, and she was someone who got what she wanted.

Her plotting skills were a little rusty. It had been a while since she'd needed to do anything more to accomplish her aims than scream at an assistant or make a phone call. Still, she thought there was a beautiful simplicity to her three-step plan, and she had no doubt it would work: 1) Find Will's new girl, if she existed; 2) Get this new girl out of the way; and 3) Get Will back.

Now Carrie wasn't stupid. She knew she and Will hadn't ended things on the best terms, but Will was smart. He knew how generous her team could be when someone was on their side.

But for now, she had to complete step one. Carrie had a hunch that her rival was one of the Longbourn girls from the Habitat for Humanity photo. When she got to campus, Carrie had furtively stalked those she viewed as the most likely candidates. She'd come to this Girly Show because, according to the campus gossip she picked up, Will visited this house fairly often. Now, hopefully, all she had to do was match the likeliest girl to one of the faces in the crowd.

EJ

It was near the end of the show, and EJ was happy. In the green room, she had successfully kept the trains running all night. She zipped people in and out of costumes and squashed any last-minute spats between performers. Now, after a quick hug from Lee, EJ was lining up the BournTones when Tessa came barreling through the double doors. "Eej, we need you right now!"

"Let me—" she began.

"No, now!" The shorter lady grabbed EJ's arm and pulled her out to the common room, where Will was sitting down at the keyboard. Her jaw dropped.

"Good evening, everyone! The organizers of the Girly Show mentioned that they needed a little interstitial entertainment in preparation for their surprise finale." He covered his mouth in mock distress. "Um, I mean . . . for reasons. In any case, I'm here to play a little piano for you. Any requests?"

A flurry of responses came from the audience before Will spoke again. "'Freebird' sounds like kind of a fun dare."

There were more shouts. "Billy Joel sounds very tempting. I'm a huge fan."

"Why?" cried someone else in the crowd.

"My mom loved Billy Joel and passed that on to me. So if you make fun of me for liking him, you're really making fun of my mother, and she's dead now." There was some uncomfortable laughter. Will sighed. "And that's why I never tried comedy." This got a genuine laugh. "Okay, no Billy Joel—he's gotten too controversial."

"Celine Dion, 'Taking Chances'!" a voice very much like Jamie's shouted.

"What a delightful suggestion, person I definitely did not pay to say that." Will placed his hands on the keys. "I must admit I was not a big fan until a couple of months ago, when a certain person helped me see that underneath a whole lot of overblown production is a quite beautiful song. Then I listened to the lyrics and realized that they just about summed up our relationship.

"Anyway, this song goes out to that someone who's become very dear to me."

"Oooh," the crowd responded, doing their best impression of a sitcom's live studio audience.

"She tells me that Bennet *Women*—emphasis hers—look out for each other, so I'm going to rely on that. Really hope you guys can keep a secret." Will placed his hands on the keyboard.

"Okay, here goes. Ella, this is for you." Then he launched into a pretty acoustic version of the song. Thankfully only a few people who knew her home name whipped around to look at her with a smirk or an impressed nod. EJ wasn't paying attention to them. She was holding too tightly to her clipboard and listening to Will's song.

The Star

At the final note, the room erupted in applause. Someone in the audience shouted, "Kiss him, EJ!"

Carrie was still watching the action through the small window in the door. But now she was surrounded by a couple of half-dressed twirlers and several members of an Indian dance troupe who'd been the last to go on. After Carrie delivered a few sharp elbows to get some breathing room, her eyes landed on a tall, chunky black girl covering her face with the sleeves of her ginormous sweater. She gurgled with shock. Her rival was nothing like she expected. "She should at least *look* like a model," Carrie muttered. "This is an insult to both of us!"

This EJ was shyly moving to the center of the room. "Way to blow up my spot, Tessa," she lightly chastised the person who'd called her out.

"I regret nothing!" the other girl shouted. "Kiss him!"

Carrie wrinkled her nose. "Or don't," she said sourly.

Now the audience had taken up the cause, chanting, "Kiss him!" until she finally did just that at the edge of the makeshift stage. When their lips met, Carrie could see the rest of the world disappear for them.

"If that's not love, it's pretty damn close," she heard one of the dancers whisper while the audience cheered.

This was unbearable. Carrie fled to the nearest bathroom. She wasn't sure if she wanted to cry or vomit. She did both, then remained in the bathroom to cheer herself up.

EJ

After the BournTones' finale, the Bennet House RAs thanked the audience for their attendance and asked them not to put anything embarrassing or personal from the night on the internet.

"Some of us have really big interviews in two weeks!" EJ squeaked.

Thankfully the crowd was mostly made up of Bennet Women and benevolent friends, who seemed to be pulling for her and Will. They dispersed to the night's parties while the organizers stayed behind to clean up. EJ found Will once more. After a long kiss, she rocked onto her toes and whispered, "As soon as we're done here, let's go back to your place." She bit him discreetly on the ear. "For . . . reasons."

Will gave her a quick tush squeeze and shouted, "Who needs help? I want to make this cleanup happen very efficiently."

Laughing, EJ went to the bathroom to wet down some rags. She leaned against the wall and took a moment to collect herself. She couldn't stop smiling. "Looks like I appreciate big romantic gestures," she giggled.

Then a voice came from behind her. "So you're Will Pak's girl now?" she spat.

"Woman, fully grown," EJ corrected reflexively. "I'd prefer to be called something more feminist than *girlfriend* but less stodgy than *significant other*, and I'd sound like that JYA student if I tried to use *partner*, not that it's that seri . . ." She trailed off and gave a little shrug.

It was clear this person did not wish her well, so she decided to speak plainly. "We are in a committed, exclusive relationship."

The other woman seemed infuriated by her last statement. She tossed her hair and went slightly red at the cheeks. EJ turned away from her and finished drying her hands. Above them, the fluorescent lights flickered and hissed. The other woman made a noise between a grunt and a groan, then met EJ at the sink. "I don't know what fantasies you've conjured up, but it won't last between you."

EJ's eyes widened, but she remembered the words of her mother ("You can't beat crazy with crazy") and swallowed her initial response. She looked the seething redhead up and down, then said, "Gosh, you're pretty. Have we met?"

That phrase was the "Bless your heart" of Bennet House, their way of saying, "You are obviously physically attractive, but otherwise too dumb/annoying/worthless to live."

The stranger turned white with anger. "Are you fucking serious?" she demanded. "You don't know who I am?"

"Should I?" EJ asked genuinely. The woman before her was pretty in an expected, head-cheerleader way—but EJ couldn't quite place her.

"I'm Carrie Dean!" she protested.

"Oh, Will's ex."

"I'm a superstar!" Carrie cried, truly galled.

The RA gave a slight gasp of recognition. "The Super Bowl, right? You, um . . . sang the anthem."

Carrie didn't answer but suddenly became fascinated with the lighting fixtures. EJ looked at her quizzically. "I thought you were a blonde."

"It's a wig. I'm considering a change. Anyway," Carrie pressed on, "I want to let you know that it won't become anything serious." She looked at EJ with evident distaste. "None of Will's friends will ever accept some chubby gold digger—especially with those ragbag clothes. No one in LA will want to know you since you're just some nerdy college feminist. You'll annoy the guys and bore the other girls. You and

Will can enjoy what you have here, but that's it. Out there: that's his world, my world, and you'll never belong."

EJ bit the inside of her cheek to maintain her calm facade. "But your world sounds so appealing," she responded dryly. "I'm a little confused as to what you're trying to accomplish here." She leaned back against the wall and folded her arms. "You didn't need to come three thousand miles to tell me that I'm not skinny and Hollywood people are shallow. I own both a mirror and a television."

"I'm here because understanding the truth is different than knowing it," Carrie Dean snapped. She looked away and huffily ran her fingers through her artificial auburn bangs. "Believe it or not, this is a friendly warning—not just for you, but for Will. He's a good friend."

She looked EJ in the eyes. "If you care about him, break up with him. Save him from himself. This"—she waved a hand vaguely in EJ's direction—"entanglement will only hurt his career. Do you want to be responsible for that?" Carrie put her hands on her hips and seemed to be awaiting EJ's instant capitulation.

Fuck that, EJ thought. She uncrossed her arms and spoke. "You're working really hard to protect an adult man from his own decisions. Whatever future Will and I have will be decided by us alone."

Carrie scoffed, but before she could speak, EJ said, "Don't waste any more of your words on me, honey. If you're so concerned about Will, why don't you go talk to him? I'm pretty sure he's still in the house."

The actress shifted uncomfortably. *Gotcha!*

Whether it was the lingering smell of cigarette smoke near the window or the undeniable clink of liquor bottles in a freshman's shower caddy, EJ could always spot the moment someone knew they were well and truly caught. "I mean, he knows you're here, right?" she continued with a small smile. "Because if he doesn't, I'd say you're less of a 'good friend' and more of a stalker with great resources."

"I'm surprising him," Carrie objected.

"And that sounds *super* likely." EJ tented her hands under her chin. "So here's a thought: how about you get the hell out. I'll forget about this pathetic attempt to intimidate me, pretend you weren't even here. That way you won't spoil your surprise, and I can go fuck my boyfriend."

Carrie flushed red, and she struggled for an insult to fling. EJ did not give her the opportunity.

"Out. Now," she insisted, making a shooing motion with her hand. The singer muttered something uncomplimentary and stomped off into the night.

EJ closed her eyes and leaned into the cool tile wall. She was suddenly tired. The adrenaline and righteous anger that carried her through that unpleasant interaction were fading fast. Now, she couldn't deny the possibility of truth in what Carrie said. Perhaps it was best that she and Will had yet to make each other any promises. EJ sighed. Then she remembered the rags still in the sink and quickly collected herself. She had cleanup to do, volunteers to thank, and bake-sale money to count. She was suddenly grateful for the distraction of work.

Will

Outside, next to the Bennet House dumpster, Will stood dumbly, staring at his phone in disbelief. Slowly, he returned it to his ear. "I'm sorry, what?" he exclaimed.

"Carrie's at Longbourn," Katerina repeated. "She thinks she's in disguise—some horrible wig—but I recognized her. I should leak the pictures I got of her looking like a madwoman. She stole my cab at the hotel."

"But we were meeting in New York in two days," he cried. "Why come here?"

"Remember what I said about her obsession, darling? I was speaking the fucking truth." She sucked her teeth in distaste. "That girl is probably skulking around your school, trying to weasel your address out of poor Lee or some such."

Will made a noise of supreme irritation and began to pace. "She has to be stopped!"

"Don't worry, darling," Katerina soothed. "I'll handle her. You just be ready to have that meeting with her tomorrow."

"Just let me know when and where." Will was fully confident in his agent's abilities, especially when she had some sort of advantage.

"Right now, go salvage your night," she advised. "Spend time with that new girlfriend of yours—the good one."

"That's a great idea. I'm going to find Ella right now." Will smiled to himself. "By the way, I've made our relationship public—at least on campus. If Carrie is around looking for a reunion, she'll be in for a nasty shock."

"That will serve her right," Katerina laughed. "And as for your girl-friend, I'll do my best to protect her privacy."

"Thanks," Will replied before disconnecting the call. He then returned inside to find EJ.

The next day's meeting/showdown was held at 9:00 a.m., in the bland conference room of a nearby Holiday Inn Express. He hoped the time and location would tell Carrie that this conversation was strictly busi-ness. At the appointed time, she swanned in, up to her usual standard: casual perfection in a diaphanous top, supertight jeans, and sunglasses, indoors. She paused at the doorframe for admiration. Will regarded her with the flat eyes of a cobra.

Shortly after Katerina's phone call last night, Will had found EJ wiping down the same table over and over. It took some coaxing, but she eventually revealed the whole of her run-in with Carrie. While she hadn't scared EJ away, his ex had succeeded in putting a damper on both EJ's and Will's triumphs. It took a vodka strawberry malt (from Cousin Nicky's), twenty minutes of piano duets, and making out dur-ing most of *Center Stage* to recover the happiness from hours before. Will's feelings toward Carrie had moved from confused vexation to seething anger.

Seemingly unaware of his hostility, Carrie approached him with open arms. "Hello, sweetness!" she cooed. "Isn't this a marvelous coincidence—"

He deftly avoided the embrace and pointed to where Katerina was waiting. "Sit," he softly ordered, gesturing to one side of the conference room table. Disappointed but not fully deterred, she took a seat opposite Will and pouted a little. Katerina, whom Carrie had yet to acknowledge, spoke with unmasked irritation.

"Young lady, you asked for this meeting and paid quite a bit of money for the privilege. What do you want?" the older woman demanded tersely.

The celebrity removed her sunglasses to glare at Katerina before turning pleading eyes to Will. "I was hoping we could speak privately."

"Why?" he barked, leaning back in the squeaking office chair. "There's nothing we have to say to each other that doesn't involve business. Also, you should be a little more respectful. Katerina is the only reason you and I are speaking in any capacity."

"So it's true?" Carrie cried, voice rising. "You've found someone else!"

His eyes narrowed dangerously. "You've got about five hundred miles of nerve," he growled. It was a phrase he'd picked up from EJ, who went slightly southern when irritated. "Do not insult my intelligence and act like you didn't harass and berate my girlfriend last night."

"She told you?" Carrie exclaimed.

"Yes, she did; what does she owe you?" Will shot back. "Besides, we don't keep important things from each other."

"Well, your 'Ella' or whatever was no angel, either," Carrie began. "And since when do you go for girls built like Serena Williams? You can't make that body type chic."

Will felt his face flush. "Do not speak of her, Carrie," he warned. "She's worth ten of you." He sat forward and placed both arms on the table. "In fact, the subject of my personal life is wholly off limits to you. We haven't been anything to each other since you dumped me by proxy, and I am happy with the status quo. The only reason I'm here is because Katerina said you wouldn't leave her alone." He sat back and folded his arms. "Now, with that established, why are we here?"

Taking in Will's, then Katerina's hard expressions, Carrie shrugged off her hopes of reconciliation. "I need intelligence—to get it or to date it," she said plainly. "Somehow my little mishap at the Super Bowl sparked the perception that I'm dumb. All of a sudden every blooper-reel flub or giggly interview has stopped reading 'cute' and started reading 'drooling idiot.'"

Katerina turned to Will. "This is about what I expected," she said.

"But why me?" he broke in.

"Right now, you've got an air of sophistication that you just can't buy, *and* you're actually smart. I need a part of that," the blonde replied. "But you know," she began slyly, "I'm still a much, much bigger star than you. Whatever my current troubles, I have the best team in the business. This would be less of a favor to me—"

Katerina broke in, cutting off the actress's attempt at charm. "Carrie's immediate prospects are too married, too short, or too unknown," she said. "And with your prior connection, you're her best shot for an easy image rehab."

Across the table, Carrie looked from Katerina to Will again before saying, "Essentially, yes."

"Right." The agent started scrolling down the screen of her iPad. "My client has made the impossibility of a romantic relationship clear, but we could move forward with the appearance of a business-centered platonic friendship."

"A heavy stress on 'appearance,'" Will interjected coldly.

Katerina continued. "Young lady, if I've recognized you, then there's no doubt someone has already tipped off TMZ or some such by now. We need to explain your presence here—separate and apart from Will. I've done a little research, and one of your biggest fans is here at Longbourn. According to her Instagram, she wants to be a triple threat, like you. She's been defending you on Twitter like it's her job since you separated yourself from Johnny. She's also in the school's prestigious drama showcase tomorrow afternoon. It's a matinee, so Sir Titus's producer friends can be back in SoHo for a late dinner.

"Here's what will happen: You'll surprise her, congratulate her, take a selfie with her. Show your fans that you reward loyalty; show everyone else that smart people can still respect your talent. If anyone asks us, we'll say you and Will had a mature discussion before you came and that you're working on an exciting new project together."

"Which is?" Carrie impatiently drummed her pointy acrylic nails on the table.

Katerina handed Carrie a small binder. "You're signing on as a producer for Will's PBS show for children. You will provide the following amount"—she slid a folded piece of paper across to Carrie—"and a theme song. You are otherwise silent. Your name will be in the credits, and you will look like you care about education and the arts."

Carrie gave a slight flinch at the number on the page.

"Oh, come now," Katerina said. "That would barely cover your shoe budget for the year. It's really a bargain." The older woman smoothed the lapels of her blazer. "Calm yourself and consider."

Carrie rocked in her chair. "It could work," she said.

"It will, but only if you agree to our next condition," Katerina replied. "That you, or more accurately, your team owes us a year of favors, no questions asked. I pick up the phone, I send an email, they move my mountain."

Carrie flicked her long blonde braid over one shoulder. "Just for Will," she interjected.

"For my roster," Katerina corrected. "Your team is indeed the best at launching a career, but Will won't need their help by summer; he's got momentum. You remember what that's like, dear." Katerina smirked slightly. Will stifled a laugh. It was nice to be on this side of the ambush.

Carrie rubbed her temples, probably thinking of how she could spin this to her momager. "Anything else I can do for you? Would you like my firstborn?"

Oh shit. Will shot Carrie a warning look. Katerina did not enjoy being sassed. The older woman didn't need his help, though. She simply folded her hands and fixed Carrie with a hard, unwavering stare until the singer/actress whispered an apology. Then, after one slow blink of recognition, Katerina spoke again.

"One more thing, Carrie—not a proposal, just a suggestion: no public boyfriends for at least six months. A smart woman can stand on her own two feet. Conversely, there is nothing people respect less than a woman defined by men."

Carrie swallowed audibly. Will suppressed a chuckle. They both knew abstinence wasn't precisely in her nature. Less kind people had put Carrie's name and *nymphomaniac* in the same sentence. Will would never do such a thing, though; he was a progressive, sex-positive man.

Reading the room, Katerina clarified her advice. "I understand. You're young, you like sex. So have lots of sex, but be discreet. Someone not in the public eye. A friend with benefits?" She tapped her pen thoughtfully. "Or better, someone you can control, a gigolo."

Will quietly snorted a laugh.

"What? They have their uses," Katerina said.

Carrie rolled her eyes. "I'll take that under advisement," she replied crisply. "Any other terms of this deal? Conditions?"

"Yes," Will replied shortly. "You stay the hell away."

Carrie started and looked at him with wide eyes. "What do you mean?"

He stood up and leaned halfway across the table. "Stay away from my girlfriend, my friends, my family—anyone in my personal sphere. I will appear friendly in public, but that's all. Remember, we are not really friends."

He returned to his seat and laced his fingers together. "If you violate this condition, I will leave the business, but not before giving a series of interviews detailing how you drove me from the industry. I will paint you as the queen of all desperate, psycho ex-girlfriends—which doesn't seem that far off base right now. I will destroy your mystique and your brand. Then I will move on with my life. Financially, I don't need this, so if you make my life difficult, I have no problem taking us both out."

Carrie inhaled deeply, then stood with all the dignity she could muster. "I'll take your proposals to my team. You'll hear from us soon."

"We'll hear from you within the hour," Katerina corrected. "Otherwise, a blind item asking 'What pop star has started stalking her exes' will go up on fourteen or so gossip sites. Perez Hilton will be the only one with the photos, though. He does not care for you. Come to think of it, neither does the head writer of *SNL*, nor your former costar who's in New York and happens to do a killer impression of you. I think together, they could make a walking joke of you by Monday. It wouldn't be too much trouble."

Will raised his eyebrows, unnerved but impressed.

"Insurance, my love," Katerina reassured her client. "We don't want to give Carrie's people time to bribe everyone."

They looked across to Carrie, but she was already out of her seat, phone in hand, striding angrily out of the conference room.

Will watched her go, shocked that he'd once thought he loved her. "Which one of us changed?"

"Both of you," Katerina responded. "You for the better and her for the worse." The older woman stood and squeezed Will's shoulder, her version of a hug. The actor squeezed her hand in thanks and rose with a slight stagger. He planned to process his feelings later.

"Think she'll play ball?" Will asked as they exited the hotel.

Before Katerina could respond, her phone buzzed. "It's a text message from Carrie's manager," she reported. "They're agreeing to our terms. Carrie may be angry, but her people understand where their bread is buttered. Give me a few minutes to call off the dogs." She walked toward her car with one ear pressed to her phone.

"Sure thing," he said. "After that, let me take you out to lunch."

"Okay, darling. I'll meet you at that gastropub in Northampton you like so much," Katerina said, then hopped into her rental car and peeled out of the parking lot.

Will got in his car and surprised himself with a loud whoop. Right now, at this moment, he was free of Carrie. She didn't have his heart, and she couldn't control his life. "Free!" he shouted out loud, pumping his fist in the air. Then he took a deep breath and called EJ.

EJ

Back at Bennet House EJ was holed up in her room, bingeing *Great British Baking Show*. She loved calm international reality shows. The stakes were always so blissfully low. All morning she'd been getting texts of congratulations from people who'd somehow heard that she was dating Will. On the one hand she wished people would stop acting like she won the lottery, but on the other, she was happy to have the support. Carrie was mean, but she was right. EJ probably didn't fit in Will's world, and for the moment, she didn't really care. There were lots of mismatched couples on campus: she and Will could just be one more. After all, they weren't entering the real world for another six weeks. EJ just wanted a chance to see if they worked.

She was texting about the whole Carrie Dean ordeal with Jamie and Tessa when Will called. He was coming to take her to lunch with Katerina.

Great, now I must try and look cute.

She went to her closet and retrieved the vintage embroidered sweater Maya got her for Christmas, her favorite skirt, purple tights, and her favorite silver flats. (They always made her look like she put in effort.) Then she showered and dressed just in time for Will's arrival. On the ride to lunch, Will told her all about his showdown with Carrie. Later, over matching salads, Katerina seemed to magically determine what EJ was most worried about.

"Part of my job is maintaining Will's privacy, and I am very good at my job. You won't be seeing your name in the headlines anytime soon." She sat back in her chair and explained: "Generally, people get the attention they want in this business. Similarly, the people who don't need the media don't get it. People do this all the time, especially the Australians. Chris Hemsworth has a wife and, like, three kids who stay out of the public eye."

Katerina signaled for the check and kept talking. She seemed to always do two things at once. "What's important right now is that you know I have your back. You are important to him, and so you're important to me, too."

EJ breathed a small sigh. Will squeezed her hand. "Thank you," she replied quietly. Ever since Carrie appeared at Longbourn, EJ had felt out of her depth. Now she had an anchor, an emergency contact. She'd take any comfort she could get in this crazy situation. They finished their salads, and Will deftly paid the check.

"Okay, I'm off," Katerina said, rising and collecting her things in one swift motion. "You two, forget Carrie, and just be with each other. I'm sure you have a lot to talk about."

And then Katerina was gone, like a tough genie in a pantsuit. EJ felt frozen to her seat. Everything that had happened over the last twenty-four hours hit her like a ton of bricks. She'd been threatened by an international celebrity. She'd told off said celebrity. Will had threatened to end someone's career for her. He was willing to walk away from his—for her. Well, maybe not just for her, but . . . It was too much.

"You're shaking," Will said, breaking her reverie.

EJ felt unsteady. "I guess I'm a little overwhelmed," she replied as she put on her spring jacket. Standing up, she let Will guide her out of the restaurant and to his car.

Once the doors were closed, Will offered an idea. "Let's just take thirty seconds to scream at the count of three."

On "three," EJ released all her pent-up anger and anxiety and bewilderment in a prolonged howl. It didn't feel so weird with Will screaming right alongside her. It lasted only thirty seconds or so, but it was very therapeutic.

"Better?" he asked, resting a hand on her knee.

EJ nodded. "Much."

Will leaned over from the driver's seat. "Good," he said. Then he kissed her. It went on for a bit. She sighed as they broke apart.

"Let's not go back to campus right now," she said, dreading the idea of other people. "Let's go . . . somewhere—" She was thinking of a longish drive, maybe to Amherst.

"Let's go to New York!" Will suggested excitedly. He reached for his phone, then showed her the screen after a series of clicks. "I can get tickets for an eight thirty p.m. flight."

Well, this escalated quickly.

EJ tried to protest, but Will had an answer for everything: the tickets would be covered by his airline miles, Monday was a holiday, she didn't have class until Wednesday, and she wasn't on duty until Thursday.

"You know way too much about my life!" she exclaimed. He wasn't wrong, though. There was no reason for her not to do this.

"I told you, I'm very observant," Will replied with a waggle of his eyebrows. Then he took her hands. "Ella, please." He flashed those dimples. "Let me whisk you away for a few days. I want to show you where I grew up, where I get my favorite cup of coffee. I want you to meet Lily."

"Wow." EJ's head was spinning again, but in a good way. If Will wanted her to meet Lily, that meant he was taking them very seriously. It really shouldn't have surprised her, though. He'd just publicly serenaded her in front of all their friends on campus.

I can be a little obtuse sometimes.

"Okay," she replied. It was worth it just to watch his face light up.

❧

She gasped when their taxi pulled up to Will's house. He'd described his home as a classic New York brownstone, which would have been impressive enough, but "the Pemberley house," as he called it, was a gorgeous Gothic revival townhome that would have been slightly too grand for an embassy. Even though it was almost midnight, she insisted on a tour. Will happily obliged, pointing out his favorite features and paintings while EJ exclaimed over all the details.

"I can't believe you *live* in a CPH Gilbert house," she said as they returned to the landing. "If they still built them like this, I would have become an architect."

"Thank you!" exclaimed a voice from the kitchen. Will's sister, Lily, emerged from the kitchen with a couple of bottles of Perrier. Handing them to Will and EJ, she said, "I've only had one friend over from FIT. She asked if Will and I plan to replace that stained-glass window with Pella for more light."

"Did you murder her to cleanse the world of her ignorance?" EJ asked almost sincerely.

"No," Lily laughed. "I just said the house is exactly as we want it."

"You're a much better person than I am." Then she added with a smile, "I'm EJ, by the way," and extended her hand. Lily waved it away and wrapped her in a hug.

"I feel like I know you already. My brother can't stop talking about you. It's always 'EJ this' and 'Ella that.'" She stepped back and adjusted her glasses. EJ noted that they matched her purple hair.

"You make him so happy," Lily whispered after releasing her. EJ gave her another quick, tight hug, in response.

Will, who'd been violently blushing as his sister spoke, piped up. "How about some takeout? Anybody hungry?"

Before long, the trio was eating delicious Indian food in the house's cavernous kitchen. Lily led the conversation—she had an openness and an ease that made EJ want to know her. She instantly understood why Will was protective of his sister and why he was so wrecked by everything that happened with Jordan. Over the course of the evening, Lily led them from dinner and conversation in the kitchen to drinks in the library, and then to playing duets on the family piano in the conservatory.

"Y'all live in the house from *Clue*!" EJ giggled. It was almost two in the morning, and she was a little punchy.

"Ooh! I love *Clue*!" Lily responded, still full of boundless enthusiasm. "We should watch the movie! I'm pretty sure—"

Will, who'd been quietly half dozing while EJ and Lily sang their way through a book of Broadway show tunes, loudly objected to his sister's new plan.

"No!" he cried. "It has been a very long day, and we"—he grabbed EJ's hand—"are going to bed."

"Okay." Lily pouted. "Good night, Will. Good night, EJ."

"Good night," EJ called as she was led to the stairs. She shook her head and turned to Will. "You get really grumpy when you're sleep deprived."

He grunted and waved vaguely in Lily's direction.

That explains so much, EJ thought, remembering Will and his milkshake at Cousin Nicky's.

Once in bed, she curled around him and smiled when Will sighed happily.

He purred into her ear, "You know you've turned me into a cuddler."

She laughed softly. "I like this," she said, beginning her slow drift into sleep. "Fuck, what are we gonna do after graduation?"

Will didn't respond, but EJ thought she felt his eyes pop open in the dark.

Will

Despite being in his own very comfy bed, it took a good bit of tossing and turning before Will got to sleep. He couldn't get EJ's words out of his head. When they started going out, he had no expectations. At best, he thought she would be the perfect rebound after Carrie Dean—an independent, ambitious woman who wasn't interested in showbiz. He imagined that they would connect, spark, and quietly fizzle before going back to their normal lives.

Instead, here he was introducing EJ to his family. He'd been shocked by how much they liked each other, how much they had in common. It wasn't just the superficial stuff like enjoying jazz or liking the same podcasts, but the important stuff: the way they saw the world, how they valued friendship, and loyalty, and good therapy. And it was nice to be in a relationship with someone who wouldn't downplay or ignore the racist stuff he regularly encountered in his career. The closer he got to graduation, the more Will knew that they needed to talk about what they each saw happening next.

We need a plan, he thought. *We'll talk about it tomorrow.* Only after making this promise to himself was Will finally able to fall asleep.

‿

It was raining on their first morning in New York, so Will and EJ spent it in his "ginormous bed." Lily delivered fresh bagels to their room before going to class, and Will had to physically stop EJ from going to the kitchen to toast hers. He stood in front of the bedroom door and held the bagels over his head protectively.

"Poppy seed, with butter, toasted: that is my standard bagel order," she said.

"You don't toast fresh bagels!" Will countered. He was holding the bag aloft. "These are perfect! These are a miracle! I will not let you ruin one."

EJ bounced on her toes, snatching at the bag, but he moved it out of her reach. "Give me my bagel!"

Will relented; he knew her hanger was real and could be dangerous. "Just try one without toasting it. Okay?" He lowered his arms and fished out the poppy-seed bagel.

"Is there butter?" she asked expectantly. Will handed her the take-away tub of butter and a plastic knife. Glancing between him and her prize, EJ sliced her bagel in half and buttered the bottom. Will dug out his plain bagel with the perfect schmear of cream cheese and watched as she ate. After the first bite EJ paused and seemed to look at her bagel in disbelief. She glanced at Will, who couldn't help his smirk, and then back at her bagel.

"Okay, fine, don't look so smug," she said before devouring the remainder of her bottom slice. She crawled back into bed and patted the space beside her.

"Your sister is a doll, by the way," she said, leaning against the head-board. "I mean, I love Maya, but I would not be bringing her bagels at God-knows in the morning, if she were home."

Will laughed, and he settled next to her. EJ was many things, but a morning person was not one of them. "She's an amazing person. I'm so glad you two get along."

"Me too," EJ agreed, chewing another bite of bagel thoughtfully. "Can we talk about this weekend? In the past two days, you had me meet Katerina and Lily. Since I already know Lee, I think I've now met the most important people in your life. Is there anyone left? I mean, I know you don't get along with your dad."

Will's shoulders fell like they always did when his dad came up. He felt a sudden need to look out the window at the rain.

"You don't have to talk about it." She placed a comforting hand on his knee.

"No, I want to." He squeezed it and sighed. "It's just a sadly typical story. My dad dumped my mom for a younger woman. That was bad enough, but what's worse is that she was the receptionist at my mother's oncologist. Mom had breast cancer. She needed to have a lump removed. It was early, so there was lots of hope, but she was still terrified. I'd never seen her so scared before."

EJ moved closer, wrapping an arm around his waist. She didn't speak, and he couldn't until she dropped a couple of encouraging kisses on his shoulder. Will found his voice and started again.

"Up to this point in my young life, even I knew that my father was . . . less than attentive. Now, suddenly he's a new man. Taking her to every appointment, showering her with gifts afterward . . . I thought he'd changed. That the cancer was bringing them together. The worst part was, she did, too." Will paused and swallowed. His anger stung more than his sorrow. His mother didn't die from the cancer. She found out about the affair and divorced his dad while going through chemo. She even had a new boyfriend when she died in the car crash. But his father's heartlessness still infuriated him.

"I never could forgive him. Still can't. Even though she survived the cancer. Mom was the one who tried to make sure we had a relationship, despite everything. After she died in the car crash, he was pretty much dead to me, too. He wasted no time moving on with the receptionist. I went to live with Lee because there was no way I could live with him

315

after that. He agreed to whatever I wanted, as long as I somehow graduated from Hanover. I think I can count on one hand how many times I've spoken to him since my high school graduation. Lily is willing to speak with them. I attended one Thanksgiving and spent the whole time trying not to flip the table. I think they're better without me."

Will heaved a sigh and leaned back against the headboard. "That's why it'll only be me and Lily at graduation." He turned to EJ wearily. "He tried to take Pemberley from us, twice: during the divorce and then after Mom died."

EJ looked at him in shock. "From his own kids?"

"Yup. Thankfully, we were protected because of my mom's iron-clad prenup." Will shook his head. "She let it slip once that she wasn't even going to bother with one but one of my great-aunts warned her that Robinson men tend to think of infidelity as a hobby. Grandma Robinson put up with it because she was Catholic but—"

EJ suddenly looked confused. "Wait, who?"

"My paternal grandma."

"Did she keep her maiden name?"

Will gave a little laugh. "There's something you should know. My dad was adopted by a wealthy middle-aged Connecticut family in the seventies. Legally, he's Daniel Robinson. My real name is Will Robinson."

EJ gaped at him. "For real?"

"Scout's honor. There was no way I was acting with my dad's name. That was one of the conditions of my release. I would have gone with my mom's last name, but Katerina said it's easy to mispronounce, which can start auditions off badly. She chose Pak."

She mulled over this small revelation. "So Will Robinson?"

"No *Lost in Space* jokes," he interjected.

"Me? I would never." She looked at him thoughtfully and said the name again. "Will Robinson . . . huh. I have to admit: EJ Davis-Robinson doesn't have the same ring as EJ Davis-Pak."

Will blinked in response. *So she is thinking beyond graduation—far beyond.* He was surprised to find that he was excited about this and not scared.

EJ tried to furiously backpedal, and it was hilarious. "Not that I'm thinking that far ahead, just talking, having fun, because I'm a fun person." She continued sputtering until she ran out of words.

"I've never seen you so flustered," he said in mocking wonder. "It was kind of beautiful."

EJ slapped his arm.

"Seriously, though, Ella," he continued. "You don't have to hide thinking about us beyond Longbourn. I'm not ready to let you go, either." He lifted their clasped hands and kissed her knuckles. "In fact, I think we should talk about the future."

Almost instantly, EJ tensed. She was more than flustered; she seemed to be panicking.

"But there's so much we don't know," she quailed. "Like where we'll even be in three months. I may be back in DC, Chicago, maybe even Scotland—in the unlikely event that I get that Fields Fellowship. And you could be literally anywhere. Either with acting or a grad program. Why focus on the darkness, when we can enjoy the sunset?"

"But," Will countered, "if we don't talk about the darkness, how are we going to find our way back to the campground . . . because we don't have flashlights, or a map, or a way out of this metaphor?" They laughed. He turned to face her and took both of her hands. "Let's just try, okay? Like it says on that poster by your door."

She shook her head. "I can't believe you're using the House commandments against me."

"Not against you, for us," he countered.

"Okay, okay," EJ agreed. "And since we're putting our cards on the table, I'm not ready to end things, either."

Will smiled. He couldn't help it; he felt like fireworks were going off in his stomach.

EJ continued. "I know a clean break after graduation is the smart thing, but then I look at you." She stroked his face and sighed. "I could happily make some really bad decisions chasing you."

They were quiet again when Will offered a compromise. "Okay, so if we don't talk about the future, capital *F*, let's talk about possible futures. Like a future in which we keep this going after graduation. Maybe one in which we're both in New York?"

"I could see that," EJ replied with a smile. "Especially if the future includes more fresh bagels."

"Could you see yourself out west?" Will asked.

"I think so." EJ leaned back against her pillow thoughtfully. "I could do San Francisco, Seattle, even Vancouver—I've heard good things." She smiled at him. "How about you?"

"I could do any of those places. I also like San Diego."

"I could try it—but not LA," EJ added firmly.

"Agreed. Never LA, not permanently anyway."

"Nashville?" EJ suggested.

"Why?"

"I have family in Tennessee. Besides, this is the time of life when you try stuff."

Will squinted. "Can't see Nashville, sorry."

"Well," EJ began in a conciliatory tone. "Should we somehow not end up in the same place, I could even see doing long distance, calling every day, seeing each other on the long weekends."

"I think I could see that, too," he agreed. "Especially if we're in the same time zone. Given my work, we'd probably have to factor in some long-distance periods, no matter what."

EJ bit her lip thoughtfully. "Yeah, but for, like, permanent long distance—not work travel—I think I could do up to three time zones, East to West Coast, but no more than that."

"And now you've identified a deal breaker," Will summarized. "See, little talks like this can be really helpful."

"It was," she agreed with a kiss. Then she looked behind Will, out the window. "You know what's perfect for a rainy day? Museums! Why don't you take me to see some art, handsome?"

Will agreed, but then EJ's phone rang.

"Dia? No, I'm not on campus, but we can talk now." She sat down on the bed and signaled that they weren't going anywhere for a little while. Will made no secret of his annoyance, but then EJ said something that stopped him in his tracks.

"Jordan's gone—with Carrie Dean?" EJ looked at Will with wide eyes. He sank into a nearby armchair. "Wow, that *is* a lot. Tell me what happened."

Jamie

It took almost a month for things at Bennet House to get back to normal after the Girly Show, and it wasn't just because of EJ and Will. On the Sunday of that weekend, Carrie Dean made a "surprise" appearance on campus to support Dia. As everyone knew at the house, Dia was chief of the Deaniacs, so this made her life. Jamie had gone to support Dia with a large contingent of Bennet Women from their floor. And Jamie was so glad she went; Dia was incredible. She had one of the best scenes onstage that night.

After the show, Jamie was giving Dia a big bouquet of flowers from their floor when who should saunter over but Carrie Dean. Knowing everything that Carrie had said and done to EJ, Jamie discreetly gave her the finger and left. Dia, however, completely melted when she met Carrie. Rumor had it that Carrie even came to the showcase after-party and hung out with Sir Titus and the class. Then *Carrie* shared the selfie she'd taken on IG. Jamie fully expected Dia to be riding the high of the showcase until she flew back to Utah for the summer, so it was a shock to see Dia looking like a heap of black eyeliner and tears for a full week after the showcase. It just didn't make any sense. Jamie was so curious that she resolved to ask EJ about it during their next waffle brunch. It didn't feel too nosy since EJ had her own Carrie Dean incident.

✑

"From what Dia told me, everything was great until her parents turned up. After talking with Dylann, Will helped fly them out," EJ explained, half whispering. "They surprised Dia in her dressing room. Her dad cried and told her he was proud of her. She was super happy, but after a while, she noticed that Jordan was being really weird. He refused to go get dinner with them even though Dia knew Jordan didn't have plans." EJ took a quick sip of her soda. "It's like Will said, Jordan can really only get his hooks into someone if they have no one else. Once he saw that Dia's family was back in her life, well, it was too much work."

Tessa gasped. "OMG, is Will the one who invited Carrie—to distract Jordan?"

EJ barked with laughter and shook her head. "*Hell* no. Carrie and Jordan meeting was just a crazy coincidence. He sure kicked Dia to the curb as soon as he got a good look at Carrie Dean, though. I guess he was desperate, starstruck, or both. Anyway, once Carrie and Jordan started talking, she totally ignored Dia and was even borderline rude to her. Never meet your idols, I guess." She shook her head. "Anyway, Carrie must have been pretty into Jordan, because she took him back to LA like a souvenir."

Jamie raised her eyebrows. "So he just dropped everything and followed Carrie Dean?"

EJ nodded. "He dropped everything, including Dia. At first, he ghosted her for like a week; then when he called, he basically tried to order Dia to lie for him and smooth things over with Sir Titus. Lots of super-manipulative bullshit about loyalty, how he carried her in class, how she owed him."

Jamie shook her head sadly. "Poor Tinkerbelle."

EJ continued the story. "Thankfully, I was able to get ahold of Dia's sister. Will flew her up and got them a spa weekend in Vermont. Dylann took Dia and basically deprogrammed her. She's been doing much better since the trip."

"Will to the rescue again?" Tessa asked, impressed.

"I know, right?" EJ replied.

Jamie put her hand up. "Wait, Dia is better?" she exclaimed. "When I last saw her, she was wearing a black veil."

EJ's head bounced between a nod and a shrug. "Yeah, but she went to all her classes, took all her exams, and packed up her room. I think she's even said something about working on cruise ships this summer. Dia came back to herself, in the end. We've seen worse, right, Tessa?"

Tessa blotted her mouth with her napkin and nodded grimly. For the first time Jamie wondered about all the stuff RAs saw that they couldn't talk about for privacy's sake. They probably knew the lives of everyone on their floor, if not everyone at Bennet House.

EJ picked up the story again. "Anyway, when she got back from Vermont, Dia told Sir Titus the truth about Jordan—and he was *pissed.* All I can say is things better work out with him and Carrie, because Jordan essentially got himself blackballed in the NYC theater community."

"Well, we can all be thankful for one thing," Tessa said. "Carrie and Jordan found each other."

Jamie sipped her iced tea and nodded. "It's beautiful when two shitty people take themselves out of the dating pool."

"We don't even have to worry about Jordan wrecking Carrie's life. From everything Will's said, Carrie's momager will have Jordan defanged before the plane lands in Cali," EJ added. "Good riddance to bad rubbish, I say."

Tessa snorted. "I swear, Eej, sometimes I think you must be twenty-two going on fifty." She shook her head with mirth. "Anyway, Jamie, you said you had news."

Indeed, she did: her postgraduate life was finally starting to come together. She knew where she was going to be in the fall. All she had to do was cross that stage, and not even her transphobic—and sexist—advisor could stop her now.

"I got the Dramaturgy Fellowship at the Shakespeare in DC, and Lee got accepted to the master's program at Johns Hopkins. We're picking those programs and staying together."

EJ screamed. Several heads whipped around, but she didn't seem to care.

"This is so great!" she said, hopping up to give Jamie a hug. "I'm so happy for you; the Shakespeare does great work. And I'm happy for Lee, too! I'm happy for the both of you—together." She clapped enthusiastically. "Just know that you can stay with my parents if you need to. I know it's in the boring suburbs, but I don't want you to ever feel trapped in a bad-roommate situation. They know you and love you," EJ assured her.

"Thanks for that, Eej."

"High fives all over the place, J!" Tessa agreed.

Jamie smiled. She was truly happy. If you'd told her a year ago that she'd be leaving campus with her first post-transition boyfriend, Jamie would have laughed in disbelief. Yet here she was, with the support of her best friends and Lee at her side. Still, she couldn't help feeling a teensy, tiny bit nervous about moving back into the real world. It was hard enough being a trans woman on campus. Yes, DC looked like it was a pretty safe city for her with a strong LGBTQ community, but you never knew—you never could know. That was just how life was, being herself in a world that was hostile to her. But even if she didn't have Bennet House anymore, she'd always be a Bennet Woman. Jamie would just have to carry that with her into the next adventure. (She was confident that she'd have EJ and Tessa, too.)

"Okay, that's enough about me. Eej, what's going on with you?" Jamie asked.

EJ picked at her afro a bit before speaking. "The good news is I've got no finals, and I'm pretty sure I'm getting some kind of 'laude' on my degree." She did a little shimmy. While normal people would have been happy just to have an engineering degree from Longbourn (it was a fucking hard program), Jamie's bestie had been talking about graduating with honors since orientation.

Tessa and Jamie both gave her high fives.

"Congrats, gir—lady; you earned it!" Tessa exclaimed.

"Thanks, doll. I'm just so relieved. When you're working toward something for four years, *happy* doesn't quite describe what you feel when everything goes right." She leaned back in her chair and sighed. "Now I just have my Fields Fellowship interview—thanks for sitting through my new presentation, by the way. It really helped."

"Of course," Jamie responded encouragingly. "Anything for the cause." She thought this fellowship would be good for Eej. Sure, she was still working way too hard, but she was inspired. She kept coming up with new ideas and writing down new areas to study when she started her grad-school program. If Jamie's bestie was destined to be a workaholic, she at least wanted her to be a happy one.

EJ nudged Tessa. "Hey, Lady T, don't you have some of your own news to share?"

Tessa nodded, brushing her new bangs out of her face. (She'd gotten herself an amazing pixie cut.) "Well, EJ already knows, but I got a yes from Bryce Canyon National Park: you are looking at their Summer Stargazing Program intern. After a semester of looking at Colin's IG pics from Sydney, I decided that I didn't want to be in a lab this summer."

"That's awesome!" Jamie exclaimed.

EJ bumped Tessa with her elbow. "If I make this road-trip thing happen, I'm going to crash on your floor," she said half-jokingly. EJ was still trying to figure out her solo cross-country trip, looking for friends to stay with at every stop between Maryland and San Diego.

Tessa placed her hands on her heart. "You will always have a place on my air mattress, Eej."

Jamie chuckled. "I want postcards from both of you, as soon as I have my new address." Her fellowship at the Shakespeare started in July.

In just a couple of months, she was going to have to be a real adult. Thankfully, her fellowship came with housing—but still!

Do I need to buy business clothes? Do I even like business clothes? Somehow the idea of getting an office wardrobe depressed her. She looked across to Tessa; something had gotten her down, too.

"We haven't discussed our bad news yet: this is our last ever Longbourn waffle brunch together." Tessa heaved a big sigh. "I'm going to miss you both so much!"

Jamie reached out and squeezed her hand. It wasn't going to be easy for Tessa next year, but at least she still had Bennet House.

Bennet House! At that thought, Jamie sat up straight and tried to catch EJ's eye.

"We'll stay in touch, hon," EJ told Tessa, pulling her into a side hug. She looked as sad as Tessa did. (EJ *really* wasn't good at goodbyes.) Jamie coughed and finally got EJ's attention.

"Especially since you'll be upholding the grand traditions of the house next year, which reminds me . . ." EJ reached under the empty chair at their table and retrieved an eleven-by-seventeen gift-wrapped box.

"Aww, you two." Tessa sighed as she ripped away the paper. Slowly she revealed their present. "Are these the house commandments, *in embroidery?*"

EJ gave another little shimmy. "I did the needlework; Jamie did the frame. She covered it in little paper butterflies and decoupaged."

Tessa gaped at EJ. "I can't believe you embroidered the whole thing—in cursive!"

"It was really relaxing," EJ replied.

Tessa then looked at Jamie warmly. "You crafted for me, J?" She laughed. "You hate crafting more than EJ hates a cappella."

Jamie couldn't help her grin. This reaction had been worth a few lousy hours at the campus craft center. "We had to give you something cool to remember us by."

Tessa teared up a little. "I know this sounds so summer camp, but you want to know what my Hearth Night wish was? That the three of us would be friends forever."

EJ dropped her head on Tessa's shoulder. "Oh no, you're gonna make me cry."

Me too, Jamie thought. So, to avoid royally fucking up her makeup, she lifted her coffee mug in a toast. "And so we will!"

"And so we will," said Tessa.

EJ took a moment to get her mug. "And so we will," she echoed. "We're goddamn Bennet Women."

Tessa went home the next day. Jamie came to realize that, as they moved out of finals and into Senior Week, every day was going to be her last "something." Like today was probably going to be the last time she and EJ were hanging out in her single, just shooting the shit. Jamie was packing up her room and moving into Lee's until graduation. EJ wasn't leaving Bennet House until she had to, but Will wasn't going to be back on campus until Senior Week, anyway. Life had come at him fast after the Girly Show.

A week before final exams, someone had posted the video of Will's piano performance online—and it blew up. (Thankfully, the thoughtful uploader had removed any mention of EJ.) Celine Dion retweeted it, and it got over a million views in three days. Suddenly, Will had his pick of TV appearances and pitch meetings. Netflix even announced that they were going to start streaming Will's old show *Band Camp*. He was presently away from campus making the most of his spike in marketability.

"Are you guys making plans?" Jamie ventured. She'd watched EJ fall for Will with the same level of excitement and trepidation that she usually reserved for Olympic figure skating. It was clear to her—even if it wasn't to them—that they were in love. But they were killing her with their mutual refusal to risk anything, Love required risk. It required someone being willing to look foolish. She wasn't sure that either of them was capable of that. Even now, watching EJ frown and hesitate, she knew that her bestie's mind was at war with her heart in how to proceed.

"We've decided not to change anything until the end of the summer," EJ replied. "By that time, I should know where I'll be living for the foreseeable future, hopefully." She plucked a bit of lint from her sundress. "For now, we're just going to enjoy what we have."

Jamie smiled, but she was unconvinced. EJ returned her smile and chuckled lightly. "I know you don't like my approach, J, but I can only be who I am."

She softened. "And I love who you are. That's why I wanted to make sure that you and I had a heart-to-heart before Senior Week and all the related craziness kicks in."

Jamie swallowed. *What do you say to someone who's been your everything for four years?* They had become friends on the first day of freshman orientation. EJ had walked her drunk ass home from every party freshman year. She was there for Jamie through her whole flippin' transition. Words couldn't contain how much EJ meant to her. Still, the moment needed something.

"I feel like I should make some sort of speech or something, but if I start talking, I'll never stop." She took EJ's hands and squeezed.

EJ sniffed. "I don't know what to say, either; nothing seems adequate." She went quiet, thinking for a bit, before making the "live long and prosper" sign with her hand. "Oh no! I'm spacing on the quote." She giggled. "Just know I'm gonna be your friend forever, okay?"

Jamie snort giggled. "Oh my God, you nerd. I thought we could get through this without a *Star Trek* reference."

EJ gave a small smile. "You're my very favorite person that I'm not related to," she offered. "If you want to see me cry, watch me try and start packing up my room."

Jamie raised her eyebrows. "*You* haven't started packing?" she exclaimed. Dorms closed in less than ten days. Usually, EJ had everything packed or sold too early and was living out of one suitcase for the last week of finals.

"I know," she wailed. "But I have the Fields Fellowship interview at MIT this Wednesday, so I'm focused on that. Then there's still Senior Week and the Gala. And, honestly, every time I get going, I'll stumble upon some sort of memento, and I end up weeping into a T-shirt." She shook her head. "I could use the help of a dear friend."

"Of course! Like I'd ever say no!" Jamie laughed. "So how are you feeling about the interview?"

"My presentation, I'm solid. I'm confident in my Q-and-A period. Now I just have to look the part. I'm going to Boston a day early for hair and nail appointments—I'd love for you to look at my top two outfits before I go."

"Anything you need, Eej," Jamie replied. "That's what friends are for."

THE INTERVIEW
AND AFTER

EJ

EJ made her way through the lobby of whatever brutalist academic building she was in before bursting into tears. The number of postgraduate uncertainties had been reduced by one: she would not be joining this year's class of Fields Fellows—not after how everything had just gone sideways in the interview.

If only I hadn't lost it in there.

She hurried to the parking lot, awkwardly half running in her dress heels, and rounded the corner to see both Jamie and Will standing outside her car with bright smiles. They'd come to surprise her. He was holding a bouquet of flowers, and Jamie had a sign that said **Go, EJ, Go!** It was mortifying. She felt the tears running down her face before she could stop them. She looked at the sign and shook her head. "Can we just drive somewhere?"

She let Jamie take the wheel and slumped into the passenger seat. They rode in tense silence, until she finally decided to tell her friends what had happened.

"Everything had gone pretty decently through the presentation. The interview questions were not great but not bad—I mean, I had an answer for everything. The problem was the last question. The youngest guy on the panel—probably some tech asshole—holds up the written portion of my presentation and says, 'This, plus the models you have there, is a hell of a lot of work for a Longbourn engineer who is also a resident advisor and does all the activities you listed. I feel I would not be doing my duty if I didn't ask: Did you have any help? Maybe a friend in the program looked it over. A boyfriend even?'"

"The fuck?" Will exclaimed.

Jamie sucked her teeth. "I wonder if he asked the parade of dudes they interviewed how much their girlfriends helped?" she said sarcastically.

"My thoughts exactly. And usually I can let this sort of thing go, but today, I couldn't hold myself back." She ran over her flat-twist updo anxiously.

"So I swallow hard, and I'm quiet for long enough that a couple panel members exchange glances; then I say, 'I'll answer the question you asked: My boyfriend is an art history major who uses an app on his phone to calculate the tip on our dinner bill. No, he didn't help with my project or my presentation. It was all my work, and it was really hard, as you acknowledged, with all my other obligations. But I'm used to it; I've been working my tail off for four years. That's because if you're a woman, especially a black woman, in the sciences, you never get to coast. There's always someone asking you to show your work or trying to poke holes in your conclusions. If the work is sound, then they ask if it's yours. After years of this, I knew I had to submit a project that was wholly mine, from conception to execution.'

"Then I turn and look directly at the tech bro. 'Now that I have answered the question you've asked, I'll respond to the one you're implying: Aren't you just here so we can say we tried to improve diversity?'"

She paused and swallowed. "I let the question hang there for a moment. 'You probably think you're the first person who has asked, but I've had three TAs, one professor, and at least a dozen of my classmates ask me this question in some form or another. Usually, I have a gracious response that demonstrates my credentials without making them feel bad for saying something so offensive *to my face*. However, I don't feel like being gracious today. I know how very, very good I am, and today, I'm not staying humble.'

"'Instead, I'd like to make a bet with this panel: You're interviewing thirty people in this final round, correct?' Someone nods. 'Okay, if my grades, my résumé, and my project are in the top five—no, make that the top three—submitted, make me a Fields Fellow. Anything less than that, pass on me. Throw out any other criteria: my glowing recommendations, my community service, even improving the diversity of the fellowship class.'

"'You may think that is a huge risk, but I know a few things most of this panel does not. You only get this lesson if you have black parents: Talent can get you into the room, but it won't help you stay; hard work can keep you in the room, but it won't win you any prizes. To soar high, to get noticed, you must be consistently excellent. That's how I know I'll win our little wager. If I wasn't one of the best, you'll see this weekend. I wouldn't have made it inside here in the first place.' Then I said thank you and left."

EJ sank into her seat and dropped her head back.

Will and Jamie were both quiet. Then her friend said, "That doesn't sound so bad, Eej. I mean, everything you said was true, and I don't think you sounded unreasonable. That was a shit question."

"Yeah," Will agreed. "And you said everything else went pretty well. I don't think that one response should knock you out."

"Trust me, it's not happening. My questioner did not appreciate me calling him out. I'm sure he's lobbying against me." EJ paused. "Even though I didn't yell, I'm sure someone in that room saw me as another angry black woman, too bitter to represent the program." She slumped miserably in her seat and stared ahead. "I didn't even find out when they're posting the winners."

Will took her hand and said, "Hey," until she met his eyes. "I'm not going to tell you to cheer up. But I do want you to know that you.

Are. Fucking. Brilliant." He punctuated his words with a kiss to each knuckle.

"Those Fields people would be lucky to have you," he continued. "If they don't get that now, they will when you're doing something incredible ten years down the road. Until then, fuck 'em."

She smiled weakly (but sincerely) in response and turned on the radio. They listened to *Ask Me Another* for the ride back to campus. Jamie dropped off EJ and Will at his sublet.

"I'm sure you kids have a bit of 'reuniting' to do. Eej, I'll drive your car back to Bennet."

EJ could only wave in thanks as Will scooped her up in a fireman's carry and brought her inside.

"I've been dreaming about this," he said before drawing her into a searing kiss.

She rested against him when they broke apart.

"I love your hair, by the way. Your braids are cool, but your afro can do so many things."

EJ smiled up at him brightly. "Thank you." She'd made a point to wear her hair out when Will got back to campus. Hair acceptance was the last hurdle they had to clear. Maya said that no black girl could feel truly secure in an interracial relationship until that happened. As per usual, she was right.

Will smiled back warmly. "Let's go to bed," he suggested. "Only to sleep—I know you're probably not in the mood right now. I'd just like to hold you."

She squeezed his hand. "You have my enthusiastic yes," EJ said, leading the way to his bedroom.

∽

It took a couple of days of moping and fried food, but eventually EJ was able to put her disappointment about the Fields Fellowship to the side and try to enjoy her last days at Longbourn. It was Senior Week, and time seemed to speed up.

First was the president's tea, where a provost congratulated her on making the Fields Fellow short list. "No matter what happens, young lady, you have been listed among the best," he said before taking the last lemon tart. This was the first comforting thing anyone had been able to reach her with since her disastrous interview. It was enough to help her truly put aside the loss.

She'd given it her best shot, and if she lost on the fellowship because she'd stood up for herself, then so be it. If she really wanted to work in sustainability, she could just tailor her job search that way. Same thing with working in historical building conservation. Once she calmed down, EJ realized there were other paths to where she wanted to go besides a Fields Fellowship. The most important thing was she now wanted something. She'd ditched the tunnel vision but found a direction for her career.

After the tea, the events just kept coming: there was Candles on the Quad, the unromantic distribution of caps and gowns, shopping for degree frames, and finally, Senior Gala (which came with much less frenzy than the Fall Formal).

Jamie wore the green gown from her mother and took lots of pictures. EJ wore a yellow A-line gown that spun beautifully. When she came down the steps at Bennet House, Will looked at her in such an openly loving way that she wanted to cry.

"You're so, so beautiful," he sighed. "And I'm so, so lucky."

"How about happy, gorgeous?" she asked. "Are you happy?"

He kissed her again in a way that helped her understand the concept of swooning. "Deliriously. Ready to go?"

She nodded. "Let's go show some pins who's boss!" They went for a round of pre-gala bowling in formal wear. Will had the best time.

At the Senior Gala, EJ danced with abandon: her best friend on one side, her boyfriend on the other. She didn't care how she looked, only the feeling as she moved. This was the promise of college fulfilled. Not the one about education and work prospects or alumni networks and informational interviews. This promise was the one made by movies, and music, and well-meaning adults who told her how much fun she'd have after high school, that one day she would feel young and beautiful and spectacularly alive. That she could unconsciously lose herself in this sea of people. She was the movement of her dress, the roll of her shoulders, and her laughing smile. She was confident and unselfconscious in a way that felt impossible 99 percent of the time. The song changed again. EJ stretched her arms upward, closed her eyes, and kept dancing.

Finally, she arrived at the day before graduation. The campus became strange, with children and strollers and the occasional dog. Parents streamed in and out of Bennet House, catching glimpses of who their daughters had been for nine months out of the year. EJ's family (Mom, Dad, Maya, and her cousin Gigi) met Will and Lily and embraced them both warmly. She gave her mother and Lily an anecdote-filled tour of Bennet House when they were supposed to be moving out while Will and Mr. Davis packed her things into the family car. Once they were done, she turned in her keys. She stood on the lawn and took one long, last look at Bennet House.

"Thank you," she whispered. "For everything."

As if in response, her phone buzzed. She had a voice mail from Stella. "Wooooooooo!" Her voice was slightly tinny through the speakers. "They just posted the winners on their website. You did it, EJ! I knew you could." EJ walked to her car and listened with a furrowed brow.

"Are you okay if I announce it when you walk tomorrow?" Stella asked. "I think it's a bigger deal than graduating summa cum laude. I mean, laudes don't get more summa than a Fields Fellowship."

Realization finally dawned. EJ dropped her phone and started screaming. Maya rushed out of the car, followed by Will and the rest of their family.

"Oh my God!" She let herself collapse back onto the grass. "Oh *my God.*" She repeated the phrase over and over as her very concerned loved ones tried to find out what had happened. She couldn't say the words herself, so she opened her email on her phone and found the acceptance letter. She handed the phone to Maya, who began to read out loud.

"'Dear Ms. Davis'"—her sister's voice was trembling—"'on behalf of the selection committee, we are pleased to inform you that you have been chosen as one of this year's Emerson Fields Fellows . . .'" She didn't get any further. Everyone else began cheering. Maya and Will each offered her a hand up. Once she was upright, her dad pulled her into a tight hug.

"I knew you could do it, Little Lizard." His voice was near tears. Her mom was full-on crying when she joined the embrace. One by one they joined the group hug, offering joyful congratulations. EJ needed them to hold her up. You could have knocked her over with a feather. She'd truly and wholly counted herself out, but she was wrong; she was wonderfully, beautifully wrong.

SUMMER

A Surprise

EJ had been home long enough to unpack from college, but she wasn't in a rush to do much else. She'd booked a solo train trip up the California coast in mid-June, but everything else was wide open. Right now, her big debate was whether she should road-trip across the country to LA or simplify her life with a five-hour flight and just see the West Coast. Part of her still wanted to do the big road trip, but another part just wasn't sure if she was up for that much solo travel in the US. She didn't feel like thinking about it, honestly. Instead, this morning she was outside, weeding her mother's vegetable garden at the rear of the house. It was pleasantly mindless work that she could do while listening to a theater podcast. She moved quickly, wanting to get it done before the mosquitoes took too much notice of her.

This peaceful exercise was interrupted by a call to the house phone. EJ dusted the damp earth off her knees and went inside.

"Hello, Davis residence," she answered, old habits never dying.

"Hi, Eej," Will greeted her.

She couldn't hold back her smile. Will just had that effect on her, even though he called at least once a day. So far dating long distance, DC to New York, hadn't been very painful. They were still together and progressing nicely. She was even getting to know Will's sister better.

"Hey, hottie, how are you?"

"Very well, my alliterative darling—I have good news and bad news."

"Oh dear, is the bad news about your Memorial Day visit?"

"No, we'll get to that in round two. My bad news is that your front tire looks really low. You should probably get some air in it soon." EJ shrieked and rushed to the kitchen window with the cordless phone. She saw Will waving from the gravel drive, then shrieked again and ran outside and saw him standing in front of a Winnebago. Will took advantage of her surprised expression to kiss her ferociously.

"I'll explain," he began after they broke apart. "Good news first?"

"Sure," she said, sliding her hands around his waist.

"I'm going to be the host of a new summer show for NBC: *Celebrity Karaoke Challenge*."

"That's amazing!" EJ exclaimed.

"Yeah, basically someone on the production team saw that Celine video, which put me on their radar, and then the first choice dropped out last minute."

EJ tilted her head and considered. "This is very good news. What's the bad news?"

"I have to be on set June twelfth."

That was bad news. So far, they'd been able to see each other every other weekend: meeting in either Philly or New York. "So this will be our first real taste of long-distance dating."

He nodded. "Training wheels will come off." They shared rueful smiles. "But"—Will squeezed her hands and made his pitch—"what if, instead of spending a week in New York before doing your America-by-rail trip, we take this baby across the country, together? If we left in two days, we'd have a leisurely ten for the drive to LA. You could stay with me in Cali and then take your train up the coast. You'd still be able to fly back home in time for your family reunion in July."

Reflexively, EJ was going to say that she couldn't afford an extra couple of weeks in LA, but then she remembered for graduation her parents, uncles, aunts, and Granny Liz all chipped in for a very generous cash gift. They highly approved of the studious striver taking her version of a summer off.

Instead she hesitated with a question. "What am I going to do in LA?"

"Disneyland?" At his girlfriend's flat expression, Will tried a different tack. "You could see the set, meet the staff, quietly stake your claim."

She tilted her head again. "I'd like to see where you work, but not in a gross territorial way. You know that."

"True," Will conceded, giving her a squeeze with the arm he still had around her waist. "You could be in a studio audience, maybe for *Jeopardy!* or *The Price Is Right*."

EJ straightened with interest. Now Will had struck gold. Children without cable grew up loving their TV for two reasons: *Sesame Street* and game shows. Still, she tried to play it cool and not envision her own hysterical run down the aisle.

"Let's say I'm persuadable. What about logistics? Will this be fun for both of us if it's just the two of us driving?"

Will stroked his chin thoughtfully. "Hm, it's too bad I hadn't thought of that—except I have!" As if on cue, Lily hopped out of the passenger side.

"Hi, EJ," she greeted her.

"Hi—you've been there the whole time? You could have come out."

Lily tossed a wry glance at her brother and adjusted her glasses. "No, I could not. This thing has been highly choreographed."

"Lily is going to come west for the summer, too."

"Katerina got us a sweet house rental when she lined this up for Will. Mom's brownstone is great, but it doesn't have a pool. Besides, I've never been to California."

EJ looked back at Will, who seemed a bit too pleased with himself. "Okay, let's say I'm amenable. It's not fair to Lily to stick her with a goopy couple. Let me call Tessa. She's going to be interning at Bryce

Canyon in Utah, and I know she got refundable plane tickets—if she's down, I'm down. I'll even cover her BoltBus from New York." EJ dug for her phone and dialed, jumping about a foot when she heard Tessa's ringtone chirp from the back of the Winnebago.

"Surprise!" Tessa cried as she hopped out.

EJ gaped at her friend, then turned back to a smirking Will. "You ridiculous person," she said, kissing him anyway. "I guess we're going on a road trip." Everyone cheered.

"Y'all come inside," EJ said, leading the way to the house. "There's lemonade, and we can start looking at itineraries—and I can tell my mom we're having people over."

"There's no need. I've booked a hotel," Will countered.

"Ha!" Tessa scoffed. "EJ's mom is the model of southern hospitality, and EJ's dad isn't just gonna let you whisk his baby to California. You're staying here, probably in the basement."

"Looks like you didn't think of everything, big bro." Lily laughed as they entered the house.

Tessa was right. EJ's parents welcomed the visitors and insisted they stay at the Davis home. Will spent his nights on the basement fold-out. Mr. Davis briefly cornered him. It was after dinner the first night. The genial man brought Will linens and a towel while the ladies were playing Scrabble in the dining room. Will went to take the linens, but Mr. Davis did not release them. Instead, he spoke.

"Rule number one: if my daughter feels unsafe, uncomfortable, or unwelcome anywhere, you leave. Follow her lead. She's been black in America longer than you've been considering what that means."

Will nodded and tried to take the sheets; they didn't budge. *He* didn't budge.

"Rule number two," Mr. Davis continued, "do not needlessly endanger my daughter's life. Be polite to police officers even if you are being treated unfairly. Same goes for any member of our government with a gun. This comes with the territory of dating a black girl. It's your problem, too."

Will swallowed hard and nodded again.

"Finally . . ." Mr. Davis stepped back and folded his arms. Will still felt frozen to the spot. "I'm not a shotgun kind of father; that sort of thing would not be effective with the strongheaded girls I raised. But that does not mean I am a laissez-faire parent, either. If I see an iceberg in the ocean of my child's happiness, I sound the alarm." Mr. Davis paused and seemed to be searching Will's face for . . . something.

"You seem to care for my baby girl, and that's good. Ordinarily, I'd leave you two alone, to see what happens. However, Ella is at that point in her life where she's making a lot of decisions—decisions that may change the direction of her whole life, and *you* are a factor. Are you aware of that?"

"Yes, sir," Will responded emphatically. He'd never called another man *sir* in his life before. "She's a factor in my decisions, too."

Mr. Davis looked at Will for another moment of prolonged silence and gave him the faintest hint of a smile, satisfied for now. "Good. I should hate to learn that you were careless in these matters."

EJ's father walked away, jovially calling, "Who wants some iced tea?" to the Scrabble combatants. Will walked down to the basement, wondering how he'd been so cowed by a husky man in a sweater vest and glasses.

On the Road

The westward-bound youth rose before dawn and were on the road by sunrise. They drove south, down Skyline Drive, windows open because it was still spring and pleasantly warm instead of miserably hot. During this first part of the trip, EJ drove and Will rode shotgun. She didn't need much navigation yet. This was the way to Grandma Jackie's house. Two hours south of Charlottesville, EJ introduced her friends to Waffle House and tried to convince them that Dollywood would be a worthwhile detour.

When they crossed into Tennessee, EJ blasted Dolly's version of the state song, "Rocky Top." Her bland middle-class Maryland accent acquired a generous dollop of honey and butter—just like it did during childhood summers at her grandma's house.

At the one gas station that still had a Slush Puppie machine, the friends switched places. Now the undergrads were driving while EJ and Will reluctantly started talking about the future. Once the euphoria surrounding EJ's triumph had dissipated, both realized that her fellowship was the worst-case scenario for their relationship.

"Where did the program place you?" Will asked, looking for a place to begin.

"University of Edinburgh—I got my wish. It was the highest-ranked one of those I applied for. That's the committee's preference, to keep the prestige."

Will nodded, and EJ stared out the window, searching the fields for cows she could smell but not see.

"When do classes start?"

"September thirtieth. When I originally applied, I was going to start my school year in January, but once I decided to take the summer off, I realized that a six-month break would be too much. Plus, Edinburgh is gorgeous in the fall." EJ shifted in her seat and continued. "I've got to be back home by August. We've got a family reunion, and I basically promised my mom a full month before I leave, mid-September."

Will nodded again, frowning a little. "With me out in LA, we pretty much have July, right?" Neither of them could say *and then it's over.*

EJ bit her bottom lip and sighed. She spoke softly, as if trying to convince herself. "I think so. I mean, super long distance just doesn't make sense. Your work and my school leave little room for a relationship as is."

"That's true," he said without conviction. Will was still strategizing.

In Knoxville, they pulled their Winnie into the parking lot of a pleasant chain hotel. Will sprang for their rooms over EJ's noisy protests about "perfectly good beds" in the trailer. He wanted some private time with his girlfriend. Also, he'd napped in enough trailers on set to know he didn't want to spend the night in one.

EJ saw his wisdom while starfishing on their king-sized bed. Later that night, she held Will tightly and kissed his shoulders, memorizing him. Will lay awake and tried to think of options.

The next morning Tessa drove while EJ navigated. EJ pointed out everything familiar on the drive as they headed to Memphis, the house her mother grew up in, only a few miles away. Auntie Celia lived there now but was out of town on a church retreat with Uncle Willy. Though EJ knew the house was empty, it felt strange to be so close and not go by. She made up for this by overloading Tessa with anecdotes.

In the back of the RV, Will and his sister quietly reviewed his options. "We could have an open relationship," he offered, blue-sky thinking. "I mean, it's only for a year."

"It's two years, remember," Lily corrected him.

"Right," Will said.

She straightened her glasses. "And I may not know EJ super well, maybe she could do an open relationship. But not you—*you* are in no way wiggly about your monogamy standards."

"I could be flexible," he protested.

"Bro, the people who can do open relationships honestly are the people that don't want monogamy. If you do want monogamy but can't have it, an open relationship isn't for you. You'll end up punishing her for taking you at your word," Lily advised.

Seeing her brother unconvinced, she forced the issue. "Okay, let's try a visualization exercise: You're walking through a forest. The trees are very tall and have bright-green leaves." Her voice was soothing, cool as a shaded pond.

"Look down the tree, down from the spidery branches, down to thick limbs, down the rough bark of the trunk. Look at the base of the tree. There is EJ sucking some guy's cock." Will's eyes popped open.

Lily continued. "She doesn't love the guy—doesn't particularly like him, but—" She looked over at her brother. He was sulky and green around the gills.

"The idea alone makes you sick to your stomach. An open relationship would not work."

"I'm not ready to say goodbye," he said.

"Then don't," she replied gently. "You have the summer. Don't say goodbye until it is goodbye."

In Memphis the four stopped for lunch and strolled down a piece of Beale. Will admitted he could see the appeal of Tennessee but still didn't know what he'd do every day. At a souvenir store, Lily bought magnets, and Tessa found a couple of postcards to decorate her door next year.

Then they drove hard to reach Little Rock by nightfall, wanting to avoid any small towns. Arriving late in the evening, they found a Days Inn flanked by a Sonic and a Dairy Queen like an answer to all prayers.

After dinner, EJ and Will went to bed early (sex) while Tessa and Lily wandered over to the Dairy Queen to see what the fuss was all about. The pair had become fast friends in the car with their similar, and often ridiculed, taste in television. Both were delighted to have long discussions on which *Real Housewives* iteration was the best without shame and spent much of the drive through Tennessee doing just that. Between traded bites of a dip cone and Butterfinger Blizzard, they discussed Will and EJ.

"How is she doing?"

"She's ecstatic about her fellowship, of course, but with the impending separation . . . not so good. However, she is determined to look strong and fine so that Will won't do anything noble. She's terrified of Will sacrificing his career and then resenting her." Tessa sipped noisily. "Him?"

"Not good. He doesn't know what to do, and he *hates* that," Lily said. "It's sad. They'd be perfect together if the timing was right."

"Honestly, I don't think things are so insurmountable," Tessa countered. "I mean, her program's only two years, that's not long for a science. After that she should have her pick of offers. If Will wants to be in LA, she can come to California. They just have to wait."

In the motel, after the afterglow, EJ opened the window a crack and adjusted the miniblinds to paint perfect stripes on Will's skin.

"It's not that long, Ella," he said, close to pleading. "Would a couple of years of really long distance be so bad?" She came back to bed and retangled their legs in the scratchy sheets. Will's eyes pressed her for an answer. EJ stroked each variegated shadow on his arm with her fingertips.

"You know, I'm not sure I would have had the guts to ask for what I wanted from the fellowship if I hadn't run into you in the gallery," EJ said. Will could see her eyes darting around the room in the darkness. "Now I have everything I asked for, and all I want is you." She shrugged shyly, rippling the sheets. "It's a terrible thing, all this wanting."

Will held his breath, waiting for EJ to finish her thought.

"Oh, my William," she whispered, on the edge of tears. "Have you seen you in the moonlight? You could ask me to do terrible things," she continued with a sniffle.

Instantly, Will understood the danger and Mr. Davis's worry. EJ, in this moment, was prepared to chuck away every important thing—for him. If they stayed together, she'd be ready to run back across the ocean the moment he said the word.

He kissed her fingertips, then placed her palm against his heart.

"I would never ask, know that—please, Ella." Then he kissed her instead of saying the words because loving her meant letting her go.

She held him close, listening for the soft snore of his slumber. Then she said the words into his hair and slept.

All the travelers were wide eyed once they crossed the Mississippi. Only Will and Tessa had been that far west—and that was by plane. None of them had seen much of the middle with their own eyes. Will drove. Simon and Garfunkel's "America" played on the stereo. EJ leaned out the window and sang to the highway.

When the quartet reached the Grand Canyon, they stared in silent awe of nature at work for thousands of years. Even Tessa, who'd frantically snapped photos out the window through much of the Painted Desert, put her camera down after a few clicks. "Sometimes you have to take a picture with your heart," she surmised. Returning to the car, everyone was very much living in the now.

California

They dropped Tessa off in Utah and then drove on to California. The less said about the traffic into LA the better, especially after days of open highway. When the party reached the adorable bungalow Katerina had secured in Toluca Lake, all were too tired and irritable to fully take it in. Only after the restorative powers of television, rest, chlorine, and bath bubbles were applied did the caravanners begin to appreciate the house's mismatched charm.

The mission-style house was full of ideas. It had faux Victorian art, art deco lamps, and 1950s tile in the kitchen. A thorough exploration of the grounds revealed a firepit and a game room, in addition to the advertised pool and a bonus pool house. Once they realized it was basically a small apartment, Lily immediately claimed it for her own. "So you two don't have to worry about being too noisy," she said, making her brother blush.

EJ called her parents to report their safe arrival. Will and Lily messaged their West Coast friends with similar news. The next day Will, EJ, and Lily met up with Lee at Venice Beach. They did the boardwalk, watching the jugglers and dodging the Rollerbladers. Lee and Lily played Frisbee while Will and EJ went to walk in the surf. They were, as Lily accurately put it, "happy California clichés." Emphasis on *happy*.

⁓

Celebrity Karaoke Challenge had been an undeniable hit. It had the univer-
sality necessary for summer shows: it could be put on in any hotel room,
vacation home, or airport lounge and please almost anyone. The show
allowed Will to be surprisingly fun and generally charming. It made him
a bona fide star. Now the BBC and PBS were coproducing his kids' show,
and ITV reached out to him to host a show that was half *Cribs*, half Sister
Wendy. As summer wound down, Will started receiving offers almost daily.
There were many hosting opportunities, a couple of three-camera sitcoms, a
Lifetime movie about Nathan Chen, and others he still had to sort through.
Katerina sent the jobs to her client as they came, with one question at the
end of every email: WHAT DO YOU WANT? He'd been asking this ques-
tion all year in therapy. Now at last he had an answer—no, a memory.

It was the morning of his first set day. EJ got up early to have breakfast with him. "My sacrifice," she said, yawning and taking down the
French press. She hummed something sweet and unrecognizable while
Will scooped yogurt and granola into bowls. He watched EJ, in a tank
top and lace undies, do what he'd dubbed her "coffee flamingo dance."
While the coffee steeped, she rose onto her toes, balancing on one leg
and pointing the suspended knee outward, then switching. Her back was
perfectly straight—proof you could take the woman out of ballet, but you
couldn't take the ballet out of the woman. Over breakfast they talked of
inconsequential things or the state of the world, he couldn't quite recall.

What he could remember was the feeling of her leg pressed against
his under the table, her good-luck kisses and her goodbye kisses. When
he closed his eyes, Will could see EJ smiling at him over her mug of
coffee as he left for the day. "If I could see her every morning, I could
be happy forever," he said to himself.

Understanding what he wanted most, Will called Katerina and
chose his next path.

A New Moon

EJ had been trying to pack for three days. Tomorrow she'd be taking the Amtrak up the California coast to Seattle before flying home. It was supposed to be one of the last great railway trips in North America, but she was having a hard time getting excited about it. All she wanted to do was rest her head on Will's chest while they filled out the crossword. She didn't want to leave, let alone say goodbye. But Will's career was finally taking off here; that meant his place was in California, and hers was not. She just had to accept it. For now, though, she was going to stall by scrolling through her pics from her last two weeks in LA.

The time in LA had gone by so quickly she needed the many photographs she'd taken to remember everything that had happened. First there were the ones from Venice Beach: Will and Lee playing Frisbee; EJ in her white one-piece with a beach ball, looking for all the world like a progressive tampon ad from the '70s. "Where did we get a beach ball?" she wondered aloud.

There was one of her, Lee, and Lily with their giant yellow name tags at a taping of *The Price Is Right*. Then there was a selfie of Will and her at Disneyland. Their mouse ears overlapped as they squeezed together to fit in the frame. EJ scrolled a bit more, stopping to admire a photo she'd taken with her good camera. It was Will, standing center stage on the set of his new show, literally basking in the spotlight. EJ thought she'd grayscale that one and have it printed and framed for his birthday.

Her favorite pictures (besides the ones of her and Will in the Pacific, or on set, or seeing *The Magic Flute* at the Hollywood Bowl) were the ones of them relaxing around Will's bungalow. Like the one of EJ and Lily on twin inflatable unicorns in the pool. Or the one of Will sitting on the front porch with a mug of coffee and a newspaper, looking like someone's dad. Or the one when he surprised her with a kiss on the cheek and she almost dropped that big bowl of popcorn. "So much happened in such a short time," EJ said aloud.

Though not enough to make up for losing him, she thought mutinously. She closed her laptop with a snap. Clearly stalling was doing her more harm than good. "Okay," she said to herself. "We are getting my junk in a suitcase right now."

After a couple of hours of laundry and folding, EJ was finally able to put her packed suitcase in the hall closet. She then heard a truly alarming car horn. When she got outside to the driveway, she had to laugh. Will, apparently sick of the rented Winnebago, rolled up in a shiny chrome Airstream trailer. He leaned out the window.

"Ready to rough it?" he asked, unashamed.

She climbed in the passenger side and leaned over for a kiss. "You did say you weren't much of a camper, but at least you're an honest man."

They arrived at the campsite in the early evening. As they set up, Will following EJ's patient instruction, he asked about the gazing conditions. She looked at the cloudless sky.

"Perfect darkness, perfect clarity." Both smiled at the familiar words.

To think I didn't even like you last fall, and now . . . She stopped that line of thinking. Things were hard enough.

∽

At sunset Earth's star was large and red, spreading fire across the sky that went pink and purple at the edges. EJ gasped at the sight of it and called Will to watch with her. He slid his arms around her waist, and they watched the sun disappear. The fire in the sky transformed into a cool blue sea. EJ turned to face Will in the twilight. She was unusually sentimental.

"That sunset was us," she began. "These past few months have brought so much color and light to my life, even in the very last moments."

Will had to kiss her, even though he contradicted her with his response.

"You really like the finality of the sunset metaphor, but I feel the need to remind you: the sun sets every day." He kissed her forehead. "All that to say: I'm not letting you go until I have to."

"What do you mean?" she asked hopefully.

"I mean I finally made a choice for my future. I've accepted a role on the next season of *Doctor Who*. The part is almost a sidekick, but it was written with me in mind. I get to do a British accent—"

"Which you love—"

"Which I love, and I'll be kicking down another door. East Asian actors are even less visible in the UK than they are here. Also, I'll be able to keep an eye on the first shows for PakMan Productions—but that's not the best part. Want to know what is?"

"Yes!" she said, full of hope.

"The best part is that the show films at Pinewood Studios . . . in London."

"Same time zone!" EJ cried in realization.

"Same time zone. I get to take a big step in my career, and I get to keep the woman I love." He looked at her tenderly. "I love you, Ella, and I'm not ready to imagine a future without you."

"I love you, too!" EJ replied. Then, giddily, she threw her arms around his neck. "I don't think I've ever been so happy!"

Will spun her around. Finally able to say the words, for some time after, they said little else. Throughout the evening they whispered them in each other's ears or shouted them until they echoed across the cooling sands. Eventually breathless, and happy, they took each other's hands and lay back to watch the stars come out.

ACKNOWLEDGMENTS

First, thanks to my mom, who read me *Jane Eyre*, *Little Women*, and the many other books that gave me a lifelong love of classic literature.

Thanks to Prince George's County Public Schools for your Write-a-Book competition. It meant more than you know.

Thanks to Mrs. Mullan, who published my short story "The Power of Mentos" in our school newspaper.

Thanks to Hill Hall, fourth floor, my freshman year. (Go, Jumbos!)

Thanks to Milady for always being willing to read what I write.

Thanks to Rosalyn for telling me to keep going.

Thanks to Lacey for introducing me to the concept of writing groups and inviting me when she started her own.

Thanks to every incarnation of the Writing Group of Awesomeness. This book would not exist without you.

Thanks to Ashley for reading each revision, through my many typos, and always offering generous critiques.

Thanks to Adele Buck for introducing me to romance-author Twitter, explaining how pitching competitions work, and helping me take myself seriously as a writer.

Thanks to the folks behind #DVPit, who helped my agent find me.

Thanks to the wonderful, kind, patient, diligent, dogged, and again wonderful Michelle Richter at Fuse Literary.

Thanks to Alison Dasho and Lindsay Faber for the energy and enthusiasm you brought to the novel.

Thanks to the amazing team at Montlake.

Finally, thanks to my wonderful husband, who proofread every draft, consoled me after every rejection, listened to every idea, and never stopped believing in this book. You were the first person to call me an author. I love you, and I'll never, ever stop.

ABOUT THE AUTHOR

Eden Appiah-Kubi fell in love with classic novels in fourth grade when her mom read her *Jane Eyre*, chapter by chapter, as a bedtime story. She's an alumna of a small New England university with a weird mascot (Go Jumbos!) and a former Peace Corps volunteer. Eden developed her fiction writing through years spent in a small Washington, DC, critique group. Today she works as a librarian and lives in the DC suburbs with her husband and hilarious daughter.